From #1 *New York Times* bestselling author Nora Roberts comes an unforgettable tale of luck and love in which the fortunes of three siblings depend on a simple twist of fate.

When the RMS *Lusitania* sank in 1915, one survivor became a changed man, giving up his life as a petty thief. But the man still kept the small silver statue he lifted, saving it as a reminder of his past and as a family heirloom for future generations. A century later, that priceless heirloom—one of a long-separated set of three—has been stolen again.

Malachi, Gideon, and Rebecca Sullivan are determined to recover their great-great-grandfather's treasure, reunite the Three Fates, and make their fortune. Their quest will take them from their home in Ireland to Helsinki, Prague, and New York, where they will meet a brilliant scholar who will aid them in their hunt—and an ambitious woman who will stop at nothing to acquire the Fates. . . .

"Satisfying . . . intriguing [and] romantic. The characters are all different and all likable. You'll become caught up in their lives, their antics and their emotions, and will miss them when they're gone."          —The State (Columbia, SC)

"Vivid characters, a strong plot."
                              —*The Providence Journal* (Providence, RI)

"A slick, snappy read."                    —*Publishers Weekly*

*Turn the page for a complete list of titles by
Nora Roberts and J. D. Robb from Berkley. . . .*

## *Nora Roberts*

## Series

*Irish Born Trilogy*
BORN IN FIRE
BORN IN ICE
BORN IN SHAME

*Dream Trilogy*
DARING TO DREAM
HOLDING THE DREAM
FINDING THE DREAM

*Chesapeake Bay Saga*
SEA SWEPT
RISING TIDES
INNER HARBOR
CHESAPEAKE BLUE

*Gallaghers of Ardmore Trilogy*
JEWELS OF THE SUN
TEARS OF THE MOON
HEART OF THE SEA

*Three Sisters Island Trilogy*
DANCE UPON THE AIR
HEAVEN AND EARTH
FACE THE FIRE

*Key Trilogy*
KEY OF LIGHT
KEY OF KNOWLEDGE
KEY OF VALOR

*In the Garden Trilogy*
BLUE DAHLIA
BLACK ROSE
RED LILY

*Circle Trilogy*
MORRIGAN'S CROSS
DANCE OF THE GODS
VALLEY OF SILENCE

*Sign of Seven Trilogy*
BLOOD BROTHERS
THE HOLLOW
THE PAGAN STONE

*Bride Quartet*
VISION IN WHITE
BED OF ROSES
SAVOR THE MOMENT
HAPPY EVER AFTER

*The Inn BoonsBoro Trilogy*
THE NEXT ALWAYS
THE LAST BOYFRIEND
THE PERFECT HOPE

*The Cousins O'Dwyer Trilogy*
DARK WITCH
SHADOW SPELL
BLOOD MAGICK

*The Guardians Trilogy*
STARS OF FORTUNE
BAY OF SIGHS
ISLAND OF GLASS

## Ebooks by Nora Roberts

**Cordina's Royal Family**
AFFAIRE ROYALE
COMMAND PERFORMANCE
THE PLAYBOY PRINCE
CORDINA'S CROWN JEWEL

**The Donovan Legacy**
CAPTIVATED
ENTRANCED
CHARMED
ENCHANTED

**The O'Hurleys**
THE LAST HONEST WOMAN
DANCE TO THE PIPER
SKIN DEEP
WITHOUT A TRACE

**Night Tales**
NIGHT SHIFT
NIGHT SHADOW
NIGHTSHADE
NIGHT SMOKE
NIGHT SHIELD

**The MacGregors**
PLAYING THE ODDS
TEMPTING FATE
ALL THE POSSIBILITIES
ONE MAN'S ART
FOR NOW, FOREVER
REBELLION/IN FROM THE COLD
THE MACGREGOR BRIDES
THE WINNING HAND
THE MACGREGOR GROOMS
THE PERFECT NEIGHBOR

**The Calhouns**
COURTING CATHERINE
A MAN FOR AMANDA
FOR THE LOVE OF LILAH
SUZANNA'S SURRENDER
MEGAN'S MATE

**Irish Legacy**
IRISH THOROUGHBRED
IRISH ROSE
IRISH REBEL

LOVING JACK
BEST LAID PLANS
LAWLESS

BLITHE IMAGES
SONG OF THE WEST
SEARCH FOR LOVE
ISLAND OF FLOWERS
THE HEART'S VICTORY
FROM THIS DAY
HER MOTHER'S KEEPER
ONCE MORE WITH FEELING
REFLECTIONS
DANCE OF DREAMS
UNTAMED
THIS MAGIC MOMENT
ENDINGS AND BEGINNINGS
STORM WARNING
SULLIVAN'S WOMAN
FIRST IMPRESSIONS
A MATTER OF CHOICE

LESS OF A STRANGER
THE LAW IS A LADY
RULES OF THE GAME
OPPOSITES ATTRACT
THE RIGHT PATH
PARTNERS
BOUNDARY LINES
DUAL IMAGE
TEMPTATION
LOCAL HERO
THE NAME OF THE GAME
GABRIEL'S ANGEL
THE WELCOMING
TIME WAS
TIMES CHANGE
SUMMER LOVE
HOLIDAY WISHES

### Nora Roberts & J. D. Robb

REMEMBER WHEN

## J. D. Robb

NAKED IN DEATH
GLORY IN DEATH
IMMORTAL IN DEATH
RAPTURE IN DEATH
CEREMONY IN DEATH
VENGEANCE IN DEATH
HOLIDAY IN DEATH
CONSPIRACY IN DEATH
LOYALTY IN DEATH
WITNESS IN DEATH
JUDGMENT IN DEATH
BETRAYAL IN DEATH
SEDUCTION IN DEATH
REUNION IN DEATH
PURITY IN DEATH
PORTRAIT IN DEATH
IMITATION IN DEATH
DIVIDED IN DEATH
VISIONS IN DEATH
SURVIVOR IN DEATH
ORIGIN IN DEATH
MEMORY IN DEATH
BORN IN DEATH
INNOCENT IN DEATH
CREATION IN DEATH
STRANGERS IN DEATH
SALVATION IN DEATH
PROMISES IN DEATH
KINDRED IN DEATH
FANTASY IN DEATH
INDULGENCE IN DEATH
TREACHERY IN DEATH
NEW YORK TO DALLAS
CELEBRITY IN DEATH
DELUSION IN DEATH
CALCULATED IN DEATH
THANKLESS IN DEATH
CONCEALED IN DEATH
FESTIVE IN DEATH
OBSESSION IN DEATH
DEVOTED IN DEATH
BROTHERHOOD IN DEATH
APPRENTICE IN DEATH

## Anthologies

FROM THE HEART
A LITTLE MAGIC
A LITTLE FATE

MOON SHADOWS
*(with Jill Gregory, Ruth Ryan Langan, and Marianne Willman)*

*The Once Upon Series*
*(with Jill Gregory, Ruth Ryan Langan, and Marianne Willman)*

ONCE UPON A CASTLE　　　ONCE UPON A ROSE
ONCE UPON A STAR　　　ONCE UPON A KISS
ONCE UPON A DREAM　　　ONCE UPON A MIDNIGHT

SILENT NIGHT
*(with Susan Plunkett, Dee Holmes, and Claire Cross)*

OUT OF THIS WORLD
*(with Laurell K. Hamilton, Susan Krinard, and Maggie Shayne)*

BUMP IN THE NIGHT
*(with Mary Blayney, Ruth Ryan Langan, and Mary Kay McComas)*

DEAD OF NIGHT
*(with Mary Blayney, Ruth Ryan Langan, and Mary Kay McComas)*

THREE IN DEATH

SUITE 606
*(with Mary Blayney, Ruth Ryan Langan, and Mary Kay McComas)*

THE LOST
*(with Patricia Gaffney, Mary Blayney, and Ruth Ryan Langan)*

THE OTHER SIDE
*(with Mary Blayney, Patricia Gaffney, Ruth Ryan Langan, and Mary Kay McComas)*

TIME OF DEATH

THE UNQUIET
*(with Mary Blayney, Patricia Gaffney, Ruth Ryan Langan, and Mary Kay McComas)*

MIRROR MIRROR
*(with Mary Blayney, Elaine Fox, Mary Kay McComas, and R. C. Ryan)*

DOWN THE RABBIT HOLE
*(with Mary Blayney, Elaine Fox, Mary Kay McComas, and R. C. Ryan)*

### Also available . . .

THE OFFICIAL NORA ROBERTS COMPANION
*(edited by Denise Little and Laura Hayden)*

# Three Fates

## Nora Roberts

JOVE
New York

A JOVE BOOK
Published by Berkley
An imprint of Penguin Random House LLC
penguinrandomhouse.com

ISBN: 9780593438602

G. P. Putnam's Sons hardcover edition / April 2002
Jove mass-market edition / April 2003
Jove mass-max edition / November 2021

Printed in the United States of America
1   3   5   7   9   10   8   6   4   2

*To Dan and Stacie:*
*May the tapestry of your lives be woven*
*with rosy threads of love,*
*the deep reds of passion,*
*the quiet blues of understanding and contentment,*
*and the bright, bright silver of humor.*

# PART ONE
## Spinning

*Oh, what a tangled web we weave,*
*When first we practice to deceive!*

SIR WALTER SCOTT

# One

May 7, 1915

HAPPILY unaware he'd be dead in twenty-three minutes, Henry W. Wyley imagined pinching the nicely rounded rump of the young blonde who was directly in his line of sight. It was a perfectly harmless fantasy that did nothing to distress the blonde, or Henry's wife, and put Henry himself in the best of moods.

With a lap robe tucked around his pudgy knees and a plump belly well satisfied by a late and luxurious lunch, he sat in the bracing sea air with his wife, Edith—whose bum, bless her, was flat as a pancake—enjoying the blonde's derriere along with a fine cup of Earl Grey.

Henry, a portly man with a robust laugh and an eye for the ladies, didn't bother to stir himself to join other passengers at the rail for a glimpse of Ireland's shimmering coast. He'd seen it before and assumed he'd have plenty of opportunities to see it again if he cared to.

Though what fascinated people about cliffs and grass eluded him. Henry was an avowed urbanite who preferred the solidity of steel and concrete. And at this particular moment, he was much more interested in the dainty chocolate cookies served with the tea than the vista.

Particularly when the blonde moved on.

Though Edith fussed at him not to make a pig of himself, he gobbled up three cookies with cheerful relish. Edith, being Edith, refrained. It was a pity she denied herself that small pleasure in the last moments of her life, but she would die as she'd lived, worrying about her husband's extra tonnage and brushing at the crumbs that scattered carelessly on his shirtfront.

Henry, however, was a man who believed in indulgence. What, after all, was the point of being rich if you didn't treat yourself to the finer things? He'd been poor, and he'd been hungry. Rich and well fed was better.

He'd never been handsome, but when a man had money he was called substantial rather than fat, interesting rather than homely. Henry appreciated the absurdity of the distinction.

At just before three in the afternoon on that sparkling May day, the wind blew at his odd little coal-colored toupee, whipped high, happy color into his pudgy cheeks. He had a gold watch in his pocket, a ruby pin in his tie. His Edith, scrawny as a chicken, was decked out in the best of Parisian couture. He was worth nearly three million. Not as much as Alfred Vanderbilt, who was crossing the Atlantic as well, but enough to content Henry. Enough, he thought with pride as he considered a fourth cookie, to pay for first-class accommodations on this floating palace. Enough to see that his children had received first-class educations and that his grandchildren would as well.

He imagined first class was more important to him than it was to Vanderbilt. After all, Alfred had never had to make do with second.

He listened with half an ear as his wife chattered on about plans once they reached England. Yes, they would pay calls and receive them. He would not spend all of his time with associates or hunting up stock for his business.

He assured her of all this with his usual amiability, and because after nearly forty years of marriage he was deeply fond of his wife, he would see that she was well entertained during their stay abroad.

But he had plans of his own, and that driving force had been the single purpose of this spring crossing.

If his information was correct, he would soon acquire the second Fate. The small silver statue was a personal quest, one he'd pursued since he'd chanced to purchase the first of the reputed three.

He had a line on the third as well and would tug on it as soon as the second statue was in his possession. When he had the complete set, well, that would be first class indeed.

Wyley Antiques would be second to none.

Personal and professional satisfaction, he mused. All because of three small silver ladies, worth a pretty penny separately. Worth beyond imagining together. Perhaps he'd loan them to the Met for a time. Yes, he liked the idea.

## THE THREE FATES

### ON LOAN FROM THE PRIVATE COLLECTION OF HENRY W. WYLEY

Edith would have her new hats, he thought, her dinner parties and her afternoon promenades. And he would have the prize of a lifetime.

Sighing with satisfaction, Henry sat back to enjoy his last cup of Earl Grey.

FELIX GREENFIELD WAS a thief. He was neither ashamed nor prideful of it. It was simply what he was and had always been. And as Henry Wyley assumed he'd have other opportunities to gaze upon the Irish coast, Felix assumed he'd remain a thief for many years to come.

He was good at his work—not brilliant at it, he'd be the first to admit, but good enough to make ends meet. Good enough, he thought as he moved quickly down the corridors of first class in his stolen steward's uniform, to have gathered the means for third-class passage back to England.

Things were just a bit hot professionally back in New York, with cops breathing down his neck due to that bungled burglary. Not that it had been his fault, not entirely. His only failing had been to break his own first rule and take on an associate for the job.

Bad choice, as his temporary partner had broken another primary rule. Never steal what isn't easily, discreetly fenced. Greed had blinded old Two-Pint Monk, Felix thought with a sigh as he let himself into the Wyley stateroom. What had the man been thinking, laying sticky fingers on a diamond-and-sapphire necklace? Then behaving like a bloody amateur by getting drunk as a sailor—on his usual two pints of lager—and bragging over it.

Well, Two-Pint would do his bragging in jail now, though there'd be no lager to loosen his idiot tongue. But the bastard had chirped like the stool pigeon he was and given Felix's name to the coppers.

It had seemed best to take a nice ocean voyage, and what better place to get lost than on a ship as big as a damn city?

He'd been a bit concerned about the war in Europe, and the murmurs about the Germans stalking the seas had given him some pause. But they were such vague, distant threats. The New York police and the idea of a long stretch behind bars were much more personal and immediate problems.

In any case, he couldn't believe a grand ship like the *Lusitania* would cross if there was any real danger. Not with all those wealthy people on board. It was a civilian vessel after all, and he was sure the Germans had better things to do than threaten a luxury liner, especially when there was a large complement of American citizens on board.

He'd been lucky indeed to have snagged a ticket, to have lost himself among all the passengers with the cops two steps behind him and closing.

But he'd had to leave quickly, and had spent nearly all his wherewithal for the ticket.

Certainly there were opportunities galore to pluck a bit of this, a bit of that on such a fine, luxurious vessel filled with such fine, luxurious people.

Cash would be best, of course, for cash was never the wrong size or the wrong color.

Inside the stateroom, he let out a low whistle. Imagine

it, he thought, taking a moment to dream. Just imagine traveling in such style.

He knew less about the architecture and design of where he was standing than a flea knew about the breed of dog it bit. But he knew it was choice.

The sitting room was larger than the whole of his third-class accommodations, and the bedroom beyond a wonder.

Those who slept here knew nothing about the cramped space, the dark corners and the smells of third class. He didn't begrudge them their advantages. After all, if there weren't people who lived high, he'd have no one to steal from, would he?

Still, he couldn't waste time gawking and dreaming. It was already a few minutes before three, and if the Wyleys were true to form, the woman would wander back before four for her afternoon nap.

He had delicate hands and was careful to disturb little as he searched for spare cash. Big bucks, he figured, they'd leave in the purser's keeping. But fine ladies and gentlemen enjoyed having a roll of bills close at hand for flashing.

He found an envelope already marked STEWARD and, grinning, ripped it open to find crisp dollar bills in a generous tip. He tucked it in the trouser pocket of his borrowed uniform.

Within ten minutes, he'd found and claimed nearly a hundred fifty dollars and a pair of nice garnet earbobs left carelessly in a silk evening purse.

He didn't touch the jewelry cases—the man's or the woman's. That was asking for trouble. But as he sifted neatly through socks and drawers, his fingers brushed over a solid lump wrapped in velvet cloth.

Lips pursed, Félix gave in to curiosity and spread open the cloth.

He didn't know anything about art, but he recognized pure silver when he had his hands on it. The lady—for it was a woman—was small enough to fit in his palm. She held some sort of spindle, he supposed it was, and was garbed in a kind of robe.

She had a lovely face and form. Fetching, he would

have said, though she looked a bit too cool and calculating for his personal taste in females.

He preferred them a bit slow of wit and cheerful of disposition.

Tucked in with her was a paper with a name and address, and the scrawled notation: *Contact for second Fate.*

Felix pondered over it, committed the note to memory out of habit. It could be another chicken for plucking once he was in London.

He started to wrap her again, replace her where he'd found her, but he just stood there turning her over and over in his hands. Throughout his long career as a thief, he'd never once allowed himself to envy, to crave, to want an object for himself.

What was taken was always a means to an end, and nothing more. But Felix Greenfield, lately of Hell's Kitchen and bound for the alleyways and tenements of London, stood in the plush cabin on the grand ship with the Irish coast even now in view out the windows, and wanted the small silver woman for his own.

She was so . . . pretty. And fit so well in his hand with the metal already warming against his palm. Such a little thing. Who would miss her?

"Don't be stupid," he muttered, wrapping her in velvet again. "Take the money, mate, and move along."

Before he could replace her, he heard what he thought was a peal of thunder. The floor beneath his feet seemed to shudder. Nearly losing his balance as the ship shook side to side, he stumbled toward the door, the velvet-cloaked statue still in his hand.

Without thinking, he jammed it into his trouser pocket, spilled out into the corridor as the floor rose under him.

There was a sound now, not like thunder, but like a great hammer flung down from heaven to strike the ship.

Felix ran for his life.

And running, he raced into madness.

The forward part of the ship dipped sharply and had him tumbling down the corridor like dice in a cup. He could hear shouting and the pounding of feet. And he tasted blood in his mouth, seconds before it went dark.

His first wild thought was, Iceberg! as he remembered what had befallen the great *Titanic*. But surely in the broad light of a spring afternoon, so close to the Irish coast, such a thing wasn't possible.

He never thought of the Germans. He never thought of war.

He scrambled up, slamming into walls in the pitch black of the corridor, stumbling over his own feet and the stairs, and spilled out on deck with a flood of others. Already lifeboats were being launched and there were cries of terror along with shouted orders for women and children to board them.

How bad was it? he wondered frantically. How bad could it be when he could see the shimmering green of the coastline? Even as he tried to calm himself, the ship pitched again, and one of the lowering lifeboats upended. Its screaming passengers were hurled into the sea.

He saw a mass of faces—some torn, some scalded, all horrified. There were piles of debris on deck, and passengers—bleeding, screaming—trapped under it. Some, he saw with dull shock, were already beyond screams.

And there on the listing desk of the great ship, Felix smelled what he'd often smelled in Hell's Kitchen.

He smelled death.

Women clutched children, babies, and wept or prayed. Men ran in panic, or fought madly to drag the injured clear of debris.

Through the chaos stewards and stewardesses hurried, passing out life jackets with a kind of steady calm. They might have been handing out teacups, he thought, until one rushed by him.

"Go on, man! Do your job! See to the passengers."

It took Felix one blank moment before he remembered he was still wearing the stolen steward's uniform. And another before he understood, truly understood, they were sinking.

Fuck me, he thought, standing in the middle of the screams and prayers. We're dying.

There were shouts from the water, desperate cries for help. Felix fought his way to the rail and, looking down, saw bodies floating, people floundering in debris-strewn water. People drowning in it.

He saw another lifeboat being launched, wondered if he could somehow make the leap into it and save himself. He struggled to pull himself to a higher point, to gain ground was all he could think. To stay on his feet until he could hurl himself into a lifeboat and survive.

He saw a well-dressed man take off his own life jacket and put it around a weeping woman.

So the rich could be heroes, he thought. They could afford to be. He'd sooner be alive.

The deck tilted again, sent him sliding along with countless others toward the mouth of the sea. He shot out a hand, managed to grab the rail with his clever thief's fingers and cling. And his free hand closed, as if by magic, over a life jacket as it went tumbling by.

Muttering wild prayers of thanks, he started to strap it on. It was a sign, he thought with his heart and eyes wheeling wild, a sign from God that he was meant to survive this.

As his shaking fingers fumbled with the jacket, he saw the woman wedged between upturned deck chairs. And the child, the small, angelic face of the child she clutched against her. She wasn't weeping. She wasn't screaming. She simply held and rocked the little boy as if lulling him into his afternoon nap.

"Mary, mother of God." And cursing himself for a fool, Felix crawled across the pitched deck. He dragged and heaved at the chairs that pinned her down.

"I've hurt my leg." She continued to stroke her child's hair, and the rings on her fingers sparkled in the strong spring sunlight. Though her voice was calm, her eyes were huge, glazed with shock and pain, and the terror Felix felt galloped inside his own chest.

"I don't think I can walk. Will you take my baby? Please, take my little boy to a lifeboat. See him safe."

He had one moment, one heartbeat to choose. And while the world went to hell around them, the child smiled.

"Put this on yourself, missus, and hold tight to the boy."

"We'll put it on my son."

"It's too big for him. It won't help him."

"I've lost my husband." She spoke in those clear, cultured tones, and though her eyes were glassy, they stayed level on his as Felix pushed her arms through the life jacket. "He fell over the rail. I fear he's dead."

"You're not, are you? Neither is the boy." He could smell the child—powder, youth, innocence—through the stench of panic and death. "What's his name?"

"Name? He's Steven. Steven Edward Cunningham, the Third."

"Let's get you and Steven Edward Cunningham, the Third, to a lifeboat."

"We're sinking."

"That's the God's truth." He dragged her, trying once more to reach the high side of the ship.

He crawled, clawed his way over the wet and rising deck.

"Hold on tight to Mama, Steven," he heard her say. Then she crawled and clawed with him while terror raged around them.

"Don't be frightened." She crooned it, though her breath was coming fast with the effort. Her heavy skirts sloshed in the water, and blood smeared over the glinting stones on her fingers. "You have to be brave. Don't let go of Mama, no matter what."

He could see the boy, no more than three, cling like a monkey to his mother's neck. Watching her face, Felix thought as he strained for another inch of height, as if all the answers in all the world were printed on it.

Deck chairs, tables, God knew what, rained down from the deck above. He dragged her another inch, another, a foot. "Just a little farther." He gasped it out, without any idea if it were true.

Something struck him hard in the back. And his hold on her slipped.

"Missus!" he shouted, grabbed blindly, but caught only the pretty silk sleeve of her dress. As it ripped, he stared at her helplessly.

"God bless you," she managed and, wrapping both arms tight around her son, slid over the edge of the world into the water.

He barely had time to curse before the deck heaved and he pitched in after her.

The cold, the sheer brutality of it, stole his breath. Blind, already going numb with shock, he kicked wildly, clawing for the surface as he'd clawed for the deck. When he broke through, gasped in that first gulp of air, he found he'd plunged into a hell worse than any he'd imagined.

Dead were all around him. He was jammed into an island of bobbing, staring white faces, of screams from the drowning. The water was strewn with planks and chairs, wrecked lifeboats and crates. His limbs were already stiff with cold when he struggled to heave as much of his body as possible onto a crate and out of the freezing water.

And what he saw was worse. There were hundreds of bodies floating in the still sparkling sunlight. While his stomach heaved out the sea he'd swallowed, he floundered in the direction of a waterlogged lifeboat.

The swell, somehow gentle, tore at the island and spread death over the sea, and dragged him, with merciless hands, away from the lifeboat.

The great ship, the floating palace, was sinking in front of his eyes. Dangling from it were lifeboats, useless as toys. Somehow it astonished him to see there were still people on the decks. Some were kneeling, others still rushing in panic from a fate that was hurtling toward them.

In shock, he watched more tumble like dolls into the sea. And the huge black funnels tipped down toward the water, down to where he clung to a broken crate.

When those funnels touched the sea, water gushed into them, sucking in people with it.

Not like this, he thought as he kicked weakly. A man wasn't meant to die like this. But the sea dragged him under, pulled him in. Water seemed to boil around him as he struggled. He choked on it, tasted salt and oil and smoke. And realized, as his body bashed into a solid wall, that he was trapped in one of the funnels, would die there like a rat in a blocked chimney.

As his lungs began to scream, he thought of the woman and the boy. Since he deemed it useless to pray for himself, he offered what he thought was his last plea to God that they'd survived.

Later, he would think it had been as if hands had taken hold of him and yanked him free. As the funnels sank, he was expelled, flying out on a filthy gush of soot.

With pain radiating through him, he snagged a floating plank and pulled his upper body onto it. He laid his cheek on the wood, breathed deeply, wept quietly.

And saw the *Lusitania* was gone.

The plate of water where she'd been was raging, thrashing and belching smoke. Belching bodies, he saw with a dull horror. He'd been one of them, only moments before. But fate had spared him.

While he watched, while he struggled to block out the screams and stay sane, the water went calm as glass. With the last of his strength, he pulled himself onto the plank. He heard the shrill song of sea gulls, the weeping prayers or weeping cries of those who floundered or floated in the water with him.

Probably freeze to death, he thought as he drifted in and out of consciousness. But it was better than drowning.


IT WAS THE cold that brought him out of the faint. His body was racked with it, and every trickling breeze was a new agony. Hardly daring to move, he tugged at his sopping and ruined steward's jacket. Bright pain had nausea rolling greasily in his belly. He ran an unsteady hand over his face and saw the wet wasn't water, but blood.

His laugh was wild and shaky. So what would it be, freezing or bleeding to death? Drowning might have been better, after all. It would be over that way. He slowly shed the jacket—something wrong with his shoulder, he thought absently—and used the ruined jacket to wipe the blood from his face.

He didn't hear so much shouting now. There were still some thin screams, some moans and prayers, but most of the passengers who'd made it as far as he had were dead. And silent.

He watched a body float by. It took him a moment to recognize the face, as it was bone-white and covered with bloodless gashes.

Wyley. Good Christ.

For the first time since the nightmare had begun, he felt for the weight in his pocket. He felt the lump of what he'd stolen from the man currently staring up at the sky with blank blue eyes.

"You won't need it," Felix said between chattering teeth, "but I swear before God if I had it to do over, I wouldn't have stolen from you in the last moments of your life. Seems like robbing a grave."

His long-lapsed religious training had him folding his hands in prayer. "If I end up dying here today, I'll apologize in person if we end up on the same side of the gate. And if I live I take a vow to try to reform. No point in saying I'll do it, but I'll give doing an honest day's work a try."

He passed out again, and woke to the sound of an engine. Dazed, numb, he managed to lift his head. Through his wavering vision, he saw a boat, and through the roaring in his ears, heard the shouts and voices of men.

He tried to call out, but managed only a hacking cough.

"I'm alive." His voice was only a croak, whisked away by the breeze. "I'm still alive."

He didn't feel the hands pull him onto the fishing trawler called *Dan O'Connell*. Was delirious with chills and pain when he was wrapped in a blanket, when hot tea was poured down his throat. He would remember nothing about his actual rescue, nor learn the names of the men whose arms had hauled him to safety. Nothing came clear to him until he woke, nearly twenty-four hours after the torpedo had struck the liner, in a narrow bed in a small room with sunlight streaming through a window.

He would never forget the first sight that greeted him when his vision cleared.

She was young and pretty, with eyes of misty blue and a scatter of gold freckles over her small nose and round cheeks. Her hair was fair and piled on top of her head in some sort of knot that seemed to be slipping. Her mouth bowed up when she glanced over at him, and she rose quickly from the chair where she'd been darning socks.

"There you are. I wonder if you'll stay with us this time around."

He heard Ireland in her voice, felt the strong hand lift his head. And he smelled a drift of lavender.

"What . . ." The old, croaking sound of his voice appalled him. His throat felt scorched, his head stuffed with rags of dirty cotton.

"Just take this first. It's medicine the doctor left for you. You've pneumonia, he says, and a fair gash on your head that's been stitched. Seems you tore something in your shoulder as well. But you've come through the worst, sir, and you rest easy for we'll see you through."

"What . . . happened? The ship . . ."

The pretty mouth went flat and hard. "The bloody Germans. 'Twas a U-boat torpedoed you. And they'll writhe in hell for it, for the people they murdered. The babies they slaughtered."

Though a tear trickled down her cheek, she managed to slide the medicine into him competently. "You have to rest. Your life's a miracle, for there are more than a thousand dead."

"A . . ." He managed to grip her wrist as the horror stabbed through him. "A *thousand?*"

"More than. You're in Queenstown now, and as well as you can be." She tilted her head. "An American, are you?"

Close enough, he decided, as he hadn't seen the shores of his native England in more than twelve years. "Yes. I need—"

"Tea," she interrupted. "And broth." She moved to the door to shout: "Ma! He's waked and seems to want to stay that way." She glanced back. "I'll be back with something warm in a minute."

"Please. Who are you?"

"Me?" She smiled again, wonderfully sunny. "I'd be Meg. Meg O'Reiley, and you're in the home of my parents, Pat and Mary O'Reiley, where you're welcome until you're mended. And your name, sir?"

"Greenfield. Felix Greenfield."

"God bless you, Mr. Greenfield."

"Wait . . . there was a woman, and a little boy. Cunning-ham."

Pity moved over her face. "They're listing names. I'll check on them for you when I'm able. Now you rest, and we'll get you some tea."

When she went out, he turned his face toward the window, toward the sun. And saw, sitting on the table under it, the money that had been in his pocket, the garnet earbobs. And the bright silver glint of the little statue.

Felix laughed until he cried.


HE LEARNED THE O'Reileys made their living from the sea. Pat and his two sons had been part of the rescue effort. He met them all, and her younger sister as well. For the first day he was unable to keep any of them straight in his mind. But for Meg herself.

He clung to her company as he'd clung to the plank, to keep from sliding into the dark again.

"Tell me what you know," he begged her.

"It'll be hard for you to hear it. It's hard to speak it." She moved to his window, looked out at the village where she'd lived all of her eighteen years. Survivors such as Felix were being tended to in hotel rooms, in the homes of neighbors. And the dead, God rest them, were laid in temporary morgues. Some would be buried, some would be sent home. Others would forever be in the grave of the sea.

"When I heard of it," she began, "I almost didn't believe it. How could such a thing be? There were trawlers out, and they went directly to try to rescue survivors. More boats set out from here. Most were too late to do more than bring back the dead. Oh sweet God, I saw myself some of the people as they made land. Women and babies, men barely able to walk and half naked. Some cried, and others just stared. Like you do when you're lost. They say the liner went down in less than twenty minutes. Can that be?"

"I don't know," Felix murmured, and shut his eyes.

She glanced back at him and hoped he was strong enough for the rest. "More have died since coming here. Exposure and injuries too grievous to heal. Some spent hours in the water. The lists change so quick. I can't think what terror of heart families are living with, waiting to know. Or what grief those who know their loved ones are lost in this horrible way are feeling. You said there was no one waiting for word of you."

"No. No one."

She went to him. She'd tended his hurts, suffered with him during the horrors of his delirium. It had been only three days since he'd been brought into her care, but for both of them, it was a lifetime.

"There's no shame in staying here," she said quietly. "No shame in not going to the funeral today. You're far from well yet."

"I need to go." He looked down at his borrowed clothes. In them he felt scrawny and fragile. And alive.


THE QUIET WAS almost unearthly. Every shop and store in Queenstown was closed for the day. No children raced along the streets, no neighbors stopped to chat or gossip. Over the silence came the hollow sound of church bells from St. Colman's on the hill, and the mournful notes of the funeral dirge.

Felix knew if he lived another hundred years he'd never forget the sounds of that grieving music, the soft and steady beat of drums. He watched the sun strike the brass of the instruments, and remembered how that same sun had struck the brass of the propellers as the stern of the *Lusitania* had reared up in her final plunge into the sea.

He was alive, he thought again. Instead of relief and gratitude, he felt only guilt and despair.

He kept his head down as he trudged along behind the priests, the mourners, the dead, through the reverently silent streets. It took more than an hour to reach the grave-yard, and left him light-headed. By the time he saw the three mass graves beneath tall elms where choirboys stood with incense burners, he was forced to lean heavily on Meg.

Tears stung the backs of his eyes as he looked at the tiny coffins that held dead children.

He listened to the quiet weeping, to the words of both the Catholic and the Church of Ireland services. None of it reached him. He could still hear, thought he would forever hear, the way people had called to God as they'd drowned. But God hadn't listened, and had let them die horribly.

Then he lifted his head and, across those obscene holes, saw the face of the woman and young boy from the ship.

The tears came now, fell down his cheeks like rain as he lurched through the crowd. He reached her as the first notes of "Abide with Me" lifted into the air. Then he fell to his knees in front of her wheelchair.

"I feared you were dead." She reached up, touched his face with one hand. The other peeked out of a cast. "I never got your name, so couldn't check the lists."

"You're alive." Her face had been cut, he could see that now, and her color was too bright, as if she were feverish. Her leg had been cast as well as her arm. "And the boy."

The child slept in the arms of another woman. Like an angel, Felix thought again. Peaceful and unmarked.

The fist of despair that gripped him loosened. One prayer, at least one prayer, had been answered.

"He never let go." She began to weep then, soundlessly. "He's such a good boy. He never let go. I broke my arm in the fall. If you hadn't given me your life jacket, we would have drowned. My husband . . ." Her voice frayed as she looked over at the graves. "They never found him."

"I'm sorry."

"He would have thanked you." She reached up to touch a hand to her boy's leg. "He loved his son, very much." She took a deep breath. "In his stead, I thank you, for my son's life and my own. Please tell me your name."

"Felix Greenfield, ma'am."

"Mr. Greenfield." She leaned over, brushed a kiss on Felix's cheek. "I'll never forget you. Nor will my son."

When they wheeled her chair away, she kept her shoulders straight with a quiet dignity that brought a wash of shame over Felix's face.

"You're a hero," Meg told him.

Shaking his head, he moved as quickly as he could away from the crowds, away from the graves. "No. She is. I'm nothing."

"How can you say that? I heard what she said. You saved her life, and the little boy's." Concerned, she hurried up to him, took his arm to steady him.

He'd have shaken her off if he'd had the strength. Instead, he simply sat in the high, wild grass of the graveyard and buried his face in his hands.

"Ah, there now." Pity for him had her sitting beside him, taking him into her arms. "There now, Felix."

He could think of nothing but the strength in the young widow's face, in the innocence of her son's. "She was hurt, so she asked me to take the boy. To save the boy."

"You saved them both."

"I don't know why I did it. I was only thinking about saving myself. I'm a thief. Those things you took out of my pocket? I stole them. I was stealing them when the ship was hit. All I could think about when it was happening was getting out alive."

Meg shifted beside him, folded her hands. "Did you give her your life jacket?"

"It wasn't mine. I found it. I don't know why I gave it to her. She was trapped between deck chairs, holding on to the boy. Holding on to her sanity in the middle of all that hell."

"You could've turned away from her, saved yourself."

He mopped at his eyes. "I wanted to."

"But you didn't."

"I'll never know why." He only knew that seeing them alive had changed something inside him. "But the point is, I'm a second-rate thief who was on that ship because I was running from the cops. I stole a man's things minutes before he died. A thousand people are dead. I saw some of them die. I'm alive. What kind of world is it that saves a thief and takes children?"

"Who can answer? But there's a child who's alive today because you were there. Would you have been, do you think, just where you were, when you were, if you hadn't been stealing?"

He let out a derisive sound. "The likes of me wouldn't have been anywhere near the first-class deck unless I'd been stealing."

"There you are." She took a handkerchief from her pocket and dried his tears as she would a child's. "Stealing's wrong. It's a sin and there's no question about it. But if you'd been minding your own, that woman and her son would be dead. If a sin saves innocent lives, I'm thinking it's not so great a sin. And I have to say, you didn't steal so very much if all you had for it were a pair of earbobs, a little statue and some American dollars."

For some reason that made him smile. "Well, I was just getting started."

The smile she sent him was lovely and sure. "Yes, I'd say you're just getting started."

# Two

*Helsinki, 2002*

SHE wasn't what he'd expected. He'd studied the picture of her on the back of her book, and on the program for the lecture—would it never end?—but there was a difference in flesh and blood.

She was smaller than he'd imagined, for one thing. Nearly delicate in her quiet gray suit that should, in his opinion, be a good inch shorter at the hem. From what he could see of her legs, they weren't half bad.

In person she didn't look nearly as competent and intimidating a woman as she did on the dust jacket. Though the little wire glasses she wore onstage added a sort of trendy intellectual tone.

She had a good voice. Maybe too good, he thought, as it was damn near putting him to sleep. Still, that was primarily the fault of the subject matter. He was interested in Greek myths—in one particular Greek myth. But Christ Jesus, it was tedious to have to sit through an hour's lecture on the entire breed of them.

He straightened in his chair and did his best to concentrate. Not on the words so much. He didn't give a rat's ass about Artemis turning some poor slob into a stag because he'd seen her naked. That only proved that women, goddesses or not, were peculiar creatures.

To his mind, Dr. Tia Marsh was damn peculiar. The woman came from money. Great gobs and hordes of money, yet instead of sitting back and enjoying it, she spent her time steeped in long-dead Greek gods. Writing about them, lecturing about them. Interminably.

She had generations of breeding behind her. Blood as blue as the Kerry lakes. But here she was, giving her endless talk in Finland, days after she'd given what he assumed was the same song and dance in Sweden, in Norway. Hyping her book all over Europe and Scandinavia.

Certainly it wasn't for the money, he mused. Maybe she just liked to hear the sound of her own voice. Countless did.

She was, according to his information, twenty-nine, single, the only child of the New York Marshes and, most important, the great-great-granddaughter of Henry W. Wyley.

Wyley Antiques was, as it had been for nearly a hundred years, one of the most prestigious antique and auction houses in New York.

It was no coincidence that Wyley's offshoot had developed such a keen interest in the Greek gods. It was his assignment to find out, by whatever means worked best, what she knew about the Three Fates.

If she'd been, well, softer, he supposed, he might have tried and enjoyed a seduction angle. It was fascinating what people would tell each other when sex was tangled into the mix. She was attractive enough, in a scholarly sort of way, but he wasn't entirely sure what button to push, romantically speaking, with the intellectual type.

Frowning a bit, he turned the book over on his lap and gave the photo another look. In it she had her sunny blond hair tucked back in some sort of bun. She was smiling, rather dutifully, he thought now. As if someone had said, "Say cheese!" It wasn't a smile that reached the eyes— very sober and serious blue eyes that suited the somewhat sober and serious curve of her lips.

Her face tapered down to a bit of a point. He might have called it elfin but for that primly styled hair and the somber stare.

He thought she looked like a woman in need of a good laugh . . . or a good lay. Both his mother and his sister would have belted him for that opinion. But a man's thoughts were his own business.

Best, he decided, to approach the prim Dr. Marsh on very civilized, very businesslike terms.

When the applause, a great deal more enthusiastic than he'd expected, broke out, he nearly cheered himself. But even as he started to rise, hands shot up.

Annoyed, he checked his watch, then settled himself for the question-and-answer session. As she was working with an interpreter, he decided the session might take the rest of his life.

He noted she took the glasses off for this portion, blinked like an owl in sunlight, and seemed to take a very long breath. The way a diver might, he mused, before plunging off a high board into a dark pool.

When inspiration struck, he lifted his hand. It was always best, he thought, to knock politely on a door to see if it opened before you just kicked it in.

When she gestured to him, he got to his feet and sent her one of his best smiles. "Dr. Marsh, I'd like to thank you first for a fascinating talk."

"Oh."

She blinked, and he saw she'd been surprised by the Irish in his voice. Good, something else to use. Yanks, for reasons that eluded him, were so often charmed silly by an accent.

"You're welcome," she said.

"I've always been interested in the Fates, and I wonder, in your opinion, if their power held individually or only because of their union."

"The Moerae, or the Fates, were a triad," she began, "each with a specific task. Clotho, who spins the thread of life, Lachesis, who measures it, and Atropus, who cuts that thread and ends it. None could function alone. A thread might be spun, but endlessly and without purpose or its natural course. Or without the spinning, there's nothing to measure, nothing to cut. Three parts," she added, sliding her fingers into an interlocking steeple. "One purpose." And closed them into a joined fist. "Alone they would be nothing but ordinary if interesting women. Together, the most powerful and honored of gods."

Exactly so, he thought as he resumed his seat. Exactly.


SHE WAS SO tired. When the Q-and-A session was finished, Tia wondered how she didn't simply stumble her way to the signing area. Despite the precautions of melatonin, diet, aromatherapy and cautious exercise, her internal time clock was running ragged.

But she was tired, she reminded herself, in Helsinki. And that counted for something. Everyone was so kind, so interested here. Just as they had been at every stop since she'd left New York.

How long ago was that? she wondered as she took her seat, picked up her pen, plastered on her author smile. Twenty-two days. It was important to remember the days, and that she was more than three-quarters of the way through this self-imposed torture.

How do you conquer phobia? Dr. Lowenstein had asked. By facing the phobia. You've got chronic shyness with whiffs of paranoia? Get out there and interact with the public. She wondered when a patient came to Lowenstein with a fear of heights if his solution was a fast leap off the Brooklyn Bridge.

Had he listened when she'd assured him she was positive she had social anxiety disorder? Perhaps agoraphobia combined with claustrophobia?

No, he had not. He'd insisted she was merely shy, and had suggested she leave the psychiatric evaluations and diagnoses to him.

As her stomach churned when the first members of the audience walked up for a word and a signature, she wished she could face Dr. Lowenstein right this minute. So she could punch him.

Still, it was better, she was forced to admit. She was better. She'd gotten through the lecture, and this time without a Xanax or a quick, guilty shot of whiskey.

The trouble was the lecturing wasn't nearly as hard as

this one-on-one business. With lecturing there was a nice cushion of distance and dispassion. She had *notes* when she lectured, a clear-cut plan that moved from Ananke to Zeus.

But when people came up to a signing table, they expected spontaneity and chat and, God, charm.

Her hand didn't shake as she signed her name. Her voice didn't quaver as she spoke. That was progress. At her first stop in London she'd been nearly catatonic by the end of the program. By the time she'd gotten back to her hotel, she'd been a quivering, quaking mess and had solved that little problem by taking a couple of pills and sliding into the safe cocoon of drug-induced sleep.

God, she'd wanted to go home. She'd wanted to run like a rabbit back to her bolt-hole in New York, lock herself in her lovely apartment. But she'd made commitments, given her word.

A Marsh never broke her word.

Now she could be glad, even proud, she'd held on, had white-knuckled her way through the first week, quivered through the second and gritted her way through the third. At this point she was nearly too exhausted from the rigors of travel to be nervous at the prospect of speaking to strangers.

Her face was numb from smiling by the time the end of the line tailed around. She lifted her gaze, met the grass-green eyes of the Irishman who'd asked her about the Fates.

"A fascinating lecture, Dr. Marsh," he said in that lovely lilt.

"Thank you. I'm glad you enjoyed it." She was already reaching for his book when she realized he'd held out a hand. She fumbled a bit, then switched her pen to her left and shook his.

Why was it people always wanted to shake hands? she wondered. Didn't they *know* how many germs were transferred that way?

His hand was warm, firm, and lingered on hers just long enough to have embarrassed heat creeping up her neck.

"Speaking of fate," he said and gave her an easy, dazzling smile. "I was pleased with mine when I saw you'd be here while I was in Helsinki on business. I've admired your work for some time." He lied without a flicker.

"Thank you." Oh God, conversation. First rule, have them do the talking. "You're from Ireland?"

"I am, yes. County Cork. But traveling just now, as you are."

"Yes, as I am."

"Traveling's an exciting part of life, isn't it?"

Exciting? she thought. "Yes, very." It was her turn to lie.

"I seem to be holding you up." He handed her the book. "I'm Malachi, Malachi Sullivan."

"It's nice to meet you." She signed his book in a careful and lovely hand, struggling to calculate how best to end the conversation and, at last, the event. "Thank you so much for coming, Mr. Sullivan." She got to her feet. "I hope your business in Finland is successful."

"So do I, Dr. Marsh."

NO, SHE WASN'T what he'd expected, and that had Malachi reevaluating his approach. He might have taken her for aloof, cool and a bit of a snob. But he'd seen the flush warm her cheeks and the occasional glint of panic in her eyes. What she was, he decided as he loitered on the corner, watching the hotel entrance, was shy.

What a woman floating in money, status and privilege had to be shy about, he couldn't say. But it took all kinds to make the world, he supposed.

The question could be asked, he admitted, why a perfectly sane man with a reasonably content life, a reasonably decent income should travel to Helsinki on the chance that a woman he'd never met might lead him to a treasure that may or may not exist?

The question, he thought, had too many layers for a single easy answer. But if he had to choose one, it would be family honor.

No, that wasn't quite enough. The second part was that he'd held Fate in his hand, and wouldn't rest until he had a hold on it again.

Tia Marsh was connected to his past and, to his way of

thinking, to his future. He checked his watch. He hoped, in very short order, they'd take the first step ahead.

It pleased him when his guess proved out. She'd come straight back to the hotel from the university, he noted as he watched her climb out of the cab. And she'd come alone.

He sauntered down the sidewalk, gauging his timing. He glanced toward her just as she turned. Once again they were face-to-face.

"Dr. Marsh." The tone of his voice, the spread of his smile were calculated for surprise and flattery. "You're staying here as well, then?"

"Ah yes. Mr. Sullivan." She remembered his name. In fact, she'd been thinking how attractive he was while she'd rubbed antibacterial lotion on her hands in the taxi.

"It's a lovely hotel. Fine service." He turned as if to walk to the door and open it for her, then stopped. "Dr. Marsh, I hope you won't think this out of line, but I wonder if I might buy you a drink."

"I . . ." Part of her brain fizzled. She'd actually woven a complex little fantasy on the taxi ride as well. One where she'd been witty and sophisticated during their conversation, and they'd ended up finishing the evening with a mad, reckless affair. "I don't really drink," she managed.

"Don't you?" Amusement touched his face. "Well, that knocks down the first approach a man might use to spend some time with an interesting and attractive woman. Would you fancy a walk?"

"Excuse me?" She couldn't keep up. He couldn't be hitting on her. She wasn't the type men hit on, particularly wildly attractive strangers with fabulous accents.

"One of the charms of Helsinki in the summer is the sun." Taking advantage of her confusion, he took her arm, gently, and steered her away from the hotel entrance. "Here it is, half past nine already, and bright as day. It's a shame to waste such a light, isn't it? Have you been down to the harbor?"

"No, I . . ." Baffled by the turn of events, she looked back at the hotel. Solitude. Safety. "I really should—"

"Have you an early flight in the morning?" He knew she didn't, but wondered if she'd have the guile to lie.

"No. No, actually, I'm here until Wednesday."

"Well then. Let me take that case for you." He slid her briefcase off her shoulder and onto his own. Though the weight surprised him, it was a smooth move. "It must be a challenge giving talks and seminars and such in a country where you don't have the primary language."

"I had an interpreter."

"Yes, she was very good. Still, it's a bit of work, isn't it? Do you wonder at such interest here in the Greeks?"

"There are correlations between the Greek gods and myths and the Norse. Deities with human failings and virtues, the adventures, the sex, the betrayals."

And if he didn't steer the conversation as he was steering her, Malachi thought, they'd be right back in lecture mode. "You're right, of course. I'm from a country that prizes its myths. Have you ever been to Ireland?"

"Once, when I was a child. I don't remember it."

"That's a shame. You'll have to go back. Are you warm enough?"

"Yes. I'm fine." The minute she said it, she realized she should have complained of a chill and gotten away. The next problem was she'd been so flustered she'd paid no attention to the direction. Now she hadn't a clue how to get back to the hotel. But surely it couldn't be difficult.

The streets were straight and neat, she noted as she worked to calm herself. And though it was moving toward ten at night, crowded with people. It was the light, of course. That lovely, luminous summer light that drenched the city in warm charm.

She hadn't even looked around until now, she admitted. Hadn't taken a stroll, done any foolish shopping, had a coffee at one of the sidewalk tables.

She'd done here what she did all too often in New York. Stayed in her nest until she had to fulfill an obligation.

He thought she looked a bit like a sleepwalker coming out of a trance as she studied the surroundings. Her arm was still rigid in his, but he thought it less likely she'd bolt now. There were enough people around to make her feel safe with him, he assumed. Crowds and couples and tourists all taking advantage of the endless day.

There was music coming from the square, and the crowd was thicker there. He skirted the bulk of it, nudging her closer to the harbor, where the breeze danced. It was there, by the edge of that deep blue water where boats, red and white, bobbed, that he saw her smile easily for the first time.

"It's beautiful." She had to lift her voice over the music. "So streamlined and perfect. I wish I'd taken the ferry from Stockholm, but I was afraid I'd get seasick. Still, I'd have been sick on the Baltic Sea. That has to count for something."

When he laughed, she glanced up, flustered. She'd nearly forgotten she'd been talking to a stranger. "That sounds stupid."

"No, it sounds charming." It surprised him that he meant it. "Let's do what the Finns do at such a time."

"Take a sauna?"

He laughed again, let his hand slide down her arm until it linked with hers. "Have some coffee."


IT SHOULDN'T HAVE been possible. She shouldn't have been sitting at a crowded sidewalk cafe, under pearly sunlight at eleven at night in a city thousands of miles from home. Certainly she shouldn't have been sitting across from a man so ridiculously handsome she had to fight the urge to glance around to be sure he wasn't talking to someone else.

His wonderful head of chestnut brown hair fluttered around his face in the steady breeze. It waved a bit, that hair, and caught glints of the sun. His face was smooth and narrow with just a hint of hollows in the cheeks. His mouth, mobile and firm, could light into a smile designed to make a woman's pulse flutter.

It certainly worked on hers.

His eyes were framed by thick, dark lashes, arched over by expressive brows. But it was the eyes themselves that captivated her. They were the deep green of summer grass, with a halo of pale gold ringing the pupil. And they stayed fixed on hers when she spoke. Not in a probing, uncomfortable way. But an interested one.

She'd had men look at her with interest before. She wasn't a gorgon, after all, she reminded herself. But somehow she'd managed to reach the age of twenty-nine and never have a man look at her in quite the way Malachi Sullivan looked at her.

She should have been nervous, but she wasn't. Not really. She told herself it was because he was so obviously a gentleman, in both manner and dress. He spoke well, seemed so at ease with himself. The stone-gray business suit fit his tall, lanky form perfectly.

Her father, whose fashion sense was laser keen, would have approved.

She sipped her second cup of decaf coffee and wondered what generous gift of fate had put him in her path.

They were talking of the Three Fates again, but she didn't mind. It was easier to talk of the gods than of personal things.

"I've never decided if it's comforting or frightening to consider your life being determined, all before you've taken your first breath, by three women."

"Not just the length of a life," Tia put in, and had to bite back the urge to warn him of the perils of refined white sugar when he added a generous teaspoon to his coffee. "The tone of it. The good and the evil in you. The Fates distribute that good and that evil justly. It's still up to a man what he does with what's inside him."

"Not preordained then?"

"Every act is an act of will, or lack of it." She moved her shoulders. "And every act has consequences. Zeus, king of the gods, and quite the ladies' man, wanted Thetis. The Moerae prophesied that her son would be more famous, perhaps more powerful in some way, than Zeus himself. And Zeus, recalling just how he'd dealt with his own father, feared siring this child. So he gave Thetis up, thinking of his own welfare."

"It's a foolish man who gives up a woman because of what may happen down the road."

"It didn't do him any good anyway, did it, since Thetis went on to mother Achilles. Perhaps if he'd followed his heart instead of his ambition, married her and loved the child, showed pride in his son's accomplishments, Zeus would have had a different fate."

What the hell had happened to Zeus? Malachi wondered, but thought it wiser not to ask. "So, he chose his own destiny by looking into the dark inside himself and projecting that on a child yet unconceived."

Her face lit at his response. "You could say that. You could also say the past sends out ripples. If you follow mythology, you know every finger dipped into the pool sends those ripples out, and they touch on those who come after. Generation after generation."

She had lovely eyes, he mused, when you got close enough to really look into them. The irises were a clear and perfect blue. "It's the same with people, isn't it?"

"I think so. That's one of the core themes of the book. We can't escape fate, but we can do a great deal to carve our own mark in it, to turn it to our advantage, or disadvantage."

"It seems mine's turned to advantage by scheduling this particular trip at this particular time."

She knew the heat was rising to her cheeks again, and lifted her cup in hopes of hiding it. "You haven't said what business you're in."

"Shipping." It was close to the truth. "It's a family business, several generations now. A fateful choice." He said it casually, but watched her like a hawk watches a rabbit. "When you consider my great-great-grandfather was one of the survivors of the *Lusitania*."

Her eyes widened as she lowered her cup. "Really? That's so strange. Mine died on the *Lusitania*."

"Is that the truth?" His astonishment was exactly the right tone. "That's a strong coincidence. I wonder if they knew each other, Tia." He touched a hand to hers, and when she didn't jolt, let it linger. "I'm becoming a champion believer in fate."

As HE WALKED with her back to the hotel, Malachi debated how much more to say, and how to say it. In the end he decided to temper his impatience with discretion. If he brought up the statues too soon, she might see through the layers of coincidence to cold calculation.

"Do you have any plans for tomorrow?"

"Tomorrow?" She could barely get over that she'd ended up having plans tonight. "No, not really."

"Why don't I pick you up about one. We'll have lunch." He smiled as he led her into the lobby. "See where it takes us."

She'd intended to pack, call home, work a bit on her new book and spend at least an hour doing her relaxation exercises.

She couldn't think why.

"That would be nice."

Perfect, he thought. He'd give her a little romance, a little adventure. A drive to the sea. And drop in the first mention of the little silver statues. At the desk he asked for her key and his own.

Before she could reach for her key, he had it in his hand and with the other pressed lightly to the small of her back, walked with her to the elevator.

It wasn't until the doors whisked shut and she was alone with him in the elevator that she tasted the first bubble of panic. What was she doing? What was *he* doing? He'd only pressed the button for her floor.

She'd broken every rule in *The Businesswoman's Travel Handbook*. Had obviously wasted $14.95 and all the hours she'd spent studying every page. He knew her room number and that she was traveling alone.

He would force himself into her room, rape and murder her. Or, *or* with the imprint of the key he could be making even now, he'd sneak in later and rape and murder her.

And all because she'd paid no attention to Chapter Two.

She cleared her throat. "Are you on four as well?"

"Hmm? No. I'm on six. I'll walk you to your door, Tia, as my mother would expect. I need to find a present for her, some glass, I'm thinking. Maybe you'll help me choose the right thing."

The mention of his mother, as he'd expected, relaxed her again. "You'll have to tell me what she likes."

"She likes anything her children buy her," he said as the elevator doors opened again.

"Children?"

"I've a brother and a sister. Gideon and Rebecca. She went biblical on the names, who knows why." He stopped at her door, slid her key into the lock. After he'd turned the knob, eased it open a crack, he stepped back.

He heard and nearly chuckled at her quiet sigh of relief. And because he'd heard it, been amused by it, he took her hand. "I have to thank you, and the gods, for a memorable evening."

"I had a lovely time."

"Until tomorrow, then." He kept his eyes on hers as he lifted her hand, brushed his lips over the knuckles. The little quiver of response did a great deal for his ego.

Shy, delicate and sweet. And as far from his type as the moon from the sun. Still, there was no reason a man shouldn't experiment with a new taste now and again.

He might just have a sip of her tomorrow.

"Good night, Tia."

"Good night." A little flustered, she backed into the door, her gaze locked with his until she stepped over the threshold.

Then she turned. And she screamed.

He was in the room ahead of her like a bullet. Under other circumstances she'd have noted and admired the speed and grace with which he moved. But at the moment, all she saw was the wreck of her hotel room.

Her clothes were strewn everywhere. Her suitcases had been slit to pieces, the bed overturned, and all the drawers dumped. Her jewelry case had its contents spilled out and its lining ripped free.

The desk in the sitting area had been ransacked as well. And the laptop that had sat on it was gone.

"Bloody hell," Malachi stated. All he could think was the bitch had beaten him to it.

Fury dark on his face, he whirled around. And one look at Tia had him biting back the rest of the oaths. She was white as a sheet, her eyes already going glassy with shock.

She doesn't deserve this, he thought. And he had no

doubt it was his hunting her down that had brought this on her.

"You need to sit down."

"What?"

"Sit." Brisk now, he took her by the arm and pulled her to a chair, dumped her in it. "We'll call security. Can you tell if anything's missing?"

"My computer." She tried to catch her breath, found it blocked. Fearing an asthma attack, she dug in her brief-case for her inhaler. "My laptop's gone."

He frowned at her while she sucked on the inhaler. "What was on it?"

She waved a hand as she drew in medication. "My work," she managed between gulps. "New book. E-mail, accounts—banking." She rooted through her bag again for pills. "I've got a disk copy of the book in here." But it was a prescription bottle she pulled out.

Malachi nipped it out of her hand. "What's this?" He read the label, and his frown deepened. "We'll just hold off on this for now. You're not going to be hysterical."

"I'm not?"

"You're not."

She felt the telltale tickle at the back of her throat that presaged a panic attack. "I think you're wrong."

"Stop that, you'll hyperventilate or some such thing." Straining for patience, he crouched in front of her. "Look at me now, breathe slowly. Just breathe slowly."

"Can't."

"Yes, you can. You're not hurt, are you? Got a mess on your hands is all."

"Someone broke into my room."

"That's right, but that's done. You gobbling down tran-quilizers isn't going to change it. What about your pass-port, any valuables. Important papers."

Because he made her think instead of react, the con-striction on her chest loosened. She shook her head. "I have my passport with me all the time. I don't travel with anything really valuable. But my laptop—"

"You'll buy another, won't you?"

Put that way, she could only nod. "Yes."

He got up to close the door. "Do you want to call security?"

"Yes, of course. The police."

"Take a minute to be sure. You're in a foreign country. A police report'll generate a lot of red tape, take a lot of time and trouble. And there'd be publicity, I'd imagine."

"But . . . someone broke into my room."

"Maybe you should go through your things." He kept his voice calm and practical as he thought it the best way to handle her. It was the way his own mother handled temper fits, and what was hysteria but a kind of temper?

"Make sure exactly what was taken." He glanced around, then toed a little white machine with his foot. "What's this?"

"Air purifier." When he picked it up, set it on the desk, she got shakily to her feet. "I can't understand why anyone would do all this for a laptop computer."

"Maybe they were hoping for more." He wandered to the door of the bathroom, glanced in.

He'd already decided the Finns deserved some sort of grand prize for the luxury of their baths. Hers, being that her room was plusher, was more spacious than his, but his didn't lack for details.

The heated floor tiles, the jet tub, the glory of the six-headed shower and towels thick and big as blankets. On her long tiled counter he saw a half dozen pill bottles, most of which proved to be some sort of vitamin or herbal remedy. There was an electric toothbrush, a travel candle, a tube of antibacterial cream. Packets of something called N-ER-G and more packets of something called D-Stress. He counted eight bottles of mineral water.

"You're a bit of a case, aren't you, darling?"

She ran a hand over her face. "Traveling's stressful, it's hard on the system. I have allergies."

"Do you now? Why don't I help you set this place back to rights, then you can take one of your pills and get some sleep."

"I couldn't possibly sleep. I need to call hotel security."

"All right." It was no skin off his nose, really, and would put more of a hitch in her stride than his. Obliging, he went to the phone and called the front desk to relay the situation.

He even stayed with her when management and security came. He patted her hand while she spoke to them, co-operatively gave his own version of the evening and his name and address, his passport number.

He had, essentially, nothing to hide.

It was nearly two A.M. before he made it back to his own room. He had a long, neat whiskey. Brooded over another.

When Tia woke the next morning, muzzy-brained, he was gone. All that was left to assure her he'd existed in the first place was a note slipped under her door.

*Tia, I hope you're feeling steadier this morning. I'm sorry but I've had to change my plans and will have already left Helsinki when you read this. The best of luck with the rest of your traveling. I'll be in touch when I can. Malachi.*

She sighed, sat on the edge of the bed and decided she'd never see him again.

# Three

MALACHI called for a meeting the minute he arrived back in Cobh. Due to the import, schedules were hastily rearranged and concerned parties made themselves available.

He stood at the head of the table as he relayed to his partners the events that took place during his stay in Finland.

When the tale was told, he sat, picked up his cup of tea.

"Well, you dimwit, why didn't you stay and give her another push?"

Since this came from the youngest partner, who also happened to be his sister, Malachi didn't take particular offense. The meeting table, in the Sullivan tradition, was the kitchen table. Before he answered, he got to his feet again, took the biscuit tin off the counter and helped himself.

"First, because pushing would've done more harm than good. The woman has more brains than a cabbage, Becca. If I'd nudged her about the statues right after she'd had her room tossed, she might very well have thought I'd had something to do with the matter. Which," he added with a scowl, "I suppose I did, indirectly."

"We can't blame ourselves for that. We aren't hooligans, after all, or thieves." Gideon was the middle child, nearly dead center at not quite two years younger than Malachi, not quite two older than Rebecca. This accident of birth had, more often than not, put him in the position of playing peacemaker between them.

He was his brother's match in height and build, but had inherited his mother's coloring. The lean, hollow-cheeked features of the Sullivans were stamped on his face, but his were set off with jet-black hair and Viking blue eyes.

He was, in his way, the most fastidious of the lot. He preferred having everything lined up in tidy columns, and because of it—though Malachi had more of a talent with figures—did duty as family bookkeeper.

"The trip wasn't wasted," he went on. "Neither the time nor the expense of it. You made contact with her, and now we've reason to believe we're not alone in our belief that she might be a likely contact to the Fates."

"We don't know if she is or isn't," Rebecca disagreed. "Because it's plain as rain it was Malachi who led them to her. Better if you'd gone hunting for the one who'd broken into her room instead of running back home."

"And how, Mata Hari, would you suggest I do that?" Malachi queried.

"Look for clues," she said with a sweep of arms. "Interrogate hotel staff. Do *something*."

"If only I'd remembered to pack my magnifying glass and deerstalker hat."

Exasperated, she sighed. She could see the sense of what he'd done, but when it came to a choice between sense and action, Rebecca would always toss sense. "All I see is we're out the price of the travel, and no better off than we were before you had your little fling with the Yank."

"We didn't have a fling," Malachi said with the edge of temper in his voice.

"Well, whose fault is that?" she shot back. "Seems to me you'd d've gotten more out of her if you'd softened her up in bed."

"Rebecca." The quiet censure came from the balance of power. Eileen Sullivan might have birthed three strong-willed children, but she had been, and always would be, the power.

"Ma, the man's thirty-one years old," Rebecca stated sweetly. "Surely you're aware he's had sex before."

Eileen was a pretty, tidy woman who took great pride in her family and her home. And when necessary, ruled both with an iron fist.

"This is not a discussion about your brother's private behavior, but a discussion of business. We agreed Mal would go and see what he would see. And so he has."

Rebecca subsided, though it wasn't easy. She adored her brothers, but there were times she could have bashed their heads together just to shake up their brains a bit.

She had the long, lean Sullivan build as well, and could be mistaken for willowy if attention wasn't paid to the strong shoulders and tough muscles under the skin she liked to pamper.

Her hair was shades lighter than Malachi's, more a gilded red than chestnut, and her eyes were a softer, mistier green. They were long-lidded and balanced a wide and stubborn mouth in a face more given to angles than curves.

Behind the eyes was a sharp, clever and often impatient brain.

She'd campaigned hard to be the one to go to Helsinki and make initial contact with Tia Marsh. She was still fuming at being outvoted in Malachi's favor.

"You'd have done no better with her," Malachi commented, reading her mind easily. "And sex wouldn't have been an option, would it? In any case, we are better off. She liked me, and she's not, I'd say, a woman easily comfortable with people. She's not like you, Becca." He moved around the table as he spoke, tugged on his sister's long curly hair. "She's not adventurous and bold."

"Don't try to soften me up."

He only grinned and tugged her hair again. "At your slowest pace, you'd have moved too fast for her. You'd've intimidated her. She's a shy one, and a bit of a hypochondriac, I think. You wouldn't have believed the stuff she had. Bottles of pills, little machines. Air purifiers, white-noise makers. It was a wonder when we went through it all for the cops. She travels with her own pillow—some allergic matter."

"Sounds a dead bore to me," Rebecca replied.

"No, not a bore." Malachi remembered that slow, sober smile. "Just a bit nervy is all. Still, when the police got there she pulled herself together. Went through the report, steady as you please, every step of it, from the time she left the hotel to go to her lecture until she walked back in again."

And hadn't, he remembered now, missed a single detail.

"She's got a brain in there," he mused. "Like a camera taking pictures and filing them in a proper slot, and a spine under all the worry."

"You liked her," Rebecca said.

"I did. And I'm sorry to have caused her the trouble. But, well, she'll get over it." He sat again, and dumped sugar in the cup of tea he'd let go nearly cold. "We'll let that end simmer a bit, at least until she's back in the States and settled. Then I might take a trip to New York."

"New York." Rebecca sprang to her feet. "Why do you get to go everywhere?"

"Because I'm the oldest. And because for better or worse, Tia Marsh is mine. We'll be more careful with step two since it appears our movements are being watched."

"One of us ought to go deal with that bitch directly," Rebecca said. "She stole from us, stole what had been in our family for more than three-quarters of a century, and now she's trying to use us to find the other two pieces. She needs to be told, in no uncertain terms, that the Sullivans won't stand for it."

"What she'll do is pay." Malachi leaned back. "And dearly when we have the other two Fates and she only the one."

"The one she stole from us."

"It'd be hard explaining to the proper authorities that she stole what had already been stolen." Gideon held up a hand before Rebecca could snap at him. "Eighty-odd years in the past or not, Felix Greenfield stole the first

Fate. I think we could come around that, legally, as there's no one to know it save us. But on the same point, we've no real proof that the statue was in our possession, and that someone with Anita Gaye's reputation would steal it from under our noses."

Rebecca gave a little sigh. "It's mortifying she did, as if we were little woolly lambs led dancing to the slaughter."

"Separate, that statue's worth no more than a few hundred thousand pounds." Because it still grated, Malachi put aside how easily he'd been duped out of the little Fate. "But all three together, that's priceless to the right collector. Anita Gaye's the right one, and in the end, it's her wool that'll be fleeced."

Sitting in the cheerful butter-yellow kitchen with his granny's chintz curtains at the window and the smell of summer grass dancing through them, he thought of just what he'd like to do to the woman who'd stolen the family symbol out of his foolish hands.

"I don't think we should wait to take step two," he decided. "Tia won't be back in New York for a couple weeks yet, and I don't want to show up on her doorstep too soon. What we need to do now is work on unraveling that thread to the second statue."

Rebecca shook back her hair. "Some of us haven't been spending their time kicking up their heels in foreign parts. I've done quite a bit of unraveling in the last few days."

"Why the hell didn't you say so?"

"Because you've been blathering on about your new Yank sweetheart."

"Oh, for Christ's sake, Becca."

"Don't take the Lord's name at my table," Eileen said mildly. "Rebecca, stop deviling your brother and preening."

"I wasn't preening. Yet. I've been searching on the Internet, doing the genealogy and so on. Day and night, by the way, and at great personal sacrifice. That was preening," she said with a grin to her mother. "Still, it's a big leap, as all we have to go on is Felix's memory of what he read on the paper with the statue. The dip in the ocean washed the ink away, and we're counting on him being clear about what he read before what had to be the most traumatic experience of his life. More, we're counting on his veracity," she decided. "And the man was, after all, a thief."

"Reformed," Eileen put in. "By the grace of God and the love of a good woman. Or so the story goes."

"So it goes," Rebecca agreed. "With the statue was a piece of paper, with a name and address in London. His claim that he committed it to memory as he thought he might stop by one night and ply his trade seems reasonable enough. More reasonable when I roll up my sleeves at the keyboard and find there was indeed a Simon White-Smythe living in Mansfield Park in 1915."

"You found him!" Malachi beamed at her. "You're a wonder, Rebecca."

"I am, as I found more than that. He had a son, name of James, who had two daughters. Both married, but the one lost her husband in the second great war and died childless. The other moved to the States, as her husband was a well-to-do lawyer in Washington, D.C. They had three children, two sons and a daughter. They lost one son when he was just a lad in Vietnam, the other hightailed it to Canada, and I haven't been able to get a line on him. But the daughter married three times. Can you beat it? She's living in Los Angeles. She had one child with husband number one, daughter. I tracked her down, too, on the information highway. She's living at the moment in Prague, with employment at some club there."

"Well, Prague's closer than Los Angeles," Malachi replied. "Couldn't have just stayed in London, could they? We're taking a leap of faith here, that the man White-Smythe had the statue to begin with, or knew how to get it. That if he had it, it's been kept in the family, or there's a record where it went. And that all being the case, we can finagle it out of their hands."

"It was a leap of faith when your great-great-grandfather gave his life jacket to a stranger and her child," Eileen put in. "To my mind there's a reason he was spared when so many were lost. A reason why that little statue was in his pocket when he was saved. Because of that, it belongs to this family," she continued with her cool, unshakable logic. "And as it's part of a piece, the others should come to us as well. It's not the money, it's the principle. We can afford a ticket to Prague to see if there's an answer there."

She smiled serenely at her daughter. "What's the name of the club, darling?"


THE NAME OF the club was Down Under, and it escaped the sloppy slide down to dive due to the vigilance of its proprietor, Marcella Lubriski. Whenever the joint would start to waver, Marcella would kick it back up to level by the toe of her stiletto heel.

She was a product of her country and her time, part Czech, part Slavic, with a drop of Russian and a whiff of German in the blood. When the Communists had taken over, she'd gathered up her two young children, told her husband to go or stay, and fled to Australia, as it seemed just far enough away.

She'd had no English, no contacts, the equivalent of two hundred dollars tucked in her bra and, as her husband had opted to remain in Prague, no father for her babies.

What she'd had was spine, a shrewd mind and a body fashioned for wet dreams. She'd put all of them to use in a strip joint in Sydney, taking it off for the drunk and the lonely and ruthlessly banking her meager pay as well as her substantial tips.

She'd learned to love the Aussies for their generosity, their humor and their easy acceptance of the outcast. She saw that her children were well fed, and if she occasionally took a private job to see that they also had good shoes, it was only sex.

Within five years, she had enough socked away to invest in a small club with partners. She still stripped, she still sold her body when it suited her. Within ten years, she'd bought out her partners and retired from the stage.

By the time the wall came down, Marcella owned the club in Sydney, one in Melbourne, a percentage of an office complex and a good chunk of a residential apartment building. She'd been pleased to see the Communists ousted from the land of her birth, but had given the matter little thought.

At first.

But she'd begun to wonder and, to her surprise, to yearn to hear her own language spoken in the streets, to see the domes and bridges of her own city. Leaving her son and daughter in charge of her Australian holdings, Marcella flew back to Prague for what she assumed would be a sentimental journey.

But the businesswoman in her smelled opportunity, and opportunities were not to be wasted. Prague would once more be a city that mixed Old World and New, would once again become the Paris of Eastern Europe. That meant commerce, tourist dollars, and getting in on the ground floor.

She bought property—a small, atmospheric hotel; a quaint, traditional restaurant. And, out of that sentiment for both her homelands, she opened Down Under.

She ran a clean place with healthy girls. She didn't mind if they took private jobs. She knew very well that sex often paid for the extras that made life bearable. But if there was a hint of drug use, employee or customer, the offender was shown the door.

There were no second chances at Down Under.

She developed a cordial relationship with the local police, regularly attended the opera and became a patron of the arts. She watched her city come to life again, with color, with music and with money.

Though she claimed she intended to return to Sydney, years passed. And she stayed.

At sixty, she maintained the body that had made her fortune, dressed in the latest Paris fashions and could spot a troublemaker at ten yards in the dark.

When Gideon Sullivan walked in, she gave him one long stare. Too handsome for his own good, she decided. And his gaze scanned the room rather than the stage, looking for something other than pretty, bouncing breasts.

Or someone.

\*    \*    \*

THE CLUB WAS slicker than he'd expected. There was plenty of bass-heavy techno music blaring, and lights flashing in concert. Onstage a trio of women were performing some sort of routine on long silver poles.

He supposed some men liked to imagine their dick as the pole, but Gideon could think of better uses for his than having a woman hanging upside down on it.

There were plenty of tables, all of them occupied. The ones nearest the stage were jammed with both men and women sipping drinks and watching the naked acrobatics.

Hazy blue smoke fogged in the light streams, but the smell of whiskey and beer was no more offensive than in his own local pub. A lot of the clientele wore black, and a lot of the black was leather, but there were enough obvious couples to make him wonder why a man would bring a date along to watch other women strip.

Though the place was somehow more middle-class than the dive he and Malachi had spent one memorable evening in on a trip to London, he was glad his mother had sent him, over Rebecca's furious objections, rather than his sister.

This was no place for a young woman of good family.

Though apparently Cleo Toliver found it suitable enough.

He moved to the bar, ordered a beer. He could see the dancers, down to G-strings and tattoos now as they swung in unison on their poles, in the mirrors behind it.

He took out a cigarette, struck a match and considered his best approach. He preferred the direct route whenever possible.

As applause and whistles broke out, he gestured to the bartender. "Cleo Toliver working tonight?"

"Why?"

"Family connection."

The man didn't respond to Gideon's easy smile, but only mopped at the bar, shrugged. "She's around." And moved off before Gideon could ask where.

So I'll wait, Gideon thought. There were worse ways for a man to spend his time than watching well-built women peel off their clothes.

"You looking for one of my girls?"

Gideon turned from the performer who was currently crawling over the stage like a cat. The woman who stood beside him was nearly as tall as he was. Her hair was Harlow blonde and coiled in complicated, lacquered twists. She wore a business suit, without a blouse, and the milky tops of her rather amazing breasts spilled out between the lapels.

He felt a twinge of guilt for noticing them when he looked at her face and realized she was more than old enough to be his mother.

"Yes, ma'am. I'm looking for Cleo Toliver."

Marcella's brows lifted at the polite address, and she signaled for a drink. "Why?"

"Begging your pardon. I'd rather speak to Miss Toliver about that, if it's all the same to you."

Without glancing at the bar, Marcella lifted the neat scotch she knew would be there. Might be handsome as sin, she mused, and have the look of a man who could handle himself in a fight. But he'd been raised to be respectful to his elders.

While she didn't necessarily trust such niceties, she appreciated them.

"You cause trouble for one of my girls, I cause trouble for you."

"I'd as soon avoid trouble altogether."

"See you do. Cleo is the next act." She downed her scotch, set down the empty and strolled away on her icepick heels.

She made her way backstage, through the smell of perfume, sweat and face paint. Her dancers shared one room lined on both sides with long mirrors and communal counters. Each made her own nest out of a section, so that the counters were a messy sea of cosmetics, pasties, stuffed toys and candy. Photographs of boyfriends, film stars and the occasional toddler were pasted to the mirrors.

As usual, the room was a gaggle of languages, of bitching, gossip and complaints. Complaints ranged from cheap tips, cheating lovers and menstrual cramps to aching feet.

In the midst of it, like a cool island, Cleo stood putting the last pins in her long, sable-colored hair. She was friendly enough with the other girls, Marcella thought, but not friends with them. She did her work and did it well, collected her money and went home alone.

So, Marcella remembered, had she in her time.

"There is a man asking about you."

Cleo's eyes, a deep, dark brown, met Marcella's in the mirror. "Asking what?"

"Just asking. He's handsome, maybe thirty, Irish. Dark hair, blue eyes. Well mannered."

Cleo shrugged shoulders currently covered in a conservative gray pin-striped suit jacket. "I don't know anyone like that."

"He asked for you by name, told Karl you were a family connection."

Cleo leaned forward to slick murderous red over her lips. "I don't think so."

"You in trouble?"

She shot the cuffs of the tailored white shirt she wore under the jacket. "No."

"If he gives you any, just signal to Karl. He'll show him out." Marcella nodded. "The Irishman's at the bar. You won't miss him."

Cleo slipped into the spike-heeled black pumps that completed her costume. "Thanks. I can handle him."

"I think this is so." Marcella laid a hand on her shoulder briefly, then moved on to break up an argument between two of the dancers over a red-spangled bra.

If she was concerned someone had come in and asked for her by name, Cleo didn't show it. She was, after all, a professional. Whether dancing *Swan Lake* or peeling it off for Euro-trash, there were professional standards for a performer.

I don't know any Irishmen, she thought as she clipped out to wait for her cue. And she certainly didn't buy that anyone remotely connected to her family would trouble themselves to ask about her. Even if they'd tripped over her bleeding body in the street.

Probably just some asshole, she decided, who'd gotten

her name from another customer and thought he might wrangle a cheap boink from an American stripper.

He was going to go home disappointed.

As her music came up, she pushed all thoughts but her routine out of her head. She counted the beats, and when the lights flashed on, Cleo erupted onto the stage.

At the bar, Gideon's hand froze in the act of lifting his beer.

She was dressed like a man. Though no one would mistake her for one, he admitted. Not if you were blind and on the back of a galloping horse. But there was something primitively erotic about the way she moved inside that traditional pin-striped suit.

The music was hot, edgy American rock, and her lighting a steamy and smoky blue. He found it clever and ironic that she'd select Bruce Springsteen's "Cover Me" to strip to.

She knew what she was about, he realized as she tugged the tailored jacket off her shoulders, moving, always moving, pulled it off.

While the others on the stage had been spinning or sliding, shaking or shimmying, this one was dancing. Sharp, complicated moves that demonstrated genuine style and talent.

Though when, with one of those sharp moves, she ripped the breakaway trousers aside, he lost track of the style for a moment.

Christ, she had legs, didn't she?

She used the poles as well, doing three fast circles with those long legs cocked up. Her hair tumbled free, past her shoulders in a straight rainfall of rich brown. He didn't see how she opened the shirt, but it was flying around her now, revealing a scrap of black lace over high, firm breasts.

He tried to tell himself they were likely manufactured, and either way they had nothing to do with him. But he found saliva pooling in his mouth when she stripped off the shirt.

To clear his throat, he sipped his beer, and watched her. She'd made him from her first turn. She couldn't see him clearly, and wasn't concerned enough to worry about it. But she knew he was there, and that his attention was on her.

That was fine. That's what she got paid for.

With her back to the audience, she slid a hand down her back, flicked open the catch of her bra. Crossing her arms over her breasts, she spun back. There was a light dew of sweat on her skin now, and a small grin—ice cold—on her lips as she made eye contact with the men in the audience she'd deemed most likely to part with folded money.

She tossed her hair back and, wearing nothing but the heels and a black G-string, lowered to a crouch so they could see what they were paying for.

She ignored the fingers sliding over her hips and registered the money tucked under the G-string.

She eased back when one overenthusiastic patron reached for her. In a move that could have been mistaken for playful, she wagged a finger at him. And thought, Asshole.

She came up in a one-armed backbend, then using her legs surged to her feet.

She played the other side of the stage in much the same way. But here she got a better look at the man at the bar. Their eyes met, held for two beats. He held up a bill, cocked his head.

Then he went back to sipping his beer.

SHE WISHED SHE'D been able to make out the denomination of the bill. But she thought it might be worth five minutes of her time to find out how much he'd pay.

Still, she took her time, cooled off in the shower, then pulled on jeans and a T-shirt. It was a rare thing for her to go out into the club after a performance, but she trusted Karl and the other muscle Marcella kept on tap to keep her from being hassled.

In any case, most of the patrons kept their attention on-stage, toward the fantasy sex, rather than scoping out the real women in the area.

Except for Slick, she thought, at the bar. He wasn't

watching the stage. Though in her professional opinion the current act was one of the more creative ones. His gaze stayed on her as she crossed to the bar. And on her face—which she gave him points for—rather than on her tits.

"You want something, Slick?"

Her voice surprised him. It was smooth and silky and without any of the hard edge he'd expected from a woman in her line of work.

Her face did credit to her body. It was hot and sultry with those dark, almond-shaped eyes and the full, red-slicked mouth. There was a little mole, a beauty mark, he supposed you called it, just at the lower end of her right eyebrow.

Her skin was dusky, adding a touch of erotic gypsy.

She smelled of soap—another illusion shattered. And sipped idly from a tall bottle of water.

"I do if you're Cleo Toliver."

She leaned back on the bar. She wore tennis shoes now rather than heels, but the jeans were black and molded tight to her hips and legs.

"I don't do private parties."

"Do you talk?"

"When I have something to say. Who gave you my name?"

Gideon merely showed her the bill again, watched her gaze flick on it and narrow in speculation. "I think this should buy an hour's conversation."

"It might." She'd reserve judgment on whether or not he was a moron, but at least he wasn't cheap. She reached for the bill, annoyed when he moved it just out of reach.

"What time do you finish here?"

"Two. Look, why don't you just tell me what you want, and I'll tell you if I'm interested."

"Conversation," he said again and tore the bill in half. He handed her one part, pocketed the other. "If you want the rest of it, meet me after closing. The coffee shop in the Wenceslas Hotel. I'll wait till two-thirty. If you don't show, we're both out fifty pounds."

He finished his beer, set down the glass. "It was an entertaining performance, Miss Toliver, and lucrative from the looks of it. But it's not every day you can make fifty pounds by sitting down and having a cup of coffee."

She frowned when he turned to walk away. "You got a name, Slick?"

"Sullivan. Gideon Sullivan. You've got till two-thirty."

# Four

CLEO never missed a cue. But neither did she believe in giving her audience the appearance she'd rushed to hit one. Theater was rooted in illusions. And life, like the big guy had said, was just a bigger stage.

She strolled toward the coffee shop at two minutes to deadline.

If some jerk with a pretty face and a sexy voice wanted to pay her for some conversation, that was fine by her. She'd already determined the exchange rate from Irish pounds to Czech koruna, using the little calculator she carried in her bag to figure it to the last haleru. In her current position, the money would go a very long way.

She didn't intend to make her living stripping off her clothes for a bunch of suckers for long. The fact was, she'd never intended to make her living, however temporary, dancing naked in a Prague strip club.

But she'd been stupid, Cleo could admit. She'd walked straight into a con, blinded by good looks and a clever line. And when a girl was flat-ass busted in Eastern Europe, in a city where she could barely manage the simplest phrase in the guidebook, she did what she could to make ends meet.

She had one thing on her side, she thought now. She never made the same mistake twice.

In that regard, at least, she was not her mother's daughter.

The little restaurant was brightly lit, and there were a few patrons scattered around the tables having coffee or a late meal. The company, such as it was, was a plus. Not that she was particularly worried about the Irish guy making a move on her. She could handle herself.

She spotted him at a corner booth, drinking coffee and reading a book, with a cigarette smoking away in a black plastic ashtray. With those dark, romantic looks, she thought, he'd pass for some kind of artist, a writer maybe. No, she decided, a poet. Some struggling poet who wrote dark, esoteric free verse and had come to the great city for inspiration as others had before him.

Looks, she thought with a smirk, were always deceiving.

He glanced up as she slid into the booth across from him. His eyes, a deep and crystal blue in the poetic face, were the type that shot straight to a woman's glands.

Good thing, Cleo acknowledged, she was immune.

"You cut it close," he commented and continued to read.

She merely shrugged, then turned to the waitress who stepped up to the booth. "Coffee. Three eggs, scrambled. Bacon. Toast. Thanks." Cleo smiled when she saw Gideon studying her over the top of his book. "I'm hungry."

"I suppose what you do works up an appetite."

He marked his place, set the book aside. Yeats, Cleo noted. It figured.

"That's the point, isn't it? Working up appetites." She stretched out her legs as the waitress poured her coffee. "How did you like my act?"

"It's better than most." She hadn't removed her stage makeup. In the bright lights she looked both hard and sexy. He imagined she knew it. Had planned it. "Why do you do it?"

"Unless you're a Broadway scout, Slick, that's my business." Watching him, she lifted a hand, rubbed her thumb and two fingers together.

Gideon took the half bill out of his pocket, then slid it under his book. "Talk first." He'd already outlined how he wanted to approach the matter with her and had decided the direct—well, fairly direct—route would work best.

"You have an ancestor on your mother's side. A Simon White-Smythe."

More puzzled than interested, Cleo sipped her coffee, strong and black. "So?"

"He was a collector, art and artifacts. There was a piece in his collection, a small silver statue of a woman. Greek style. I represent a party that's interested in obtaining that statue."

Cleo said nothing as her breakfast was served. The scent of food, particularly food she wasn't going to have to pay for, put her in a cooperative mood.

She scooped up a bite of egg, picked up a slice of bacon. "Why?"

"Why?"

"Yeah. This client got a reason for wanting some little silver woman?"

"Sentimental reasons, primarily. There was a man back in 1915 who was traveling to London to purchase it from your ancestor. He made an unwise choice in his mode of transportation," Gideon added as he helped himself to Cleo's bacon. "And booked passage on the *Lusitania*. He went down with it."

Cleo studied the selection of jams and settled on black currant. She slathered a slice of toast generously as her mind worked through the story.

Her grandmother on her mother's side, the one family member who'd been human and humorous, had been a White-Smythe by birth. So his story gelled, as far as it went.

"Your interested party's waited over eighty years to track down this statue?"

"Some are more sentimental than others," he said evenly. "You could say this man's fate was determined by that small statue. My job is to locate it and, if it remains in your family, to offer a reasonable price for it."

"Why me? Why not contact my mother? You're a generation closer that way."

"You were closer geographically. But if you've no knowledge of the piece, that's my next step."

"Your client sounds pretty screwy, Slick." Her lips

curved as she bit into her toast. Her eyebrows winged up, making the beauty mark a velvet period on a sexy exclamation point. "What's his definition of a reasonable price?"

"I'm authorized to offer five hundred."

"Pounds?"

"Pounds."

Jesus, Jesus, she thought as she continued to eat with every appearance of calm. That kind of money would fatten her get-out-of-Dodge fund. More, it would help her get back to the States without losing face.

But the man must have tagged her as an idiot if he thought she was buying his story from top to bottom.

"A silver statue?"

"Of a woman," he said, "about six inches high, holding a kind of measuring spool. Do you know it or not?"

"Don't rush me." She signaled for more coffee and continued to plow her way through the eggs. "I might have seen it. My family has a lot of dust catchers, and my grandmother was the world title holder. I can check on it, if you add another fifty to that," she said with a nod toward the note sticking out from under Yeats.

"Don't wind me up, Cleo."

"A girl's got to make a living. And the extra fifty's less than it would cost your client to send you to the States. Plus, my family's more likely to cooperate with me than a stranger."

Which is bullshit, of course, she thought.

Considering his options, Gideon slid the half bill across the table. "You'll get the other fifty if and when you earn it."

"Come by the club tomorrow night." She plucked up the bill, stuffed it into her jeans pocket.

Not an easy feat, Gideon mused, as those jeans appeared to be painted on.

"Bring the money." She slid out of the booth. "Thanks for the eggs, Slick."

"Cleo." He closed a hand over hers, squeezed just hard enough to be sure he had her attention. "You try to hose me, it's going to make me irritable."

"I'll remember that." She tossed him an easy grin, tugged her hand free, then strolled out with a deliberate swing of hips.

She made a statement, Gideon mused. Any man with a single red corpuscle would want to fuck her. But only a fool would trust her.

Eileen Sullivan hadn't raised any fools.


CLEO WENT STRAIGHT to her apartment, though calling the single room an apartment was like calling a Twinkie a fine dessert. You had to be either really young or stupidly optimistic.

Her clothes were hung on the iron rod that was screwed into a water-stained wall, stuffed into the banana-crate-sized dresser with its missing drawer, or tossed where they landed. She'd decided the problem with growing up with a maid was you never learned to be tidy.

Even with its single dresser, cot-sized bed and lopsided table, the room was crowded. But it was cheap and boasted its own bath. Such as it was.

While the room wasn't to her taste—and she was neither really young nor in any way optimistic—she could cover the weekly rent with one night's tips.

She'd installed the dead bolt lock herself after one of her neighbors had tried to muscle his way into her room for a free show. It gave her a considerable sense of security.

She switched on the light, tossed her purse aside. She went to the dresser, pawing her way through the top drawer. She'd had a considerable wardrobe when she'd landed in Prague, and a great deal of it had been new lingerie.

Bought, she thought viciously as she shoved through silk and lace, to delight one Sidney Walter. The prick. Then again, when a woman let herself spend a couple grand on undies because she was hot for a man, she deserved getting screwed. In every possible sense.

Sidney had certainly obliged her, Cleo thought now. Heating up the sheets in the presidential suite of the priciest hotel in Prague, then strolling away with all her cash and her jewelry and leaving her with a hefty hotel bill.

Leaving her, she added, flat broke and mortified.

Still, Sidney wasn't the only one who could cash in on an opportunity when it slapped him in the face. She smiled to herself as she yanked out a pair of athletic socks, unrolled them.

The little silver statue she uncovered was badly tarnished, but she remembered what it looked like when it was shiny and clean. Smiling to herself, Cleo rubbed a thumb over the face with absent affection.

"You don't much look like my ticket out of here," she murmured. "But we'll see."

SHE DIDN'T SHOW until nearly two the following afternoon. Gideon had just about given up on her. As it was, he nearly didn't recognize her when she finally came out into the broiling sunlight.

She wore jeans, a low-cut black top that offered peeks of her midriff. So it was her body he made out first. She'd pulled her hair back in a thick braid, shielded her eyes with dark, wraparound glasses and, walking briskly in some sort of thick-soled black boots, melded with pedestrian traffic.

About damn time, he thought as he followed her. He'd been stuck kicking his heels for hours waiting for her. Here he was in one of the most beautiful, most cultured cities in Eastern Europe, and he couldn't risk the time to see anything.

He wanted to drop in on the Mucha exhibit, to study the Art Nouveau foyer of the Main Station, to wander among the artists on the Charles bridge. Because the woman apparently slept half the day, he'd had to make do with reading a guidebook.

She didn't window-shop, never paused at the displays of crystal or garnets that flashed in the brilliant sunlight. She walked steadily, down sidewalks, over the cobbled bricks of squares and gave her shadow little time to admire the domes, the baroque architecture or the Gothic towers.

She stopped once at a sidewalk kiosk and bought a large

bottle of water, which she stuffed in the oversized purse on her shoulder.

Gideon regretted, when she kept up the clipped pace and the sweat began to run down his back, that he hadn't followed her lead.

He cheered a bit when he realized she was heading toward the river. Maybe he'd get a look at the Charles after all.

They passed pretty, painted shops thronged with tourists, restaurants where people sat under umbrella tables and cooled off with chilled drinks or ice cream, and still those long legs of hers climbed steadily up the steep slope to the bridge.

The breeze off the water did little to bring relief, and the view, while spectacular, didn't explain what the hell she was doing. She didn't so much as glance at the grandeur of Prague Castle or the cathedral, never paused to lean on the rail and contemplate the water and the boats that plied it. She certainly didn't stop to haggle with the artists.

She crossed the bridge and kept going.

He was trying to decide if she was heading to the castle, and if so why the hell she hadn't taken a bloody bus, when she veered off and walked breezily downhill to the street of tiny cottages where the king's goldsmiths and alchemists had once lived.

They were shops now, naturally, but that didn't detract from the charm of low doorways, narrow windows and faded colors. She cut through the tourists and tour groups as the uneven stone street climbed again.

She turned again, walked onto the patio of a little restaurant and plopped down at a table.

Before he could decide what to do next, she turned around in her chair and waved at him. "Buy me a beer," she called out.

He ground his teeth as she turned away again, stretched out her long, apparently tireless legs, then signaled to the waiter by holding up two fingers.

When he sat across from her, she offered a wide smile. "Pretty hot today, huh?"

"What the hell was this all about?"

"What? Oh this? I figured if you were going to follow me around, the least I could do was show you a little of the city. I was planning to hike up to the castle, but . . ." She tipped down her glasses and studied his face. It was a little sweaty, a lot pissed off, and down-to-the-ground gorgeous. "I figured you could use a beer about now."

"If you'd wanted to play tour guide, you could've picked a nice cool museum or cathedral."

"Hot and cranky, are we?" She tipped her sunglasses back in place. "If you felt compelled to follow me, you could've asked me to show you around today and bought me lunch."

"Do you think about anything but eating?"

"I need a lot of protein. I said I'd meet up with you tonight. You tailing me like this makes me think you don't trust me."

He said nothing, just stared at her stonily as the beers were served and he downed half of his in one long swallow.

"What do you know about the statue?" he said when he set his glass down.

"Enough to figure you wouldn't have followed me on a two-mile jaunt in high summer if it wasn't worth a lot more to you than five hundred pounds. So here's what I want." She paused, snagged the waiter again and ordered another round of beer and a strawberry sundae.

"You can't eat ice cream with beer," Gideon said.

"Sure you can. That's the beauty of ice cream; it goes with anything, any time. Anyway, back to business. I want five thousand, USD, and a first-class ticket back to New York."

He lifted his glass again and polished off the first beer. "You're not going to get it."

"Fine. Then you don't get the girl."

"I can get you a thousand, once I see the girl. And maybe five hundred more when she's in my hands. That's the cap."

"I don't think so." She clucked her tongue when he pulled out his cigarettes. "Sucking on those is why you had trouble with an afternoon stroll."

"Afternoon stroll, my ass." He blew out a stream of

smoke while the fresh beers and her ice cream were served. "You eat like that on a regular basis, you're going to be fat as a hog."

"Metabolism," she said with a mouthful of ice cream. "Mine runs like a rabbit. What's the name of your client?"

"You don't need names, and you needn't think they'll deal with you directly. You go through me, Cleo."

"Five thousand," she said again and licked her spoon. "And a first-class flight back home. You come up with that, I'll get you the statue."

"I told you not to hose me."

"She's wearing a robe, right shoulder bared, with her hair in a curly updo. She's wearing sandals, and she's smiling. Just a little. Sort of pensive."

He closed a hand over her wrist. "I don't negotiate till I see her."

"You don't see her till you negotiate." He had good, strong hands. She appreciated that in a man. There were enough calluses on them to tell her he worked with them and didn't make his living hunting up art pieces for sentimental clients.

"You've got to get me home if you want her, don't you?" It was reasonable. She'd spent time working out the reasonable angles. "To go home, I've got to quit my job, so I need enough money to tide me over until I get another one back in New York."

"I imagine there're plenty of titty bars in New York."

"Yeah." Her voice chilled. "I imagine there are."

"It's your choice of profession, Cleo, so spare me the hurt feelings. I need proof she exists, that you know where she is and that you can acquire her. We don't move forward on terms until that time."

"Fine, you'll get your proof. Pay the check, Slick. It's a long walk back."

He waved a hand for the waiter and reached for his wallet. "We'll have a taxi."

SHE BROODED OUT the side window of the taxi on the drive back. Her feelings weren't hurt, she told herself. She did honest work, didn't she? Hard, honest work. What did she care if some Irish jerk looked down his nose at her?

He didn't know anything about her, who she was, what she was, what she needed. If he thought her feelings got bruised because of one rude comment, he was underestimating her.

She'd spent nearly her entire life as an outcast from her own family. A stranger's opinion didn't matter to her.

She'd get him his proof, and he'd pay her price. She'd sell him the statue. She didn't know why the hell she'd kept the damn thing all these years anyway.

Good luck for her she had, she decided. The little lady was going to get her home and give her some breathing space until she snagged a few auditions.

She'd have to shine the thing up. Then she'd sweet-talk Marcella into letting her use that little digital camera and the computer. She'd take a picture, then send it through, print it out. Sullivan wouldn't know where it came from, and he'd never guess she had what he wanted tucked in her purse for safekeeping.

Figured he was dealing with a loser, did he? Well, he was sure going to find out different.

She shifted as they made the turn toward her building. "Come by the club," she said without looking at him. "Bring cash. We'll do business."

"Cleo." He clamped a hand on her wrist as she pushed open the cab door. "I apologize."

"For what?"

"For making an insulting comment."

"Forget it." She climbed out, headed straight toward her building. Funny, she thought, the apology had gotten under her skin even more than the insult.

She turned on her heel and headed down the block again without going back to her apartment. She'd go to the club a little early, she decided. After a quick stop for some silver polish.

IT WAS STILL shy of seven when she walked in. She skirted the stage and headed down the short hall that led to

Marcella's office. Marcella answered the knock with a quick bark that made Cleo wince.

Asking Marcella for a favor was always problematic, but asking when Marcella was in a snarly mood could be downright dangerous.

Still, Cleo poked her head into the ruthlessly organized office. "Sorry to interrupt."

"If you were sorry, you would not interrupt." Marcella continued to hammer at the computer keyboard on her desk. "I have work. I am a businesswoman."

"Yes, I know."

"What do you know? You dance, you strip. This is not business. Business is papers and figures and brains," she said, tapping a finger on the side of her head. "Anybody can strip."

"Sure, but not everybody can strip so people will pay to watch. Your door's increased since I stepped onstage and took my clothes off in here."

Marcella peered over the straight rims of her half-glasses. "You want raise?"

"Sure."

"Then you're stupid to ask for one when I'm busy and in bad mood."

"But I didn't," Cleo pointed out, and closed the door behind her. "You asked. I just want a favor. A very small favor."

"No extra night off this week."

"I don't want a night off. In fact, I'll trade you an extra hour onstage for the favor."

Now Marcella gave Cleo her full attention. The books could wait. "I thought it was a small favor."

"It is, but it could be important to me. I just want to borrow your digital camera for one picture, and your computer to send it. It'll take, what, ten minutes. You get an hour back. That's a good trade."

"You send a picture out for another job? You want to use my things to get work in another club?"

"No, it's not for a job. Christ." Cleo huffed out a breath. "Look, you gave me a break when I was in trouble. You gave me some professional pointers and helped me through the first night's queasies. You dealt straight with me. You deal straight with everybody. Going behind your back to a competitor isn't how I pay that back."

Marcella pursed her slick red lips, nodded. "What do you need to take a picture of?"

"It's just a thing. It's a business deal." When Marcella's gaze narrowed, Cleo sighed. "It's not illegal. I've got something someone wants to buy, but I don't trust him enough to let him know I've got it with me." At Marcella's steely stare, Cleo dug into her bag. "Nag, nag, nag," she muttered under her breath.

"There is nothing wrong with my hearing or my English."

"This." Cleo held up the newly polished statue.

"Let me see." Marcella wagged a finger until Cleo walked over and put it in her hand. "Silver. Very nice. Needs polishing."

"I got most of the gunk off."

"You should care better for your things. Sloppy. This is pretty," she mused and tapped at it with a red-slicked fingernail. "Solid silver?"

"Yeah, it's solid."

"Where do you get?"

"It's been in my family for years. I've had it since I was a kid."

"And this man—the Irishman," she assumed. "He wants it."

"Apparently."

"Why?"

"I'm not sure. He's got a story that may or may not be true. Doesn't matter to me. I've got it, he'll pay for it. Can I use the equipment?"

"Yes, yes. This is an heirloom?" Marcella frowned as she turned the statue over in her palm. "You would sell your heirloom?"

"Heirlooms only count if family counts."

Marcella set the statue on the desk, where it glinted in the lamplight. "That is a hard heart, Cleo."

"Maybe." Cleo waited while Marcella unlocked a desk drawer, took out the camera. "But it's also a hard truth."

"Get your picture, then put on your costume. You can put in the extra hour now."

THIRTY MINUTES LATER, Cleo zipped up the tight black leather skirt that went with the bustier and silver-studded black jacket. The little whip worked well with the outfit, and Cleo gave it a testing flick that made the other girls jump and bitch at her.

"Sorry." Turning to the mirror, she straightened the dog collar she'd strapped around her neck and ran a hand over the hair she'd sleeked back into a tight bun at the base of her neck.

A couple of good head shakes would free it, so she'd have to be careful it didn't tumble down off cue. She added a little more black eyeliner, then practiced pivots and pliés in the high-heeled boots.

She was executing a spread-leg squat, shifting her weight from side to side, when Gideon burst in. Several of the girls called out comments or made kissing noises.

"Let's go." He snagged her hand and hauled her to her feet.

"Go?"

"Let's move. I'll explain later."

"I'm on in three minutes."

"Not tonight you're not." When he started to drag her to the door, she shifted her body, angled it, and jammed an elbow into his gut.

"Hands off."

"Goddamn it." He'd think about the pain later, and how to pay her back for it. But for now he caught his breath as the others in the dressing area cheered and whistled. "They've already been to your place. Your landlady's in the hospital with a concussion. They can't be more than five minutes behind me."

"What the hell are you talking about?" She took a step back from him. Another. "Who's been to my place?"

"Somebody who wants a particular item and isn't as nice as I am about how they get it." He grabbed her arm again. "They slapped your landlady around before they bashed her in the head. You want to wait for them to try it with you, or are you coming with me? You've got ten seconds to decide."

Impulse, Cleo thought, had always gotten her in trouble. Why should tonight be any different? She snagged her purse. "Let's go."

He moved fast, heading out into the corridor, then dragging her to the right. "No, not out the front," he said. "They could already be out there. We'll go out the back."

"Back door locks from the inside. We go out that way, and there's trouble, we can't get back in."

He nodded, then opened the back door far enough to look out. The alleyway dead-ended to the left, and didn't that just figure. But he could see nothing and no one at the mouth of it. "How fast can you move in those things?" he asked, gesturing toward the boots.

"I can keep up with you, Slick."

"Then move." He pulled her out, kept a hand like a vise on her arm as he jogged down to where the alley opened onto the street. When they came out on the street, he shot a quick glance in either direction, swore and turned a hard right. He slid an arm around her waist.

"Just keep walking. Two men across the street. One heading toward the club, the other for the alley. Don't look back!"

But she already had, and made out both of them quickly enough. "We could take them."

"Christ. Just walk. If we're lucky, they didn't see us come out that way."

At the corner he glanced back. "So much for luck." He switched his grip to her hand. "Here's your chance to prove you can keep up."

He ran, and when they were halfway down the block, yanked her out in the street and across traffic. Brakes squealed, horns blasted. Cleo felt the wind from a fender that missed her by inches.

"You crazy son-of-a-bitch." But when she looked back she saw a man trying to thread his way between cars. She didn't slow down. The heels of her boots skidded and slipped over the uneven bricks. If she could have spared ten seconds, she'd have dragged them off and run barefoot.

"There's only one," she called out. "There are two of us."

"The other's somewhere." Following instinct, he pulled her into a restaurant, raced with her past a number of startled diners and through the kitchen and out the back onto the narrow street.

"Oh baby." It was nearly a prayer when he spotted the sleek black motorcycle parked against the back of the building. "Give me a hairpin."

"You start that thing with a hairpin, I'll kiss your ass." But panting a bit, she dragged one out of her hair.

Her hair tumbled free as he used the pin to pry off the ignition box. Within ten seconds, he had it hot-wired and was swinging his leg over.

"Get on. You can kiss my ass at a more private moment."

Her skirt hiked up to crotch level as she climbed on so her black G-string pressed snug against his butt. He ignored that, as best he could, and the way her breasts pressed into his back as he whipped the bike into a tight circle and flew toward the mouth of the alley with the roar of a serious engine.

She strapped her arms around him and let out a whoop when they shot down the street. At the corner, he nearly ran over the toes of the man who'd pursued them. Cleo got a good, close look at his shocked and furious face, and laughed wildly as Gideon leaned into the turn.

"They've got a car!" she called out, straining to see behind her as the wind whipped her hair into her face. "The other guy must've gotten the car, the one you nearly creamed's getting in it."

"That's all right." Gideon swung around another corner, punched it, then bulleted down the first side street. "We'll lose them on this."

Using the map in his head, he maneuvered out of the city. He wanted an open road, the dark, and the quiet. He wanted five damn minutes to think.

"Hey, Slick." Her voice was close to his ear. He could smell her, a pungent and erotic combination of female and leather. He could be sure now that her breasts, and they were beauties, were the ones God had given her.

"What? I've got to concentrate here."

"You just go right ahead. I wanted you to know I'm not interested in the five thousand anymore."

"You don't sell that statue to me, they'll keep after you."

"We'll talk about the why of that when we're not so busy." She looked behind her, at the lights and glow of Prague. "But the five thousand's off the table." She leaned into him again. "Because I just became your fucking partner."

To seal the deal she nipped lightly at his ear. And laughed.

# Five

"YOU lost track of them."

Anita Gaye leaned back against the butter-soft leather of her desk chair and examined her manicure. The phone call did not please her.

"Were my instructions unclear?" she asked in a low, silky voice. "Which part of 'locate the woman and find out what she knows' didn't you understand?"

Excuses, she thought as she listened to her employee's apologetic explanation. Incompetence. It was really very annoying.

"Mr. Jasper?" she interrupted in the most pleasant of tones. "I believe I told you 'by any means.' Do you need a definition of that phrase? No? Well then, I suggest you find them, and quickly, or I'll be forced to think you're not half as clever as a second-rate Irish tour guide."

She broke the connection, then to calm herself swiveled in the chair to gaze out at her view of New York. She enjoyed being able to watch the noise and bustle of the city, while being removed from it.

She enjoyed more knowing she could leave her plush corner of the elegant brownstone, stroll directly onto Madison Avenue, wander into any of the tony shops and have whatever her whim dictated.

And be recognized, admired, envied, as she did so.

There had been a time, not so many years before, when she'd been out there on the streets, rushing over the pavement, hounded with worries about rent payments, credit card bills and how to stretch her paycheck into one more good pair of shoes.

Standing with her nose pressed to the window, she thought now, knowing she was better, smarter, worthier than any of the ladies-who-shopped inside that cool, fragrant air, trailing pampered fingers over hand-stitched silks.

She'd never had a doubt she'd be on the other side, the *right* side of the glass. She'd never had a doubt she was meant to be.

She'd had something a great many of the workforce lacked as they'd scrambled to their next hive. A towering ambition and a nearly violent belief in self. She'd never intended to work her life away just to put a roof over her head.

Unless the roof was spectacular.

She'd always had a plan. A woman, Anita thought as she pushed back from the rosewood desk, was a man's toy, his doormat or his punching bag if she didn't have a plan. And most often, a combination of the three.

With a plan, and the brains to implement it, he became hers.

She'd worked hard to get where she was. If marrying a man old enough to be her grandfather wasn't work, she didn't know the meaning of the word. When a twenty-five-year-old woman had sex with a sixty-six-year-old man, the woman—by God—worked.

She'd given Paul Morningside his money's worth. For twelve long, laborious years. Dutiful wife, faithful assistant, elegant hostess and live-in whore. He'd died a happy man. And not a minute, in Anita's estimation, too soon.

Morningside Antiquities was hers now.

Because it always entertained her, she took a turn around her office, letting her heels sink into the faded wool of the Bokara carpet, click lightly on polished wood. She'd selected every piece personally, from the George III settee to the T'ang horse riding on a shelf of the Regency breakfront.

It was a mix of styles and eras that appealed to her, an elegant and distinctly female melding, all in superior taste. She'd learned a great deal from Paul, about value, continuity and perfection.

The colors were soft. She saved the bold and splashy for other areas, but her downtown office was done in quiet female tones. The better to seduce clients and competitors.

Best of all, she thought as she picked up an opal snuff box, everything in the room had once belonged to someone else.

There was such a thrill in possessing what had been another's. It was, to her mind, a kind of theft. A legal one. Even a distinguished one. What could be more exciting?

She was perfectly aware that after fifteen years, three of them as head of Morningside, some continued to consider her little more than a gold digger.

They were wrong.

There had been gossip, there had been snide comments when Paul Morningside had fallen for a woman more than forty years his junior.

Some had passed her off as a bimbo.

They'd been very wrong.

She had been, and was, a beautiful woman who knew exactly how to exploit her attributes. Her hair was flamered, and at forty, she wore it in a sleek, chin-length sweep to play up smooth, round cheeks and a full, deceptively soft mouth. Her eyes were bright blue and Kewpie-doll wide. Many who'd looked into them found them guileless.

They were wrong, too.

She had pale, flawless skin, a small, streamlined nose. And a body a former lover had described as a walking wet dream.

She presented the package carefully. Tailored suits for business, fashionably elegant gowns for social occasions. Throughout her marriage she'd been meticulous about her behavior, public and private. There might have been some who whispered, but there were no whiffs of scandal, no questionable behavior attached to Anita Gaye.

Some might continue to look askance, but they accepted her invitations, and they issued them to her in return. They patronized her company, and paid well for the privilege.

Inside the package was the brain of a born operator. Anita Gaye was the dedicated widow, the society hostess, the respected businesswoman. She intended to live the part for the rest of her days.

It was, she mused, the longest con on record.

Gold digger, she thought with a quiet laugh. Oh no, it had never been just about money. It had been about position and power and prestige.

It was no more about dollars and cents than owning something was about filling space on a shelf. It was about status.

She crossed to a Corot landscape, pushed a mechanism hidden in the frame to lever out the painting. With quick fingers she punched in her security code on the keypad behind it, input the combination to the safe.

For her own pleasure, she took out the silver Fate.

And hadn't it been fate, she reflected, that had had her traveling to Dublin, spending those few weeks overseeing the opening of a Morningside branch there? Just as it had been fate that had urged her to take an appointment with one Malachi Sullivan.

She'd known of the Three Fates. Paul had told her the story. He'd had an endless supply of long-winded, tedious stories. But this one had caught her interest. Three silver statues, forged, some said, on Olympus itself. That, of course, was nonsense, but legend added a luster, and a value, to objects. Three sisters, separated by time and circumstances, falling into various hands over the years. And separated, they were no more than pretty bits of art.

But if and when they were brought together . . . She ran her fingertip over the shallow notch in the base, where Clotho had once linked to Lachesis. Together, they were beyond price. And some, a gullible some in Anita's mind, said that together they were beyond power. Wealth beyond imagining, control of one's own destiny unto immortality.

Paul hadn't believed they existed. A pretty story, he'd claimed. A kind of Holy Grail for collectors of antiquities.

She'd passed it off as well. Until Malachi Sullivan had asked for her professional opinion.

It had been child's play to seduce him into seducing her. Then to blind his caution with lust until he trusted her enough to put the statue into her hands. For tests and assessments, she'd told him. For research.

He'd told her enough, more than enough to assure her that she could take the statue from him with impunity. What could he do—some middle-class Irish sailor, descended by his own accounting from a thief—against a woman of her unimpeachable reputation?

Stealing outright, she thought now, had been a glorious rush.

He'd made noise, of course, but her money and position, and the miles of ocean between them, insulated her against any trouble he could stir. As she'd expected, he'd quieted down again in a matter of weeks.

What she hadn't expected was for him to outmaneuver her—even temporarily—for the other two pieces of the prize. She'd wasted time delicately questioning Wyley Antiques's current owners while he had zeroed in on Tia Marsh.

He got nothing from her, Anita knew now. There hadn't been time. There'd been nothing in her hotel room, nothing on her laptop that pertained to the statues, or to her ancestor.

And nothing in the more discreet search of her New York apartment. Still, she believed Tia was a key, one worth turning in any case.

She'd pursue that personally, she decided. Just as she would pursue the New York thread of Simon White-Smythe personally. She'd leave her incompetent employees to track down the black sheep of that family, while she courted the cream of it.

Once she had the second Fate, she'd use all her resources, all her energies, by any means, to find and acquire the third.

*　*　*

TIA SPENT THE first twenty-four hours after the flight home sleeping or shuffling around her apartment in her pajamas. Twice she woke up in the dark without a clue where she was. And, remembering, had hugged herself in sheer joy before snuggling back into her pillow and sleep.

The second day, she indulged in a long bath—lukewarm water and plenty of lavender oil—then changed into fresh pajamas and went back to sleep.

When she was awake and wandering the apartment, she'd stop to touch something—the back of a chair, the side of a table, the round dome of a paperweight. She would think, Mine. My things, my apartment, my country.

She could open the drapes and look out on her view of the East River, enjoy the look of the water that always managed to soothe and thrill her. Or close them again and imagine herself in a lovely, cool cave.

There was no one waiting for her, no need to dress, to style her hair, to gear up mentally and emotionally for an appearance.

She could, if she wanted, stay in her pajamas for a week and talk to no one. She could lie in her own, wonderful bed and do nothing but read or watch television.

Of course, that was bad for the back. And, of course, she needed to fix proper meals and reacquaint her system with basic routine. She was running low on echinacea, too, and really needed to go out and buy some fresh bananas if she didn't want her potassium level to dip.

But she could make it one more day. Just one more. Because the prospect of having no conversations whatsoever, even with a clerk at the market, was so wonderful it was worth the risk of a potassium dip.

To relieve her guilt for not phoning her family, not stirring herself to travel the few blocks to see her mother, she sent her parents an e-mail. Then she confirmed her next appointment with Dr. Lowenstein the same way.

She loved e-mail, and offered thanks that she lived in an age in which it was possible to communicate without speaking.

Despite all her travel precautions, she was pretty sure

she was coming down with a cold. Her throat was a bit scratchy, her sinuses a little stuffy. But when she took her temperature—twice—it was dead normal.

Still, she took some extra zinc, more echinacea and made herself a pot of chamomile tea. She was just settling down with it and a book on homeopathic remedies when her doorbell chimed.

She nearly ignored it. It was guilt that had her setting cup and book aside. It could very well be her mother, who tended to drop by unannounced. And who would, certainly, let herself in with her key if Tia didn't answer.

It was guilt as well that had her glancing around and wincing. Her mother would see that she'd been lounging around like a slug for days. She wouldn't criticize—or she would mask her criticism so expertly in indulgence that Tia would, she knew, end up feeling like a self-centered, lazy child.

Worse, if she sniffed out even a hint of the cold Tia was sure she was brewing, she would make a terrible fuss.

Resigned, Tia peered out the peephole. And squeaked.

It wasn't her mother.

Flustered, she pushed a hand through her hair and opened the door to a man she'd nearly convinced herself she'd imagined.

"Hello, Tia." If Malachi thought it odd she was answering the door in her pajamas at three in the afternoon, his warm smile didn't show it.

"Um . . ." Something about him seemed to cross-wire the circuits in her brain. She wondered if it was chemical. "How did you . . ."

"Find you?" he finished. She looked a bit pale, he thought, and sleepy. The woman needed some fresh air and sunshine. "You're in the book. I should've called, but I was in the neighborhood. More or less."

"Oh. Well. Ah." Her tongue wouldn't cooperate on more than one syllable. She made a helpless gesture of invitation and had closed the door behind him before she remembered she was wearing pajamas. "Oh," she said again, and clutched the lapels together. "I was just . . ."

"Recuperating from your travels, I expect. It must be lovely, being home."

"Yes. Yes. I wasn't expecting company. I'll just change."

"No, don't." He snagged her hand before she could rush off. "You're perfectly fine, and I won't keep you long. I was worried about you. I hated leaving you so abruptly. Did they find who broke into your hotel room?"

"No. No, they didn't. At least not yet. I never thanked you properly for staying with me through all the questioning and paperwork."

"I wish I could've done more. I hope the rest of your trip went well."

"It did. I'm glad it's over." Should she offer him a drink? she fretted. She couldn't possibly, not while wearing pajamas. "Did you . . . Have you been in New York long?"

"I've just arrived. Business." She had the drapes pulled over the windows, he noted. The place was dim as a cave but for the reading lamp on the table by the sofa. Still, what he could see was tidy as a church and quietly pretty. As she was, despite the prim cotton pajamas.

He was, he realized, more pleased to see her than he'd expected to be. "I wanted to look you up, Tia, as I've been thinking about you the last few weeks."

"Really?"

"Yes, really. Would you have dinner with me tonight?"

"Dinner? Tonight?"

"It's short notice, I know, but if you're not busy I'd love to have an evening with you. Tonight." He moved in, just a little. "Tonight. Tomorrow. As soon as you're free."

She'd have considered it all a hallucination, but she could smell him. Just a hint of his aftershave. She didn't think she'd identify men's aftershave in a hallucination. "I don't have any plans."

"Brilliant. Why don't I pick you up at seven-thirty?" He released her hand, wisely opting to retreat before she could think of an excuse. "I'll look forward to it."

While she stood, staring at him, he let himself out.

* * *

"IT'S JUST DINNER, Tia. Relax."

"Carrie, I asked you to come over and help, not advise me to do the impossible. What about this?" Tia turned from her closet, holding up a navy suit.

"No."

"What's wrong with it?"

"Everything." Carrie Wilson, a streamlined brunette with skin the color of melted caramel and ebony eyes, angled her head. "It's fine if you're going to address the board of directors on fiscal responsibility. It's dead wrong for a romantic dinner for two."

"I never said it was romantic."

"You're going out with a great-looking Irishman you met in Helsinki who stayed by your side during a criminal investigation and who has shown up on your doorstep in New York the minute he hit the States."

Carrie's voice had the rapid-fire punch of a machine gun as she lounged on the bed. "The only way it could be more romantic would be if he'd shown up on a white charger with the blood of a dragon on his sword."

"I just want to look reasonably attractive," Tia replied.

"Honey, you always look reasonably attractive. Let's swing the hammer and ring the bell." She unfolded herself from the bed and plunged into Tia's closet.

Carrie was a stockbroker. Tia's stockbroker. Somehow during their six-year association they'd become friends. She was Tia's image of the modern, independent woman, the type who normally would have intimidated Tia into muscle spasms.

And had until they'd discovered a mutual interest in alternative medicine and Italian shoes.

Thirty, divorced, professionally successful, Carrie dated a string of interesting, eclectic men, could analyze the Dow Jones or Kafka with equal authority and vacationed solo every year, selecting the location by sticking a pin in an atlas.

There was no one Tia trusted more in matters of finance, fashion or men.

"Here, the classic little black number." Carrie pulled out a simple sleeveless sheath. "We'll sex it up a bit."

"I'm not looking for sex."

"That, as I've told you for years, is your core problem." She stepped out of the closet, then studied Tia. "I wish we had more time. I'd call my stylist, get him to squeeze you in."

"You know I don't go to salons. All those chemicals, and the hair flying everywhere. You don't know what you might pick up."

"A decent haircut, for one thing. I'm telling you, you'd really open your face up, accent your bone structure and your eyes if you'd just get that mop whacked off."

Carrie tossed the dress on the bed, then gathered Tia's long hair in her hand. "Let me do it."

"Not as long as I still have a brain wave pattern," she chided. "Just help me get through the evening, Carrie. Then he'll go back to Ireland or wherever, and things'll get back to normal."

Carrie hoped not. As far as she was concerned her friend had entirely too much normal in her life.

MALACHI THOUGHT THE flowers were a nice touch. Pink roses. She struck him as the type for pink roses. He was afraid he was going to have to rush her a bit, and he regretted that. She also struck him as the type for slow, rather sweet seductions. And oddly, he thought he'd enjoy seducing her, slowly.

But he couldn't spare the time. He wasn't at all sure he should have left home, not before Gideon had returned. The fact that Anita had managed to track down the Toliver woman worried him.

Was it another case of her trailing their path, or were their routes just coinciding? Either way, he was absolutely sure that Anita would move on Tia soon. If she hadn't already.

He needed to get his pitch in, to lure Tia over to his side before Anita could confuse matters.

So here he was, toting a dozen pink rosebuds to the door of Wyley's ancestor while his brother was God-knew-where with one of White-Smythe's.

He'd have preferred striding to Anita's door, and leading with his boot there. If he hadn't promised his mother—who had the good sense not to want her oldest son locked in a foreign jail—he'd have done just that.

Still, when it came down to it, spending the evening having dinner with a pretty woman was a better bet than dragging one all over Europe as Gideon was doing.

He knocked, waited, then was caught off balance when she opened the door. "You look fantastic."

Tia struggled not to tug at the hem of the little black dress that Carrie had ruthlessly shortened a full two inches. Carrie had chosen the opera-length pearls, too, and was responsible for the hairstyle that added a few wispy bangs and whisked the rest away in a long fall down the back.

"Thank you. Those are lovely."

"I thought they suited you."

"Would you like to sit down? Have a drink before we go? I have some wine."

"I'd like that, yes."

"Well, I'll just put these in some water." She restrained herself from mentioning she was relatively sure she'd inherited her mother's allergy to roses. Instead, she chose an old Baccarat vase from her display cabinet. She carried them back into the kitchen, setting them aside while she got out the bottle of white she'd opened for Carrie.

"I like your place," Malachi said from behind her.

"So do I." She poured a glass, turned to offer it. As he was closer than she'd anticipated, she nearly plowed the glass into his chest.

"Thanks. I think the hardest aspect of traveling is not having your own things about you. The little things that comfort you."

"Yes." She let out a quiet breath. "Exactly." To keep busy, she filled the vase with water, then began to arrange the flowers in it, one by one. "That's why you caught me in pajamas this afternoon. I was wallowing in being home. In fact, other than the limo driver, you were the first person I'd spoken to since I got back."

"Is that right?" So Anita hadn't beaten him, after all. "Then I'm very flattered." He picked up one of the roses, handed it to her. "And I hope you'll enjoy the evening."

She did. A great deal.

The restaurant he'd chosen was quiet, with soft lighting and discreet service. Discreet enough that the waiter hadn't blinked when she'd picked her way through the menu, ordering a salad, without dressing, and requested her fish be broiled without butter and served without the accompanying sauce.

Because he'd ordered a bottle of wine, she accepted a glass. She rarely drank. She'd read several articles on how alcohol destroyed brain cells. Of course, a glass of red wine was supposed to counteract that by being good for your heart.

But the wine was so soft, and he managed to put her so completely at ease, that she never noticed how often her glass was topped off.

"It's so interesting that you live in Cobh," she said. "Another tie to the *Lusitania*."

"And indirectly to you."

"Well, my great-great-grandparents were brought back here for burial. But I suppose, like so many of the others, they were taken to Cobh, or Queenstown then. It was foolish, really, for those people to make that crossing during wartime. Such an unnecessary risk."

"We never know what another considers necessary, or a risk, do we? Or why some lived and some died. My ancestor wasn't from Ireland, you know."

She nearly missed what he was saying. When he smiled at her, just that way—slow and intimate—his eyes seemed impossibly green. "He wasn't?"

"No, indeed. He was born in England, but lived most of his life here in New York."

"Really?"

"After the tragedy, he was nursed back to health by a young woman who was to become his wife. It's said the experience changed him. Word is, he was a bit of a loose cannon before it happened. In any case, his story's been passed down through the family. It seems he was interested in a certain item he'd heard was in England. Seeing as you're an expert on Greek myths, you might have heard of it. The Silver Fates."

Struck, she set down her fork. "Do you mean the statues?"

His pulse jumped, but he nodded easily. "I do, yes."

"Not The Silver Fates. The Three Fates. Three separate statues, not one, though they can be linked by the bases."

"Ah well, stories take on a life of their own, don't they, over generations." He cut another bite of his beef. "Three pieces, then. You know of them?"

"I certainly do. Henry Wyley owned one, and it went down with the *Lusitania.* According to his journal, he was going to England to buy the second of the set and to, hopefully, follow a lead on finding the third. It seemed so interesting to me as a child to think that he'd essentially died for those pieces that I looked up the Fates."

He waited a beat. "What did you find?"

"Oh, about the statues, next to nothing. In fact, it's most commonly believed they don't really exist. For all I know Henry had something else entirely." She moved her shoulders. "But I found out about the Fates of mythology, and kept reading. The more I read, the more fascinated I was by the gods, and the half gods. I had absolutely no talent for the family business, so I turned an interest into a career."

"Then you have Henry to thank for that."

She'd always thought the same. "You're right, I do."

He lifted his glass, tapped it to hers. "To Henry, then, and his pursuit of the Fates."

He let the conversation wind into other areas. Damn it, she was pleasant company when she loosened up. The wine added a sparkle to her eyes, a pretty glow to her cheeks. She had a mind that was quick enough to jump into any area, and a subtle and dry wit when she forgot to be nervous about what came out of her mouth.

He gave himself an hour to simply enjoy her company, and didn't circle back to the Fates until they were in the cab heading back to her apartment.

"Did Henry note down in his journal how he planned to acquire the other statues?" Idly, Malachi toyed with the ends of her hair. "Weren't you curious if they existed? If they were real?"

"Mmm. I don't remember." With the wine spinning gently in her head, she relaxed against him when he slid an arm around her shoulders. "I was thirteen, no, twelve, when I first read it. It was the winter I had bronchitis. I think it was bronchitis," she said, lazily now. "I always seemed to have something that kept me in bed. Anyway, I was too young to think about heading off to England to find some legendary statue."

He frowned. It seemed to him that was precisely what a twelve-year-old girl should have thought of doing. The adventure of it, the romance of it would have made a perfect fantasy for a housebound child.

"After that, I was too steeped in gods to worry about artifacts. That's my father's area. I'm hopeless at business. I've no flare for figures or for people. I'm a crushing disappointment to him."

"That's not possible."

"It is, but it's nice of you to say it isn't. Wyley Antiques paid for my education, my lifestyle and my piano lessons, and I've given nothing back, preferring to write books on imaginary figures rather than accept the weight and responsibilities of my legacy."

"Writing books about imaginary figures is an art, and a time-honored profession."

"Not when you're my father. He's given up on me, and as I've yet to latch onto a man long enough to produce a grandchild for him, he despairs that on his retirement, Wyley's will pass out of the family."

"A woman's not required to birth a child for the sake of a bloody business."

She blinked a bit at the temper in his voice. "Wyley's isn't just a business, it's a tradition. Oh my, I shouldn't have had so much wine. I'm rambling."

"You're not." He paid the driver when they pulled to the curb. "And you shouldn't worry so much about pleasing your father if he can't see the value of who you are and what you do."

"Oh, he's not . . ." She was grateful for the firmness of Malachi's hand as she climbed out of the cab. The wine made her limbs feel loose and disconnected. "He's a wonderful man, amazingly kind and patient. It's just that he's so proud of Wyley's. If he'd had a son, or another daughter with more business skills, it wouldn't be so difficult."

"Your thread's been spun, hasn't it?" He led her into the elevator. "You are what you are."

"My father doesn't believe in fate." She shook back her hair, smiled. "But maybe he'd be interested in the Fates. Wouldn't it be something if I research and manage to find one of them? Or two. Of course, they don't have any serious significance unless they're complete."

"Maybe you should read Henry's journal again."

"Maybe I should. I wonder where it is." She laughed up at him as they walked toward her door. "I had the best time. That's twice now I've had the best time with you, and on two continents. I feel very cosmopolitan."

"See me tomorrow." He turned her into him, slid a hand up her back to the nape of her neck.

"Okay." Her eyes fluttered closed as he drew her closer. "Where?"

"Anywhere." He whispered it, then touched his lips to hers.

It was a simple matter for a man to deepen a kiss when a woman was all but melting around him. It was easy to take as much as he wanted when she sighed and wrapped her arms around him.

And when what she gave back was sweet and warm and unbearably soft, it was damn near impossible not to want more.

He could have more, he thought as he changed the angle of the kiss. He had only to open her door, step inside with her. Already there was a purr in her throat and a quiver along her skin.

And he couldn't do it. She was half-drunk and criminally vulnerable. Worse, somehow worse, the want for her was a great deal more personal than he'd bargained for.

He eased her back with the sudden, certain knowledge that his plans had just suffered a major snag. And the snag could become a large and tangled knot.

"Spend the day with me tomorrow."

She felt as if she were floating. "Don't you have work?"

"Spend the day with me," he repeated and tortured himself by leaning her back against the door and taking her mouth again. "Say yes."

"Yes. What?"

"Eleven. I'll be here at eleven. Go inside, Tia."

"Go where?"

"Inside." God help him. "Inside," he repeated as he fumbled a bit with her lock. "Damn it, one more." He yanked her back against him, kissed her until the blood was roaring in his head. "Lock the door," he ordered and, giving her a little shove inside, shut it smartly in his own face before he could change his mind.

# Six

TIA wasn't sure if it was curiosity or lust that drove her to look for the old journal. Whichever it was, it was a powerful force to make her face her mother in the middle of the day.

She loved her mother, sincerely, but any session with Alma Marsh was wearing on the nerves. Rather than risk a germ-crawling taxi, she walked the eight blocks to the lovely old town house where she'd spent her childhood. She was so energized, so full of the delight of the last two days and Malachi, she didn't even think about the pollen count.

The air was thick as a brick, and so miserably hot it wilted her crisp linen blouse before she'd walked cross-town to Park Avenue. But she strolled along, as she headed uptown, humming a tune in her mind.

She *loved* New York. Why hadn't she ever realized how much she loved the city, with its noise and traffic, its crowded streets. Its *life*. There was so much to see if you just looked. The young women pushing baby carriages, the boy walking a group of six little dogs that pranced along like a parade. The sleek, black, hired cars taking ladies to lunch, or home again after a morning's shopping. And look how gorgeous the flowers were along the avenue, and how smart the doormen looked in their uniforms as they stood outside the buildings.

How had she missed all this? she wondered as she turned onto her parents' pretty, shady street. Simple. On the rare times she actually walked outside of her own three-block radius, she kept her head down, her purse in a stranglehold and imagined herself being mugged, or run over by a bus that jumped the curb.

But she'd walked yesterday with Malachi. They'd strolled up Madison Avenue, had stopped at a little sidewalk café for cold drinks and careless conversation. He talked to everyone. The waiter, the woman beside them with, of all things, a miniature poodle in her lap.

Which could hardly be sanitary.

He talked to shop clerks in Barneys, to a young woman debating over scarves in one of the terrifying boutiques Tia usually avoided. He struck up conversations with one of the guards at the Met, and the sidewalk vendor where he'd bought hot dogs.

She'd actually eaten a hot dog—right on the street. She could hardly get over it.

For a few hours she'd seen the city through his eyes. The wonder of it, the humor in it, the grit and the grandeur.

And she was going to see it again tonight, with him.

She was nearly skipping by the time she reached her parents' house. There were flowerpots flanking the entrance. Tilly, the housekeeper, would have planted and tended them. She remembered now that she'd wanted to help plant the pots once. She'd been about ten, but her mother had worried so about dirt, allergies and insects that she'd given up the idea.

Maybe she'd buy a geranium on the way home. Just to see.

Though she had a key, Tia used the bell. The key was for emergencies, and using it meant decoding the alarm, then explaining why she'd done so.

Tilly, a sturdy fireplug of a woman with stone-gray hair, answered quickly.

"Why, Miss Tia! What a nice surprise. All settled in,

then, after your trip? I really enjoyed the postcards you sent me. All those wonderful places."

"A lot of places," Tia agreed as she stepped into the cool, quiet air. She kissed Tilly's cheek with the easy comfort she felt for few. "It's good to be home."

"One of the best parts of traveling is coming home, isn't it? Don't you look pretty today," Tilly said, surprise in her voice as she studied Tia's face. "I think traveling agreed with you."

"You wouldn't have said that a couple of days ago." Tia set her purse on a table in the foyer, glanced at the Victorian mirror above it. She *did* look pretty, she realized. Sort of rosy and bright. "Is my mother available?"

"She's upstairs in her sitting room. You go right up, and I'll bring you both something cold to drink."

"Thanks, Tilly."

Tia turned to the long sweep of stairs. She'd always loved this house, the elegant dignity of it. It was such a combination of her parents—her father's great love for antiques, her mother's deep need for organized space. Without that combination, that balance, she supposed, it might have been a hodgepodge, a kind of sub-shop for Wyley's. As it was, the furnishings were arranged with an eye for style as well as beauty. Everything had its place, and that place rarely changed.

There was something comforting in that continuity, that stability. The colors were pale and cool. Rather than flower arrangements, there were lovely statuary, wonderful old bowls filled with chunks of polished, colored glass.

Ladies' gloves, jeweled handbags, hat pins, cuff links, watch fobs, snuffboxes were displayed behind ruthlessly clean glass. Temperature and humidity were strictly maintained by a climate-control system. It was always seventy-one degrees, with a ten percent humidity rate, inside the Marsh town house.

Tia paused outside her mother's sitting room door, knocked.

"Come in, Tilly."

The moment Tia opened the door, her spirits dropped. She caught the faint scent of rosemary, which signaled her mother was having one of her difficult mornings. Though the window glass was treated to filter out UV rays, the drapes were drawn. Another bad sign.

Alma Marsh reclined on the silk-cushioned recamier with an eyebag draped over her upper face.

"I think I have one of my headaches coming on, Tilly. I shouldn't have tried to answer all that correspondence at one time, but what can I do? People will write you, won't they, and then you have no choice but to respond. Would you mind getting my feverfew? Perhaps I can ward off the worst of it."

"It's Tia, Mother. I'll get it for you."

"Tia?" Alma slid the eyebag aside. "My baby! Come give me a kiss, dear. There couldn't be any better medicine."

Tia crossed over and gave Alma a light kiss on the cheek. She might have been having one of her spells, Tia thought, but her mother looked, as always, perfect. Her hair, nearly the same delicate shade as her daughter's, was glossy and swept back in gentle waves from a face suitable for a cameo. It was delicate, lovely, unlined. Though she tended to be thin, her body was turned out with casual elegance in a soft pink blouse and tailored trousers.

"There now, I feel better already," Alma said as she shifted to sit up. "I'm so glad you're home, Tia. Why, I didn't get one moment's rest while you were gone. I was so worried about you. You took all your vitamins, didn't you, and didn't drink the tap water? I hope you demanded nonsmoking suites in all your hotels, though God knows they don't enforce that. Just come in and spray after some horrible person's spewed carcinogens into the air. Pull open the drapes, dear, I can barely see you."

"Are you sure?"

"I can't indulge myself," Alma said heroically. "I've a dozen things to do today, and now that you're here . . . Well, we'll make time for a nice visit, and I'll work harder later. And you, you must be exhausted. A delicate system like yours suffers under the demands of travel. I want you to arrange for a complete physical right away."

"I'm fine." Tia moved to the windows.

"When the immune system's compromised, as yours must be, it can take several days before you recognize the symptoms. You make that appointment, Tia, for my sake."

"Of course." Tia drew open the drapes, relieved when light poured into the room. "You don't have to worry. I took very good care of myself."

"Be that as it may, you can't . . ." She trailed off when Tia turned around. "Why, you're all flushed! Are you feverish?" She leaped off the daybed, clamped a hand over Tia's brow. "Yes, you feel a little warm. Oh, I knew it! I knew you'd catch some foreign germ."

"I'm not feverish. I got a bit hot on the walk over, that's all."

"You walked? In this heat! I want you to sit down, sit down right here. You're dehydrated, courting heatstroke."

"I'm not." But she thought she might feel just a little dizzy after all. "I'm perfectly fine. I've never felt better."

"A mother knows these things." Revived, Alma waved Tia to a chair and marched to the door. "Tilly! Bring up a pitcher of lemon water and a cold compress, and call Dr. Realto. I want him to examine Tia right away."

"I'm not going to the doctor."

"Don't be stubborn."

"I'm not." But she was beginning to feel a bit queasy. "Mother, please, sit down before you aggravate your headache. Tilly's bringing up cold drinks. I promise, if I feel the least bit ill, I'll phone Dr. Realto."

"Now what's all this fuss?" Tilly came in, carrying a tray.

"Tia's ill, you only have to look at her to see it, and she won't have the doctor."

"She looks just fine to me, blooming like a rose."

"It's fever."

"Oh, now, Miss Alma, girl's got some color in her cheeks for a change, that's all. You sit down and have some nice iced tea. It's jasmine, your favorite. And I've got some lovely green grapes here."

"You washed them in that anti-toxin solution?"

"Absolutely. I'm going to put your Chopin on," she added when she set down the tray. "Real low. You know how that always soothes your nerves."

"Yes, yes, it does. Thank you, Tilly. What would I do without you?"

"Lord only knows," Tilly said under her breath and added a wink for Tia as she walked out.

Alma sighed and sat. "My nerves haven't been good," she admitted to Tia. "I know you felt this trip was important for your career, but you've never been so far away for so long."

And according to Dr. Lowenstein, Tia thought as she poured the tea, that was part of the problem. "I'm back now. And all in all, it was a fascinating trip. The lectures and signings were well attended, and it helped clear out some of the cobwebs I've been dealing with about the new book. Mother, I met this man—"

"A man? You met a man?" Alma came to attention. "What kind of man? Where? Tia, you know perfectly well how dangerous it is for a woman alone to travel, much less to hold conversations with strange men."

"Mother, I'm not an imbecile."

"You're trusting and naive."

"Yes, you're right, so when he asked me to go back to his hotel room to discuss the modern significance of Homer, I went like a lamb to the slaughter. He ravished me, then passed me to his nefarious partner for sloppy seconds. Now I'm pregnant and I don't know which one is the father."

She didn't know why she'd said it, honestly didn't know how all that had burst out of her mouth. She felt her own headache coming on as Alma went white and clutched her chest.

"I'm sorry, I'm sorry. But I wish you'd give me some credit for common sense. I'm seeing a perfectly nice man. We have an interesting connection that goes back to Henry Wyley."

"You're not pregnant."

"No, of course not. I'm simply seeing a man who shares my interest in Greek myths, and who, coincidentally, had an ancestor on the *Lusitania*. A survivor."

"Is he married?"

"No!" Shocked, insulted, Tia got to her feet to pace. "I wouldn't date a married man."

"Not if you *knew* he was married," Alma said significantly. "Where did you meet him?"

"He attended one of my lectures, and he had business here in New York, so he looked me up."

"What sort of business?"

Growing more frustrated by the minute, Tia pushed at her hair. It felt suddenly, abominably heavy. As if it were smothering her brain. "He's in shipping. Mother, the point is that in talking about the Greeks, and the *Lusitania*, we touched on the Three Fates. The statues? You've heard Father mention them."

"No, I can't say I have, but someone asked me about them just the other day. Who was it?"

"Someone asked you about them? That's odd."

"It's neither here nor there," Alma said irritably. "It was in passing, at some function your father dragged me to though I was feeling unwell. That Gaye woman," Alma remembered. "Anita Gaye. She has a hard look about her, if you ask me. And no wonder, marrying a man forty years older, and so blatantly for his money no matter what anyone says. Well, more fool he. She's fooled your father, of course. Women like that always fool men. A good businesswoman, he says. A credit to the antiquity community. Hah! But where was I? I can't concentrate. I'm just so out of sorts."

"What did she ask you?"

"Oh, for heaven's sake, Tia, I dislike speaking to the woman so can hardly be expected to remember some irritating conversation with her about some silly statues I've never heard of. You're just trying to change the subject. Who is this man? What's his name?"

"Sullivan. Malachi Sullivan. He's from Ireland."

"Ireland? I've never heard of such a thing."

"It's an island, just northwest of England."

"Don't be sarcastic, it's very unattractive. What do you know about him?"

"That I enjoy his company and he appears to enjoy mine."

Alma let out a long-suffering sigh. One of her best weapons. "You don't know who his family is, do you?

Well, I'm sure he knows who yours is. I'm sure he knows very well who you come from. You're a wealthy woman, Tia, living alone—which worries me to distraction—and a prime target for the unscrupulous. Shipping? We'll see about that."

"Don't." Tia's voice snapped out, surprising Alma into lowering herself back into her chair. "Just don't. You're not going to have him investigated. You are not going to humiliate me again that way."

"Humiliate you? What a thing to say. If you're thinking of that . . . that history teacher, well, he wouldn't have been so angry and upset if he'd had nothing to hide. A mother has a right to look after her only child's welfare."

"Your only child is nearly thirty, Mother. Couldn't it be, just on a wild whim of fate, couldn't it be that an attractive, interesting, intelligent man chooses to go out with me because he finds me an attractive, interesting, intelligent woman? Does he have to have some dark, underlying motive? Am I such a loser that no man could want a normal, natural relationship with me?"

"A loser?" Sincerely shocked, Alma gaped. "I don't know what puts ideas like that in your head."

"No," Tia said wearily and turned toward the windows. "I bet you don't. You needn't worry. He's only in New York a few days. He'll be going back to Ireland soon and it's unlikely we'll see each other again. I can promise if he offers to sell me some bridge over the River Shannon or pops up with a great investment opportunity, I'll turn him down. Meanwhile, I was wondering if you know where Henry Wyley's journal might be. I'd like to study it."

"How should I know? Ask your father. Obviously my concerns and advice are worthless to you. I don't know why you bothered to come by."

"I'm sorry I upset you." She turned back, walked over to kiss Alma's cheek again. "I love you, Mother. I love you very much. You get some rest."

"I want you to call Dr. Realto," Alma ordered as Tia walked away.

"Yes, I will."

She lived dangerously and took a cab downtown to

Wyley's. She knew herself well enough to be certain if she
went home in her current mood she would brood, and
eventually decide her mother was right—about the state of
her health, about Malachi, about her own pitiful appeal to
the opposite sex.

Worse, she wanted to go home. To draw the drapes,
huddle in her cave with her pills, her aromatherapy and a
cool, soothing gel bag over her eyes.

Just, she thought in disgust, like her mother.

She needed to keep busy, to keep focused, and the idea
of the journal and the Fates was a puzzle that would keep
her mind occupied.

She paid the cabdriver, slid out and stood for a moment
on the sidewalk in front of Wyley's. As always, she felt a
rush of wonder and pride. The lovely old brownstone with
its leaded windows and stained-glass door had stood for a
hundred years.

When she'd been young, her father—over Alma's dire
predictions and dark warnings—had taken her with him
once a week. Into that treasure trove, into that Aladdin's
cave. He'd taught her, patiently she thought now, about
eras, styles, woods, glass, ceramics. Art, and the bits and
pieces people collected that became, in time, an art of its
own.

She'd learned, and God, she'd wanted to please him.
But she'd never been able to please them both, never been
able to stay on her feet in that subtle and constant tug-of-
war her parents had played with her.

And she'd been afraid of making a mistake and embarrassing him, had been tongue-tied with clients and customers, baffled by the inventory system. In the end, her
father had deemed her hopeless. She could hardly blame
him.

Still, when she stepped inside, she felt another wave of
pride. It was so beautiful, so perfectly lovely. The air
smelled lightly of polish and flowers.

Unlike the house uptown, things changed here all the
time. It was a constant surprise to see a familiar piece
missing, a new one in its place, and a kind of thrill when
she recognized the changes, identified the new. She

moved through the foyer, admiring the curves of the set-tee—Empire period, she decided, 1810–1830. The pair of gilt-gesso side tables were new stock, but she remembered the rococo candlesticks from her visit before she'd left for Europe.

She stepped into the first showroom and saw her father.

Seeing him always struck her with pride, and wonder, too. He was so robust and handsome. His hair was silver, and thick as mink pelt, his eyebrows black as midnight. He wore small, square-framed glasses, and behind them she knew his eyes would be dark and clever.

His suit was Italian, a navy pinstripe that was tailored for his strong frame.

He turned, glanced her way. After an almost impercep-tible hesitation, he smiled. He passed an invoice to the clerk he'd been speaking to and crossed to her.

"So, the wanderer returns." He bent to kiss her cheek, his lips barely meeting her skin. She had a rush of memory of being tossed high in the air, of squealing with terrified pleasure, of being caught again by those big, wide hands.

"I don't mean to interrupt you."

"It doesn't matter. How was your trip?"

"It was good. It was very good."

"Have you been by to see your mother?"

"Yes." She shifted her gaze, stared hard at a display cabinet-on-chest. "I've just come from there. I'm sorry, we had a disagreement. I'm afraid she's upset with me."

"You had a disagreement with your mother?" He took his glasses off and polished the lenses with a snowy white handkerchief. "I believe the last time that happened was sometime in the early nineties. What did you argue about?"

"We didn't really argue. But she may be upset when you get home tonight."

"If your mother isn't upset every other evening, I think I've walked into the wrong house."

He gave her an absent pat on the shoulder that told her his mind was already moving away from her.

"I wonder if I could talk to you a minute about some-thing else? The Three Fates?"

His gaze and his attention snapped back to her. "What about them?"

"I had a conversation the other day that reminded me of them. And of Henry Wyley's journal. It sparked my interest when I was a child, and I'd like to read it again. In fact, I've been thinking I may be able to work a section on the mythology of those pieces into my new book."

"The interest may be timely. Anita Gaye brought them up in a conversation a few weeks ago."

"So Mother told me. Do you think she has a line on one of the other two that still exist?"

"If she does, I couldn't get it out of her." He slid his glasses back on and gave her a wolfish smile. "And I tried. If she locates one of the others, it would be of some interest in the community. Two, and she'll make a reasonable splash. But without all three, it's no major find."

"And the third, according to the journal, must be lost in the North Atlantic. Still, I'm interested. Would you mind if I borrowed the book?"

"The journal is of considerable personal value to the family," he began, "as well as its historic and monetary value given its age and author."

Another time, she would have backed off. "You let me read it when I was twelve," she reminded him.

"I had some hope you'd show an interest in the family history and the family business when you were twelve."

"And I disappointed you. I'm sorry. I'd very much appreciate seeing the book. I can study it here if you'd prefer I didn't take it home."

He made a little hiss of impatience. "I'll get it for you. It's up in the vault."

She sighed when he strode off, then retreated back into the foyer to sit on the edge of the settee and wait for him.

When he came back down the stairs, she rose. "Thank you." She pressed the soft, faded leather to her breast. "I'll be very careful with it."

"You're very careful with everything, Tia." He walked to the door, opened it for her. "And that's why, I think, you disappoint yourself."

* * *

"WHERE DID YOU go?" Malachi danced his fingers over the back of Tia's hand and watched her attention shift back to him.

"Nowhere important. Sorry. I'm not very good company tonight."

"That's for me to decide." What she'd been, all evening, was broody. So far she'd barely touched her polenta, though he was sure it had been prepared following her specific instructions. It was clear to him that her mind kept drifting, and when it did, a sadness came over her face that made his heart ache.

"Tell me what's troubling you, darling."

"It's nothing." It warmed her when he called her darling. "Really. Just a family . . ." She couldn't call it an argument. No voices had been raised, no angry words tossed. "Disagreement. I managed to upset my mother and irritate my father, all in the space of a couple of hours."

"How did you do that?"

She poked at her polenta. She hadn't told him of the journal yet. As it was, by the time she'd gotten back to her apartment, she'd been too tired, too depressed, to open it. She'd wrapped it carefully in an unbleached cloth and had tucked it in her desk drawer. In any case, she thought, it wasn't the journal that had caused the problem. It was, as usual, herself.

"My mother wasn't feeling well, and I spoke out of turn."

"I'm forever speaking out of turn to mine," Malachi said easily. "She just gives me a cuff, or that terrifying look mothers develop while you're still in the womb, I imagine, and goes about her business."

"It doesn't work that way with mine. She's worried about me."

Worried I'm endangering my health, worried I'm letting myself care about a man I know little to nothing about. "I had a lot of health problems as a child."

"You seem pretty healthy to me now." He kissed her fingers, hoping to tease her out of her mood. "I certainly feel . . . healthy when I get close to you."

"Are you married?"

The absolute shock on his face gave her the answer, and made her furious with herself for asking the question.

"What? Married? No, Tia."

"I'm sorry, I'm sorry. I'm an idiot. I mentioned to my mother that I was seeing someone, and before I knew it you were married and after my money, and I'm having some wild, illicit affair that will leave me penniless and heartbroken, and probably suicidal."

He let out a breath. "I'm not married, and I'm not interested in your money. As to the affair, I've been giving that considerable thought, but I'll have to rearrange my plans for the rest of this evening if getting you into bed could result in leaving you broke, heartbroken and suicidal."

"Jesus." She wrung her hands. "Why don't we skip all of that and you can just shoot me now and put me out of my misery."

"Why don't we skip dinner instead and go back to your flat so I can get my hands on you. I give you my word that when we're done, you won't be after jumping out the window."

She had to clear her throat. She had an urge, an outrageous one, to lean over and slide her tongue over the long, strong line of his cheekbone. "Maybe I should get that in writing."

"Happy to."

"Why, it's Tia Marsh, isn't it? Stewart Marsh's daughter."

It was a voice Malachi would never forget. His fingers tightened convulsively on Tia's as he shifted, looked up and met Anita Gaye's glittering smile.

# Seven

MALACHI's grip on her hand was enough to make Tia jolt. But she got over that quickly enough, as the fact that she couldn't put a name to the face of the woman smiling sharply enough to drill holes in her brought on a quick spurt of social panic.

"Yes. Hello." Tia struggled furiously for the connection. "How are you?"

"I'm wonderful, thanks. You won't remember me. I'm Anita Gaye, one of your father's competitors."

"Of course." Conflicting emotions trickled through the wash of relief. Malachi's grip on her fingers had eased slightly, but still held firm. Anita's eyes glittered like suns, and her companion looked politely bored.

Tia began to wonder if the strangling tension she felt came from a source other than her own social clumsiness. "It's nice to see you. This is Malachi Sullivan. Ms. Gaye," she began, shifting to Malachi, "is in antiques. As a matter of fact—" She had to bite back a yelp when his hand vised on hers again. "Ah, she's one of the top dealers in the country," she finished weakly.

"You flatter me. It's nice to meet you, Mr. Sullivan." There was a laugh in her voice, but the tone of it made

Tia want to shiver. It was so predatory. "Are you in the business . . . of antiques?"

"No." The single syllable was clipped and as rude as a slap. Anita only purred and touched a hand lightly to Tia's shoulder.

"Our table's ready, so I won't keep you. We must have lunch sometime soon, Tia. I read your last book and was just fascinated. I'd love to discuss it with you."

"Of course."

"Give your parents my best," she added, and sent one last, laughing look at Malachi as she glided away.

Deliberately, Tia drew her hand from his, then reached for her water glass to soothe her throat. "You know each other."

"What?"

"Don't." She set her glass down again, then folded her hands together in her lap. "You must think me the perfect fool, both of you. She's never said two words to me in my life. Women like her don't notice women like me. I'm not her competition."

His blood was up, which made it difficult to think clearly. "That's a ridiculous thing to say."

"Stop it." She gathered herself, let out a breath. "You knew each other, and you were surprised, you were angry when she came over. And you were afraid I was about to mention the Fates."

"That's a great deal of conclusions for such a short interlude."

"People who stay in the background tend to develop good observation skills." She couldn't look at him, not yet. "I'm not wrong, am I?"

"No. Tia—"

"This isn't the place to discuss it." Her voice was dismissive, as was her slight shift away from him when he touched her arm. "I'd like you to take me home."

"All right." He signaled for the check. "I'm sorry, Tia, it's—"

"I don't want an apology. I want an explanation." She rose and, because her legs were unsteady, kept moving. "I'll wait outside."

She didn't speak in the cab, which was just as well. He needed time to figure out how and where to begin. He should have anticipated Anita would muck up the works; he should have anticipated her making a move. And he'd wasted valuable time. Wasted it, he admitted, because he enjoyed being with Tia and hadn't been able to make himself push her too hard and fast toward the goal.

And, he thought, because the longer he knew her, the more he wished he'd approached the whole matter differently. Instead he'd tangled himself up in lies.

Still, she was a reasonable woman. All he had to do was make her understand.

She ignored the hand he offered to help her out of the cab. He began to feel a little sick. When they reached the door to her apartment, he braced for her to try to slam it in his face, but she walked inside, left it open, and walked straight across the room to the windows. As if, he thought, she still needed air.

"It's a complicated business, Tia."

"Yes, deceit and underhanded behavior often are." She'd had time to think. Concentrating on the puzzle of it helped distance her from the hurt. "It all deals with the Fates. You and Ms. Gaye want them. I'm a link. She'd work on my parents, and you . . ." She turned back now, her face cool and set. "You'd work on me."

"It's not like that. Anita and I are in no way partners."

"Oh." She nodded. "Competitors, then, working against each other. That does make more sense. Did you have a lovers' spat?"

"Christ." He rubbed his hands over his face. "No. Listen to me, Tia, she's a dangerous woman. Ruthless, completely unscrupulous."

"And you're just loaded with scruples? I suppose you misplaced all those scruples when you lured me away from my hotel in Helsinki, spent all that time charming me, making me believe you were interested in me so someone could break into my hotel, search it. Did you really think I carried clues to the Fates around on a book tour?"

"I didn't have anything to do with the break-in. That was Anita. I'm not a fucking criminal."

"Oh pardon me. Just a fucking liar, then?"

He reined in his fury. What right did he have to be pissed off? "I can't deny I lied to you. I'm sorry for it."

"Oh, you're sorry? Well, that's different, then. All is forgiven."

Malachi slid his hands into his pockets, balled them there. The woman facing him wasn't the soft, sweet, slightly neurotic one who'd snuck under his skin. This woman was coldly furious and tougher than he'd believed. "Do you want an explanation, or would you rather just pound on me?"

"I'll have the first, and reserve my right to the second."

"Fair enough. Can we sit?"

"No."

"Be easier if you pounded on me first and got it out of your system," he responded. "I told you some of the truth."

"You'll have a long wait for your medal of honor, Malachi. Is that your name, or did you make it up?"

"It's my name, goddamn it. You want to see my bloody passport?" He began to pace now as she stood cool and still. "I did have an ancestor on the *Lusitania*. Felix Greenfield, who survived and married Meg O'Reiley and settled in Cobh. The experience changed his life, turned it around and made something out of him. He worked the fishing boats with his wife's family, had his children, converted to Catholicism and by all accounts was quite devout about it."

He paused, ran his fingers—as she'd allowed herself to imagine doing herself—through his thick chestnut hair. "Before that time, before the ship sank under him, he wasn't such an admirable man. He'd booked passage on that particular vessel as he was on the run from the police. He was a thief."

"Blood tells."

"Oh, stop it. I've never stolen a flaming thing." The insult grated and had him whirling on her.

He didn't look so much the cultured gentleman now, Tia thought dispassionately. Despite the handsome suit, he looked more the brawler. "I don't think you're in a position to be so touchy."

"I come from a good family. We may not be as fancy and fine as yours, but we're not thieves and bandits. Felix was, and I can't be blamed for it. In any case, he turned a corner. It just happened he turned it after he'd taken a few items from the stateroom of the Henry W. Wyleys."

"The Fate." She had to wait until her mind could absorb it. "He took the Fate. It was never lost."

"It would've been if he hadn't pinched it, so you might want to consider that in the grand scheme of things. He didn't know what it was, only that it was pretty and shiny and it, well, it called to him, so to speak. It was passed down through the family, along with the story, and kept as kind of a good-luck charm."

Fascinating. Fantastic. Beneath the hurt and fury, she felt interest stirring. "And it came to you."

"It came to my mother, and through her to myself and my brother and sister at this point."

He was calmer now. He was Catholic enough himself to feel some of the weight of the lies lift by the confessing of them. "I had some curiosity about it, and there's where I made my fatal mistake. I took it to Dublin. I thought to have it identified, if possible, appraised certainly My sister, who has a knack for such things, said that she'd see what she could find out through researching books and on the Internet. But I took it with me, impatient, and walked like a sheep into Morningside Antiquities."

"You showed it to Anita."

"Not at first, no. I told her about it. Why shouldn't I?" he asked, frustrated all over again. "She was supposed to be an expert on such things, and a reputable businesswoman. I didn't burst out with the history of it right off, but over the next few days . . ."

He trailed off as impotent embarrassment shimmered around him.

"Yes. I can fill in the blanks." Because it made it worse, it somehow, perversely, made it better. She wasn't the only one who could be blinded stupid by her own hormones. "She's very beautiful."

"So's a mako shark to some points of view." There was bitterness there, for the woman who'd duped him, and for the one who stood placidly with the dark river at her back.

"Well, she got enough of it out of me before I noticed the teeth. She came by my hotel so she could see it privately. She thought that would be best. Naturally I agreed because she'd already demonstrated a keen personal interest in me. She uses sex the way other women use lipstick," he declared. "Putting it on and taking it off on a whim. I handed it right over to her."

She thought of Anita Gaye. Sharp, sexy, confident. Predatory. Yes, she could understand why even a clever man might be a fool around her. "No receipt?"

"I might have thought to ask for one if she hadn't been undoing my trousers at the time. We had sex, and we had wine. Or I had wine. The bitch must've put something in it because I didn't wake up until past noon the next day. She was gone, and so was the Fate."

"She drugged you?"

He caught the edge of disbelief, set his teeth. "I don't pass out near to twelve hours on a bounce and two glasses of wine. I didn't believe it myself at first. I went to Morningside and was told she was in meetings and unavailable. I left messages there and at her hotel. She never returned them. When finally I managed to contact her after she'd come back to New York, she told me she had no idea who I was or what I was talking about, and not to bother her again."

It wasn't easy hazing the image of him and Anita romping in a hotel bed, but she worked at it so she could think clearly. "You're telling me that Anita Gaye, of Morningside Antiquities, drugged you unconscious after sleeping with you, then stole from you, then denied ever meeting you?"

"I've just said so, haven't I? Made a fool of me in the bargain, using sex, pretending to care—" He broke off when he caught Tia's arch look.

"Yes, it's mortifying, isn't it?"

"This wasn't the same." But his stomach pitched nearly to his knees. "Not at all the same."

"Just because we didn't get to the . . . 'bounce' doesn't change the intent, or the result. You could've approached me directly, honestly. You chose not to."

"I did. As far as I knew you might've been as calculating as she was. Or, failing that, how could I know if you wouldn't get it into your head to push some claim on the Fate?"

He lifted his hands. What had seemed perfectly reasonable, certainly necessary at the time, now looked very cold, and very ugly.

"It may not have come to me by a tidy route, Tia, but it's been ours for almost ninety years. And when we found out about there being three of them, and what that meant, it changed things considerably. Part of it's just wanting back what's ours, and the other, well, damn it, we're talking a lot of money. Great pots of money. We can use it. Ireland's booming at the present, and if we had more to work with, we could expand our business."

"Your shipping business?" she asked dryly and saw he had the grace to look embarrassed.

"It's boats anyway. We run tours out of Cobh and around the Head of Kinsale. Still have a hand in fishing as well. I thought you'd be more comfortable with me if you believed I was in your circle of things."

"So, you considered me shallow."

He let out a breath, met her eyes directly. "I expected you to be. I was wrong."

"You were going to come back here with me tonight, go to bed with me. That's cold. That's despicable. You used me, right from the beginning, a means to an end, as if I had no feelings. I never mattered to you at all."

"That's not true." He crossed to her then, and though she held her arms rigidly at her sides, gripped her hands. "I won't have you think that."

"When you came up to me the first time, when you smiled at me, asked me to go for a walk, it meant nothing to you. I meant nothing. All you wanted was to see if I could be of any use, nothing more or less."

"I didn't know you. At first, you were just a name, just a possibility. But—"

"Please. Is this the part where you tell me everything changed once you got to know me, to care about me? Spare us both that particular cliché."

"I got tangled up being with you, Tia. That wasn't part of my plan."

"Your plan's a mess. Let go of my hands."

"I'm sorry I hurt you." It was pitiful, but he could think of nothing else. "I swear to God I never meant to."

"Let go of my hands," she repeated. When he did, she stepped back. "I can't help you, and wouldn't now if I could. But you can comfort yourself that I'll be no help to Anita Gaye, either. I'm useless to both of you."

"You're not useless, Tia. Not to anyone. And I'm not speaking of the Fates."

She only shook her head. "It's all we have to speak of. Now I'm tired. I'd like you to go."

"I don't want to leave it like this."

"I'm afraid you'll have to. I really have no more to say to you, at least nothing more that would be the least bit constructive."

"Throw something, then," he suggested. "Punch me, yell at me."

"That would make it easier for you." She needed her cave, her solitude. And some scrap of pride. "I asked you to go. If you have any conscience about what you've done, you'll respect that."

Without a choice, he went to the door. He turned, studying her as she stood framed by the window. "The first time I looked at you," he said quietly, "really looked at you, Tia, all I could think was you had the loveliest and saddest eyes. I haven't been able to get them out of my head since. This isn't over, none of it's over."

She let out a long breath when the door shut behind him. "That's for me to say."

THE STREETS WERE steep in Cobh. Like San Francisco, they speared up from a bay at a leg-aching angle. At the top of one was a pretty house painted a pale water-green with a colorful dooryard garden behind a low, stone wall.

There were three bedrooms, two baths, a living room with a TV that needed upgrading and a comfortably sprung couch covered with blue-and-white checks. There was a small parlor and a dining room as well, both used only for company. There, the furniture was ruthlessly polished and the lace curtains were soft with age.

On the wall of the parlor were pictures of John F. Kennedy, the current pope and the Sacred Heart of Jesus. That particular trio had always made Malachi so uneasy, he rarely sat in the room unless given no choice.

Until he'd turned twenty-four and had moved into the set of rooms over the boathouse, he'd lived in that same house, shared one of the bedrooms with his brother and fought with his sister over her time in the upstairs bath.

As long as he could remember, the kitchen was the gathering place. It was the kitchen he paced now, while his mother peeled potatoes for dinner.

He'd been back only two days, and on the first he'd been buried in work. He'd taken out one of their two tour boats himself, as Rebecca had pointed out he hadn't pulled his weight in that area for a good chunk of the summer. Then he'd hacked through paperwork until he couldn't see straight.

He'd put in a full twelve-hour day, and another ten on his second day home. But he hadn't been able to work off the anger, or the guilt.

"Wash these potatoes off," Eileen ordered. "It'll give you something to do besides brood."

"I'm not brooding. I'm thinking."

"I know brooding when I see it." She opened the oven, checked the roast. It was Malachi's favorite, and she'd made the Sunday meal in the middle of the week in hopes of cheering him up. "The girl had a perfect right to toss you out on your ear, and you'll just have to live with it."

"I know it, but you'd think she'd see the logic of it all after sleeping on it. At least give me the chance to make it up to her. She wouldn't answer the damn phone or the door. Probably tossed out the flowers I sent. Who knew she had such a hard side to her?"

"Hard side, my aunt Minnie. Bruised feelings is what she has. You made it personal when you should've kept it businesslike."

"It got personal."

Eileen turned back and softened. "Yes, I see it did. That's the wonder of living, isn't it, never knowing when something or someone's going to turn you down a different road." She started peeling the carrots that would go around the roast with the potatoes. "Flowers never worked on me either when your father was in the doghouse."

Malachi smiled a little. "What did?"

"Time, for one thing. A woman's got to sulk a bit and know a man's suffering for his sins. And after that a good crawling's in order. I like a man who knows how to grovel."

"I never saw Da grovel."

"You didn't see everything, did you?" Eileen chided.

"I hurt her, Ma." He set the potatoes aside to drain. "I didn't have the right to hurt her that way."

"You didn't, no, but you didn't start it all with that in mind." She wiped her hands on a dish towel, hung it back over a hook. "You were thinking of the family, and your own pride. Now you've got her to think of as well. You'll know what to do next time you see her."

"She won't see me again."

"If I thought a son of mine gave up so easily, I'd cosh you over the head with this skillet. Haven't I worries enough with Gideon off with that dancer?"

"Gideon's fine. At least he's made contact with a connection in all this who's still speaking to him."


"YOU SON-OF-a-bitch!"

She was speaking to him, all right, in a low growl as she planted her fist squarely on his jaw. The sucker punch shot Gideon hard on his ass on the grimy rug outside the door of the dingy room in the last of the fleabag hotels they'd booked.

He tasted blood, saw stars and heard what sounded like the "Hallelujah Chorus" ring in his ears.

He swiped at his lip and eyed her maliciously as she stood, in a black bra and panties, with her hair still dripping from what the hotel laughingly called a shower.

"That's it." He got slowly to his feet. "For the good of mankind, I have to kill you now. You're a bloody menace to society."

"Come on then." She rocked on the balls of her feet, lifted her fists. "Take your best shot."

He wanted to. Oh, how he wanted to. For five hideous days he'd crisscrossed Europe with her in tow. He'd slept in beds that made the cots in the youth hostels of his short, carefree holiday after passing his A levels seem like celestial clouds. He'd tolerated her demands, her questions, her complaints.

He'd ignored the fact that he shared very close, even intimate quarters with a woman who got paid to dance naked, and whose body ensured she'd be well paid for the task. He'd behaved like a perfect gentleman even when she'd been deliberately provocative.

He'd fed her—and Christ could she eat—and made certain she had the best shelter his dwindling budget would allow.

What did she do? She punched her fist in his face.

He took a step toward her, his hands bunched at his sides. "I can't hit a woman. It pains me more than I can say, but I can't do it. Now move aside."

"Can't hit a woman." She lifted her chin, daring him. "But you don't have any trouble stealing from one. You took my earrings."

"That's right." He couldn't hit her, but he did give her a good shove so he could step in and slam the door. "And I got twenty-five pounds for them. You eat like a horse, and I'm not made of money."

"Twenty-five?" Her outrage doubled. "I paid three hundred and sixty-eight dollars for those, after an hour's hard bargaining in the jewelry exchange on Fifth. You're not only a thief, you're a sucker."

"And you've vast experience hocking earrings, have you?"

She didn't, but she was sure she could have done better. "Those were eighteen-carat, Italian gold."

"Now they're going to be fish and chips at the pub, and a night's lodging in this hellhole. You keep hammering at me about being partners, but you don't contribute anything."

"You could have asked."

"Sure, you'd've handed them over if I'd asked. You, who takes her handbag into the flaming shower with her."

Her full, taunting mouth curled. "You've just proven I was smart to do so."

Disgusted, he grabbed a shirt, tossed it to her. "Put something on, for Christ's sake. Have some respect for yourself."

"I've plenty of respect for myself." She'd forgotten she was in her underwear. She tended to miss fine details when the red haze of temper came over her. But now, the contempt in his tone had her heaving the shirt across the room. "I want that twenty-five pounds."

"You're not getting it. You want to eat, get some clothes on. You've got five minutes." He started toward the bath. He should've known better than to turn his back on her.

She leaped on him, wrapping those long legs like steel bands around his waist, yanking his head back by the hair until lights exploded in front of his eyes.

He spun, tried to buck her off. She clung like a burr and managed to hook an arm around his throat. With his windpipe in danger of being crushed, he reached up, got a good hank of her hair himself. Her howl when he pulled it was pure satisfaction.

"Let go! Let go of my hair!"

"You let go of mine," he choked out. "Now."

They circled, her heaped on his back, both of them cursing, both of them yanking. He rammed into the side of the bed, lost his balance. When he hit, he landed on top of her, hard enough to knock the wind out of her and loosen her grip. Before she could recover both, he flipped and pinned her.

"You've got a screw loose," he muttered, struggling to

hold her arms when she started to fight back. "Dozens of screws loose. It's twenty-five pounds, for God's sake. I'll give you twelve and five if you're so crazed for it."

"My earrings," she panted. "My money."

"For all you know I'm a desperate man. For all you know I could bash you on the head and take a hell of a lot more than a pair of earrings."

She sniffed, derisively, then, inspired, tried a new strategy. Tears threatened to spill down her cheeks. That wide, lush mouth trembled. "Don't hurt me."

"I'm not going to hurt you. What do you take me for? Don't cry, come on now, darling." He released her arm to brush a tear away.

She attacked like a wildcat. Teeth, nails, flying limbs. She caught a glancing blow off his temple, shot an elbow into his ribs. In his struggle to defend himself, he rolled off the bed, with her on top of him.

Grunting, sweating, stunned with pain, he managed to pin her a second time before he realized she was breath-less with laughter.

"What is it about a few tears that makes guys all gooey?" She grinned up at him. Christ, he was cute. All pissed off and poetical. "Your mouth's bleeding, champ."

"I know it."

"I guess that was worth twenty-five pounds. But I'm not settling for fish and chips. I want red meat," she demanded.

Then she saw that focused, narrowed look that meant one thing from a man. Her belly muscles quivered in response.

"Uh-oh," she murmured.

"Damn it, Cleo." He crushed his throbbing, bleeding mouth to hers. She tasted of sin and smelled like a rain-washed garden. Beneath his, her mouth opened, and it took every bit as greedily. Her limbs wrapped around him again, but silkily this time. She arched, center to center in a slow, sinuous invitation.

He lifted his head and looked down at her. Her hair, all that warm, damp sable, was spread over the thin, burn-scarred carpet. Her lashes were still set with those mock tears. He wanted to devour her, one quick gulp, no matter how it might make his belly ache afterward. He was rock hard and randy.

And he found himself blocked by the same set of values that had prevented him from striking her.

"Damn it," he said again and pushed off her to sit with his back braced against the bed.

Baffled, she levered onto her elbows. "What's the matter?"

"Get dressed, Cleo. I said I wouldn't hurt you. I won't use you, either."

She sat back up on her heels as she studied him. His eyes were closed, his breath ragged. She had good reason to know he was aroused. But he'd stopped. Stopped, she realized, because despite the toughness, the cool calculation she'd recognized in him, he was decent. Right down to the marrow.

"You're the genuine article, aren't you?"

He opened his eyes to see her smiling thoughtfully. "What?"

"Just one question. Did you back off because I'm a currently unemployed stripper?"

"I backed off because whatever you say about partnerships, I'm responsible for you being here. For you having to run out of Prague and across the continent to England with the clothes on your back. I made the choice to go after these statues, and to take the consequences knowing someone was going to try to stop me, however they could. You didn't have the choice."

"That's what I thought," she replied. "That means I'll just have to take you down again."

"Cut it out," he warned when she slithered like a snake into his lap.

"You can just lie back and take it." She ran her tongue over his jaw. "Or you can participate. Up to you, Slick. But either way, I'm having you. Umm, you're all hot and sweaty." When he clamped his hands on her wrists, she just continued to use her mouth. "I like it. This'll go easier on you if you cooperate."

She rocked on him, then covered his mouth with hers when he moaned.

"Touch me." It had been so long since she'd had a man's hands on her. Since she'd wanted them on her. "Touch me."

In one rough move, he had her on her back again, and his hands were everywhere. The floor was hard as rock, smelled of stale smoke, but they rolled over it as she tugged at his shirt, as she dug her nails into his back.

She'd wanted this. Even knowing it was stupid, it was pointless, she'd wanted him. Every time she'd felt his gaze linger on her, every night she'd lain awake knowing he was lying awake an arm's length away, she'd wanted him.

The good, solid weight of him pressed her into the un-yielding floor, those strong, hard hands streaked over her. She bowed up when he dragged her bra down to her waist, moaned in pleasure when his mouth ravaged her breast.

Her body was a banquet. Sleek and curvy with generous breasts, endless legs. He'd wanted to feast since he'd first seen her strut onstage in her man's clothes with that know-ing smirk on her fabulous face.

He couldn't think about how it was a mistake. He could only think how much he needed to feed.

He found her mouth again, and pain and pleasure warred through him. She was dragging his jeans down, raking her nails over his hips. And his blood was a raging hammer blasting against his heart, in his head.

Then he was inside her, rammed deep, and she was al-ready coming around him on a wild, wet burst.

"Jesus!" Her eyes flew open and were nearly black with shock. "Jesus, what was that?"

"I don't know, but let's try it again." Even as she shud-dered, he drove himself into her in fast, nearly violent strokes. He heard her gasp for air, saw the fresh flush of heat flood her cheeks. Then she was matching him, beat for frantic beat.

And on the instant when he lost himself in her, she dragged his mouth back to hers.

# Eight

CLEO lay facedown and crossways on a mattress that had all the yield of concrete. Her lungs had stopped wheezing, and the roar of blood in her ears had subsided to a pleasant hum.

She'd had her first sexual experience at sixteen when, after a fight with her mother, she'd let Jimmy Moffet do what he'd been begging her to let him do for three months.

The earth hadn't moved, but as initiators went, Jimmy had been all right.

In the eleven years since, she'd had better, and she'd had worse, and she'd learned to be selective. She'd learned what pleasured her own body and how to guide a man to satisfy her needs.

She'd made some mistakes, of course, Sidney Walter being the most recent and the most costly. But by and large she thought she had a good, healthy sex drive and a reasonably discriminating taste in bed partners.

It was true that drive had diminished radically during her stint as a performer at Down Under, but strip clubs tended to show men and sex at their most basic and ordinary. In the same way, she imagined that experience had only honed her discrimination.

It certainly seemed to have worked this time around.

Gideon Sullivan not only knew how to make the earth move, he had it doing the merengue. And the tango. And the rumba. The man was a regular Fred Astaire in the sheets.

It was, she decided, going to add a nice dimension to this odd business partnership of theirs.

Not that he considered it a partnership, but she did. And that's what counted. Plus, she had an ace in the hole. She opened her eyes and looked at the purse that sat on the pockmarked dresser.

Make that a queen in the hole, she mused. A silver queen.

She intended to deal squarely with him when the time came. Probably. But experience had taught her it was wise to keep something in reserve. For all she knew, if she told Gideon about the statue, he'd take off with it just as he had her earrings.

Damn it, she'd really liked those earrings.

Of course, he didn't seem to be a total prick. The man had ethics when it came to sex, and she respected that. But money was a whole different ball game. It was one thing to heat the sheets with a man she'd known less than a week, and another to trust him with a potential gold mine.

Smarter, much smarter to keep her own counsel and pump him for information.

She rolled over, scraped her teeth along his hip since it was handy. "I didn't realize you Irish guys had such stamina."

"Guinness for strength." His voice was rough with sleep. "Christ Jesus, and I do need a beer."

"You've got a nice build here, Slick." To please herself she walked her finger up his thigh. "You work out?"

"Like at a gymnasium? No. Bunch of sweaty guys and terrifying machinery."

"You run?"

"If I'm in a hurry."

She laughed and slithered up to his chest. "So what do you do back in Ireland?"

"We have boats." He stirred himself to trail fingers into her hair. He really liked all that dense, dark hair of hers. "Tour boats, fishing boats. Sometimes I run tourists around, sometimes I fish, and half the time I'm hammering one of the bloody boats into proper repair."

"That explains these." She pinched his biceps. "Tell me more about the Fates."

"I told you already."

"You told me some of the history stuff. But that doesn't tell me how you're so sure they're worth a lot of money. Why it's worth our time to try to track them down. I've got an investment here, too, and I don't even know for certain who the hell chased me out of Prague."

"I know they're worth a lot of money, first, because my sister, Rebecca, researched them. Becca's a demon with research and facts and data."

"No offense, Slick, but I don't know your sister."

"She's brilliant. Has so much information in her brain I'm always expecting it to start spilling out of her ears. It was she who pushed the whole idea of the touring business on the family. She was only about fifteen and here she comes up to Ma and Da with all these figures and projections and systems she'd put together. The economy was going to boom, she was sure of it. And with Cobh already of interest to tourists because of the *Titanic* and the *Lusitania,* and the fine scenery and harbor, we'd only have the more of them as time went on."

She forgot for a moment that she was luring him into giving her more information. "They listened to her?" The idea of parents paying any attention to the ideas of a child seemed both fascinating and ridiculous.

"Sure they listened to her. Why wouldn't they? 'Twasn't as if they jumped up shouting, 'Well, of course, if Bec says to do it, then we must.' But it was discussed and picked over and hammered at until the conclusion was reached that she had a fine notion there, one worth exploring."

"My parents wouldn't have listened." She settled her head on his chest. "Of course, by the time I was fifteen, we'd stopped having what you could define as conversations."

"Why would that be?"

"Ah, let's see. Oh right, I remember. We don't like each other."

Curious, and struck by the sheer bitterness in her tone, he rolled them over so he could see her face. "Why do you think they don't like you?"

"Because I'm wild, argumentative, nasty and wasted the many opportunities they offered me. Why are you smiling?"

"I was just thinking the first three seem to be why I'm starting to like you. What opportunities did you waste?"

"Education, social advancements, all of which I squandered or threw back in their faces, depending on my mood."

"Hmm. And why don't you like them?"

"Because they never saw me." The minute she said it, she was embarrassed. Where in hell had that come from? To counter it, she wiggled under him and danced her fingers over his ass. "Hey, as long as we're here . . ."

"What did you want them to see?"

"It doesn't matter." She rubbed her foot over his calf in long strokes, lifted her head enough to take a quick nip at his mouth. "We washed our hands of each other some time ago. They pretty much washed hands of each other, too. Stopped pretending to be married when I was sixteen. My mother's been married twice since. My father just whores around—discreetly."

"It's rough on you."

"Nothing to do with me." She jerked a shoulder. "Anyway, I'm more interested in now, and whether you've got one more round in you before we go get that beer."

He wasn't so easily distracted once he'd pinned to a point. But he lowered his head to nibble at her throat. "How'd you end up in Prague, working at that club?"

"Stupidity."

He lifted his head. "That's a wide area in my experience. What specific form?"

She huffed out a breath. "If I'm not going to get laid again, I want to take a shower."

"I like to know more about the woman I'm making love with than her name."

"Too late, Slick. You already fucked me."

"The first time I fucked you," he said in a cool, steady

voice that made her feel ashamed. "The second time it was more. If we go on this way, there'll be more yet. That's how it works."

It sounded, quite a bit, like a threat. "Do you complicate everything?"

"I do, yes. It's a talent of mine. You said they didn't see you. Well, I'm looking at you, Cleo, and I'm going to keep looking until I see clearly. Let's see how you deal with that."

"I don't like being pushed."

"That's a problem, then, as I'm pushy." He rolled off her. "You can have the shower first, but make it snappy. I'm half starved to death and dying for a beer."

He folded his hands on his belly, shut his eyes.

Frowning, Cleo climbed off the bed. On her way to the bath, she shot him one last curious look, then grabbed her purse and shut herself in the bathroom.

Confused her, Gideon thought. That was fine as she sure confused the hell out of him.

HE WAITED UNTIL they were settled at one of the low tables in the pub, she with her tough little steak, he with the better choice of fish and chips.

"Being as your family's of New York society, would you know Anita Gaye?"

"Never heard of her." The steak required a great deal of work, but she wasn't going to complain about it. "Who is she?"

"You know Morningside Antiquities?"

"Sure. It's one of those old, snooty places where rich people pay too much for things that used to belong to other rich people." She tossed back her mass of hair. "Me, I like bright, shiny and new."

He grinned. "That's a damning description, particularly by a rich person."

"I'm not rich. My family is."

Privately, he thought anyone who paid more than three hundred American dollars for something that dangled from the earlobes was either rich or foolish. Possibly both. "No inheritance?"

She shrugged, sawed at the beef. "I've got a nice pile due when I hit thirty-five. That won't keep me in beer and pretzels for the next eight years."

"Where'd you learn to dance?"

"What does Morningside have to do with our current situation?"

"All right then. Anita Gaye is, at the moment, in charge of Morningside, being the widow of the former proprietor."

"Wait a minute, wait a minute." She wagged her fork. "I remember something about that. Old dude marries sharp young chick. Worked for him or something. My mother got all righteous about it, lunched on the horror for weeks. Then when he kicked off, there was a whole second round. I was still speaking, on rare occasions, to my mother then. She was back in New York between husbands. And I said something like, if the bimbo saw to it the old goat died happy, what's the diff? She, my mother, got all pissed off about it. I guess that was one of our last bouts before we did the Pontius Pilate routine."

"Washed your hands of each other?"

"Bingo."

"Over someone else's dead husband?"

"Actually, the hand-washing came when her latest husband got a little grabby with my tits and I was annoyed enough to tell her about it."

"Your stepfather touched you?" His tone was filled with moral outrage.

"He wasn't my stepfather right at that point. And it was more of a grab boobs, squeeze boobs, resulting in my knee rammed into his groin sort of event rather than touching. I said he'd come on to me, and he, in a rare use of gray matter, countered that I'd come on to him. She bought his side, foul language issued from all interested parties. I left, she married him, and they moved to his turf. L.A."

She shrugged, lifted her beer. "End of sentimental family saga."

He touched the back of her hand. "I suppose she deserves him, then."

"I suppose she does." She shook it off, drank down beer. "So Anita Gaye applies to us because . . . She's the one who backed the muscle who went after us in Prague?" Cleo pursed her lips. "Maybe not such a bimbo."

"She's a calculating, devious woman. And a thief. She has one of the Fates because she stole it from us. From my brother, specifically. She wants all three and won't quibble about the method of acquiring them. That's something we'll use against her. We get to the other two first, then we negotiate."

"So, there's no client. It's your brother."

"My family," he corrected. "Malachi, my brother, is working on another angle, and my sister's researching a third. The trouble we're having is, whatever route we take, Anita Gaye's right there. A step ahead, a step behind, but always close. She's anticipated us, or she has another source of information. Or, more troubling, she's got a way of keeping tabs on us."

"Which is why you and I have been staying at crappy hotels, paying cash, and you've been using a bogus name."

"Which can't go on much longer." He sipped his own beer while scanning the crowded, noisy pub. "I'm reasonably sure we've lost her, for now. It's time you got to work." His lips twitched, then curved. "Partner."

"Doing what?"

"You said you recalled seeing the Fate, which means it's still in your family. So I think the best approach is to start off with a phone call, a nice daughterly call, I think, with just a hint of contrition and apology."

She stabbed one of his chips with her fork. "That's not even funny."

"Wasn't meant to be."

"I'm not calling home like some repentant prodigal."

He only smiled at her.

"I'm not."

"After your story, I'm no fonder of your mother than you are. But you'll call her if you want a fifth of the take."

"A fifth? Check your math, Slick."

"Nothing wrong with my figures. There are four of us, and one of you."

"I want half."

"Well, you can want the world on a string, but you won't get it. A fifth of potentially millions of pounds should be enough to hold you until you reach the ripe age of thirty-five. Are things so strained between you she'd refuse a collect call? Or perhaps you'd do better with your father."

"Neither of them would accept charges if I were calling from the third level of hell. But I'm not making the call anyway."

"You are. We'll just have to put the call on a credit card. How's yours holding up?" When she folded her arms over her chest, stared stonily, he shrugged. "We'll put it on mine, then."

"I'm not doing it."

"Best to find a phone box," he decided. "If Anita has some way of tracking my card, I'd as soon not put a target on my back. Hopefully, we'll be out of London by tomorrow in any case. You need to work in the statue, so I'm thinking a bit of sentiment there. Missing the familiar things of home, that kind of thing. You play it right, maybe one of them'll wire you some money."

"Listen to me. I'll speak very slowly and in short syllables. They wouldn't give me a dime, and I'd slit my own throat before I asked them to."

"Don't know till you try, do you?" He tossed some money on the table. "Let's find a phone box."

How did you argue with someone who didn't argue back but simply kept moving forward like a big, shiny steamroller?

Now she was in a real fix and had very little time to wheedle her way out of it.

She didn't waste her time talking to him as they walked through the light rain that turned the streets glossy black. She had to use her head, calculate her choices.

She could hardly tell him, Gee, no point in calling Mom or Dad because—ha ha—I happen to have the statue right here in my purse!

And if she called—and she'd rather be staked to an anthill than do so—her parents would probably speak to her. Coldly, dutifully, which would only piss her off. If she maintained her temper and asked about the statue, they'd ask her if she was doing drugs. A common inquiry. And she'd be reminded, stiffly, that the little silver statue had stood in her room at home for years. A fact they would know, as her room had been searched weekly for those drugs, which she'd never done, or any sign of immoral, illegal or socially unacceptable behavior.

Since neither of those choices appealed to her, she had to come up with a third.

She was still calculating when he pulled her out of the rain and into a shiny red phone booth. "Take a minute to think about what you're going to say," he advised. "Which one do you think might be best? Mum in Los Angeles? Da in New York?"

"I don't have to decide because I'm not going to call either of them or say anything."

"Cleo." He tucked her wet hair behind her ear. "They really hurt you, didn't they?"

He said it so quietly, so sweetly, she had to elbow her way around and stare out into the rain. "I don't need to call them. I know where it is."

He leaned down, brushed his lips over her hair. "I'm sorry this is hard for you, but we can't keep knocking around from place to place this way."

"I said I know where it is. Get me to New York."

"Cleo—"

"Damn it, stop patting me on the head like I'm a puppy. Give me some goddamn room in here." She used her elbow again to shove him back, then dug into her purse. "Here." She pushed the scanned photograph into his hands.

He stared at it, then lifted his gaze and stared at her. "What the hell is this?"

"The wonders of technology. I made a call from Down Under after our little sight-seeing jaunt. Had a picture taken of it and sent to me on Marcella's computer. I figured you'd cough up the money I wanted, and the ticket, once you had proof I could get my hands on it. The chase scene changed things. Having a couple of goons come after me upped the stakes."

"You didn't bother to show it to me until now."

"A girl needs an edge, Slick." She could hear the temper—the cold fire of it—licking at the edges of his voice. She didn't mind it. "I didn't know you from Jack the Ripper when we drove out of Prague. I'd have to be pretty stupid to toss all my cards on the table until I had a handle on you."

"Got one now?" he said softly.

"Enough of one to know you're supremely pissed, but you'll choke it back. First, because your mother raised you not to hit girls. Second, because you need me if you want to hold that thing in three dimensions instead of in a picture."

"Where is it?"

She shook her head. "Get me to New York."

"How much money do you have?"

"I'm not paying—"

He simply grabbed her purse. She dug her fingers into it like talons and yanked back.

"All right, all right. I've got about a thousand."

"Koruna?"

"Dollars, once they're exchanged."

"You've got a thousand fucking dollars in here, and you haven't parted with a single flipping cent since we started?"

"Twenty-five pounds," she corrected. "Earrings."

He shoved out of the phone booth. "You've just upped your investment, Cleo. You're paying to get us to New York."

WHEN ANITA GAYE wined and dined a client, she did so superbly. In general, she considered such matters a business investment. When the client was an attractive, desirable man she'd yet to lure into bed, she considered it a challenge.

Jack Burdett intrigued her on a number of levels. He

wasn't as polished, as smooth, nor was his pedigree as sterling as the men she normally chose for her escorts.

But he was, precisely, the type she often preferred as a lover.

Dark blond hair fell as it chose around a strong, roughly hewn face that was more compelling than handsome. There was a faint scar running along the side of his mouth, a kind of crescent rumor said he'd gotten from flying glass during a bar fight in Cairo. The mouth itself had a sensual, almost hedonistic curve that told her he'd be demanding in bed once she got him there.

He had a tough build to go with that tough face. Broad shoulders and long arms. She knew he boxed as a hobby, and thought he would strip down to his trunks very nicely.

His family had had money once—a few generations back, on his mother's side. Lost, Anita knew, in the stock market crash of '29. Jack hadn't been raised in luxury, and had built his own tidy fortune with his electronics and security firm.

A self-made man, she thought, sipping her wine. Who at the age of thirty-four earned a sturdy seven figures a year. Enough to indulge his other hobby. Collecting.

He'd been married once, and divorced. He owned, among other things, a rehabbed warehouse in SoHo, and lived alone in one of the lofts when he was in the city. He traveled extensively, for both business and pleasure.

He collected, most particularly, antique art pieces with a clearly documented history.

With the first Fate tucked in her safe, Anita hoped Jack Burdett could offer her a path to the others.

"So, tell me all about Madrid." Her voice purred out just over the quiet strains of Mozart. She'd had her staff set up the table for two on the little garden terrace off the third-floor drawing room of her town house. "I've never been, and always wanted to go."

"It was hot." He sampled another bite of the Chateaubriand. It was perfect, of course, as was the wine, the level of the music, the light scent of verbena and roses. And the face and form of the woman across from him.

Jack never trusted perfection.

"I didn't have much time for recreation. The client kept me busy. A few more that paranoid and I can retire."

"Who was it?" When he only smiled and continued to eat, she pouted. "You're so frustratingly discreet, Jack. I'm hardly going to race off to Spain and try to get through your security and rob the man."

"My clients pay me for discretion. They get what they pay for," he added. "You should know."

"It's just that I find your work so fascinating. All those complicated alarm systems, infrared this and motion-detecting that. Come to think of it, with your expertise, you'd make a hell of a burglar, wouldn't you?"

"Crime pays, but not nearly well enough." She wanted something from him, he decided. The intimate meal at home was the first tip-off. Anita liked to go out, where she could see and be seen.

If he'd let ego rule him, he might have convinced himself what she had on her mind was sex. Though he had no doubt she'd enjoy sex, nearly as much as she'd enjoy using it, he imagined there was more here.

The woman was a ruthless operator. It wasn't something he held against her. But neither did he intend to become another trophy on her very crowded shelf, or another tool in her formidable arsenal.

He let her guide the conversation. He was in no hurry for her to get to whatever point she had. She was an attractive companion, and an interesting one who was knowledgeable about art, literature, music. Though he didn't share a great many of her tastes, he appreciated them.

In any case, he liked the house. He'd liked it more when Paul Morningside had been alive, but a house was a house. And this one was a jewel.

A jewel that maintained its dignity and its style decade after decade. And could, he assumed, continue to maintain that dignity regardless of its mistress. The Adam fireplaces would always be stunning frames for simmering fires. The Waterford chandeliers would continue to drip sparkling light on gleaming wood, glinting glass and hand-painted china no matter who warmed themselves by the flame or turned the switch for the lamp.

The Venetian side chairs would be just as lovely no matter who sat in them.

It was one of the aspects he most appreciated about the continuity of the old and the rare.

Not that he could fault Anita's taste. The rooms were still elegantly furnished with the art, the antiques, the flowers placed just so.

No one would ever call it homey, he supposed, but as livable galleries went, it was one of the finest in the city.

As he'd designed and installed the security, he knew every inch of it. As a collector, he approved of how that space was used to display the beautiful and the precious, and rarely refused an invitation.

Still, by the time they'd reached the dessert and coffee stage, his mind was beginning to drift toward home. He wanted to plop down in his underwear and catch a little ESPN.

"I had an inquiry from a client a few weeks ago that might interest you."

"Yeah?"

She knew she was losing him. It was frustrating, infuriating and strangely arousing to have to work so hard to keep a man's attention. "It was about the Three Fates. Do you know the story?"

He stirred his coffee, slow, circular motions. "The Three Fates?"

"I thought you might have heard of them, since your collection runs to that type of art. Legendary, so to speak. Three small silver statues, depicting the Three Fates of Greek mythology." When he only watched her politely, Anita told him the story, carefully picking her way through fact and fantasy in the hope of whetting his appetite.

Jack ate his lemon torte, made appropriate noises, asked the occasional question. But his mind had jumped very far ahead.

She wanted him to help her find the Fates, he mused. He knew of them, of course. Tales of them had been among his bedtime stories as a child.

If Anita was interested enough to hunt them down, it meant she believed all three were still accessible.

He finished off his coffee. She was going to be very disappointed.

"Naturally," she continued, "I explained to my client that if they ever existed, one was lost with Henry Wyley, which negates the possibility of a complete set. The other two seem to be lost in the maze of history, so even the satisfaction of locating two-thirds of the set would take considerable effort. It's a pity when you think what a find they would be. Not just in financial worth, but artistically, historically."

"Yeah, it's a shame all right. No line on the other two?"

"Oh, hints now and then." She moved her bare shoulders, swirled her after-dinner brandy. "As I said, they're legendary, at least among high-end dealers and serious collectors, so rumors about their whereabouts pop up occasionally. The way you travel, and the contacts you've made around the world, I thought you might have heard about them."

"Maybe I haven't asked the right people the right questions."

She leaned forward. Some men might have thought the candlelight flickering in her eyes made them dreamy, romantic. To Jack they were avaricious.

"Maybe you haven't," she agreed. "If you do, I'd love to hear the answers."

"You'll be the first," he assured her.


WHEN HE GOT back to his loft, he stripped off his shirt, turned on the TV and caught the last ten minutes of the Braves crushing the Mets. It was a keen disappointment, as he'd had twenty on the Mets, which just went to show you what happens when you bet on sentiment.

He muted the screen, then picked up the phone and made a call. He asked the right person the right questions, and had no intention of sharing the answers.

## Nine

HENRY W. Wyley, Tia discovered, had been a man of diverse interests with a great lust for life. He had, she supposed, due to his working-class background, put a great deal of stock in status and appearances.

He hadn't been a man to pinch pennies, and though by his own admission had enjoyed the attributes of young, comely females, had remained faithful to his wife throughout their more than three decades of marriage.

That, too, she imagined, stemmed from his working-class roots and mores.

As a writer, however, he could have used a good editor.

He would ramble on about some dinner party, describing the food—of which he seemed inordinately fond—in such detail she could almost begin to taste the lobster bisque or rare roast beef. He talked of other guests until she could begin to imagine the music, the fashions, the conversations. And just when she'd lose herself in the moment, he'd shift into business mode and list, painstakingly, his current investments and interest rates, along with his own pedantic views on the politics that drove them.

He was a man, Tia learned, who loved his money and loved spending it, who doted on his children and grandchildren and considered good food one of life's greatest pleasures.

His pride in Wyley Antiques was paramount, and his ambition to make it the most prestigious dealer a steady drive. Out of that ambition had come his interest, and his desire, for the Three Fates.

Here, he had done his research. He'd tracked Clotho to Washington, D.C., in the fall of 1914. A large section of the journal was devoted to his delighted boasting of wheeling and dealing, and his ultimate purchase of the silver Fate for four hundred twenty-five dollars.

Highway robbery, he'd called it, and Tia could only agree.

He had, by his own account, all but stolen the statue that would be, in less than a year, stolen from him in turn.

But old Henry, unaware of his own fate, kept his ear to the ground. He seemed to delight in the hunt every bit as much as he did in the anticipation of a seven-course meal.

In the spring of that next year, he had linked Lachesis to a wealthy barrister named Simon White-Smythe, Mansfield Court, London.

He booked passage for himself and his wife, Edith, on the doomed ship, believing he would finagle the second Fate for himself, for Wyley's, then follow his next lead, toward Atropus, to Bath.

Uniting the Three Fates was his great ambition. For the sake of art, yes, but more for the sheen it would layer over Wyleys and his family. And, Tia thought, even more than that, for the sheer fun of it all.

As she read, Tia made her own notes. She'd check his facts, use his detailing to find more.

She had an ambition and an anticipation of her own now. Though they had sprung out of injured pride and anger, they were no less formidable than her ancestor's.

She would track down the Fates, and would—in a manner she'd yet to completely pin down—reclaim Henry's property.

She would find them with meticulous research, consistent logic, careful cross-referencing, just as he had done.

When she had them, she would astonish her father, one-up the oh-so-clever Anita Gaye and skewer the detestable Malachi Sullivan.

When her phone rang, she was sitting at the desk in her office, her glasses perched on her nose as she sipped a protein supplement. As usual when she was working, she told herself to let the machine pick up. And as usual, she worried it might be some sort of emergency only she could handle.

She fretted over that for two rings, then gave in.

"Hello?"

"Dr. Marsh?"

"Yes."

"I'd like to speak to you about your work. Specific areas of your work."

She frowned at the phone, at the unrecognizable male voice. "My work? Who is this?"

"I think we have a mutual interest. So . . . what are you wearing?"

"I beg your pardon?"

"I bet you've got on silk panties. Red silk—"

"Oh, for heaven's sake." She slammed down the phone. Embarrassed, shaken, she hugged herself and rocked. "Pervert. That's it. I'm getting an unlisted number."

She picked up the journal again. Set it down. You'd think being listed as T. J. Marsh would be enough to protect a woman from rude, disgusting calls by sick people.

She brooded over it and pulled out the white pages to look up the phone company's business office when her doorbell chimed.

Her first reaction was annoyance at the interruption, and on its heels rushed a paralyzing fear. It was the man on the phone. He would break into her apartment, attack her. Rape her. Then slit her throat from ear to ear with the large, jagged-edge knife he carried.

"Don't be stupid, don't be stupid." She rubbed a hand over her mouth as she got to her feet. "Obscene phone callers are idiots, nuisances who hide behind technology. It's just your mother, or Mrs. Lockley from downstairs. It's nothing."

But she inched her way out of the office, staring at the front door as she crossed the room. With her heart hammering, she eased up on her toes and looked through the peep.

The sight of the big, tough-faced man in a black leather jacket had her gasping, spinning around with her hand to her throat, which she imagined was about to be cut. She looked around wildly and grabbed the closest weapon. Armed with a bronze figure of Circe, she squeezed her eyes tight.

"Who are you? What do you want?"

"Dr. Marsh? Dr. Tia Marsh?"

"I'm calling the police."

"I am the police. Detective Burdett, ma'am, NYPD. I'm holding my shield up to the judas hole."

She'd read a book once in which the homicidal maniac had shot one of his victims through the peephole. A bullet in the eye and straight into the brain. Shaking now, she jerked toward the peep and away again, trying to get a look without risking a violent death.

It looked like proper identification.

"What's this about, Detective Burdett?"

"I'd just like to ask you a few questions, Dr. Marsh. If I could come in? You can leave the door open if you'd be more comfortable."

She bit her lip. If you couldn't trust the police, she told herself, where were you? She set the bronze aside and unlocked the door. "Is there a problem, Detective?"

He smiled now, a friendly, reassuring gesture. "That's what I'd like to talk to you about." He stepped inside, pleased that she felt safe enough to shut the door behind him.

"Has there been some trouble in the building?"

"No, ma'am. Could we sit down?"

"Yes, of course." She gestured to a chair, then perched on the edge of another when he sat.

"Nice place."

"Thank you."

"I guess you get your taste for antiques and such from your father."

The blood drained out of her face. "Is something wrong with my father?"

"No. But this has something to do with your father's line of work, and yours. What do you know about a set of silver statues known as the Three Fates?"

He saw her pupils dilate. That quick jolt of shock. And knew his instincts here were on target. "What is this about?" she demanded. "Is this about Malachi Sullivan?"

"Does he have something to do with the Fates?"

"I hope you've arrested him," she said bitterly. "I hope you have him in jail this minute. And if he gave you my name thinking I'd help him wheedle out, you're wasting your time."

"Dr. Marsh—"

He saw the instant she made him, heard the quick gasp an instant before she tried to leap up. He was faster, and pinned her back in the chair.

"Take it easy now."

"You're the one who called on the phone. You're not a cop at all. He sent you, didn't he?"

Jack had expected tears, screams, and was impressed when she stared holes through him instead.

"I don't know your Malachi Sullivan, Tia. My name's Jack Burdett, Burdett Securities."

"You're just another liar, and a pervert on top of it." Fury was shrinking back, and she could feel her throat closing. "I need my inhaler."

"You need to stay calm," he corrected when she started to wheeze. "I've done business with your father. You can check with him."

"My father doesn't do business with perverts."

"Listen, I'm sorry about that. Your phone's tapped; when I realized it, I said the first thing that came to mind."

"My phone is not tapped."

"Honey, I make my living knowing this stuff. Now, I want you to relax. I'm going to give you my phone; it's secure. I want you to call the Sixty-first Precinct and ask for Detective Robbins, Bob Robbins. You ask him if he knows me, if he'll vouch for me. If he doesn't, you tell him to send a radio car to this address. Okay with that?"

She pressed her lips together. He had hands like rock,

she thought, and a cold expression on his face that warned her she wasn't going to get away. "Give me the phone."

He eased back, reached one hand into his jacket and took out both a small phone and a business card.

"That's my company. I'd let you call your father for another reference, but I don't know if his phones are secure."

She kept her attention on Jack as she contacted information. "I want the number for the Sixty-first Precinct in Manhattan. I want you to connect me."

Jack nodded. "Ask for the Detectives Division, Bob Robbins."

She did, and worked on her breathing. "Detective Robbins? Yes, this is Tia Marsh." She spoke clearly, gave her address down to the apartment number.

Good, Jack thought. She wasn't an idiot.

"There's a man in my apartment. He gained entrance by impersonating a police officer. He says his name is Jack Burdett and that you'll reassure me as to his character." She lifted her brows. "About six-two, two hundred thirty. Dark blond hair, gray eyes. Yes, a small scar, right side of the mouth. I see. Yes, I see. I couldn't agree more, thank you."

She tilted her ear away from the phone for a moment. "Detective Robbins confirms that he knows you, that you're not a psychopath, and assures me he'll be happy to kick your butt for impersonating an officer, as well as issue a warrant for your arrest should I want to pursue that option. He also says you owe him twenty dollars. He'd like to speak with you."

"Thanks." Jack took the phone, and a step back. "Yeah, yeah. I'll fill you in first chance I get. What fake ID? I don't know what you're talking about. Later." He broke the connection, pocketing the phone. "Okay?" he asked Tia.

"No, it's not okay. It's certainly not okay. Excuse me."

She popped out of the chair and marched out of the room. Because he wasn't entirely sure she wasn't going for a weapon, Jack followed her.

She opened a cupboard in the kitchen, and his brows shot up at the rows of pill bottles. She snagged aspirin, wrenched open the refrigerator. "I have a tension headache, thank you very much."

"I apologize. I couldn't risk the phone. Look." He lifted the kitchen portable off its stand, opened the mouthpiece. "See this? It's a tap—decent quality."

"Since I wouldn't know a listening device from a horned toad, I'll just have to take your word, won't I?"

His research hadn't indicated she was quick. "Guess you will. I'd be careful what I said on this line."

"Why should I take your word, Mr. Burdett?"

"Jack, make it Jack. Got any coffee?" Her withering look made him shrug. "Okay. Anita Gaye." He smiled when she slowly lowered the water bottle. "Thought that would ring a bell. Odds are she's the one who got your phone tapped. She wants the Fates, and you and your family have a connection to them. Henry Wyley's statue of Clotho wasn't lost on the *Lusitania*, was it, Tia?"

"If you and Anita are friends, ask her."

"I didn't say we were friends. I'm a collector. That's something you can confirm with your father, but I'd appreciate it if you'd do it face-to-face so Anita isn't tracking my moves. I've bought some nice pieces from Wyley's. The latest was a Lalique vase, molded. Six nude maidens pouring water from urns. I like naked women," he said with a chuckle. "Sue me."

"I thought you liked red silk panties."

"I haven't got anything against them."

"I can't help you, Mr. Burdett. You might as well go back and tell Ms. Gaye she's wasting her time with me."

"I don't work with or for Anita. I work for myself, and I have a personal interest in the Fates. Anita dropped some bait on me, gotta figure she's hoping I'll do some of her legwork and lead her to them. She miscalculated. She's covering bases with you, too," he added, gesturing toward the phone. "I'm betting you know something she doesn't. I think we can help each other out."

"Why should I help you, even if I could?"

"Because I'm really good at what I do. You tell me what you know and I'll find them. That's what you want, isn't it?"

"I haven't decided what I know."

"Who's Malachi Sullivan?"

"That's one thing I'm sure of." Sure because the mere mention of his name made her chest tight. "He's a liar and a cheat. He claimed that Anita duped him, but for all I know they're thick as . . . thieves," she decided.

"Where would I find him?"

"I assume he's back in Ireland. Cobh. But I'd prefer he was roasting in hell."

"What's his connection?"

She hesitated, then could find no reason not to elaborate. "He claims that Anita stole one of the Fates from him, but as his tongue would probably turn black if it tasted truth, I've reason to doubt that. Now, this has been very interesting, but you've interrupted my work."

"You've got my card. You think about it, get in touch." He started out, then turned and looked back at her. "If you know anything, be careful where you step. Anita's a snake, Tia, the kind that likes to gulp down soft, pretty things."

"And what are you, Mr. Burdett?"

"I'm a man who respects and appreciates the whims of fate."

Malachi Sullivan, he thought as he walked out

It looked as if Jack was going to take a trip to Ireland.

IT WAS A long trip from London to New York. Longer when you were wedged into a center seat the size of a postage stamp between a woman whose legs were nearly as long as your own and a man who used his elbows like switchblades.

Gideon tried to bury himself in his book, but even Steinbeck's brilliant prose couldn't compete. So he spent the hours thinking, winding his way through the morass of the situation he, and his family, had gotten themselves into.

He survived the flight, then shuffled brainlessly through the agony of customs and baggage retrieval.

"You're sure about this friend of yours," he asked Cleo.

"Look, you asked me to come up with a friend in the

city who'd put us up for a few days, no questions, no hassles because you're too cheap to spring for a hotel. That's Mikey."

"I can't afford a bloody hotel at this point, and I don't know how you can trust a grown man named Mikey."

"You're just cranky." Cleo took deep gulps of air as they walked through the terminal. It was airport air, but it was New York. "You should've slept on the plane. I slept like a log."

"I know it, and for that single act, I'll hate you till my dying day."

"Bitch, bitch, bitch. It won't bother me a bit." She stepped outside, into the choking exhaust and helacious noise. "Oh baby, I am back!"

He'd hoped to doze in the cab, but the driver had some sort of eye-twitching Indian music on the radio.

"How long have you known this Mikey?"

"I don't know. Six, seven years, I guess. We've done some gigs together."

"He's a stripper?"

"No, he's not a stripper," Cleo retorted. "He's a dancer, and so am I. Look, I've done Broadway." Briefly, but she'd done it. "We were partnered up in the revival of *Grease*. Did the road tour."

"The two of you have a thing going?"

"No." She tucked her tongue in her cheek. "Mikey's a lot more likely to hit on you than on me."

"Oh. Wonderful."

"You're not homophobic, are you?"

"I don't think so." He was too tired to search his social conscience. "Just remember the cover story and stick to it."

"Shut up, Slick. You're spoiling my homecoming."

"Been a week with the woman," he grumbled as he shut his eyes. "Not once does she use my name."

Cleo glanced over at him and found herself smiling. He was all rumpled and tapped out and so damn cute with it. He'd be feeling a whole lot better in a day or two, after she implemented her plan.

He wasn't the only one who'd spent time thinking on the flight.

The first order of business was getting the statue to a nice, secure place. Say a bank box. Then she'd contact Anita Gaye and get down to serious negotiations. She figured she could settle for a cool million. And being a stand-up gal, she intended to split it with Gideon.

Sixty-forty.

Oh, he'd bitch about it, but she'd bring him around. A bird in the hand, after all. He was never going to finesse the first Fate from a woman like Gaye. Not in this lifetime. And if he wanted to go chasing off after the third, well, he'd have financial backing.

She was doing him a favor. Payback, to her way of thinking, for getting her to New York, and for finding her a way to plump up her bank account. Six hundred thousand would tide her over very nicely.

After he'd calmed down, maybe he'd hang in New York for a few weeks. She'd like to show him around. Show him off, too.

Despite the heat, Cleo rolled down the window so New York could slap her in the face. The blast of horns was music as the cab inched its way in jerks through crosstown traffic.

By the time they pulled to the curb in front of Mikey's building off Ninth, she was riding on such a high she didn't think to complain when Gideon told her to pay the driver.

"So what do you think?" she demanded.

"About what?" he asked groggily.

"New York. You said you hadn't been here before."

He looked around numbly. "It's crowded. It's noisy, and everybody looks annoyed about something."

"Yeah." Cleo felt sentimental tears clog her throat. "It's the best." She danced up to the call box at the entrance to the building and pressed Mikey's button.

Moments later there was a long, vaguely obscene sucking sound that made Cleo laugh. "Mikey, you perv. Buzz me in. It's Cleo."

"Cleo? Damn! Get your fine, firm ass in here."

The buzzer sounded, locks clicked, and Cleo dragged open the door. There was a tiny closet of a lobby and a dull gray elevator that made suspicious grinding noises as the doors opened. But Cleo, apparently unconcerned, stepped right on and pushed a button for the third floor.

"Mikey's from Georgia," Cleo told Gideon. "From a fine upstanding family full of doctors and lawyers. Since we both ended up being an embarrassment to our parents, we bonded fast."

At the moment, Gideon didn't care if Mikey came from Georgia or the moon, whether he was gay or had three heads. As long as he had a shower with hot running water and an available bed.

When the doors ground open again, Gideon got a glimpse of a tall, dark-skinned man wearing a red muscle shirt, tight black pants and an explosion of glossy dreadlocks. He let out a ululant howl that had Gideon bracing for attack, then moved like lightning.

Cleo was plucked off her feet and swung around. Before Gideon could react, she was plunked down again, then whipped into some sort of dance—he thought it was a kind of jitterbug—that spun her and her partner down the narrow hallway.

She didn't miss a beat and ended the impromptu number with her arms wrapped around his neck and her legs around his waist.

"Baby doll, where have you *been*?"

"Everywhere. Jesus, Mikey, you look great."

"Damn right I do." He kissed her, one cheek, the other, then with a humming smack on the lips. "You look like you've been dragged through the street and dumped on the curb."

"Could use a shower." She rested her head on his shoulder. "So could my friend."

Mikey angled his head, his body and gave Gideon a long, piercing look. "Mmm, what *have* you brought me, Cleopatra?"

"His name's Gideon." Enjoying herself, Cleo ran her tongue over her top lip. "He's Irish. I picked him up in Prague. I'm keeping him for a while."

"He's fucking gorgeous."

"Yeah. He's got some personality flaws, but in the looks department, he's aces. Come on, Slick, don't be shy."

"Does that mean the show's over for now?"

"Moves well," Mikey commented when Gideon came down the hall. "Lovely accent."

"So's yours."

At Gideon's response, Mikey's lips spread in a huge, toothy grin. "Come inside. I want to hear everything." And though in Gideon's opinion the man was built like a toothpick, he carried Cleo's not unsubstantial weight into the apartment.

"It's humble," he added, setting Cleo down, patting her ass. "But it's home."

Gideon didn't see humble. What he saw was color, from the navy blue walls and white trim, the dozens of theater posters, the wildly geometric pattern in the rug. The couch was white leather, big as a boat and piled with plump, multicolored pillows.

He imagined falling facedown on it and sleeping for the rest of his life.

"Cocktails," Mikey announced. "Tall, frosty cocktails."

"I think Slick here could use a tall, frosty shower first," Cleo said. "Go ahead, back through the bedroom there, on the right."

He glanced at Mikey, got a friendly wave of invitation. "Help yourself, handsome."

"Thanks." Gideon hauled his duffel with him and left them alone.

"Gin and tonics, I think." Mikey crossed to the glossy white bar. "Lots of ice, lots of gin and a whiff of tonic for form. Then you can tell Daddy all."

"Sounds perfect. Mikey, can we bunk here a couple days?"

"*Mi casa,* and all that, sugarplum."

"It's a hell of a story." She crossed over to the bedroom door, angled her head in until she heard the shower start. Then, easing the door shut, she walked back to the bar and told him the whole of it.

Gideon was wet and naked when she stepped into the

bathroom with a gin and tonic. "Thought this might come in handy."

"Thanks." He took the glass, downed the contents in one grateful gulp. "Do we stay?"

"We stay," she confirmed. "In fact, he's generously offered you his bed."

Gideon remembered it from his pass through to the shower. Big, soft, red. And so appealing at that point he'd barely blinked at the mirrors on the ceiling over it. "Do I have to sleep with him?"

She laughed. "No, you get me. Go ahead, tune out for a few hours."

"I will. In the morning, we're going to work out how to get our hands on the Fate. I'm too punchy to think straight now."

"Then get some sleep. Mikey and I can spend some time catching up before he leaves for the theater. He's in the chorus of *Kiss Me, Kate*."

"Good for him. Tell him I appreciate the hospitality."

Still naked, still damp, Gideon went to the bed, crawled in and conked out.

HE WOKE TO the sounds of horns and the rumble of garbage trucks. While his brain caught up he stared in mild fascination at the reflection in the overhead mirror. The red sheets hit him at the waist so that he looked as if he'd been cut in two during the night.

No, he corrected. Like they had.

Cleo was sprawled over him, her hair swept back, black against red, so that it seemed to melt into the sheets. Her skin was shades darker than his own so that the arm she'd flung over his chest, the long curve of her shoulder, the long line of her back lay like gold dust against the white of him and the glossy scarlet sheets.

He remembered the dreamy sensation of her sliding into bed sometime in the night. Of her sliding over him in the dark. And him sliding into her.

She hadn't spoken, not a word. He hadn't been able to see her. But he'd known the shape of her, and the taste.

Even the scent. What did it mean, he wondered, when he knew her so instantly, so intimately in the dark?

He'd have to think about it, eventually. Just as he'd have to analyze why, with a bed as big as a lake, they'd tangled together in sleep, and held on.

But for now there were other things to think about. A man couldn't trust his brain until it had been primed with coffee. .

He started to ease away and was surprised and oddly touched when Cleo shifted closer and snuggled in. It made him want to cuddle right back, and perhaps wake her so he could make proper use of the mirror on the ceiling.

Won't do, he thought and, giving her a careless kiss on the top of her head, untangled himself.

He tugged on jeans and, leaving her sleeping, went out to find the kitchen.

His first jolt of the day didn't come from caffeine, but from seeing Mikey stretched out on the white leather couch all but buried in the colorful pillows, his own dreadlocks and a sheet of bright emerald green.

Though it felt awkward, the desire for coffee was stronger than his sense of propriety. Gideon skirted the couch and moved as quietly as possible into the kitchen.

It was like a page from a catalogue, all glossy and spotless with a number of canny-looking devices tidily arranged on the counter. He opened cupboards, found dishes of navy and white, in perfectly alternating stacks. Glasses, arranged according to type and size. And finally, when he was on the point of whimpering, a bag of coffee. He opened it, swore under his breath when he stared into a bag of fragrant beans.

"What the hell do I do with these? Chew them?"

"You could, but it's easier to grind them."

Gideon jolted, spun and stared.

Mikey was wearing a pair of gold briefs that barely covered his balls.

"Ah . . . sorry. Didn't mean to wake you."

"I sleep like a cat." Mikey plucked the bag from Gideon's hand and poured some of the beans into a grinder. "Nothing like the smell of freshly ground beans," he said over the noise of it. "Did you sleep well?"

"I did, yes, thanks. We shouldn't have kicked you out of your own bed."

"Two of you, one of me." He sent Gideon a sidelong look as he measured out water. "You must be starving. How about some breakfast to go with this? I'm in the mood for French toast."

"That'd be brilliant. It's kind of you to let us drop in on you this way."

"Oh, Cleo and me, we go back." With a careless wave, Mikey started the coffee, then turned to get eggs and milk from the refrigerator. "That girl's my honey. I'm so glad to see her back, and hooked up with someone with style. I warned her about that Sidney character. He looked tasty, no argument there, but he was all flash, no substance. And what does he do but steal her money and leave her high and dry." He made disapproving sounds while he cracked eggs into a bowl. "And in Prague, of all places. But she told you all about that."

"Not really." And Gideon was fascinated. "You know Cleo. She tends to skim over the details."

"Wouldn't have run off with that rat bastard, excuse my French, if her daddy hadn't told her, again, how she was wasting her time, how she was embarrassing herself and the family."

"How?"

"Dancing. Theater." He said it with a deliberately dramatic air, doing a fluid leg extension as he got down coffee mugs. "Fraternizing with people like me. Not only a black man, but a *gay* black man. A gay, black, dancing man. I mean, *really*. Cream, sugar?"

"No, thanks. Just straight." He winced. "That is—"

Mikey let out a rollicking laugh. "Me, I like a whole *lot* of sugar. He wouldn't like you, either," Mikey added as he handed Gideon a mug. "Our Cleopatra's daddy."

"No? Well, fuck him." Gideon lifted his mug in toast, then drank. "Ah, God be praised."

"Drink up, honey." Mikey dipped thick slices of sourdough bread in the egg batter. "You and me, we're going to get along just fine."

And they did. Plowing through half a loaf of bread, a pot of coffee and nearly a quart of the orange juice Mikey squeezed fresh.

By the time Cleo staggered out of the bedroom, Gideon no longer found anything odd about the gold briefs, the tattoo of a dragon on Mikey's left shoulder blade or being called honey by another man.

# PART TWO
## Measuring

*I have measured out my life*
*with coffee spoons.*

T. S. ELIOT

# Ten

"SUGARPLUM, I'm not sure you're doing the right thing here."

"I'm doing the smart thing," Cleo insisted. "The smart thing's always the right thing."

"Whatever's going on between you and Gideon is going to get screwed up." Mikey shook his head as they hit the bustle of Broadway and squeezed through the eastbound crosswalk traffic. "I've got a good feeling about you two, and you're going to fuck it over before you get it started."

"You're too romantic for your own good."

"Can't be," he disagreed. "Romance turns sex into art. Without it, it's just a messy, sweaty business."

"That's why you get your heart broken, Mikey, and I don't."

"A little heartbreak would do you good."

"Don't sulk." Because she knew he would, she slid an arm around his waist as they turned on the corner of Seventh and Fifty-second and headed north. "Besides, I'm doing this for him as well as myself. Once Anita's got the Fate, she'll leave him alone, and he'll have a big fat pile of money out of it. The statue *is* mine, after all. I don't have to share, but I'm going to."

She gave him a quick squeeze as she swung into the

bank. "Let's make this as fast as we can. If I don't meet him by one, he's going to ask questions, and," she added, dropping her voice as they stepped into the quiet lobby, "he's got something going himself right this minute, or he'd never have agreed so easily to me heading out to run some errands without him."

"Your trouble, Cleopatra, is you're a cynic."

"You try working a few months in a strip club in the Czech Republic," she chided. "We'll see if you come out of it with a Pollyanna complex."

"You didn't go into this with one," he pointed out, and she gave him a smirk as she stepped up to a teller.

"I need to get a safe-deposit box."

WHEN SHE WALKED back out on Seventh, the Fate was safely locked in the vault. Both she and Mikey had keys. That, she'd calculated, was the smartest move. If there was any trouble, which she didn't anticipate, he could retrieve the statue in her stead.

"Okay, now I make the call, set up the meet. Someplace public," she added as she held out a hand for Mikey's cell phone. "But where it's unlikely anyone we know will come by and recognize us."

"It's like a spy thriller." And because he loved a good melodrama, Mikey grinned as he handed her his phone.

"It's business. And I've got the perfect spot for it." She pulled out the scrap of paper on which she'd written the number for Morningside, and dialed as they walked toward Sixth. "Anita Gaye, please. It's Cleo Toliver. I think she'll recognize the name and speak with me. Now. If she doesn't, just tell her I'm calling to discuss the price of fate. Yes, that's right."

With her destination already in mind, she turned south on Fifth. And lost Mikey briefly when he glued himself to a jewelry store window.

"Stay with me, and don't be such a girl." She gave one of his dreads a tug. "This is serious business."

"Ooh, you sound all cold and tough," Mikey commented. "Like Joan Crawford or—no, no Barbara Stanwyck in *Double Indemnity*. A woman with balls."

"Shut up, Mikey," she ordered and bit back a snicker as Anita Gaye came on the line.

"Cleo." The voice didn't sound cold or tough, but soft and warm as velvet. "I can't tell you how delighted I am to hear from you."

Cleo considered it a good sign Anita had agreed to the terms of the meeting without hesitation. She thought of the wild race across Europe and shook her head. Men, she decided. They had to flex their muscles, turn a simple business deal into an altercation.

No wonder the world was so screwed up.

SHE FELT A little foolish with her choice of arenas. But Mikey was getting such a kick out of it all now, she deemed it worth it.

"*An Affair to Remember*. Cary Grant, Deborah Kerr." He stood on the observation level of the Empire State Building, arms spread, dreads flying. "That's romance, baby."

And the difference between them, Cleo mused, was that the spot reminded her not of poignant romance but of King Kong's fatal obsession with Faye Wray.

She considered Faye Wray's character a moron. Cringing and screaming on the ledge—waiting for the big, strong man to rescue her, Cleo thought, instead of getting her ass moving when the idiot ape set her down.

Well, it took all kinds.

"You go stand over there, keep me in sight. When she shows, I'll give you a sign if she gives me any grief. Then you can hulk over and help me out." She checked the Wonder Woman watch Mikey had lent her. "She'll be here any minute. If she's on time, we'll stay on schedule. I've got a good half hour before I'm supposed to meet Gideon."

"What are you going to tell him?"

"Same old, same old, until I have the cash in hand. I can

stall him for another twenty-four hours, and that's the deadline I'll give Anita."

"A million smackeroos is a lot to put together in a day, Cleo."

"We're talking Morningside here, and that spells beau-coup *dinero*. She wants the Fate, she'll find a way. I'm go-ing to stand over there and practice looking bored."

She wandered to the safety rail, leaned back on it and watched the elevator through the glass. Tourists swarmed the souvenir shop inside or stood outside snapping pic-tures, shoving coins into the telescopes.

She wondered if anyone who lived in the city ever came here unless they were dragged along by out-of-towners. And she wondered why anyone felt compelled to come all the way up here when all the action, all the life, all the meaning was down on the streets.

Her belly tightened when she saw the spiffy-looking woman step out of the elevator. Anita had said she'd be wearing a blue suit. The number was blue all right— smoke blue with a long, sleek jacket, a tube of a skirt cut at a conservative length.

Valentino, Cleo decided. All richly understated and whispering of class.

She waited while Anita slipped on dark glasses and stepped out into the wind. Watched while the woman scanned the area, the faces, and honed in on her.

She shifted the slim leather portfolio bag on her shoul-der and crossed over. "Cleo Toliver?"

"Anita Gaye." Cleo accepted the handshake while the two women measured each other.

"I almost expected to have to exchange passwords." There was a trace of humor in the tone as Anita glanced around. "You know, this is the first time I've been up here. What *is* the point?"

Since it so clearly mirrored her own sentiments, Cleo nodded. "You got that right. But it seemed like a good place to do a little private business in a public place. A place where we'd both feel comfortable."

"We'd both feel more comfortable at a table at Raphael's, but I imagine Gideon's filled you with trepidation about dealing with me." Anita spread her arms, looking chic, attractively windblown and amused. "As you can see, I'm no threat."

"The muscle you had chase us down in Prague didn't seem very friendly."

"An unfortunate miscommunication, which often happens when you're dealing with men, doesn't it?" Anita tucked her hair behind her ear. "My representatives were instructed to stop by your place of employment and speak to you. No more, no less. Apparently Gideon, and they, became a little overexcited. In point of fact, Cleo, my representatives thought you were being abducted, and pursued."

"Is that right?"

"A miscue, as I said. In any case, I'm happy you're back in New York safe and sound. I'm sure you and I can discuss the matter without the histrionics." She glanced around again. "Gideon's not with you?"

"I brought someone else, in case of histrionics." She could see Mikey over Anita's shoulder. He stood several feet away elaborately flexing his biceps. "First, what made you track me down and instruct your representatives to speak with me?"

"A hunch, after considerable research. Both are vital in my business. This meeting today makes me assume both were accurate. Do you have the Fate, Cleo?"

If there'd been more time, Cleo would've made her work harder, for form's sake. "I've got it in a safe place. I'm willing to sell it. One million dollars, cash."

Anita let out a laughing breath. "A million dollars? Gideon certainly told you some fairy tales."

"Don't try to hose me, Anita. You want the statue, that's the price. Nonnegotiable. That gives you two of three since you've already stolen one from Gideon's brother."

"Stolen?" Annoyance flashed through her as she turned to pace. As she paced, she scanned the others on the deck, trying to pick out Cleo's backup. "Those Sullivans. I should sue them for slander. Morningside's reputation is above reproach. And so is mine," she added tightly as she stopped to face Cleo again. "I *purchased* that statue from

Malachi Sullivan and will be happy to produce the signed receipt. For all I know he may very well have told his brother some trumped-up story and kept the money for himself. But I will not have them spreading vicious lies about my company."

"How much did you pay him?"

"Less." She seemed to draw herself in. "Considerably less than your asking price."

"Then you got a bargain first time out. You get number two, you pay. You can have her in your hands tomorrow, three o'clock, right here in this spot. You bring the cash, I bring the girl."

"Cleo." Anita's lips curved thinly. "I've dealt with the Sullivans. How do I know you're not as underhanded as they? I have no assurance you actually have the Fate."

Saying nothing, Cleo reached in her bag and took out the photograph.

"Lachesis," Anita murmured as she studied the photo. "How do I know this is authentic?"

"I guess you play your hunch. Look, my grandmother gave it to me when I was a kid. She had a couple of loose screws and thought about it like a doll. Up until about a week ago, I considered it a sort of good-luck charm. A million buys me a hell of a lot of luck."

Anita continued to study the picture as she considered her options. The rundown confirmed what Cleo's father had told Anita during a long evening of perfectly prepared coq au vin, a superior Pinot Noir and mediocre sex. Interestingly, the man hadn't known that his daughter was in New York, or had been in Prague. In fact, he couldn't have been less informed or concerned about his only child's whereabouts or well-being.

Which meant, handily, no one was likely to look if Cleo Toliver suddenly disappeared.

"I assume the Fate is yours, legally."

Cleo arched her eyebrows. "Possession and all that."

"Yes." Anita smiled and couldn't have agreed more. "Of course."

She took the picture back, tucked it in her bag. "Your call, Anita."

"That's a lot of money in a short amount of time. We can meet tomorrow—that table at Raphael's. You bring the statue so I can examine it, I'll bring a quarter million as deposit."

"All, straight exchange, right here at three. Or I put it on the open market."

"I'm a professional dealer—"

"I'm not," Cleo interrupted. "And I've got another appointment. Fish or cut bait."

"All right. But I'm not carrying that kind of cash into this place." She looked around, a faint line of annoyance between her perfect eyebrows. "A restaurant, Cleo. Let's be civilized. You pick the spot if you don't trust me."

"That's reasonable. Teresa's in the East Village. I've got a yen for some goulash. Make it one o'clock."

"One o'clock." Anita offered her hand again. "And if you decide to give up the theater, I could use someone like you at Morningside."

"Thanks, but I'll stick with what I know. See you tomorrow."

She waited until Anita was back in the elevator. Then she counted to ten, slowly. When she turned to where Mikey was waiting, she broke out in a grin

She did a quick tap-shuffle in his direction. "Kiss me, baby, I'm rich!"

"She went for it?"

"All the way. Put up a struggle, but not much of one. Overreacted to some stuff, underreacted to others." She hooked her arm through Mikey's. "She's not as good as she thinks she is. She'll cough up the dough because I've got what she wants."

"I never got the chance to hulk and look mean."

"Sorry, you'd've been great." She walked with him through the souvenir shop to the elevators. "You know the first thing I'm going to do when I get the money? I'm throwing a big, kick-ass party. No, first I'm buying a place, then I'm throwing a big, kick-ass party."

"Guess you won't be heading out to the cattle calls anymore."

"You kidding?" She squeezed in the elevator car with

him. "Let me wallow in it for a week, maybe two. Then I'm going to every audition my agent can push me into. You know how it is, Mikey. Gotta dance."

"I can get you a shot at the chorus of *Kiss Me, Kate*."

"No shit? That'd be great! When?"

"Let me put the word in with the director tonight."

"Told you my luck was changing." She rode on it all the way down to ground level.

"I've got to split," she said on the street. "Go meet Slick."

"Why don't you come to the show tonight? I'll get you a couple house seats and introduce you to the director."

"Cool. I love you, Mikey." She gave him a long, noisy kiss. "Look, I'll meet you back at your place in a few hours. I'm going to buy a big bottle of champagne."

"Buy two. We'll get toasted after the show."

"That's a deal. I love you, Mikey."

"I love you, Cleopatra."

He headed west, she headed east. As she crossed the street, she glanced back, laughing like a loon when he threw her a kiss. With a spring in her step she started uptown. Right on schedule, she thought. She'd meet Gideon on the east corner of Fifty-first and Fifth, maybe grab some pizza. She'd tell him she needed another day or two to get the statue.

He wouldn't like it, but she'd smooth it out. And when she handed him four hundred thousand dollars the next day, he'd have no room to bitch.

She'd talk him into staying in New York for a while. Maybe Mikey was right about the thing between them. Not the romance part, that wasn't in the cards. But she had a good feeling when she was with him. She liked the steady side of him as much as she liked the reckless one. What was wrong with wanting a little more time with both?

The glint from a jewelry display caught her eye, had her moving toward the window. She'd buy Mikey something to thank him for the help. Something extravagant.

She brooded over the gold neck chains—too ordinary— and the flash of stones—too gaudy. Slowing her pace, she browsed from window to window, then let out a little *ah ha!* at the wink of a thin gold anklet with ruby cabochons.

Tailor-made for Mikey, she decided and tilted her head in hopes of seeing the price tag tucked discreetly under the chain.

She froze that way, her nose all but pressed to the window, her body in a slight dip as she caught a reflection in the glass.

She knew that face. Though he was turned away from her in profile, as if studying the traffic, she recognized him. They'd all but run over him on the street in Prague.

Shit, shit, shit! She straightened, then moved casually on, as if to study the offerings in the next display. He didn't follow, but angled his body a little more toward her.

Anita fucking Gaye, she thought. So businesslike, the professional dealer. And she'd sent out one of her goons. Well, that was fine, that was great, because this was New York. This was *her* turf.

She sauntered as if she had all the time in the world. He was following now, she noted, and careful to keep pace. She kept sauntering right into the International Jewelry Exchange, meandering into the babble of voices, down the crowded aisles between booths. He kept half the store between them, shaking his head, scowling when the merchants began their pitch.

And she sprinted. Her long legs ate up the distance to the side door. She was through it and loping across the street and muscling aside a man who was about to climb into a cab.

While he stumbled back, shouted at her, she slammed the cab door. "Step on it! Get me five blocks down in under a minute, I got twenty dollars." She pulled a bill out of her pocket, waved it even as she glanced over and saw her tail running across the street. For added incentive, she shoved the twenty into the security slot. "Move!"

He moved.

"Cut over to Park," she ordered, swiveling around on her knees to watch out the rear window. "Go up to Fifty-first and cut back to Fifth. Yeah, baby." She waved as he charged down the cross street. "Already huffing and puffing."

Still she watched until they hit Madison. When they turned onto Park, she dropped back down on the seat.

"Fifty-first and Fifth," she repeated coolly. "Drop me on the east corner."

"That's a hell of a ride, lady, for a couple blocks."

"You get what you pay for."

She popped out on the corner, grabbed Gideon's hand.

"You're late," he began, but she was already running. "What's going on?"

"Taking a subway ride, Slick. You haven't been to New York until you do."

Summer tourists were thronged around Rockefeller Center. All the better for cover, she decided—if they needed it. Then she whipped him down the stairs of the subway stop at 50 Rock.

"My treat," she added and dug out the fare for both of them. When they were through the turnstiles on the platform, she caught her breath. "We'll get off at Washington Square. Bop around the Village. Give you a real tour, grab some lunch."

"Why?"

"Because a girl's gotta eat."

"Why did we run like maniacs into the tube to ride a train to a village?"

"*The* Village, you alien. And we're taking a ride to make sure I've thrown off the shadow. I was doing a little window-shopping on Fifth, and who should I see but one of our friends from Prague."

He grabbed her as the rumble of the approaching train shook the air. "Are you sure?"

"Absolutely. He's got a face like a pie plate. Flat, round and shiny. I ditched him, but maybe he circled around, so better safe than sorry."

She pushed through into the car, dropped down on a seat. She patted the place beside her.

"What have you done, Cleo?"

"What do you mean, what've I done? I just told you. Imagine that asshole thinking he could tag me in my city."

"And he just happened to be walking down the same street at the same time as you? I don't think so."

"Actually, Fifth is an avenue as opposed to a—"

His hand tightened on her arm, a hard warning. "What have you done? Where's Mikey?"

"Hey, ease up, pal. We ran some errands, hung out a little. It's a free country. I did some window-shopping on the way to meet you, and he headed home to catch a nap. Mikey's not a morning person and you had him up at dawn."

"How did she know where to find you?"

"Look—"

"You said you ditched him. Just one? What about the other guy?"

He was really bumming out her triumphant mood. "How the hell do I know? Are they joined at the hip?"

"How long after you and Mikey split up did you see him?"

"Jesus, a few minutes. A couple of blocks. What's the big . . ." But she trailed off as it struck her. "You think the other one moved on Mikey? That's crazy. He's not part of this."

But she'd made him part of it, she realized, and the arm Gideon gripped began to tremble.

"Okay, so maybe they'll follow him, maybe they will. We'll just get off at the next stop and I'll call him on his cell phone, clue him in. He'll lose a tail as easy as I did. He'll get a kick out of it."

But her hands were like ice by the time she pushed her way out at the Thirty-fourth Street stop, got to a phone. And her fingers shook as she punched in the numbers. "You've got me spooked," she grumbled. "Wait till I tell Mikey. He'll laugh his bony ass off. Answer, damn it. Answer the phone."

But in two rings his cheerful and recorded voice came on.

"I'm busy, honey, hopefully making sweet love. Leave a message and Mikey will get back to you." He made his signature kissing sound that ran right into the beep.

"He's turned it off." She took a calming breath, then another. "He's home, taking a nap, and he turned off his pocket phone, that's all."

"Ring him on the land line, Cleo."

"I'm just going to wake him up." She dialed. "He hates it when you wake him up from a nap."

The phone rang four times. She was braced for another recording when he answered. The instant she heard his voice, she knew he was in trouble.

"Mikey—"

"Don't come back here, Cleo!" There was a shout, a crash, and she heard him call her name again. "Run."

"Mikey." A second crash and the short scream had her hand going wet on the receiver. Even when the phone went dead in her ear, she kept shouting his name.

"Stop. Stop it." Gideon pried the phone out of her fingers.

"They're hurting him. We have to get there. We have to help him."

"Call the police, Cleo." He clamped his hands on her shoulders before she could run. "Call them now. Give them his name, his address. We're too far away to help."

"The police."

"Don't give your name," he added as she fumbled to hit 911. "Just his. Make sure they hurry."

"I need the police. I need help." She ignored the calm voice of the emergency operator. "Mikey—Michael Hicks, four-forty-five West Fifty-third, apartment three-oh-two. Just—just off Ninth Avenue. You have to hurry. You have to help. They're hurting him. They're hurting him."

Gideon depressed the receiver as she began to cry. "Hold it together. Just hold it together. We're going. Which train do we take? What's the fastest way to get there?"

Nothing could be fast enough, not with that scream of pain and terror echoing in her head. She all but flew the blocks from the subway stop, but it wasn't fast enough.

Relief spurted through her when she spotted the two radio cars outside Mikey's building. "They got here," she managed. "New York's finest."

Uniforms were already setting up barricades, and a small crowd was gathering.

"Don't say anything," Gideon warned with his lips against her temple. "Let me ask."

"There should be an ambulance. He needs to get to the hospital. I know they hurt him."

"Just stay quiet, and I'll find out." Gideon kept his arm tight around her as they stepped up to the barricade.

"What's going on?" He glanced toward a bike messenger who was straddling his ride and snapping a wad of gum.

"Dude got killed in there."

"No." Cleo shook her head slowly from side to side. "No."

"Hey, I should know. I was heading in to make my delivery when the cops came back out. Said I had to hang out and be interviewed and shit 'cause they had a homicide on the third floor. Suit cops are coming, you know, like on *NYPD Blue*? One of the uniform dudes told me this black guy got his face and head all bashed to shit."

"No. No. No," she said again, her voice rising as Gideon pulled her away.

"Keep moving, Cleo. We're just going to keep moving for a little while."

"He's not dead. That's a lie, a stupid, fucking lie. We're going to his show tonight. He's getting us house seats. We're going to get shit-faced on champagne. He is *not* dead. We were just . . . it was only an hour ago. I'm going back. I've got to go back."

He needed to get her some place quiet, some place private. Gideon wrapped both arms around her to hold her still. Where the hell did you find quiet in a city like this? "Cleo, you listen to me, just listen to me. We can't stay here. It isn't safe."

When she let out a low moan, when her knees buckled, he took her weight. He half dragged, half carried her down the street. "We need to get inside somewhere. You need to sit down."

He scanned the street, the shops, and spotted a bar. There was nothing, he decided, like an urban dive for a little privacy.

He pulled her inside, keeping his arm banded around

her. There were only three patrons, all hunched at the bar. None of them even bothered to glance over as he poured Cleo into a dim corner booth.

"Two whiskeys," he ordered. "Doubles." He dragged out bills, slapped them on the bar.

He carried the glasses back to where she was curled in a ball in the corner of the booth. He slid in beside her, took her chin firmly in his hand and poured half the shot down her throat.

She choked, sputtered, then simply laid her head down on the table and sobbed like a baby.

"It's my fault. It's my fault."

"I need you to tell me what happened." He lifted her head again, held the glass to her lips. "Take another drink and tell me what you did."

"I killed him. Oh God, oh God, Mikey's dead."

"I know it." He picked up his own untouched glass of whiskey and urged it on her. Better drunk, he thought, and half passed out than hysterical. "What did you and Mikey do, Cleo?"

"I asked him. He'd have done anything for me. I loved him. Gideon, I loved him."

Now, he thought, in grief, she finally used his name. "I know you did. I know he loved you."

"I thought I was so smart." Her tears plopped on his hand as he made her take another swallow. "I had it all figured out. I'd sell that bitch the Fate, skin her for a million dollars, give you a nice cut to keep you happy and dance in the goddamn street."

"Christ. You contacted her?"

"I called her, set up a meet. My turf. Top of the fucking Empire State," she continued with her voice slurring now with liquor. "Like King goddamn Kong. Mikey went with me, just in case she got testy. But she didn't. Butter wouldn't melt. Didn't have a good word to say about you or your brother, but that's beside the point. Gonna give me a million dollars tomorrow, cash money. I give her the little lady. Sensible deal, no harm, no foul. Mikey and I got a good laugh out of it. I told him the whole story, you know."

"Yeah, I got that."

"Gonna split it with you, Slick, sixty-forty." She swiped at tears and smeared mascara over her cheek, over the back of her hand. "You got a four-hundred-thousand-dollar bird in the hand, why beat around the fucking bush, right?"

He couldn't work up any anger. Not when she was shattered. He pushed her hair back from her damp cheeks. "No, I guess you don't."

"But she was never gonna give me the money. She played me. Mikey's dead because I was too stupid to know it. I'll never forgive myself, never, not for as long as I live. He was harmless. Gideon, he was harmless and sweet, and they hurt him. They hurt him."

"I know it, darling." He drew her head down on his shoulder, stroking her hair as she cried. He thought of the man who'd fixed French toast that morning, had given up his bed to a stranger because a friend had asked.

Anita Gaye would pay for it, he promised himself. It was no longer just about money, about principle, it was about justice.

So he stroked Cleo's hair, drank the last swallow of the whiskey.

He could think of only one place to go

# Eleven

D R. Lowenstein had his own problems. They included an ex-wife who had successfully skinned him in the divorce, two children in college who were under the delusion he owned a grove of money trees and an administrative assistant who'd just demanded a raise.

Sheila had divorced him because he'd spent more time working on his practice than his marriage. Then she had sucked the financial benefits of that practice up like a Hoover.

The irony of it had been lost on her. Which, Lowenstein decided, only proved he was well rid of the humorless bitch.

But that was neither here nor there. As his son, who changed majors as often as he changed his socks, was given to say, it was only money.

Tia Marsh had money. A steady stream of interest and dividends and mutual funds. As well as, he supposed, a reasonably substantial trickle of royalties from her books.

And God knew the woman had problems.

He listened to her now as she sat tidily in the chair facing him and told a convoluted tale of sneaky Irishmen, Greek myths, historic disasters and thievery. When she ended with a police impersonator and tapped phones, he rubbed his steepled fingers on his thin blade of a mouth and cleared his throat.

"Well, Tia, you've certainly been busy. Tell me, what do you think fate represents in this context?"

"Represents?" Finding the courage to tell the tale, and telling it, had used up most of her steam. For a moment, Tia could only stare. "Dr. Lowenstein, it's not a metaphor, it's statues."

"Determining your own fate has always been one of your core dilemmas," he began.

"You think I'm making this up? You think this is all some complicated delusion?" The insult of it kicked her energy level back up again. Certainly she had delusions, or else why would she be here. But they were much more simplistic, much more ordinary.

And he, at two hundred fifty dollars for a fifty-minute hour, should know it.

"I'm not *that* crazy. There was a man in Helsinki."

"An Irishman," Lowenstein said patiently.

"Yes, yes, an Irishman, but he could have been a one-legged Scotsman, for all that matters."

He smiled, gently. "Your month of travel was a big step for you, Tia. I believe it opened you up to yourself. To the imagination you often stifle. The challenge now will be to channel and refine that imagination. Perhaps, as a writer—"

"There was a man in Helsinki," she said again, between her teeth. "He came to New York to see me, pretended a personal interest in me when, in fact, he was only interested in my connection to the Three Fates. Those Fates are real, they exist. I've documented it. My ancestor owned one and was traveling to England on the *Lusitania* to acquire the second. That's fact, documented fact."

"And this Irishman claims his ancestor, also aboard the ship, stole the statue."

"Exactly." She huffed out a breath. "And that Anita Gaye stole the statue from him—the Irishman. I can't substantiate that. In fact, I had strong doubts about it until Jack Burdett came to see me."

"The one who pretended to be a police detective."

"Yes. See, it's not that complicated if you just follow the steps in a linear fashion. My problem is I'm not sure what to do about it, what step to take next. If my phones are tapped, it seems to me I should report it. But then there'll be all sorts of awkward questions, won't there, and if the phones are, subsequently, untapped, Ms. Gaye will know that I know she had them tapped, then I lose the advantage of working behind the scenes, so to speak, to find the other two Fates."

She took a long breath. "And I don't actually talk on the phone that much anyway, so maybe I should leave it alone for now."

"Tia, have you considered that your reluctance to report this stems from your subconscious knowledge that there is nothing wrong with your phones?"

"No." But his calm, patient question planted the seed of doubt in her mind. "This isn't paranoia."

"Tia, do you remember calling me from your hotel in London at the beginning of your tour and telling me you were afraid the man staying down the hall was stalking you because twice he rode in the elevator with you?"

"Yes." Mortified, she dropped her gaze to her hands. "But that was different. That *was* paranoia."

Except for all she knew, for all anyone knew, she thought, she'd been right and had had a lucky escape from a crazed British stalker.

"You've made great strides," he continued. "Important ones. You faced down your travel phobia. You confronted your fear of dealing with the public. You spent four consecutive weeks exploring yourself and your own capabilities, and expanded your safety zone. You should be proud of yourself."

To show he was proud of her, he leaned over, patted her arm lightly. "Change, Tia, change creates new challenges. You have a tendency, as we've discussed before, to manufacture scenarios within your mind—exotic, complicated scenarios wherein you're surrounded or beset by some sort of danger or threat. A fatal illness, an international plot. And so beset, you retreat, constrict that safety zone to your apartment. I'm not surprised that finding yourself in familiar surroundings again, dealing with the natural physical and mental fatigue of a long, demanding trip, you'd need to revert to pattern."

"I'm not doing that," she said under her breath. "I can't even see the pattern anymore."

"We'll work on that during our next session." He leaned over to pat her arm again. "It might be best if we go back to our twice-weekly sessions for the time being. Don't think of that as a step back, but as a new beginning. Angela will schedule you."

She looked at him, the kindly face, the trim beard, the dash of gray at the temples. It was like, she realized, being indulged and dismissed by an affectionate parent.

If there was a pattern in her life, she thought as she got to her feet, this was it.

"Thank you, Doctor."

"I want you to continue your relaxation and imagery exercises."

"Of course." She picked up her purse, walked to the door. And there, turned. "Everything I just told you is a hallucination?"

"No, Tia, of course not. I believe it's all very real to you, and a combination of actual events and your very creative imagination. We'll explore it. In the meantime, I'd like you to consider why you find living inside your head more comfortable than living outside it. We'll talk about it during our next session."

"It's not comfortable inside my head," she said quietly. She stepped into his outer office. And kept on going.

He hadn't believed a word she'd said. And worse, she discovered as she rode the elevator down to the lobby, he'd stirred up doubts so she wasn't sure she believed herself.

It had happened. She was *not* crazy, damn it. She wasn't some sort of loony who wore aluminum foil on her head to keep out the alien voices, for God's sake. She was a mythologist, a successful author, a functioning adult. And, she added as temper began to rise, she was sane. Felt saner, steadier, stronger than she'd ever felt in her life.

She wasn't hiding in her apartment. She was working there. She had a goal, a fascinating one. She would prove she wasn't delusional. She'd prove she could stand on her own two feet, that she was a healthy—well, moderately healthy—woman with a good brain and a strong will.

As she strode out on the street, she whipped out her cell phone, punched in a number. "Carrie? It's Tia. Get me an emergency appointment at your salon. When? Now. Right now. It's coming off."

"ARE YOU SURE about this?" Carrie was still winded from her six-block dash from her Wall Street offices to Bella Donna.

"Yes. No."

Tia clutched Carrie's hand as they sat in two of the streamlined leather chairs in the salon's waiting area. There was loud techno-rock blaring, and one of the stylists, a rail-thin woman dressed all in black, had her hair arranged in a terrifying magenta cloud.

Already she could feel her air passages shutting down as they were assaulted with the beauty shop scents of peroxide and polish remover and overheated perfume.

The sound of hair dryers blowing was like plane engines. She was going to get a migraine, hives, respiratory arrest. What was she doing here?

"I'd better go. I'd better go right now." She fumbled in her bag for her inhaler.

"I'm going to stay with you, Tia. I'm going to see you through this every step of the way." Carrie had canceled two meetings to see to it. "Julian's a genius. I swear it." She squeezed Tia's free hand as Tia sucked on the inhaler. "You're going to feel like a new woman. What?" she asked when Tia mumbled.

Removing the inhaler, Tia tried again. "I said, I'm just getting used to the old one. This is a mistake. I only did it because I was so upset with Dr. Lowenstein. Look, I'll pay for the appointment, but I—"

"Julian's ready for you, Dr. Marsh." Another wand-slim, black-clad female came out.

Didn't anyone here weigh over a hundred pounds? Tia thought frantically. Wasn't anyone over twenty-three?

"I'll take her back, Miranda." In the bright, cheerful voice mothers use when they drag their children to the dentist chair, Carrie hauled Tia to her feet. "You're going to thank me for this. Trust me."

Tia's vision blurred as they walked past operators, customers, past gleaming black shampoo bowls and sparkling glass displays holding dozens and dozens of sleekly packaged products. Dimly she heard overlapping chatter and a cackle of laughter that sounded just a bit insane.

"Carrie."

"Be brave. Be strong." She steered Tia toward a large cubical done in dazzling black and silver. The man who stood by the big leather chair was short, sleek as a greyhound, with white-blond hair cut like a skullcap.

For some reason, he made her think of a very hip Eros and that didn't comfort her a bit.

"So," he began in a voice that bit down on vowels with the teeth of a native New Yorker, "this is Tia, at last." He took one look at her pale face and judged his quarry. "Louise! Some wine here. Sit."

"I was just thinking that maybe—"

"Sit," he interrupted Tia, then leaned over to kiss Carrie's cheek. "Moral support?"

"You bet."

"Carrie and I have been plotting endlessly on how to get you in my chair." He got her there, finally, by simply nudging her backward. "And from the looks of this . . ." He fingered a lock of hair that had come loose from its knot. "It's not a moment too soon."

"I really don't think I need—"

"Let me be the judge of what you need." He took one of the wineglasses Louise brought in, handed it to her. "When you go to the doctor, do you tell him what you need?"

"Actually, ha, yeah, I do. But—"

"You have lovely eyes."

She blinked them. "I do?"

"Excellent brow line. Very nice bones," he added and began to touch her face with smooth, very cool fingertips. "Sexy mouth. The lipstick's wrong, but we'll fix that. Yes, it's a fine face we've got here. Dull, outdated hair." With a couple of tugs, he had the pins out and the heavy weight of it tumbling free.

"It doesn't suit you at all. You're hiding behind your hair, my Tia." He swiveled the chair around so she was facing the mirror, and his head was close to hers. All but cheek to cheek. "And I'm going to expose you."

"You are? But don't you think . . . What if there's nothing particularly interesting to expose?"

"I think you underestimate yourself," he chided. "And expect everyone else to do the same."

While she was blinking over that she found herself being shampooed by one of the slender shop girls in one of the glossy black sinks. By the time she thought to ask if they used hypo-allergenic products, it was too late.

Then she was back in the chair, facing away from the mirror with a glass of very nice white wine in her hand. He talked to her. Asked her what she did, who she dated, what she liked. Every time she gave a noncommittal answer or asked what he was doing with her hair, he asked another question.

When at one point she made the mistake of looking down and seeing the piles of shorn hair littering the floor, her breath began to hitch. Little white dots danced in front of her eyes, and from a distance she heard Carrie's alarmed voice.

The next thing she knew Julian pushed her head between her knees, holding it there until the roar of her heartbeat slowed. "Steady, honey. Louise! I need a cold cloth here."

"Tia, Tia, snap out of it."

She opened her eyes to find Carrie crouched on the floor in front of her. "What? What?"

"It's a haircut, okay? Not brain surgery."

"A traumatic event's a traumatic event." Julian laid a cool, damp cloth on the back of Tia's neck. "Now, I want you to sit up slowly. Deep breath now. That's the way. Now another. There now, tell me about this Irish guy Carrie mentioned."

"He's a bastard," Tia said weakly.

"We all are." The scissors began to snip again, frighteningly close to her face. "Tell me all about it."

So she did, and when his reaction was shock, fascination, delight—so very different from Lowenstein's—she forgot about her hair.

"Incredible. You know what you have to do, don't you?"

She stared up at him as he clicked her chair back. "What?"

"You have to go to Ireland, find this Malachi and seduce him."

"I do?"

"It's perfect. You track him down, seduce all pertinent information on the statues out of him, then you add that to what you've dug up, and you're ahead of everyone. We're going to put in a few highlights, jazz it up a bit, especially around her face."

"But I can't just . . . go. Besides, he isn't really interested in me that way. And more to the point, it's not right to use sex as a weapon."

"Sweetie, when a woman uses it on me, I'm usually grateful. You have wonderful skin. What are you using on it?"

"Oh, well, right now I'm using this new line I read about. All natural ingredients. But you have to keep the products refrigerated, which is a little inconvenient."

"I have something better. Louise! BioDerm, full skin care treatment. Normal."

"Oh well, I always do a patch test before I use another new—"

"Not to worry." He dipped a flat brush in a small bowl and came up with a dab of pale purple goo. "You just lie back and relax."

It wasn't easy to relax when a strange woman was rubbing creams on your face, and your hair—what was left of it—was full of goop and aluminum foil. And no one would let you look in the mirror.

But he gave her another glass of wine, and Carrie stayed loyally within arm's reach.

Somehow she was talked into having her eyebrows waxed and dyed to give them more definition, then after her hair was rinsed, into a full makeup treatment. By the time Julian was wielding the blow dryer on her she was so tired, so tipsy, she nearly nodded off in the chair.

Whoever claimed an afternoon at the salon was a luxury had a sick sense of humor.

"Keep your eyes closed," Julian ordered, and the wine sloshed around in her head a little as her chair revolved. "Now, open up and take a look at Tia Marsh."

She opened her eyes, looked in the mirror and felt a fast slam of pure panic.

Where did she go?

The woman who stared back at her had a sunny cap of hair, with a snazzy fringe down to dramatically arched eyebrows. Her eyes were enormously and richly blue, her mouth wide and boldly red. And when Tia's jaw dropped, so did hers.

"I look . . . I look like Tinkerbell."

Once again Julian lowered his head so that his was close to hers. "You're not far wrong. Fairies are fascinating, aren't they? Clever and bright and unpredictable. That's how you look."

Carrie's face joined theirs in the mirror so that for a dizzy second, Tia imagined herself with three heads, none of which was actually hers. "You look fabulous." A tear trickled down Carrie's cheek. "I'm so happy. Tia, look! Really look at yourself."

"Okay." She took a huge breath. "Okay," and reached up gingerly to touch the nape of her neck. "It feels so strange." She shook her head a little, laughed a little. "Light. But, it doesn't look like me."

"Yes, it does. The you that was hiding. Give me some photo ID," Julian demanded.

Baffled, she dug in her purse, in her wallet, and took out her bank card.

"Which," he asked, "do you want to be?"

Tia stared at the photo, stared at the mirror. "I'll take everything you used on me today, and another appointment in four weeks."

*  *  *

SHE'D SPENT FIFTEEN hundred dollars. Fifteen hundred on nothing more than vanity. And, Tia thought as she sat in the cab with her shopping bag brimming with beauty products, she didn't feel guilty about it.

She felt exhilarated.

She couldn't wait to get home and look at herself in the mirror again. And again. Because she couldn't, she slid her hand into her purse, clicked open her compact. Holding the mirror inside the bag to shield her foolishness from the cabdriver, she tilted it up. And grinned at herself.

She wasn't ordinary at all. Not beautiful, certainly, but not by any means ordinary. She was even pretty in an odd sort of way.

Caught up with herself, she didn't register that they'd stopped in front of her building until Rosie O'Donnell's recorded voice reminded her to take all her belongings. Flustered, Tia dropped her compact back into her purse, fumbled with the fare she would normally have had ready, then, juggling her bag and her purse, climbed out.

As a result, she dropped her purse on the sidewalk, had to scoop the contents hurriedly back in. When she straightened, took a step toward her building, she nearly plowed into the couple who'd stepped into her path.

"Dr. Marsh?"

"Yes?" She answered without thinking, as she was looking at the beautiful, tall brunette who'd obviously been crying.

"We need to speak with you," he began, and the Irish in his voice finally got through. As did, when she shifted her gaze to his face and homed in on the family resemblance, the name.

"You're a Sullivan." She said the name as some might an oath, with bitter passion.

"I am, yes. Gideon. This is Cleo. If we could come up to your flat for a minute?"

"I don't have anything to say to you."

"Dr. Marsh." He put a hand on her arm as she turned.

She whipped back, surprising them both with the speed and the fury. "Take your hand off me or I'll start screaming. I can scream very loud, and very long."

As he was a man who understood and respected a woman's temper, he lifted his free hand, palm out, in a gesture of truce. "I know you're angry with Mal, and I don't blame you for it. But the fact is, we've got nowhere else to go right at the moment, not that's safe. We're in trouble here."

"That doesn't concern me, and neither do you."

"Let her alone, Slick." Cleo said it wearily, weaving a little from the whiskey. "It's all fucked anyway."

"You've been drinking." Outraged—and conveniently forgetting two glasses of afternoon wine—Tia sniffed. "You've got some nerve, coming around here drunk, accosting me on the street. You want to get out of the way, Mr. Sullivan, before I call the police."

"Yeah, she's been drinking." With his own temper rising, Gideon took Tia's arm again. "Because I saw to it as it was the only way I knew to numb her enough for her to deal with having her closest friend murdered. Murdered because of the Three Fates, murdered because of Anita Gaye. You can walk away from that, Dr. Marsh, but it doesn't stop you being part of it."

"He's dead." Cleo's voice was flat and dull, and in it Tia heard the ravages of grief. "Mikey's dead, and hassling her won't bring him back. Let's just go."

"She's sick, and she's tired," Gideon said to Tia. "I'm asking for her, let us come in. She needs a place until I can think what to do."

"I don't need anything."

"Come in. Damn it." Tia dragged a hand through her newly styled hair. "Come on." She streamed in ahead of them, jammed the button for the elevator.

Didn't it just figure that Malachi Sullivan would find some way to ruin her triumphant day?

"I'm grateful to you, Dr. Marsh."

"Tia." Inside, she jammed the button for her floor. "Since your friend's very likely to pass out on my floor, why be formal? I hate your brother, by the way."

"I understand. I'll let him know next time I see him. I almost didn't come up to you outside. Mal said you had long hair."

"I used to." She led the way down the hall to her apartment. "How did you recognize me?"

"Well, he said, too, that you were blond and delicate and pretty."

With an unladylike snort, she opened the door. "You can stay until she feels better," Tia began and set aside her purse and shopping bag. "Meanwhile you can tell me what you're doing here and why you expect me to believe Anita Gaye murdered anyone."

His face hardened, and in it Tia saw the resemblance again. Malachi's had taken on that same look of barely restrained violence in her trashed hotel room in Helsinki.

They might be very attractive, musically voiced men, she thought. But that didn't mean they weren't dangerous.

"She didn't do it personally, but she's responsible. Is there a place Cleo can lie down?"

"I don't need to lie down. I don't want to lie down."

"All right, then, you'll sit down."

Tia frowned as Gideon dragged Cleo to the sofa. His voice was rough, she noted, not particularly kind despite the lovely lilt of it. But he handled the brunette gently, as a man might some fragile antique glass.

And he was right to get her off her feet, Tia decided. The woman was sheet-white and shaky.

"You're cold," she heard him say. "Now do what you're told for once. Put your feet up." He hauled them up himself, pulled the throw off the back of the sofa and tucked it around her.

"I'm sorry for this," he said to Tia. "I couldn't risk a hotel, even if I had enough of the wherewithal for one just now. I haven't had time to think since everything happened. It was a quest, you see. An adventure, with some annoyances and expenses, to be sure, and a risk of a fist in the face or ass-kicking. But it's different now. Now there's murder."

"I'm sick." Cleo pushed off the couch, swayed. "I'm sorry. I'm sick."

"There." Tia pointed to a door on the left and felt a twist of sympathetic nausea in her own belly as Cleo lurched for it. Gideon was two steps behind her and got the door slammed in his face.

He stood, staring helplessly at it, then lowered his brow to the door.

"I guess it's the whiskey. I poured it into her because it was all I could think of."

He was grieving, too. She could see that now. "I'm going to make tea."

He nodded. "We'd be grateful."

"Come in the kitchen where I can see you, and start explaining."

"My brother said you were a fragile kind of thing," Gideon commented as he followed her into the kitchen. "He's not usually so wrong."

"He's the same one who claimed one of New York's most respected dealers is a thief. Now you add murder."

"It's not a claim, it's a fact."

With restless movements, he paced back to the doorway, looked toward the powder room door, paced back.

His brother, Tia noted, was more contained. At least, she amended, as far as she knew.

"She took what wasn't hers," Gideon continued. "And because she wants more, she's upped the stakes beyond anything that can be justified. A man's dead. A man I met only yesterday, one who gave me his bed because his friend asked him. A man who fixed me breakfast just this morning. A man who's dead only because he was loyal to a friend."

"How did you meet Cleo?"

"I tracked her down in Europe."

"Who is she in this?"

"She's connected to the second Fate."

"How?" she demanded.

"Through ancestry. She comes down from the White-Smythes. One was a collector in London."

All right, Tia mused. All right. Another piece of the puzzle in place.

"You recognize the name." Gideon's statement proved to Tia she'd have to work on her acting skills. "You've looked into it, then."

"I think, under the circumstances, I should be the one asking the questions."

"And I'll answer them. If I could use your phone first off. I need to call my family."

"No, I'm sorry."

"I'll call collect."

"You can't use the phone. It's tapped. Or maybe it's tapped. Or maybe I'm just having a big, complicated hallucination after all."

"I'm sorry? Bugged? Your phone's bugged?"

"According to another surprise visitor." She turned around. "I think, all in all, I'm really taking this very well, don't you? I mean, here I am, with a couple of strangers in my apartment—one who is currently being sick in my powder room and the other telling me fantastic stories in the kitchen. And I'm making tea. I think even Dr. Lowenstein would agree that's progress."

"I'm not following you."

"Why should you? Tell me why you believe Anita's responsible for this man's death."

"I'm responsible." Cleo stood, braced against the doorway. She was still very pale, but her eyes were clear again. "He'd be alive if it wasn't for me. I got him involved."

"I'm the one who got you involved," Gideon reminded her. "So you might as well hang it on me."

"I'd like to, but it won't wash. I was double-crossing you. I'd justified it, and you were going to get your share, but I was doing a shuffle on you, and I pulled Mikey into it. She must've had them watching the street, so when we came down after I made the deal with her, Mikey goes his way, I go mine. They split up and tail us, only I make my shadow and, being so goddamn clever, lose him. Only Mikey's clueless, so he just bops on home, and that bastard takes him down there. If he hadn't been with me, they wouldn't have known he existed."

"None of us knew she'd resort to murder," Gideon told her.

"Well, we know now." She looked at Tia.

"If this is true, why haven't you gone to the police?"

"And tell them what?" Gideon jammed his hands in his pockets. "That we believe a respected businesswoman is directly responsible for the murder of a young black dancer? A murder that very likely took place while she was at some public place or in some meeting? And we tell them we know this because she's stolen a statue while in Dublin and agreed to buy another? I suppose we can tell the police they'll just have to take our word on it when they ask for proof of any sort. No doubt they'll clap the cuffs on her."

"Regardless, you expect me to believe you." Tia lifted the sputtering kettle off the burner.

"Do you?" Gideon asked.

She looked at him, then at Cleo. "Yes, I guess I do, but I intend to research if insanity runs in my family. There's a pull-out sofa in my office here. You can use that tonight."

"Thanks."

"It isn't free," she told Gideon and lifted the tea tray. "From this point on, I stop being a tool and become an active participant in this little . . . quest."

Cleo smiled as Tia carted the tray into the living room. "Translated, Slick, the doc just informed you she's your fucking partner."

"Yes, I did. Lemon or sugar?"

# Twelve

"AN accident." Anita studied the two men who had come to the private entrance of her office. It served her right, she supposed, for selecting brawn over brains. But really, she'd given them such a simple task, with such specific, follow-the-dots instructions.

"The guy went nuts on me." Carl Dubrowsky, the shorter, stockier of the two, had a belligerent expression on his pockmarked face. He'd been a bouncer at a club before Anita had enlisted him to handle a few pesky chores.

She'd had reason to know he'd needed a job and wouldn't quibble about a few minor legalities, as he'd been arrested twice for assault and had barely beaten a charge of manslaughter.

Such activities didn't look well on a résumé.

She studied him now as he stood in one of the dark, Savile Row suits she'd paid for. You can dress them up, she thought. But you can't take them out.

"Your instructions, Mr. Dubrowsky, were to follow Ms. Toliver, and/or any companions she might have brought with her to our meeting. To detain her and/or those companions only if it should become necessary. And to, most important, retrieve my property, using persuasion of a physical nature if such action was warranted. I don't be-

lieve there were any instructions in there to fracture anyone's skull."

"It was an accident," he repeated stubbornly. "I tailed
the black guy and Jasper took the girl. Black guy went to
the apartment, like I said. I went in behind him, like I said.
Had to soften him up a little so he'd pay attention while I
was asking him about the statue. Went through the place
looking for it, didn't find it, so I softened him up some
more."

"And you let him answer the phone."

"Figured maybe it was the girl, and I'm thinking I put
the arm on him while she's on the hook, maybe she'll
talk—or with Jasper on her, she could maybe take off for
the piece you're after. Guy starts screaming, warns her off,
so I gave him a good jab. Fell wrong, is all. Guy fell
wrong and fucked himself."

"I've warned you about your language, Mr.
Dubrowsky," she said coolly. "I see the problem here is
that you attempted something in an area where you have
no skill. You attempted to think. Don't do so again. And
you, Mr. Jasper." She paused for a long-suffering sigh.
"I'm very disappointed. I had more faith in you. This is
the second time you haven't been able to keep up with a
second-rate stripper."

"She's got fast feet. And she ain't as dumb as you
think."

Marvin Jasper was flat-faced and kept his hair in the
same needle-sharp buzz cut he'd worn as an MP during
his stint in the army. He'd hoped to turn that into a stint
with the police force but had washed out during the psych
test. He was still bitter about it.

"Apparently she has brains enough to outmaneuver
both of you. Now she could be anywhere, and so could the
Fate."

Moreover, she thought, the police were involved. She
had no doubt Dubrowsky had been foolish enough to
leave some sort of evidence behind. Fingerprints, a stray
hair, something that would, eventually, tie him to the murder. Something that could, potentially, tie her.

That would never do.

"Mr. Jasper, I want you to go back, keep a surveillance on this apartment where Mr. Dubrowsky had his accident. Perhaps she'll go back there. If you see her, I want her taken. Quickly and quietly. Then contact me. I have a place where we can discuss business in private. Mr. Dubrowsky, you'll come with me. We'll go prepare for that business."

ONE OF THE advantages of marrying a wealthy, older man was that wealthy, older men so often had myriad holdings. And clever businessmen often kept those holdings buried under a morass of corporations and twisting red tape.

The warehouse in New Jersey was just one of the many. Anita had sold it only the day before to a developer who planned to open one of those cavernous discount stores.

One-stop shopping, she mused as she drove across the cracked concrete. She wasn't planning on shopping, but she was going to take care of her task with one, final stop.

"Sure is out in bumfuck," Dubrowsky muttered, and in the dimming light pulled back his lips in a sneer at her prissy order to watch his language.

"We can keep her here for several days, if necessary." Anita crossed to the loading bay doors, careful not to catch the heels of her Pradas in the cracks. "I want you to go over the security, to make certain once we have her in, she won't get out."

"No problem."

"These loading doors operate electrically and require a code. I'm more concerned with the side doors, the windows."

He pursed his lips, studied the sooty block of the building. "She'd have to be a monkey to get to the windows, and you got riot bars on them."

She studied them as if weighing his opinion. Paul might have left her a number of properties, but Anita had taken the time to tour them all. Inside and out. "What about around the sides?"

He trudged around, turning the corner. Weeds sprung up

through the broken stone, and though he could hear the sound of traffic from the turnpike, it was a distant whoosh. Bumfuck, he thought again, shaking his head.

"Broken lock on this side door," he called out.

"Is there?" She knew it. She'd had a complete and extensive report from the appraisal. "That's a problem. I wonder if it's locked from the inside."

He gave it a hard shove, shrugged. "Might be. Or it's jammed or something."

"Well, we won't . . . No," she said after a moment's thought. "Best to see if we can get in through it so we know what has to be done. Can you push or kick it in?"

He was built like a bull and proud of it. Proud enough that he didn't think to ask why she didn't just unlock the damn door.

Slamming his bulk against the thick wood soothed the ego she'd scraped raw in her office. He hated the bitch, but she paid well. That didn't mean he was going to tolerate getting sniped at by a woman.

He imagined she was the door, gave it one good kick and snapped the thin bolt lock on the inside.

"Like paper," he claimed. "Gonna want to put a steel door on here, a police lock if you want to keep out vandals and shit."

"You're quite right. It's dark inside. I have a flashlight in my bag."

"Light switch right here."

"No! We don't want to advertise we're here, do we?" She aimed the thin beam inside, scanned the room. It was another concrete box, dark, dusty and smelling of rodents.

It was, she thought, perfect.

"What's that?"

"What?"

"Over there in the corner," she said, gesturing with her light.

He walked over, kicked listlessly. "Just an old tarp. You want us to keep her out here for any time, you gotta think about how we're going to get food out here."

"You won't have to worry about it."

"Ain't no Chinese carry-out on the corner," he began as he turned. He saw the gun in her hand, held as steady as the pencil light. "What the fuck?"

"Language, Mr. Dubrowsky," she said with a *tsk*. And shot him.

The gun kicked, the sound echoed, and both sent a thrill through her. He took a lurching step toward her, so she shot him again, then a third time. When he was down, she stepped very carefully around the blood spilling into a slow river on the concrete floor. Tilting her head like a woman considering a new bauble in a shop window, she sent one more bullet into the back of his head.

It was a first for her, a killing. Now that it was done, very well done, her hand shook lightly and her breath came fast and shallow. She shined the light in his pupils, just to be sure, to be absolutely sure. The beam bobbed a bit, but she bore down and saw that his eyes were open and staring. And empty.

Paul had been like that after she'd waited out his final heart attack with his medication tight in her fist. She didn't consider that killing. That, she thought now as she steadied herself, had been patience.

She stepped back, took the old broom from the corner and meticulously brushed at the dust, smearing any footprints on her backward trip to the door. Taking out a lace trimmed handkerchief, she wiped the broom handle before tossing it aside, then covered her hand with the silk and lace to pull the door closed.

It was a bad fit now, she mused, as Dubrowsky had conveniently jarred the jamb. An obvious break-in, an obvious murder.

Finally, she wiped off her dead husband's unregistered Beretta and heaved it as far as she could into the scrubby brush bordering the lot. The police would find it, of course. She wanted them to find it.

There was nothing to tie her here but the fact that her husband had once owned the building. There was nothing to tie her to some nasty little man who'd made his living breaking arms. There were no records of employment, no tax forms, no witnesses to their dealings. Except for Jasper. She didn't think he'd run to the police when he heard his associate had been shot.

No, she had a feeling Marvin Jasper would become a sterling employee. Nothing like a little incentive to inspire loyalty and hard work.

She walked back to her car, and inside smoothed her hair, freshened her lipstick.

She drove away thinking that it was absolutely true if you wanted something done right, you did it yourself.


JACK AWOKE TO church bells. The pretty peal of them brought him out of a sound sleep on top of the bedspread and made him aware of the steady flow of the breeze through the window he'd left wide open.

He liked the smell of it, the hint of sea it carried. He lay as he was a moment, letting it wash over him until the bells faded to echoes.

He'd arrived in Cobh too early to do anything more productive than admire the harbor and get the general lay of the land.

What had once been a port that had given so many of the country's immigrants their last look at their homeland was now more of a resort town. And pretty as a postcard. He had a strong view of the low street, the square and the water from his windows. On another trip he would have taken his time absorbing the place, acquainting himself with the rhythms of it, with the locals. He enjoyed that aspect of traveling, and traveling alone.

But in this case there was only one local he had any interest in. Malachi Sullivan.

He intended to find out what he needed to know, make his second stop, and be back in New York within three days. Anita Gaye needed watching, and he'd do a better job of it in New York.

When he was finished here, he intended to contact Tia Marsh again as well. The woman might know more than she realized or more than she'd let on.

Business aside, he'd make time for a pilgrimage before

he left Cobh. He checked his watch and decided to order up coffee and a light breakfast before he showered.

The room service waiter had a face full of freckles.

"And isn't it a fine, fresh day?" he said as he set up the meal. "You can't do better for sightseeing. If you'd be needing any arrangements made for touring, Mr. Burdett sir, the hotel's happy to see to it for you. We might have rain tomorrow, so you'll want to take advantage of the weather while you have it. Now, is there anything else I can do for you?"

Jack took the little folder holding the bill. "Do you know a Malachi Sullivan?"

"Ah, it's a boat tour you're wanting, then."

"Sorry?"

"You want to tour around to the head of Kinsale, where the *Lusitania* was sunk. Fine views, even if it's a sad place all in all. Tours run three times daily this time of year. You've missed the first boat, but the second leaves at noon, so you've plenty of time for that. Would you like us to book that for you?"

"Thanks." Jack added a generous tip. "Does Sullivan run the tour himself?"

"One Sullivan or the other," the boy said cheerfully. "Gideon's away just now—that's the second son—so it's likely to be Mal or Becca, or one of the Curry crew, who are in the way of being cousins to the Sullivans. It's a family enterprise, and a fine value for the money. We'll see to the booking for you, and you've only to be down the dock by a quarter to noon."

SO HE HAD time to wander a bit after all.

He picked up his tour voucher at the front desk, pocketed it while he headed out. He walked down the steeply sloped street to the square, where the angel of peace stood over the statues of the weeping fishermen who mourned the *Lusitania*'s dead.

It was a powerful choice in memorials, he thought, the rough-clad men, the shattered faces. Men who'd made their living from the sea and had cried for strangers taken by it.

He supposed it was very Irish, and he found it very apt.

A block over was a monument to the doomed *Titanic,* and her Irish dead. Around them were shops, and the shops were decked with barrels and baskets of flourishing flowers that turned the sad into the picturesque. That, he thought, was probably Irish as well.

Along the streets, in and out of shops, people strolled or moved briskly about their business.

The side streets climbed up very impressive hills and were lined with painted houses whose doors opened straight onto the narrow sidewalks or into tiny, tidy front gardens.

Overhead the sky was a deep and pure blue with the waters of Cork Harbor mirroring it.

Boats were being serviced at the quay, the same quay, his pamphlet told him, as had been in service during the era that White Star and Cunard ran their grand ships.

He walked down to the dock and took his first study of Sullivan's tour boat.

It looked to seat about twenty, and resembled a party boat, with its bold red canopy stretched over the deck to protect passengers from the sun. Or around here, he assumed, the rain. The seats were red as well, and a cheerful contrast to the shiny white of the hull. The red script on the side identified it as *The Maid of Cobh.*

There was a woman already on board, and Jack watched as she checked the number of life jackets, seat cushions, ticking items off on a clipboard as she worked.

She wore jeans faded to nearly white at the stress points, and a bright blue sweater with the sleeves shoved up to her elbows. In them she appeared slim and slight. There was a shoulder-length tumble of curls spilling out of her blue cap. The hair color his mother would have called strawberry blond.

A pair of dark glasses and the cap's brim shielded most of her face, but what he could see—a full, unpainted mouth, a strong curve of jawline—was a nice addition to the view.

She moved forward, her steps quick and confident as

the boat swayed in its slip, and continued her checklist on the bridge.

She sure as hell wasn't Malachi Sullivan, Jack surmised, but she had to be a link to him.

"Ahoy, *The Maid*," he called out and waited on the dock while she turned, head cocked, and spotted him.

"Ahoy, the dock. Can I help you with something?"

"I'm going out." He took the voucher out of his pocket, held it up where the frisky wind whipped at it. "Is it okay to come aboard now?"

"You can, sure if you like. We won't be leaving for about twenty minutes."

She tucked the clipboard under her arm and walked over, prepared to offer him a hand on the long step from dock to deck. She realized he wouldn't need it. He moved well, and was fit enough, she concluded. Quite fit enough, she thought as she admired the strong build.

She admired the leather bomber jacket he wore as well, the fact that it was soft and battered. She had a weakness for good texture.

"Do I give this to you?" he asked.

"You do indeed." She accepted the voucher, then turned over her clipboard, flipping a page to the passenger list. "Mr. Burdett, is it?"

"It is. And you're . . ."

She glanced up, then shifted the clipboard again to take the hand he offered. "I'm Rebecca. I'll be your captain and tour guide today. I've yet to start the tea, but I'll have it going shortly. Just make yourself comfortable. It's a fine day for a sail, and I'll see you have a good ride."

I'll bet you will, he thought. Rebecca, Becca for short, Sullivan. She'd had a tough little hand and a good firm grip. And a voice like a siren.

After she tucked the clipboard in a bracket, she headed back to stern, turned into a tiny galley. When he followed, she sent him a friendly smile over her shoulder.

"Would this be your first visit to Cobh, then?"

"Yes. It's beautiful."

"It is, yes." She set a kettle on the single burner, then

got out the makings for tea. "One of the jewels of Ireland, we like to think. You'll get some of the history during the tour. There's but twelve passengers on this trip, so I'll have plenty of time to answer any questions you might have. You're from America, then?"

"Yes. New York."

Her mouth turned down in a sulk. "Seems everybody's going or coming from New York these days."

"Sorry?"

"Oh, it's nothing." She gave a little shrug. "My brother just left for New York this morning."

Well, hell, Jack thought but kept his expression neutral. "He's having a holiday?"

"It's business. But he'll see it all, won't he? Again. And I've never." She pulled off her sunglasses, hooked them on her sweater while she measured the tea.

Now he got a good, close look at her face. It was better, he decided, even better than he'd anticipated. Her eyes were a cool and misty green against skin as white and pure as marble. And she smelled, since he was close enough to catch her scent, like peaches and honey.

"It's very exciting, isn't it, New York City? All the people and the buildings. Shops and restaurants and theaters, and just everything and more all jammed into one place. I'd like a look at it myself. Excuse me, the others are starting to queue up on the dock. I need to check them in."

He stayed back at the stern, but he turned, slowly, to watch her.

She felt him watching her as she checked in the passengers, made them welcome. When they were settled, she introduced herself, made the standard safety announcements. Just as the cathedral bells began to ring the noon hour, she cast off.

"Thanks, Jimmy!" She waved to the dockhand who secured her line, then eased the boat out of the slip and into Cork Harbor. Piloting one-handed, she took up a microphone.

"It's my mother, Eileen, who's going to be entertaining you for the next little while. She was born here in Cobh, though we're forbidden to discuss the year of that happy event. Her parents were born here as well, as theirs before them. So she's in the way of knowing the area and the history. It happens I know a bit about it all myself, so if you've any questions when she's finished talking to you, just shout them out. We've a good, clear day, so your trip should be smooth and pleasant. I hope you enjoy it."

She reached up, flipped on the lecture her mother had recorded, then settled in to enjoy the trip herself. With her mother's voice speaking of Cobh's fine natural harbor, or its long vitality as a port that had once been the assembly point for ships during the Napoleonic Wars, as well as a major departure point in the country for its emigrants, she piloted the boat so its passengers could have the pleasure of seeing the town from the water, and appreciate the charm of it, the way it was held in its cup of land, its streets rising sharply to the great neo-Gothic cathedral that cast its shadow over all.

It was a clever, even a slick operation, Jack decided. All the while with the charm of simplicity. The daughter knew how to handle the boat, and the mother knew how to deliver a lecture and make it seem like storytelling.

He wasn't learning anything he didn't already know. He'd studied the area carefully. But the friendly voice over the mike made it all seem more intimate. That was a gift

The ride was smooth, as promised, and there was no faulting the scenery. As Eileen Sullivan began to speak of May seventh, he could almost see it. A shimmering spring day, the great liner plowing majestically through the sea with many of its passengers standing at the rail, looking— as he was—at the Irish coast.

Then that thin stream of white foam from the torpedo streaking toward the starboard bow. The first explosion under the bridge. The shock, the confusion. The terror. And fast on its heels, the second explosion in the forward.

The wreckage that had rained down on the innocent; the tumble of the helpless as the ship listed. And, in the twenty horrible minutes that followed, the cowardice and heroism, the miracles and the tragedies.

Some of his fellow passengers snapped cameras or ran video recorders. He noted that a few of the women blinked at tears. Jack studied the smooth plate of the sea.

*Out of death and tragedy,* Eileen continued, *came life and hope. My own great-grandfather was on the* Lusitania *and by grace of God survived. He was taken to Cobh and nursed back to health by a pretty young girl who became his wife. He never returned to America, or went on to England, as he had planned. Instead he settled in Cobh, which was then Queenstown. Because of that terrible day I'm here to tell you of it. While we grieve for the dead, we learn to celebrate the living, and to respect the hand of fate.*

Interesting, Jack thought, and gave his attention to Rebecca for the rest of the tour.

She answered questions, joked with the passengers, invited the children to come up and help steer the boat. It had to be routine for her, Jack reflected. Even monotonous. But she made it all seem fresh and fun.

Another gift, he decided. It seemed the Sullivans were full of them.

He asked a question or two himself because he wanted to keep her aware of him. When she maneuvered the boat into its slip again, he calculated he'd gotten his money's worth.

He waited while she talked to disembarking passengers, posed for pictures with them.

He made sure he was the last off.

"That was a great tour," he told her.

"I'm glad you enjoyed it."

"Your mother has a way of bringing it all into focus."

"She does." Pleased, Rebecca tipped back the brim of her cap. "Ma writes the copy for the brochures, and the ads and such. She's a gift with words."

"Are you going out again today?"

"No, I'm done with it till tomorrow."

"I was planning to head up to the cemetery. It seems the way to round out the tour. I could use a guide."

Her brows went up. "You don't need a guide for that, Mr. Burdett. It's signposted, and there are markers giving the history as well."

"You'd know more than the markers. I'd like the company."

She pursed her lips as she studied him. "Tell me, do you want a guide or do you want a girl?"

"If I get you, I get both."

She laughed and went with impulse. "All right, then, I'll go with you. But I'll need to make a stop first."

She bought flowers, enough that he felt obliged to offer to carry at least some of them. As they walked, she'd call out a greeting, or answer one.

She might have looked slight in the oversized sweater, but she strode up the steep hills effortlessly and, during the two-mile hike, kept up a running conversation without any hitches in breath.

"Since you're flirting with me, Mr. Burdett—"

"Jack."

"Since you're flirting with me, Jack, I'm going to assume you're not a married man."

"I'm not married. Since you ask, I'm going to assume that matters to you."

"It does, of course. I don't have flirtations with married men." She cocked her head as she studied his face. "I don't generally have them with strange men, either, but I'm making an exception because I liked the look of you."

"I liked the look of you, too."

"I thought you must, as you stared at me more than the scenery during the tour. I can't say I minded. How'd you happen by the scar here?" she asked and tapped a finger to the side of her own mouth.

"A disagreement."

"And do you have many?"

"Scars or disagreements?"

She laughed up at him. "Disagreements that lead to scars."

"Not so far."

"What is it you do back in America?"

"I run my own security company."

"Do you? Like, bodyguards?"

"That's an aspect. We're primarily electronic security."

"I love electronics." She narrowed her eyes when he

glanced down at her. "Don't give me that indulgent look. Being a woman doesn't mean I don't understand gadgetry. Do you do private homes or places like banks and museums?"

"Both. All. We're worldwide." He didn't brag about his company as a rule. But he wanted to tell her. The way, he realized with some chagrin, a high-school quarterback wanted to impress the head cheerleader. "And we're the best. In twelve years, we've expanded from one branch in New York to twenty internationally. Give me another five and when people think security, they'll think Burdett, the way they think Kleenex for tissues."

She didn't consider it bragging, she considered it pride. And she was one to appreciate and respect a person's pride for his own accomplishments. "It's a good feeling, to make your own. We've done that as well, on a smaller scale, of course. But it suits us."

"Your family?" he asked, reminding himself to stick to the point.

"Yes. We've always made our living from the water, but it was fishing only. Then we tinkered our way into a tour boat. One, to start. We lost my da a few years back, and that was hard. But as my mother's fond of saying, you have to find the right in the wrong. So I started thinking. We had the insurance money. We had strong backs and good brains. Tourism helped turn Ireland around, economically speaking. So what could we do to cash in on that."

"Harbor tours."

"Exactly. The one boat we ran was doing a reasonable business. But if we used the money and bought two more, well then. I ran the figures and calculated the potential outlay and income and such. So now Sullivan Tours runs the three for touring, and the fishing boat as well. And I'm thinking it's time to add another package that would include just what we're doing now. A guided walk along the funeral route and to the cemetery where the *Lusitania* dead are buried."

"You run the business end of it?"

"Well, Mal, he does the people part—the promotion

and glad-handing, as he's best at it. Gideon keeps the books because we make him, but he prefers overseeing the maintenance and repairs, as he's the organized sort and can't stand anything not perfectly shipshape, so to speak. My mother handles the copy and correspondence and keeps us all from killing each other. As for me, I have the ideas."

She paused, nodded toward the stones and high grass of the graveyard. "Do you want to wander a bit on your own? Most do. The mass graves are up ahead with those yew trees. There were elms there first, but the yews replaced them. The graves are marked with three limestone rocks and bronze plaques, and there are others—twenty-eight others—individual graves for those who died. Some are empty as they never recovered the bodies."

"Are these for them?"

"These," she said and took the flowers from him, "are for my own dead."

# Thirteen

THE cemetery stood on a hill surrounded by green valleys. Gravestones were stained with lichen, and some were so old that wind and rain had blurred their carvings. Some stood straight as soldiers, and others tipped like drunks.

The fact that they did both, that there was no static order to it all, Jack thought, made the hill all the more poignant, all the more powerful.

The grass, still thick with summer, rose in wild hillocks and lifted the scent of living, growing things as it waved in the breeze. And on countless graves, flowers grew or were laid. Some wreaths were sheltered in clear plastic boxes, and others held little vials of holy water taken from some shrine.

He found the sentiment oddly touching even as it puzzled him. What possible help could holy water offer to the occupants of a graveyard?

He saw fresh flowers spread beneath stones that had stood for ninety years and more. Who, he wondered, brought daisies to the old, old dead?

Because there was no way he could reasonably refuse Rebecca's obvious desire for some time alone, he walked through the cemetery to the brilliant green carpet of smooth and tended grass sheltered by the yews. He saw the stones with their brass plaques. Read the words.

A heart would have had to be stone not to be moved. While his was, he believed, contained, it wasn't hard. There was a connection here, even for him, and he wondered why he'd waited so long to come to this place, to stand on this ground.

Fate, he thought. He supposed it was fate, once again, that had chosen his time.

He looked back, over the stones, over the grass, and saw Rebecca laying another bouquet on another grave. Her cap was off now, out of respect, he assumed, and stuffed in her back pocket. Her hair, that delicate reddish gold, danced in the breeze that stirred the grass at her feet. Her lips were curved in a quiet and private smile as she looked down at a headstone.

And looking at her across the waving grass, the somber stones, he felt his contained heart give a single hard lurch. Though he was shaken by it, he wasn't a man to ignore trouble, whatever its form. He walked toward her.

Her head came up, and though her mouth stayed gently curved, he sensed a watchfulness in her now. Did she feel it, too? he wondered. This strange tug and pull, almost—if he believed in such things—a kind of recognition.

When he reached her, she shifted the last two bouquets to her other hand. "Holy ground is powerful ground."

He nodded. Yes, he realized. She'd felt it, too. "Hard to disagree with that right now."

She studied his face as she spoke, the hard, strong lines of it that fit together made something less than handsome, and something more. And his eyes, his smoky, secret eyes.

He knew things, she was sure of it. And some of them were marvels.

"Do you believe in power, Jack? Not the kind that comes from muscle or position. The kind that comes from somewhere outside a person, and inside him as well."

"I guess I do."

This time she nodded. "And so do I. My father's there." She gestured to a black granite marker bearing the name Patrick Sullivan. "His parents are living yet, and in Cobh, as are my mother's. And there are my great-grandparents, John and Margaret Sullivan, Declan and Katherine Curry. And their parents are here as well, a ways over there for my father's side."

"You bring them all flowers?"

"When I walk this way, yes. I stop here last. My great-great-grandparents, on my mother's side." She crouched to lay the flowers at the base of each stone.

Jack looked over her head, read the names.

Fate, he thought again. Sneaky bitch.

"Felix Greenfield?"

"Don't see many names like Greenfield in Irish grave-yards, do you?" She laughed a little as she straightened. "He was the one my mother spoke about on the tour, who survived the *Lusitania* and settled here. So I stop here last, as if he hadn't lived through that day, I wouldn't be here to bring him flowers. Have you seen what you wanted to see?"

"So far."

"Well then, you'd best come home with me and have some tea."

"Rebecca." He touched her arm as she turned. "I came here looking for you."

"For me?" She scooped back her hair and schooled her voice to stay smooth despite the sudden trip of her heart. "That's a fine romantic sort of thing to say, Jack."

"I should've said I came looking for Malachi Sullivan."

The laughter in her eyes vanished. "For Mal? Why is that?"

"Fate."

He saw the flash of fear run across her face, then with admiration, he watched it harden and chill. "You can go back to New York City and tell Anita Gaye she can kiss my ass on the way to hell."

"I'd be happy to, but I'm not here because of Anita. I'm a collector, and I have a . . . personal interest in the Fates. I'll match whatever Anita's paying your family and add ten percent."

"Paying us? Paying?" Her cheeks went hot with fury. Oh, when she thought of how everything inside her body had softened and hummed just with looking at him! "That thieving bitch. Now look! Look, you've got me standing over my own dead ancestor and swearing. Since I am, I'll finish by telling you to go to hell as well."

He sighed a bit as she loped around graves and toward the road.

"You're a businesswoman," he reminded her when he caught up. "So let's try to have a discussion. Failing that, I'll point out I'm bigger and stronger than you are. Don't make me prove it."

"So that's the way of it?" She whipped around on him. "You're going to threaten and bully me? Well, try it and see if you don't end up with another scar or two for your trouble."

"I just asked you not to make me bully you," he pointed out. "Why did your brother go back to New York this morning?"

"That's none of your flaming business."

"Since I've just traveled three thousand miles to see him, it is my flaming business." Rather than fight fire with fire, he kept his tone quiet and reasonable. "And I can tell you, if he's gone to see Tia Marsh, he's not going to get a very warm reception."

"A lot you know about it, as she's paying his fare. As a loan," she added with a sniff. "We're not leeches or money-grubbers. And he's been half sick since Gideon called to tell him about the murder."

"What?" This time his hand clamped like steel on her arm. "What murder?"

She was mad as a hornet and because of it wanted to spit and kick at him. The bastard had stirred up something in her, had started stirring it from that first careless *ahoy*. But she saw something else in him now, something cold and determined. And that something else was hearing of murder for the first time.

"I'm not telling you a bloody thing until I know who you are and what you're about."

"I'm Jack Burdett." He took out his wallet, flipped out his driver's license. "New York City. Burdett Security and Electronics. You got a computer, you can do a Net search."

She took the wallet, studied the identification.

"I'm a collector, just like I said. I've done some security work for Morningside Antiquities, and I've been a client. Anita dangled the Three Fates in front of me like bait because she knows it's the sort of thing I'm interested in, and that I have a tendency to find things out."

As she continued to flip through his wallet, he struggled for patience. Then just nipped it out of her fingers, shoved it back in his pocket.

"Anita's mistake was in assuming I'd find them for her, or that she could break through my own security measures and keep track of my movements. Who the hell is dead?"

"That's not enough. I'll do that Web search. Let me tell you something, Jack, I have a tendency to find things out as well."

"Tia Marsh." He fell into step beside Rebecca as she strode down the hill. "You said she paid for your brother's flight to New York. She's okay, then?"

Rebecca slanted him a look. "She's fine and well as far as I can tell. You know her, do you?"

"Only met her once, but I liked her. Did anything happen to her parents?"

"No. It has something to do with someone else altogether, and I'm not giving you names until I'm sure you've no part in it."

"I want the Fates, but not enough to murder. If Anita's behind that, it changes the complexion of things."

"You don't sound as if you'd put such a thing past her."

"She's a spider," Jack said simply. "I liked her husband, did some work for him. I've done work for her, too. I don't have to like all my clients. How did your brother get tangled up with her?"

"Because she—" She broke off, scowled. "I'm not saying. How did you get Malachi's name, unless she gave it to you?"

"Tia mentioned him." He walked in silence for a while. "Listen, you and your family seem to have a nice business going here," he continued. "You should think about letting this go. You're out of your league with Anita."

"You don't know me or my league. We'll have the

Three Fates before it's done, that's a promise. And if you're such an interested collector, you can prepare yourself to ante up for them."

"And I thought you weren't a money-grubber."

Because she heard the humor in his voice, it didn't ruffle her feathers. "I'm a businesswoman, Jack, as you pointed out yourself. And I can wheel and deal as well as anyone. Better than most. I've done my research on the Fates. The complete set at auction at a place like Wyley's or Sotheby's could go for upwards of twenty million American dollars. More, if the right publicity spin's put on it."

"An incomplete set, even two-thirds of the three, would only net a fraction of that, and only from an interested collector."

"We'll have the three. We were meant to."

He let it go and kept pace with her brisk march up a long hill at the very edge of town. At the top was a pretty house with a pretty garden, and a pretty woman tending it.

She straightened, shielded her eyes with the flat of her hand. When she smiled in greeting, Jack caught the resemblance around the mouth.

"Well, Becca darling, what have you brought home with you?"

"Jack Burdett. I invited him home for tea before I knew he was a liar and a sneak."

"Is that so?" Eileen's smile didn't dim in the slightest. "Well, an invitation's an invitation after all. I'm Eileen Sullivan." She extended her hand over the garden gate. "Mother to this rude creature."

"It's nice to meet you. I enjoyed your talk during the tour."

"It's kind of you to say so. You're from America?" she added as she opened the gate.

"New York. I'm in Cobh as I was hoping to talk to your son Malachi, regarding the Three Fates."

"Sure, you have no trouble spilling it all out to her in a lump," Rebecca scolded. "With me it's all flirtation and pretense."

"I said I liked the look of you, and since you don't strike

me as a stupid woman, you'd know if a man looks at you and doesn't like what he sees, he's got a serious problem. Boiled down, that means there was flirtation but no pretense. I've annoyed your daughter, Mrs. Sullivan."

Amused, intrigued, Eileen nodded. "That's easily done. Maybe we should talk inside before the neighbors start wagging about it. Kate Curry's already peeking out the window. So, you've come from New York," she continued as she started up the short walk to the door. "Have you family there?"

"Not anymore. My parents moved to Arizona several years ago. They like the weather."

"Hot, I suppose. No wife, then?"

"Not anymore. I'm divorced."

"Ah." Eileen led the way into the company parlor. "That's a pity."

"The marriage was the pity. The divorce was a lot easier on both of us. You have a good home, Mrs. Sullivan."

She liked the way he put it. "Yes, I do, and you make yourself comfortable in it. I'll see about that tea, then we'll talk. Rebecca, entertain our guest."

"Ma." With a withering glance at Jack, Rebecca hustled after Eileen.

He could hear the whispers from the hallway where they stood. Argued, he decided with a grin. He couldn't make out the words, until the last of them. That was clear.

"Rebecca Anne Margaret Sullivan, you get in the company parlor and show some manners this minute, or I'll know the reason why."

Rebecca stomped back in, flung herself in the chair across from Jack's. Her face was full of storms, and her voice full of ice. "Don't think you'll get around me because you got around my mother."

"Wouldn't dream of it. Rebecca Anne Margaret."

"Oh, stuff it."

"Tell me why your brother went back to New York. Tell me why you think Anita's involved in a murder."

"I'll tell you nothing at all until I've had a whack at my computer and seen how much of what you've told me is the truth."

"Go ahead, do it now." He waved a hand. "I'll cover for you with your mother."

Rebecca weighed her mother's wrath against the burn of her own curiosity. Knowing she'd pay for it dearly, she got to her feet. "If one single thing you've said doesn't match, I'll boot you out personally."

She walked to the doorway, and Jack saw her send an uneasy glance down the hall, where her mother had gone, before she charged up the steps.

Because he sympathized with a child's healthy fear of her mother, he rose and wandered back to the kitchen.

"I hope you don't mind." He stepped in while Eileen cut cake into neat squares. "I wanted to see the house."

"I heard that girl go upstairs, and after I told her not to."

"My fault. I told her to go ahead and run a check on me. You'll both feel more comfortable once she does."

"If I didn't feel comfortable now, you wouldn't be in my home." She tapped a long-bladed knife against the side of the cake plate, smiling a little when his gaze dropped to it. "I know how to judge a man when I look him in the eye. And I know how to take care of my own."

"I believe you."

"Good. Now I know why I went and baked this cake this morning, though the boys aren't about to eat it." She turned to the stove to finish the tea. "For company, it's the parlor. For business, it's the kitchen."

"Then I guess it's the kitchen."

"Have a seat, and have some cake. When the girl gets going on that computer, there's no telling when she'll show her face again."

He couldn't remember the last time he'd had homemade cake, or eaten in a kitchen that wasn't his own. It relaxed him, and made the time he normally would have marked pass easily.

It was thirty minutes or more before Rebecca sailed in and pulled up a chair. "He's who he says he is," she said to her mother, "so that's something." When she reached for a piece of cake, Eileen slapped her hand away.

"You don't deserve any sweets."

"Oh, Ma."

"Whatever your age, Rebecca, you don't disobey your mother without consequences."

Her brows drew together, but she left the cake alone. "Yes, ma'am. I'm sorry." She shifted her gaze, and the darts in it, to Jack. "I wonder what you'd be needing with a flat in New York, and another in Los Angeles, and still a third in London."

Though she surprised him, he sipped his tea. It had taken more than average computer skills to dig that deep. "I travel a lot, and prefer my own place to hotels when I can manage it."

"And what does the man's personal business have to do with this, Becca?"

At her mother's censorious tone, she bristled. "I've got to know the nature of him, don't I? He shows up here this way, just after Mal's left, and after that horrible business in New York, where he admits he's just come from."

"I'd have done the same," he told her with a nod. "And more."

"I intend to do more. But more takes time. What I did find was that you checked into your hotel here early this morning, driving a rental car. And you'd booked your room two days ago. That's before the trouble in New York, so I can't see what one has to do with the other."

He leaned forward now. "Tell me who was murdered."

"It was a young man named Michael Hicks," Eileen told him. "God rest him."

"Was he working with you?"

"He was not." Rebecca huffed out a breath, then added, "It's a complicated business."

"I'm good at complications."

Rebecca looked at her mother.

"Darling, someone has died." Eileen laid a hand on her daughter's. "An innocent young man, by all accounts. Everything changes because of it. All this has to be put right again. If there's a chance Jack can help do that, we have to take it."

Rebecca sat back, studied Jack's face. "Will you help see she pays for what she's done?"

"If Anita had anything to do with murder, I'll see she pays. You have my word on it."

Rebecca nodded and, because she still wanted cake, folded her hands on the table. "You tell it, Ma. You're better at telling."


EILEEN WAS GOOD at telling and, Rebecca discovered, Jack Burdett was good at listening. He asked no questions, made no comments, only sipped his tea and kept his attention on Eileen while she spoke.

"And so," she finished, "Malachi's gone back to New York City to do what needs to be done."

Jack nodded, and wondered if this nice, cozy family had any conception of what they'd gotten themselves into. "So this Cleo Toliver has the second Fate."

"It wasn't perfectly clear if she had it or knew where it was. The boy who died was a dear friend of hers, and she's blaming herself over it."

"And Anita knows who she is, but not where. At the moment."

"As it stands," Eileen confirmed.

"It'd be wise to keep it that way. If she's killed once, it'll be easy to kill again. Mrs. Sullivan, is it worth it to you? To risk your family?"

"Nothing's worth my family, but they won't be stopped now. I'd be disappointed in them if they did. There's a young man dead, and that has to be accounted for. This woman can't steal and murder without an accounting."

"How did she get the first Fate away from you?"

"How do you know she did?" Rebecca demanded. "Unless she told you herself."

"You told me," he said mildly. "You called her a thief. And you put flowers on the grave of your great-great-grandfather, one Felix Greenfield, who'd been aboard the *Lusitania*. Up until recently, I believed the first Fate to have been lost along with Henry W. Wyley. The way this plays out, the Fate and your ancestor were spared. How did he manage it? Did he work for Wyley?"

"Felix wasn't the only one who survived," Rebecca began.

"Oh, Becca, for pity's sake, the man's got a brain in his head, and he's used it. I'm afraid Felix stole the statue. He was a bit of a thief, but he reformed. He slipped the little thing in his pocket just as the torpedo hit. Though it might seem self-serving, I like to think it was meant."

"He stole it." A grin spread over Jack's face. "That's perfect. Then Anita steals it from you."

"That's different," Rebecca insisted. "She knew what it was, and Felix didn't. She used her dead husband's business reputation when Mal took it to her for appraisal. Then she used her body to dull his common sense—and him being a man, it was easily done. She made a fool out of all of us and that . . . well, we'll have an accounting for that as well."

"If this is a matter of pride, you'd better rethink. She'll eat a tasty morsel like you alive."

"She can try. And she'll choke."

"Pride isn't a luxury," Eileen said quietly. "And not always a kind of vanity. Surviving when others died changed Felix. It, you could say, made a man out of him. The Fate was a symbol of that change, and it stood for it in our family for five generations. Now we know what it is, beyond that symbol, and we believe the three should be brought back together. That was meant as well. Maybe there's profit in it, and we won't turn from that. But it's not for greed. It's for family."

"Anita has the first, and knows—or thinks she knows—how to get the second. You're in her way."

"And the Sullivans aren't so easily pushed aside as she might think," Eileen said. "Felix floated freezing on a broken crate while one of the grandest ships ever built sank behind him. He survived, while it didn't. While more than a thousand others didn't. And he had that little silver figure in his pocket. He brought it here, and we'll have it back."

"If I help you do that, help you put the three together, will you sell it to me?"

"If you meet the asking price," Rebecca began, but her mother cut her off with one sharp look.

"If you help us, we'll sell it to you. You have my word on it," she said and extended her hand over the table.

HE WANTED TIME to think it through, so stayed over in Cobh another day. It gave him the opportunity to make a number of calls, begin a number of background checks on the players in what Jack was finding a very interesting game.

He trusted Eileen Sullivan. While he was attracted to Rebecca, he didn't have the same instinctive faith in the daughter as he did in the mother. Because he wanted a second run at her, Jack bought another ticket for the tour and strolled down to the dock.

She didn't look pleased to see him. The cheerful expression she wore while chatting with passengers went cold and hard when her gaze shifted, landed on him.

She snatched the voucher out of his hand. "What are you doing back here?"

"Maybe I can't keep away from you."

"Bollocks. But it's your money."

"I'll give you ten pounds more for a seat on the bridge and some conversation."

"Twenty." She held out a hand. "In advance."

"Distrusting and mercenary." He dug out twenty pounds. "Careful, I could fall in love with you."

"Then I'd have the pleasure of grinding your heart into dust. For that, I'd refund your twenty. Take your seat, then, and don't touch anything. I've got to get started."

He waited, let her wonder and stew as she maneuvered into the harbor and set her mother's recording.

"Looks like rain," he commented.

"We've a couple hours yet. You don't strike me as a man who makes the same trip twice without good reason. What do you want?"

"Another invitation to tea?"

"You won't get it."

"Now that's cold. Other than me, have you noticed any-one hanging around, taking this tour, walking by your house, maybe showing up along your daily routine?"

"You think we're being watched?" Rebecca shook her head. "She doesn't do it that way. She's not worried about what we're doing here in Cobh. She's concerned with what one of us might be doing when we're not at home. She tracked my brothers when they went off, and I think she did that through the airline tickets—the credit card, you know. It's not that difficult to get such information if you're clever with the computer."

"It's not simple either."

"If I can do it, she, or someone she pays, can as well."

"And can you?"

"I can do damn near anything with a computer. I know, for instance, that you were divorced five years ago, after one year and three months of marriage. Not such a long time."

"Long enough, apparently."

"I know your address in New York City, should I want to pay a call sometime in the future. I know you went to Oxford University and graduated in the top ten percent of your class. That's not too bad," she added. "Considering."

"Thanks."

"I know you have no criminal record, at least none that shows on a surface look, and that your company, which you started twelve years ago, has a strong, international reputation and has given you an estimated net—net, mind you—worth of twenty-six million American dollars. And that," she said with the first hint of laughter in her eyes, "isn't so very bad either."

He stretched out his legs. "That's a lot of digging." And very impressive work, he thought.

"Oh, not so very much." She waved it—and the six hours she'd spent at her keyboard—off. "And I was curious."

"Curious enough to take a trip to Dublin?"

"Why would I want to go to Dublin?"

"Because I'm going, tonight."

"Is that a proposition, Jack? And while my mother's voice is coming through the speaker?"

"It is, but whether it's personal or business is up to you. There's someone in Dublin I need to see. I think it'll be worth your while to tag along."

"Who would this be?"

"You want to find out, have a bag packed and be ready by five-thirty. I'll come by for you."

"I'll think about it," she replied, but was mentally packing her bag.

# Fourteen

"I know I'm leaving you shorthanded, Ma."

"That's not what concerns me." Eileen frowned as Rebecca rolled up a sweater like a sausage and stuffed it into her bag. "I said I had a good feeling about Jack Burdett, and that I trusted him to be an honest man, but that doesn't mean I feel easy about my daughter going off with him after one day's acquaintance."

"It's business." Rebecca debated between jeans and trousers. "And if it were Mal or Gideon heading out like this, you wouldn't think twice."

"I'd think twice, as they're as precious to me as you. But as you're a daughter instead of a son, I'm thinking three or four times. That's the nature of things, Rebecca, and there's no point in getting sulky over it."

"I know how to take care of myself."

Eileen laid a hand on Rebecca's tumbled curls. "You do, yes."

"And I know how to handle men."

Eileen lifted her eyebrows. "Those you've had dealings with up to now. But you haven't dealt with the likes of this one before."

"A man's a man," Rebecca said dismissively, and ignored her mother's hearty sigh. "Mal and Gideon have been traipsing all over the world while I stay here, at the wheel or the keyboard. It's time I had some part of the adventure of it, Ma. Now I've a chance to, if only to go as far as Dublin for it."

She's always fought to stand toe-to-toe with her brothers, Eileen thought. And had worked for it. Earned it. "Take an umbrella. It's raining."

She was packed and walking out the front door when Jack pulled up. She wore a light jacket against the steady rain and carried a single duffel. He appreciated both promptness and efficiency in a woman, and the independence that had her tossing the bag in the backseat before he could walk around to take it from her.

She kissed her mother, then ended up exchanging a hard, swaying hug before climbing into the car.

"It's my only girl I'm trusting you with, Jack." Eileen stood in the rain, laid a hand on his arm. "If I come to regret it, I'll hunt you down like a dog."

"I'll take care of her."

"She can take care of herself or she wouldn't be going with you. But she's my only daughter and my youngest child, so I'm putting the weight of it on you."

"I'll have her back tomorrow."

Telling herself to be content with that, Eileen stepped back and watched them drive away in the rain.

SHE'D EXPECTED THEY'D drive all the way to Dublin and had prepared herself for the tedium of it. Instead he drove to Cork airport and turned in the rental car, and she prepared instead for the short flight.

She wasn't prepared for the little private jet, or for Jack himself to take the controls.

"Is it yours?" She ordered her nerves to quiet as she took her seat in the cockpit beside him.

"The company's. Simplifies things."

She cleared her throat as he went over his checklist. "And you're a good pilot, are you?"

"So far," he replied absently, then shot her a glance. "You've flown before?"

"Of course." She blew out a breath. "Once, and on a big plane where I wasn't required to sit beside the pilot."

"There's a parachute in the back."

"I'm trying to think if that's funny or not." She kept her hands folded as he was given clearance and began the taxi to his assigned runway. When he picked up speed, she watched the gauges, and when the nose of the plane lifted, her stomach gave one quick shudder.

Then smoothed out.

"Oh, it's something, isn't it?" She strained forward, watching the ground fall away. "Not like a big plane at all. It's better. How long does it take to get a pilot's license? Can I have a go at the wheel?"

"Maybe on the way back, if we have clear weather."

"If I can pilot a boat in a storm, I ought to be able to fly a little plane in a shower of rain. It must be grand being rich."

"It has its advantages."

"When we have the Fates and sell them to you, I'm taking my mother on a holiday."

It was interesting, he thought, that that would be her first priority. Not that she would buy a fancy car or fly to Milan to shop, but that she would take her mother on vacation.

"Where to?"

"Oh, I don't know." Relaxed now despite the turbulence, she eased back to peer at the stacks of clouds. "Someplace exotic, I think. An island like Tahiti or Bimini, where she can stretch out under an umbrella on the beach and see blue water while she drinks some silly thing out of a coconut shell. What's in those things anyway?"

"The road to perdition."

"Is it now? Well then, that'll be good for her as well. She works so hard, and she never complains about it. Now we've been throwing money around right and left when by rights it should be in the bank so she can feel secure."

She paused, then shifted to look at him. "What she said to you yesterday, that it wasn't about greed. That's the truth for her. I might be greedy, though I prefer to think of it as practical, but she's not."

Greedy? No, a greedy woman didn't fantasize about

taking her mother to a tropical island and getting her plastered on coconut drinks.

"Is that your way of telling me when you get the statue back you'll skin me over the purchase price?"

She only smiled. "Let me have a go at the wheel there, Jack."

"No. Why haven't you asked me why we're going to Dublin?"

"Because you wouldn't tell me, and I'd be wasting my breath."

"That's refreshing. I'll tell you this instead. I did background checks on you and your brothers, and on Cleo Toliver."

"Is that so?" Her voice cooled.

"You ran me, Irish, so let's call it tit for tat. Toliver had some light smears on her juvenile record—underage drinking, shoplifting, disorderly conduct. Basic teenage-rebellion-type stuff. She got plugged into the system because her parents didn't rush to get her out again."

"What do you mean?" A combination of shock and outrage warred inside her. "That they let her go to jail? Their own child?"

"Juvie's not jail, but it's close enough. Her parents divorced, and her mother likes to remarry. She bounced between the two of them, then took off when she hit eighteen. No dings on her adult record, so she either cleaned up her act or got better at avoiding the cops."

"You're telling me this because you think with her background, her record, she might be a problem for us. If Gideon thought that, he'd have said so."

"I don't know Gideon, and I prefer drawing my own conclusions. Speaking of your brothers, they're both clear as far as legal difficulties. And you, you're as pure as your skin."

She jerked her head back when he reached over to brush a fingertip down her cheek. "Mind your hands."

"What is it about Irishwomen and their skin?" he said as if to himself. "Makes a man want to lap it up, especially when it smells like yours."

"I don't mix flirtations and business," she said stiffly.

"I do. As often as possible. Being a practical woman, I'd think you'd appreciate the efficiency of multitasking."

She had to laugh. "Well now, I'll admit that's a unique line, Jack. But if you think the sophisticated world traveler can lure the naive village girl with clever lines, you've mistaken the matter."

"I don't think you're naive." He turned his head, met her eyes. "I think you're fascinating. And more, I'm curious about what I felt run through me when I looked over the high grass and old stones of a cemetery and watched you lay flowers on a grave. I'm very curious about that, Rebecca, and I always satisfy my curiosity."

"I felt something, too. That's as much why I've come with you as wanting to know what's in Dublin. But don't think you can maneuver me, Jack, because you can't. I've a goal to meet, for myself, for my family. Nothing can get in the way of it."

"I didn't think you'd admit it." He gave his attention to his instruments. "That you'd felt something. You're a straightforward woman, Rebecca. A straightforward woman who knows computers, who can pack for a last-minute trip in a single bag and be on time. Where have you been all my life? We're about to start our approach," he said before she could answer.

THERE WAS ANOTHER rental car waiting at Dublin airport, and this time Jack hauled up Rebecca's bag before she could grab it herself. She didn't comment on it, nor on the conversation they'd had in the plane. She wasn't sure either would be safe topics at the moment.

She didn't speak at all until he headed away from the city instead of toward it.

"Dublin's the other way," she pointed out.

"We're not actually going into the city."

"Then why did you say we were?"

Her suspicious nature was just one more thing he found appealing. "We flew into Dublin, and now we're driving a few miles south. When we're done, we'll drive back and fly out of Dublin."

"And where might we be spending the night?"

"At a place I haven't been to for a couple of years. You'll have your own room," he added, "with the option of sharing mine."

"I'll take my own. Who's paying for it?"

He grinned, lightning fast, in a way that engaged his whole face and made her want to trace a finger over that faint, crescent scar.

"That won't be a problem. It's pretty country," he commented, gesturing at the rising green hills that shimmered through the thinning rain. "Easy to see why he decided to retire here."

"Who?"

"The man we're going to see. Tell me, do you share your mother's belief that the Fates are a kind of symbol?"

"I suppose I do."

"And that they belong together for reasons more than their monetary, even artistic value?"

"Yes. Why?"

"One more. Do you agree that what goes around comes around?"

She blew out an impatient breath. "If you're meaning there are cycles and circles to things, I do."

"Then you're going to appreciate this." He took the car up a hill, then around to a pretty road lined with dripping hedgerows and painted bungalows with thriving gardens.

The road climbed again, turned again, and he swung into a short drive beside a lovely stone house where the chimney was smoking and the gardens were a small sea of beauty.

"Your friend lives here?"

"Yeah."

Even as Jack stepped out of the car, the door of the house opened. An old man stood in the doorway, leaning on a cane and grinning. He had a monk's fringe of snowy hair topping a wide face lined with deep creases. Silver-framed glasses slid down his nose.

"Mary!" His voice croaked like a frog. "They're here," he shouted, and came forward even as Jack hurried to him.

"Don't come out in the rain."

"Hell, boy, little rain doesn't hurt. Everything else does at my age, but not a bit of wet." He caught Jack in a one-armed embrace.

Rebecca saw now the old man was quite tall, but bent a bit with age. His big hand reached up to lie across Jack's cheek and looked, despite its size, fragile there, and somehow sweet.

"I've missed you," Jack said, and leaned down in an easy, unself-conscious gesture Rebecca admired and kissed the old man lightly on the lips. "This is Rebecca Sullivan."

He shifted his body, and again she noted the gentleness in him when he slid a hand under the man's arm.

"Well, you said she was a beauty, and so she is." He reached out and took her hand, simply held it. And she saw with puzzled embarrassment the sparkle of tears come into his eyes.

"Rebecca, this is my great-grandfather."

"Oh." At sea, she managed a smile. "It's nice to meet you, sir."

"My great-grandfather," he repeated. "Steven Edward Cunningham, the Third."

"Cunningham?" Her throat snapped closed. "Steven Cunningham? Sweet Jesus."

"It's a great pleasure to welcome you into my house." Steven stepped back, blinking at tears. "Mary!" he shouted again. "Deaf as a post," he stated, "and she's forever turning her bloody hearing aid off. Run up and get her, Jack. I'll take Rebecca into the parlor. She's fussing with your room," he said as he led Rebecca away. "Been fussing since Jack called to say you were coming."

"Mr. Cunningham." Off balance, she walked blindly into a neat parlor where everything gleamed, and sank at his urging into the deep cushions of a wing-backed chair. "You're the same Steven Cunningham who . . . who was on the *Lusitania*?"

"The same as who owes his life to Felix Greenfield."

"And you're Jack's—"

"Great-grandfather. His mother's my granddaughter. And here we are. Here we are," he repeated and pulled a handkerchief from his pocket. "I'm sentimental in my old age."

"I don't know what to say to you. My head's spinning." She lifted a hand to her temple as if to hold it in place. "I've heard of you all my life. And somehow always thought of you as a little boy."

"I was just three when my parents made that crossing." He sighed deeply, then tucked the handkerchief away. "I can't be sure how much I actually remember, or how much I think I remember because my mother told me the story so often."

He walked over to a polished gateleg table crowded with framed photographs and lifted one, brought it to Rebecca. "My parents. It's their wedding photo."

She saw a handsome young man with a dashing mustache and a woman, hardly more than a girl, glorious in silk and lace and her bridal glow.

"They're beautiful." Tears threatened to spill. "Oh, Mr. Cunningham."

"My mother lived another sixty-three years, thanks to Felix Greenfield." Steven took his handkerchief out again and gently pressed it into Rebecca's hand. "She never remarried. For some there's only one love in a lifetime. But she was content, and she was productive, and she was grateful."

"The story's true, then." Composing herself, she handed him the photograph.

"I'm proof of that." He turned at the sound of footsteps on the stairs. "Here comes Jack with my Mary. When she's done fussing over you, we'll talk about it."

MARY CUNNINGHAM WAS indeed deaf as a post, but in honor of the occasion, she turned her hearing aid on. Rebecca was given a lovely room with fresh flowers in china vases and invited to rest or freshen up before supper.

She did neither, but simply sat on the side of the bed hoping her mind would settle. It was Jack who knocked on her door fifteen minutes later. Rebecca stayed where she was and studied him.

"Why didn't you tell me?"

"I thought it would mean more this way. It did to him, and that matters to me."

She nodded. "I think in my heart, I always believed it happened just as I'd been told. But in my head, I wasn't so sure. I want to thank you for bringing me here, for giving me this."

He crossed over, crouched in front of her. "Do you believe in connections, Rebecca? In the power of them, even the inevitability of them?"

"I'd have to, wouldn't I?"

"I'm not a sentimental man," he began, but she laughed and shook her head.

"I saw you with Steven, then with Mary, so don't tell me you're not sentimental."

"About people who matter to me, but not about things. I don't romanticize." He took her hand, felt her brace. "I looked at you. That's really all it took."

"It's confusing." She managed to keep her voice steady, though her heart was humming in her throat. "This maze of circumstances that links our families."

"It's more than that."

"I'd like to keep things simple."

"Not a chance," he told her as he drew her to her feet. "Besides, I like complications. Life's bland without them. You're a hell of a complication."

"Don't." She pressed a hand to his chest as he pulled her closer, and felt like an idiot. "I'm not being coy, I'm being careful."

"You're trembling."

"Oh, you enjoy that, don't you? Getting me all stirred up and confused."

"Damn right." He gave her one hard tug. It brought her to her toes, had her sucking in a breath for an oath. Then his mouth was on hers, hard and hot and hungry enough to blur the curse into a small sound of shock.

He kissed like a man accustomed to taking, with a ruthless skill that had her pulse pumping fast and her belly quivering with need. Though the reaction stupefied her, she felt her own bones go liquid.

And so did he.

His hands dived into her hair, used it to draw her head back. "The first time I saw you," he said. "That's never happened to me before."

"I don't know you." But her lips were warm with the taste of his, her body primed for the weight of him. "I don't sleep with men I don't know."

He lowered his head, skimmed his teeth lightly over her throat. "Is that a firm policy?"

"It used to be."

He nipped his way along her jaw. "We're going to get to know each other very quickly."

"All right. That's all right. Don't kiss me again now. It isn't proper, not with them downstairs this way, Jack. They're waiting supper for us."

"Then we'll go down."


THEY SETTLED IN the small dining room made charming with china figures and antique glass. The walls were decorated with a collection of old, floral-patterned plates.

"You have such a lovely home," Rebecca complimented Mary. "It's so nice of you to let me come."

"It's a treat for us." Mary beamed and helpfully cocked her ear in Rebecca's direction. "Jack never brings his girls to see us."

"Doesn't he?"

"No, indeed." She had the soft music of Ireland in her voice. "We only met the one he married twice, and once was at the wedding. We didn't like her very much, did we, Steven?"

"Now, Mary."

"Well, we didn't. She had a cold streak, if you ask me, and—"

"The roast is perfect, Gram."

Distracted, Mary sent Jack a twinkling look. "You always favored my pot roast."

"I married you for it," Steven said with a wink. "Like a lot of young men, I did the Grand Tour when I was done with university," he told Rebecca. "Outside of Dublin, I stayed at a small inn and met my Mary, whose parents ran it. I fell in love with her over pot roast, and ended my tour then and there. It took me two weeks to convince her to marry me and move back to Bath."

"You exaggerate. It took you only ten days."

"And we've been married now sixty-eight years. We lived in America for a time. In New York. My father's family had fallen on very hard times. They'd never recovered from the crash of 'twenty-nine. One of my daughters married an American and settled there. It's her daughter who's Jack's mother."

He reached over to lay his hand over Mary's. "We've had four children, two sons and two daughters. They gave us eleven grandchildren, and they six great-grandchildren and counting. Every one of them owes their life to Felix Greenfield. That one unselfish and courageous act set the rest in motion."

"He didn't intend it. The way it's been told in my family," Rebecca explained. "He only wanted to live, to survive. He was panicked when he found the life jacket. He thought only of saving himself, then he saw your mother, and you, trapped in the debris. He said she was so calm, so beautiful in the midst of all the horror. And she held you close to comfort you, and you her, without even crying for all you were just a little thing. And he couldn't turn away."

"I remember his face," Steven said. "Dark eyes, white skin already smeared with smoke or soot. My father was gone. I didn't see it happen, or don't remember. That she'd never speak of. But we fell when the ship lurched. She was carrying me, and we fell. She twisted herself to keep me from hitting the deck. She always had a limp when she tired after that."

"She was a brave and wonderful woman," Rebecca said.

"Oh, she was. And I think her courage met Felix Greenfield's that day. The ship was sinking, and the deck tilting higher and higher. He pulled her up it, trying to get us to one of the lifeboats. But the boat lurched again, and though he tried to reach us—I see his face even now as he called out and tried to get to her—we fell into the water.

Without the life jacket he'd given us, we wouldn't have had a prayer."

"Even with it, it's a miracle. He said she was hurt."

"She broke her arm shielding me as we went into the water, and as I said, she'd already badly twisted her leg. She wouldn't let me go. I had barely a scratch. The miracle," he said, "was my mother and Felix Greenfield. Because of them, you could say the thread of my life has been long and productive."

When Rebecca stared, Jack lifted his water glass. "Which brings us to the Fates. Did I tell you my great-great-grandfather had a small antique shop in Bath?"

A chill ran over Rebecca's skin. "You didn't mention it, no."

"Yes, indeed." Steven polished off his roast beef. "Inherited it from my grandfather. We were going to visit my mother's parents there. My grandmother wasn't well. After my father was lost, we stayed in Bath rather than returning to New York. Because of that I developed quite an interest in antiques and made my own living through them, in the same shop my grandfather had. Another twist of fate that owes its run to Felix."

He crossed his knife and fork tidily over his plate. "I can't tell you how fascinated I was when Jack told me Felix stole one of the Three Fates from Henry Wyley's stateroom just before he saved my life. Mary dear, are we going to have that apple pie in the parlor?"

"Never can wait for his pie. Go on and settle in, then, I'll bring it along shortly."

Questions were tripping over her tongue, but her mother had drummed manners into her. "I'll help you clear, Mrs. Cunningham."

"Oh, there's no need."

"Please, I'd like to help."

Mary shot Jack an arched look as everyone got to their feet. "The one you married never offered to clear a dish, to my recollection."

While the dishes were seen to, Rebecca was treated to a full rundown of Jack's ex-wife. She'd been beautiful, brainy and blond. An American lawyer who, according to Mary, worried more about her career than hearth and home. They'd taken their time marrying and had divorced, in her opinion, in a finger snap and without even the heart for battling over it.

Rebecca made appropriate noises and filed the information away. She was interested; in fact, she was dying to know everything. But she couldn't juggle the matter in her brain with thoughts of the Fates.

She wheeled in the dessert tray herself and held back the barrage of questions that raced through her mind.

"This one's been raised right," Mary said with approval. "Your mother must be a fine woman."

"She is, thank you."

"Now, if the two of you don't finish what you've started and give this poor child the rest of it, I'll do it myself."

"Connections," Jack said. "We've talked about them, haven't we, Rebecca?"

"We have."

"The little shop in Bath was called Browne's. It was established in the early eighteen hundreds and catered, for a number of years, to the gentry who came to Bath for the waters. Often, its clientele were those who needed to liquidate possessions into cash, discreetly. So its stock was varied and often unique. While discreet, it was a carefully run business, and records were meticulously kept. According to them, in the summer of 1883, a certain Lord Barlow sold a number of trinkets and artifacts to Browne's. Among them was a small silver statue, Grecian style, of a woman holding a pair of scissors."

"Holy Mary, Mother of God."

"My grandfather was proprietor of Browne's when Wyley made his last crossing," Steven continued. "I have no way of knowing if he'd been in touch with my grandfather regarding the Fate. I first learned of them when I was a young man, enthusiastically studying my trade. I was interested in the legend of the statue and whether or not the one Browne's had purchased so long before had been authentic. When I heard that Wyley had owned one of the

THREE FATES    217

set, and had, by all accounts, taken it with him on the ship, I was more fascinated."

"But even if the statue Browne's had bought was authentic," Jack put in, "its value was diminished as the first Fate was, by all accounts, lost along with Wyley. So what was left was an intriguing connection to another *Lusitania* passenger, and a piece of a legend."

"Was it real? Where is it now?" Rebecca demanded.

"My mother never tires of family history." Rather than answering, Jack rose to put another log on the parlor fire. "I was raised on it, and the sinking of the *Lusitania,* the legend of the Fates were part of all that. And, I came by my own interest in antiques naturally," he added, laying a hand on Steven's shoulder. "When Anita mentioned the Fates, it stirred my interest in them again, enough that I phoned my mother and asked her to confirm the stories she'd told me. Enough for me to arrange for an overdue visit here, with a stop in Cobh to check out Sullivan and pay my respects to Felix Greenfield."

He crossed to a satinwood display cabinet, opened it. "Imagine my surprise when I discovered the Sullivans were just one more connection, to this."

He turned and held up the third Fate.

"It's here." Though her legs felt like rubber, Rebecca rose. "It's been here all along."

"Where it's been," he said as he held it out for her, "since Granddad closed the doors of Browne's twenty-six years ago."

She held it in her cupped hand, testing the weight, studying the cool, almost sorrowful silver face. Gently, she ran her thumb over the shallow notch in the right corner of the base. Where, Rebecca knew, Atropus would link with Lachesis.

"Another thread, another circle. What will you do now?"

"Now, I take it with me back to New York, negotiate with Cleo Toliver for hers, then figure out how to get yours back from Anita."

"It's good you remember the first is mine." She gave the statue back to him. "I'll be going to New York as well."

"You'll be going back to Cobh," he corrected. "And staying an ocean away from Anita."

She angled her head. "I'll be going to New York, with you, or on my own, for I'm damned if you or my brothers will finish this off without me. You'd best resign yourself, Jack, that I won't be tucked in a corner to wait while the men do the work. I pull my own weight."

"There now." Mary cut her husband a second slice of pie. "What did I tell you? I like this one much better than the one you married, Jack. Sit down and finish your pie, Rebecca. Of course you're going with him to New York."

Her expression was smug as Rebecca turned away and sat. She forked up a bite of pie. "Thank you, Mrs. Cunningham. I wonder if I should stop in Dublin and buy some clothes for the trip, or wait and buy some things in New York. I've only packed one change of clothes."

"Oh, I'd wait if you can. You'll have such a fine time shopping in New York, won't you?"

"It's not a damn vacation," Jack snapped.

"Don't interrupt your Gram," Rebecca said mildly.

"Let it go, boy." Steven waved a hand. "You're outnumbered."

# Fifteen

MALACHI knew exactly how he would handle Tia, from his initial greeting, to his overall tone of approach. He would apologize again, of course. There was no question about that. And he would use all the charm and persuasion at his disposal to soften her stance toward him.

He owed her; there was no question of that either. For the financial backing, but more, much more, for the help she'd given his brother.

That he could repay by keeping their association completely professional, friendly but reserved. He thought he understood her well enough to know that was the way she'd prefer it.

Once they were on the proper footing again, they would get down to business.

He and Gideon would move into a hotel. Naturally they couldn't continue to impose on her privacy. But he hoped he could convince her to allow the Toliver woman to stay. In that way, he'd be assured they were both safe. And, almost as important, that they were out of his way.

A bit worn from the trip, he knocked briskly on her apartment door. And hoped her sense of hospitality would run to a cold beer.

Then she opened the door, and he forgot the beer and his carefully outlined approach.

"You've cut your hair." Without thinking, he reached out to dance his fingers over the short ends of it. "Just look at you."

She didn't jerk back. That was the willpower she'd been working on for hours. But she stepped back, stiffly. "Come in, Malachi. Set your bags down," she invited. "I hope your flight went well."

"It was fine. It suits you, you know. The hair. You look wonderful. I missed seeing you, Tia."

"Do you want a drink?"

"I would, please. I'm sorry, I haven't even thanked you for fronting me the means to fly over."

"It's business." She turned and walked into the kitchen.

"You've changed more than your hair."

"Maybe." Assuming he'd prefer a beer, as his brother did, she pulled one out of the refrigerator, shifted to get a glass from the cupboard. "Maybe I've had to."

"I'm sorry, Tia, for the way I handled things."

Proud of herself, she popped the top of the beer and poured it into the glass without the slightest tremor in her hand. "The way you handled me, you mean."

"Yes. I could make excuses for it." He took the glass she held out to him. Waited for her gaze to meet and hold his. "I could even make you accept them, but I won't bother. I regret lying to you more than I can tell you."

"There's no point in hashing it over at this stage." She started to walk back into the living room and stopped when he stepped over to block her.

"It wasn't all a lie."

Though her color came up, her voice was cool and brisk. "There's no point in discussing that either. We have a mutual interest, and a mutual claim, on a particular piece of art. I intend to use my resources, and yours, to get it back. That's àll there is to discuss."

"You're making it easier on me."

"Oh?" She cocked her head to what she hoped was a sarcastic angle. "How?"

"By not being vulnerable, I don't have to worry so much about bruising you."

"I had thin skin once. That doesn't seem to be one of my problems anymore. Now, house rules." This time she skirted quickly around him and began to breathe easier as soon as she had some distance. "No smoking in the apartment. You can use the terrace or, as Gideon is just now, the roof. He and Cleo had a good case of cabin fever working up, so I suggested they use the roof for a while. It's not as confining as the terrace, and it's safe."

He started to tell her he and his brother would go to a hotel, then changed his mind. If she wasn't bothered, why should he be?

"I quit smoking two years ago, so it's not a problem for me."

"Good, you'll live longer. You clean up after yourself, and that includes dishes, laundry, papers, whatever. I like a tidy space. You'll have to sleep on the couch, as Gideon and Cleo have the spare bed. That means you'll have to be prepared to get up at a reasonable hour in the morning."

Because she was starting to sound more like Tia, he began to enjoy himself and sat on the arm of the couch. "What's reasonable?"

"Seven."

"Ouch."

"You and Gideon will have to work out a shower schedule. You'll have use of the small bathroom. Cleo can share mine, but it and my bedroom are off limits to you and your brother. Clear enough?"

"Crystal, darling."

"I'm keeping a record of expenses. The flight, of course, and food, any other transportation. You will pay me back."

That irritated him enough to have him push to his feet. "We fully intend to pay you back. We're not leeches. I can get a bank loan and clear it up straightaway."

Feeling small, she turned away. "That's not necessary. I'm angry with you. I can't help it."

"Tia—"

"Don't." Alerted by the gentle tone, she whirled back.

"Don't *soothe* me. I can be angry with you and do what needs to be done. I'm very good at working around unstable emotions. Now, do you cook?"

He raked a hand through his hair. "After a fashion."

"Good, Cleo doesn't. That leaves you, Gideon, me and takeout. Now we can—" She broke off, glancing over as she heard the key in the lock.

Cleo came in first, looking a bit sweaty, outrageously sexy and suspiciously rumpled. Her smile was slow and considering as she sized up Malachi. "So, this must be big brother."

"Mal." Gideon strode in behind her, and the two men caught each other in a hard, unself-conscious hug. "It's good to see you. We've got a fucking mess on our hands."

It took thirty minutes, and another beer, to bring him up to date.

"I don't see what business this Burdett has sticking his nose in it." Malachi brooded into his second beer, then got up to pace. "It just adds another complication."

"If he hadn't stuck his nose in, I wouldn't know my phones are tapped, would I?" Tia rose, picked up the glass Malachi had set down and put a coaster under it.

"He *says* they're tapped."

"Why would he make it up? In any case, I went to see my father this morning and asked him about Jack. My father confirms who he is, and that he's a serious collector. And the police detective vouched for him."

"You're just pissed off because there's another guy in the mix." Cleo fluttered her lashes and took a sip of Gideon's beer when Malachi turned to scowl at her. "It's the testosterone thing, and nobody blames you for it. Tia, you got any cookies in here?"

"Um, I think I have some sugarless wafers."

"Honey, we really need to talk. Life should never be about sugarless wafers. Now, before you climb up my ass," she said to Malachi, "remember we've had a little more time to think about Burdett and his place in all this. He knows Anita," she continued, ticking off the points on her fingers. "He knows security, and he's interested in the Fates. We hope to sell mine, and the third when we get it.

The way I see it, you've got two potential buyers now instead of one. We can have our own private auction."

"I might not like having another player in the game," Gideon put in, "but it makes sense, Mal. Anita's been tracking us right along. Could be this Burdett helps us with that end. And Tia's father says how he's got money, so we sell to him. I'd rather that than have any more dealings with that bitch Anita. Besides all this, I called Ma from the pay phone down the street to check in, and she's met him. She trusts him, and that's enough for me."

"I'll decide that for myself. You said he left you a business card, Tia?" Malachi drummed his fingers on his thigh as he worked out the details in his mind. "I'll ring him up and have a meeting with him, face-to-face. And if he's such a bloody security expert, he can fix these damn phones so we're not running down to a phone box every time we turn around."

"You need some carbs," Cleo decided. "You got carbs around here, right?"

"Ah . . ." Tia glanced nervously toward her kitchen. "Yes, I—"

"Don't worry. I'll root around. I get pissy when my carbs are low," she said sympathetically to Malachi.

"I'm not being pissy."

She unfolded herself and walked over to pinch his cheeks. "Since we're the ones you're pissing on, handsome, we should know. You Sullivans don't travel very well. Slick there was ragged out when we got here, too. You're pretty, aren't you?" She cocked her head. "You guys have some superior DNA."

She teased a laugh out of him. "You're quite the package, aren't you?"

"Damn right. Hey, Tia, let's just order some pizza. Couple larges with the works ought to do it."

"I don't really eat—" She broke off when Cleo turned and gaped at her.

"If you're about to tell me you don't eat pizza, I'm getting a gun and putting you out of your misery."

It didn't seem the time to discuss fat grams, or the fact that she suspected she might be allergic to tomato sauce.

"If the phones are tapped and I order two large pizzas, isn't that going to seem strange to whoever's listening since I'm supposed to be here alone?"

"So, they'll think you're a greedy pig. Let's live dangerously."

"And besides, I have a two o'clock lunch appointment, which I should be leaving for right now."

"Who are you meeting?" Malachi asked as she walked into the bedroom. "Tia?"

"Bedroom's off limits," Gideon muttered before his brother could follow. "She's very strict about it."

"She's not acting like herself." He jammed his hands in his pockets and frowned at the bedroom door. "I don't know as I like it."

"Figuring on what's been going on around here the past couple of days, you could cut her a break. She took us in," Cleo reminded him. "She sure as hell didn't have to. You messed with her head. Hold on." She held up a hand when he spun around and snarled. "I'm not saying I wouldn't have played it the same way, but when you've already got low-self-esteem issues, having a guy fuck with you can really screw you up."

"That's quite an analysis in a short order."

"You dance naked for a few months, you learn a lot about people." She shrugged. "We're going to like each other fine after we get to know each other better, sweetheart. I already like your baby brother, and your taste in women," she added, nodding toward the bedroom door.

"Later you can explain to me how dancing naked turns you into a psychologist, but for now . . ." Malachi banged a fist on the bedroom door. "Tia, where the devil are you going?"

The door opened, and she hurried out. He caught the drift of the perfume she'd just sprayed on. She'd painted her lips as well, and slipped into a streamlined black blazer. A small and unwelcome curl of jealousy formed in his gut. "Who are you meeting for lunch?"

"Anita Gaye." She opened her purse to check the contents. "I can call the pizza in from a phone booth on the way."

"Cool. Thanks. Great jacket," Cleo commented.

"Really? It's new. I wasn't sure if . . . well, it doesn't matter. I should be back by four or four-thirty."

"Just one bloody minute." Malachi beat her to the door, slammed a hand on it. "If you think I'm having you walk out of here and have lunch with a woman we know hires killers, you've lost your fucking mind."

"Don't swear at me, and don't tell me what you'll have me do." Nerves hopped in her stomach and urged her to shrink back, but she held her ground. "You're not in charge of me, or of this . . . consortium," she decided. "Now move aside. I'm going to be late."

"Tia." Since anger didn't work, he switched smoothly to charm. "I'd be worried about you, is all. She's a dangerous woman. We all know how dangerous now."

"And I'm weak and foolish and out of my league."

"Yes. No. Oh, Christ." He held up a hand, though he was tempted to strangle her, or himself, with it. "Just tell me what you're trying to do here."

"Have lunch. She called and asked me. I agreed. I assume she thinks she can pump some information out of me regarding the Fates and Henry Wyley. And you. I'm perfectly aware of her agenda, as she's never spoken above twenty words to me before in her life. However, she isn't and won't be aware of mine. I'm not the moron you think I am, Malachi."

"I don't think that of you. Tia—" He bit back an oath when he noted neither Cleo nor his brother had the courtesy to pretend they weren't listening. "Let's go up on the roof and talk about this."

"No. Now, unless you plan to wrestle me to the ground and tie me in a closet, I'm going out to have lunch."

"Atta girl, Tia," Cleo said under her breath and earned an elbow in the ribs from Gideon.

"Mal," Gideon said quietly, "ease back now."

When he did, Tia wrenched open the door.

"Don't forget the pizza," Cleo called out just before Tia slammed it in Malachi's face.

"If that woman hurts her—"

"What's she going to do?" Cleo demanded. "Stab Tia

with her salad fork? Cool your jets a minute and think. This is smart. Odds are Anita thinks Tia's a dork, when *she's* the one who'll be out of her league. Smart money says Tia comes back with a lot of information, while Anita slinks off with nothing."

"She's bloody brilliant, Mal," Gideon confirmed. "And we need her. You should relax."

"Right." But he knew he wouldn't until Tia came back.


EVEN WITH HER active fantasy life, Tia had never imagined herself as a kind of spy. Sort of a double agent, she decided as she arrived exactly on time for lunch. And all she had to do was be herself to pull it off. Shy, jittery, anal and boring, she thought as she was shown to her table.

Some secret agent.

Naturally Anita was late because, in Tia's experience, women who weren't shy, jittery, anal and boring were most often late for appointments. Because they had a life, she supposed.

Well, she sure as hell had a life now and still managed to be prompt.

She ordered mineral water and tried not to look conspicuous and, well, jittery, as she sat alone in the quiet elegance of Café Pierre, for the next ten minutes.

Anita swept in—there was really no other word for that stylish and urbanely rushed entrance—wearing a gorgeous suit the color of ripe eggplant and a spectacular necklace fashioned from complicatedly braided gold and chunks of amethyst.

"I'm so sorry I'm late. I hope you haven't been waiting long." She leaned down and air-kissed Tia's cheek before sliding into her chair and setting her cell phone beside her plate.

"No, I—"

"Trapped with a client and couldn't shake loose," Anita interrupted. "Vodka martini," she told the waiter. "Stoli, straight up, dry as dust, two olives." Then she sat back, let out the long breath of a woman about to decompress. "I'm so glad we could do this. I so rarely have the chance to have a non-business lunch these days. You look well, Tia."

"Thank you. You—"

"You've done something different, haven't you?" Anita pursed her lips, tapped her crimson fingertips on the table as she tried to put a clearer picture of Tia in her mind. "You've changed your hair. Very flattering. Men make such a to-do about long hair on a woman. I can't think why," she added, tossing back her own luxurious locks. "Now, tell me all about your travels. It must have been fascinating lecturing all over Europe. Tiring though. You look just exhausted. But you'll bounce back."

You're really a champion bitch, aren't you? Tia thought and sipped her water as Anita's martini was served. "It was a difficult and fascinating experience. You don't see as much of the world as you might think. You're in airports and hotels, and the lecture venues."

"But still, there are benefits. Did you meet that gorgeous Irishman you were dining with while you were traveling?"

"Actually, I did. He attended one of my lectures in Europe, then looked me up when he had business here in New York. He was awfully handsome, wasn't he?"

"Extremely. And he was interested in mythology?"

"Hmm." Tia picked up her menu, scanned her choices. "Yes, very much. Particularly in the groupings. The Sirens, the Muses, the Fates. Do you suppose I could get this grilled chicken salad without the pine nuts?"

"I'm sure. Are you still in touch with him?"

"With who?" Tia tipped down her menu, tipped down her reading glasses. Smiled vaguely. "Oh, with Malachi. No, he had to go back to Ireland. I thought he might call, but I suppose . . . It is three thousand miles, after all. Men don't generally call me after a date when they live in Brooklyn."

"Men are such pigs. The Amazons had the right idea. Use them for sex and propagation, then kill them." She laughed, then turned to the waiter when he stepped up to the table. "I'll have the Caesar salad, a mineral water and another martini."

"Um . . . do you use free-range chicken?" Tia began,

and deliberately turned the ordering of a simple salad into a major event. She caught Anita's smirk out of the corner of her eye and considered it a job well done.

"It's interesting, you talking about the Fates," Anita said.

"Was I?" Tia slipped off her glasses, put them carefully in their case. "I thought it was Amazons—though, of course, they weren't gods, or Greek. Still, they were a fascinating female culture, and I've always—"

"The Fates." Anita managed to polish off her first martini through clenched teeth.

"Oh yes. Female power again. Women, sisters, who determine the length and quality of life for gods and for men."

"With your interest, and your family background, you'd have heard of the statues."

"I've heard of a lot of statues. Oh!" Tia exclaimed innocently and swore she could hear Anita's teeth grinding. "The Three Fates. Yes, of course. In fact, one of my ancestors was reputed to have owned one—I think it was Clotho, the first Fate. But he died on the *Lusitania* and by all accounts had it with him. It's very sad if it's true. Lachesis and Atropus have nothing to measure and cut without Clotho to spin the thread. Then again, I know more about the myths than antiques. Do you think the statues exist? The other two, I mean."

"I suppose I'm romantic enough to hope they do. I thought someone with your knowledge, and your connections, might have some ideas."

"Gosh." Tia bit her lip. "I hardly ever paid any attention to that sort of thing. Which is what I told Malachi when we talked about it."

"He talked to you about the statues, then?"

"He was interested." Gingerly, Tia picked through the basket of warm bread and rolls. "He collects mythological art. Something he started doing on one of his business trips to Greece some years ago. He's in shipping."

"Is that so? A handsome, wealthy Irishman, with an interest in your field. And you haven't called *him*?"

"Oh, I couldn't." As if flustered, Tia stared down at the tablecloth and fiddled with the collar of her jacket. "I wouldn't feel comfortable calling a man. I never know what to say anyway. Besides, I think he was disappointed I couldn't give him any help with the Fates. The statues, that is. I was very helpful with the myths, if I do say so myself. And with one of them at the bottom of the Atlantic, they'd never be complete, would they?"

"No."

"I suppose if they were—complete, that is—they'd be quite valuable."

"Quite."

"If Henry Wyley hadn't taken that trip, at that time, on that ship, who knows? But then again, that's fate. Maybe you could find one of them, if they still exist or ever did. You must have all kinds of sources."

"I do, and I happen to have an interested client. I always hate to disappoint a client, so I'm doing what I can to verify their existence, and to track them down."

Anita nibbled delicately on a roll as she watched Tia. "I hope you won't mention that to—was it Malachi?—if he calls you again. I wouldn't like him to scoop me on this."

"I won't, but I don't think it'll be an issue." Tia put a lot of wind into her sigh. "I did tell him I'd heard, oh, some time ago, that someone in Athens claimed to have Atropus. That's the third Fate."

With her heart pounding at her own improvisation, Tia carefully studied her salad for flaws.

"In Athens?"

"Yes, I think someone spoke about it last fall. Or maybe it was last spring. I can't quite remember. I was doing some research on the Muses. Those are the nine daughters of Zeus and Mnemosyne. They each have their own specialty, such as Clio, who—"

"What about the Fates?" Anita demanded.

"What about the what? Oh." Tia laughed a little and sipped her water. "Sorry, I suppose I tend to run off on tangents. It's so irritating to people."

"Not at all." Anita imagined herself just leaning over and choking the boring twit to death over her salad. "But you were saying?"

"Yes, it must have been in the spring of last year." Face intent, she dribbled a stingy amount of dressing on her salad. "I really wasn't looking for information on the Fates, certainly not on the art pieces. I only paid attention to be polite. This source I contacted . . . what was his name? Well, it doesn't matter as he wasn't nearly as much help as I'd hoped. With the Muses, that is. But during the conversation he mentioned that he'd heard this person in Athens had Atropus. The statue, not the mythological figure."

"I don't suppose you remember the name of the person in Athens?"

"Oh my, I'm not good with names." With an apologetic glance at Anita, Tia forked up salad. "In fact, I don't think it came up at all, as it was just something mentioned in passing. And it was so long ago. I remember it was Athens only because I've always wanted to go there. Plus, it seemed logical that one of the statues would be there. In Greece. Have you ever been?"

"No." Anita shrugged. "Not yet."

"Neither have I. I don't think the food would agree with me."

"Did you mention this to Malachi?"

"About Athens? No, I don't think I did. It didn't occur to me. Oh my! Do you suppose I should have? Maybe, if I'd thought of it, he'd have called me again. He really was terribly handsome."

Idiot, Anita thought. Imbecile. "Anything's possible."


TIA FELT GIDDY. The way she imagined a woman might feel after committing adultery in a sleazy motel with a younger, unemployed artist while her stuffy, dependable husband presided over a board meeting.

But no, she decided as she quick-footed it into her apartment building, that sort of giddiness would come *before* the actual adultery, on the way to the sleazy, rent-by-the-hour motel. After, you'd feel guilty and ashamed and in need of a long shower.

Or so she imagined.

Still, she'd lied, deceived—and figuratively screwed someone—and she didn't feel guilty in the least. She felt powerful.

And she liked it.

Anita detested her. Did people think she couldn't tell when they found her boring and annoying and basically stupid? Well, it didn't matter, she assured herself as she rode, on a cloud of triumph, to her floor. It didn't matter in the least what a woman like Anita thought of her. Because she, Tia Marsh, had won the round.

She sailed into the apartment, prepared to crow, and found only Cleo, sprawled on the sofa watching MTV.

"Hey. How'd it go?"

"It went well. Where is everyone?"

"They went to call their mother. Irish guys have a real thing for their mothers, don't they? Then they're going to pick up some stuff—ice cream. They just took off a couple minutes ago."

Cleo glanced at the television screen before switching it off.

"So, what went down with Anita?" Cleo questioned.

"She thinks I'm a brainless neurotic who's grateful for any scrap of attention a real person tosses my way."

Cleo rolled off the couch—a fluid grace Tia admired hopelessly. "I don't. Not that it matters, but I think you're a smart, classy ass-kicker who just hasn't tried out her boots yet. Want a drink?"

The description had Tia gaping so that she didn't register being invited to drink in her own apartment. "Maybe. I don't really drink."

"I do, and this seems like the time for it. We'll chug down a glass of wine and you can fill me in."

Cleo opened a bottle of Pouilly-Fumé, poured two glasses. And listened. Somewhere during that first glass, Tia realized the only person who listened to her with the same focused interest was Carrie. Maybe, she thought, that's why they were friends.

"You sent her to Athens?" Cleo let out a hoot of laughter. "That's fucking brilliant."

"It just seemed . . . I guess it was."

"Damn right." Cleo shot up a hand, so fast and close, Tia's head jerked back as if to avoid a slap. "High five!"

"Oh. Well." With a giggle, Tia slapped palms.

"You're going to have to go through all this again with the boys," Cleo continued. "So since we've got this girl moment before they get back, give me the dish on Malachi."

"The dish?"

"Yeah. I know you're pissed at him, and personally if I were you I'd want to boil his balls for breakfast, but he's really gorgeous. How are you going to play him?"

"I'm not. I wouldn't know how, so I'm not. This is business."

"He's got a good case of the guilts over you. You could use that." Cleo dipped a finger into her wine, licked it off. "But it's not just guilt. He's got the hots for you, too. Guilty hots, that gives you some major power."

"He's not attracted to me that way. It's just pretense so I'll help."

"You're wrong. Listen, Tia, there's one thing I know. Men. I know how they look at a woman, how they move around a woman, and what's going on in their sex-obsessed brains when they do. That guy wants to slurp you up like soda pop, and since he's guilty for fucking with you, that makes him edgy, frustrated and stupid. You could have him sitting up and begging like a Labrador, you play your cards right."

"I don't have any cards," Tia began. "And I don't want to humiliate him." Then she thought of how she'd felt when she'd realized he'd lied to her. Used her. She took another sip of her wine. "Well, maybe I do. A little. But I don't think it's relevant. Men don't have the same urges about me as they do for women like you."

She stopped, appalled, and set down her glass. She should *not* drink. "I'm so sorry. I didn't mean to . . . I meant that as a compliment."

"Relax. I got it. You got more going on than you think. Brains, goofiness, repression."

"None of those sound very sexy."

"They're working just fine on big brother. Then you've got that dreamy wood-nymph look going for you."

"Wood nymph? Me?"

"Honey, you ought to look in the mirror more often. You're really hot."

"No, I'm really very comfortable . . ." She trailed off when Cleo collapsed in wild laughter. "Oh. *Hot.*" Laughing herself now, she peered closely at Cleo's face. "Are you drunk?"

"Nope, but I might work on that later." She leaned back. She didn't make friends easily, at least not with other women. But there was something about Tia.

"I always wanted to look like you," Tia blurted out.

"Me?"

"Tall and sultry and exotic. And built."

"We all work with what we got. And what you've got is making big brother's glands go loop-de-loop. Take my word. Listen." Cleo leaned closer. "When they get back, I'm going to drop a little bombshell. Slick's not going to like it, and big brother's already looking at me sideways. I could use some help. Support, a distraction, whatever you've got."

"What is it?"

Cleo started to speak, then heard the key in the lock. Tia saw something move over her face that might have been grief, might have been regret. Then she tossed back the last of her wine. "Countdown," she mumbled.


"ATHENS?" GIDEON BROKE into a delighted, almost demented grin. "Athens?" he repeated and plucked Tia out of her chair, kissed her enthusiastically on the mouth. "You're a bloody genius."

"I, uh . . . Well." Her ears buzzed. "Thanks."

"A bloody genius," he said again, and swung her in a quick circle before he shot that grin at his brother. "And you were worried Anita would gobble her down like lunch. We've a certified mastermind here."

"Set her down, Gideon, before you bruise her. That was clever," Malachi said to Tia. "Clever and quick."

"It was logical," she corrected and, with her head spinning just a bit, and rather pleasantly, sat again. "I don't know if she'll actually go to Greece, but she'll certainly look there."

"It gives us some breathing space," Malachi agreed. "Now what do we do with it? Rebecca's doing what she does to get background information on this Jack Burdett. We'll leave that, and him, to her for now. Seems the first thing, logically speaking, is to figure out how Cleo's to get the White-Smythe Fate. We'll want to do that quietly, without putting Anita on the scent, then get it into a safe, secure place."

"That's not a problem." Cleo didn't take a deep breath, but she did brace herself, did shift her gaze until she met Gideon's directly. "I've already got it, and it's already in one."

# Sixteen

"You had it all along?" Shell-shocked and with temper just starting to bubble beneath, Gideon stared at Cleo. "From the beginning?"

"My grandmother gave it to me when I was a kid." She felt the bats beating wings in her stomach. "She'd started to get pretty spacey, so I guess she didn't think of it as more than a kind of doll. It's been like my good-luck piece. It went where I went."

"You had it in Prague."

"Yeah, I had it." Because the steady, quiet tone of his voice made her feel a little sick, she poured another glass of wine.

"I never heard the story. The Three Fates deal. If that part of it ever came down through my mother's family, it didn't get as far as me. I didn't know what it was until you told me about it."

"And wasn't it lucky for you I came along and educated you?"

She decided the bitter edge of the words, delivered with just the perfect dip of contempt, was as effective as a jab in the gut. "Look, Slick, some guy chases me down at work, starts asking about my good-luck charm, gives me the song and dance about big money and Greek legends, I'm not handing it over to him on a platter. I didn't know you."

"Got to know me, didn't you?" He leaned over, clamping his hands on the arms of her chair, caging her in with his body. "Or do you make a habit of rolling around on a hotel floor with strangers?"

"Gideon."

"This isn't for you." He whipped his head around, flicked the keen edge of his fury over his brother to silence any interference. Then snapped it back to Cleo.

"You knew me well enough for that. You knew me well enough, didn't you, when we shared the bed Mikey gave us hours before he died."

"That's enough." Though her hands were ice cold with fear, Tia used them to pull on Gideon's arm. It was, she realized, like trying to pry open a steel wall with her fingers. "He was her friend. She loved him. However angry you are, you know that, and you know you haven't the right to use him to hurt her."

"She used him. And me."

"You're right." Cleo lifted her chin, not in defiance but in a kind of invitation. Punch me, she seemed to say, I'd prefer it. "You couldn't be more right. I overestimated myself, underestimated Anita. And Mikey's dead. However much disgust and rage you've got working in you for me right now, it doesn't touch what I've got for myself."

"It might come closer than you think." He shoved himself away from her.

"Okay." Something inside her broke, something she hadn't realized was there to be damaged. "Okay. I screwed up with you. I figured I'd cut a deal with Anita, take the money and hand you your share. Everybody's happy. I figured, well, he'll be a little pissed I did it behind his back, but when he's got all that green in his hands, how can he complain?"

When he turned back, violence shimmering almost visibly around him, Tia stepped between them. "Stop. Think. What she did made sense. If she'd been dealing with a normal businesswoman, even a dishonest one, it made sense. None of us could have predicted how far Anita would go."

"What she did was lie." He ignored Tia's tugging hand. "To all of us."

"It started with lies." Tia's voice had just enough punch behind it to have Gideon glancing at her. "Trust and full disclosure's been the main problem here all along. We're all splintered in different directions, with different goals. Different agendas. And as long as we stay that way, Anita has the advantage. She has one direction, and one goal. Unless we agree on ours, she's going to win."

"That's right." Malachi laid a hand on Tia's shoulder, and though she stiffened, she didn't pull away. "I'm no more pleased about how we got to this point than any of the rest of us. We all, well, all but Tia here, have reasons for regrets. We can stew about them. Or we can punch a few walls. Gid."

His voice gentled and he waited until his brother turned those angry eyes on him. "Remember the punching bag Da set up at the boatyard? We called it Nigel," he said to the women. "And we beat hell out of it instead of each other. Most of the time."

"We're not boys now."

"We're not, no. So instead of sulking off, or finding a handy Nigel, why don't we start from here? The good news is we have the second Fate. And where might this bank be, Cleo?"

"Over on Seventh." She dug into her jeans pocket for the key she'd put there that morning. "I have to get it. I have to sign and show ID to get into the box. I can do it in the morning."

"*We'll* do it in the morning," Gideon corrected. "Right now I want some air. I'm going up to the roof."

Cleo sat where she was when the door slammed behind him. Then as the shards of what had broken inside her stabbed, she got to her feet. "That went real well." Appalled that her voice broke, she bore down. "I'm going to take a nap."

When the office door shut behind her, Tia pushed her

hands through her hair. "Oh boy. I never know what to do. I never know what to say."

"You did and said exactly right. Stop shoving yourself down, Tia. It's irritating."

"Well, pardon me. I'm going to go see if I can help Cleo."

"No, that's the easy way." With a small sigh, he touched her shoulder again. "I'll go talk to Cleo, you try Gideon. Let's see if we can make this mess we've created into some sort of unit."

He started for the office door, then turned. "You were brilliant with Anita," he said, then knocked briskly and opened the door without waiting for an invitation.

Cleo lay on her back, on the unmade pullout. She wasn't crying, but she knew she was working up to a good, explosive jag. "Look, I've had enough of the Sullivan brothers for this act. Let's consider this intermission."

"That's too bad because the show's not over." He lifted her feet, sat, then dropped them into his lap. "And because this Sullivan brother is willing to admit he might have done exactly as you did. I wouldn't be proud of it, would look back from here and see all the places where I went wrong, when I should've turned right instead of left. But that wouldn't change a fucking thing, would it?"

"Are you being nice to me so I'll cooperate? Go, team, go?"

"That'd be a nice benefit, but the fact is, you've had a hell of a time, and I'm part of the reason why. Gideon now, he's not as devious-natured as you and me. Not that he's a doormat or a fool, but he's more inclined to say what he thinks and is often annoyed everyone doesn't do the same. He has a refined sense of fair play, our boy."

Knowing it, hearing Malachi say it, didn't go far toward mollifying her. "People who play fair mostly lose."

"Don't they just?" He laughed a little and began to rub her feet in a friendly way. "But when they win, they win clean. That matters to him. You matter to him."

"Maybe *did* matter."

"Matter still, darling. I know my brother, so I know that.

But not knowing you so well, I have to ask. Does he matter to you?"

She tried to tug her foot out of his hand, but he held it firmly, kept on rubbing. "I wasn't trying to screw him out of the money."

"That wasn't my question. Does he matter to you?"

"Yeah, I guess he does."

"Then I'll give you a piece of advice. Fight back. Use shouts and oaths until you've burned him out, temper-wise. Or use tears and drown it. Either works with him."

She shoved a second pillow under her head. "That's going back to devious, isn't it?"

"Well." He patted her foot. "Do you want to win or lose?"

The crying jag had backed off, enough for her to sit up, sniffle once and study him. "I wasn't sure I'd like you. It's handy, all things considered, that I do."

"That's mutual. So tell me, as it's a subject that's been preying on my mind. Do most of the women who work as strippers have the body God gave them, or what medical science can provide?"

TIA WASN'T HAVING as much luck with Gideon. For a time, she just sat quietly in one of the little iron chairs in the roof garden. She rarely came up here, as she didn't trust the air or the height. Which was a pity, she thought, as she so loved the view of the river.

As she was a woman accustomed to being ignored, she sat while Gideon stood at the stone rail, smoking and brooding in silence.

"We spent days and nights together, running all over goddamn Europe, and she had it in that fucking purse of hers all along."

Okay, Tia mused, he speaks. That was a start. "It belongs to her, Gideon."

"That's not the point." He spun around, ridiculously handsome, Tia thought, wrapped in his fury. "Did she think I'd cosh her on the head and steal it from her? Sneak out with it in the night after making love with her and leave her in some ugly room alone?"

"I can't answer that. I wouldn't have had the nerve to go with you in the first place, or the presence of mind to protect myself—which is what she did. I . . . this is going to sound sexist, but it's different for a man to go running around Europe with a woman than it is for that woman to go running around with a man. It's riskier and it's scarier. It just is."

"I won't argue that, but we weren't together a week when . . . things changed between us."

"Sex is, in some ways, another scary risk." She felt heat sting her cheeks as he frowned at her now. "If it had been a matter of using you—which is what you're thinking—she'd have been the one to sneak out with Lachesis in the night. Instead she brought you here."

"Then went behind my back and—"

"Made a mistake," Tia finished. "One that cost her more than it cost you. You and I know what shape she was in when you brought her here. We're the only ones who know that. And maybe I'm the only one who could see how you were with her. How gentle and kind. How loving."

He made a short, rude sound and crushed the cigarette under his heel. "She was drunk and sick because I made her that way. What was I supposed to do? Shove her about?"

"You took care of her. And when I heard her wake up crying in the middle of the night, you took care of her again. She was probably too tangled up in her own grief to know that. I've never been in love," she said, taking a few cautious steps toward him, and the wall. And the drop. "So I could be wrong thinking that you're in love with her. But I know what it is to have feelings for someone stirred up, then be hurt by them."

"Mal's sick over that, Tia." He took her hand, not realizing her instinctive resistance was for the height and not for the gesture. "I promise you."

"This isn't about that. I'm just saying that when you're not so mad, or so hurt, you should try to look at it from her side. Or if you can't, at least resolve yourself enough so we can work together."

"We'll work together," he promised. "I'll deal with the rest of it."

"Good. Good." Why was it people nervous about heights couldn't resist looking down from tall buildings? she wondered. Compelled, she stared down at the street until her head spun. She managed a shaky step back, then another. "Whew. Vertigo."

"Steady now." He took her arm when she swayed. "You're fine."

"I guess I will be. More or less."

CLEO DIDN'T HAVE a chance to try out Malachi's advice. It was hard to fight—words or tears—with someone who avoided you as if you carried the plague. It was hard to have a showdown with a man who'd rather spend the night sleeping on the roof of an apartment building in New York than share a corner of the bed with you.

It hurt, in parts of her she hadn't known she had to hurt. And was worse because she was afraid she deserved it.

"Go there, get it, come back," Malachi repeated as a gritty-eyed Gideon gulped down a second cup of morning coffee.

"So you've said already."

"Best not to take a straight route either way. The bank's near enough . . . the other flat," Malachi decided, with a glance at Cleo. "She might have people watching that general area yet."

"We kept these guys off our asses all over Europe." Gideon set his empty cup on the counter, then, at Tia's meaningful clearing of the throat, picked it up again and rinsed it out in the sink. "We can handle this."

"Just watch your back. And the rest of you as well."

Gideon nodded. "Ready?" he asked Cleo.

"Sure."

Tia linked her fingers together, barely resisted wringing them when Gideon and Cleo walked out her door. "You don't need to worry about them," she said as much to herself as Malachi.

"No. They can handle themselves all right." But he stuck his hands in his pockets and wished, passionately, he hadn't given up smoking. "It'll be good to see it, have a good look at it. Be sure it's authentic."

"Yes. Meanwhile, I have a lot of work to catch up on."

"This is the first time we've been alone, really. There are things I'd like to say."

"You've said them."

"Not all of them. Not things I thought of after you'd given me the boot."

"They're not applicable now. I haven't been able to work on my book for days. I'm behind schedule. You can watch television, listen to the radio, read a book. Or go up and jump off the roof. It's all the same to me."

"I appreciate the ability to hold a grudge." He moved, smoothly, into her path as she started toward her office. "I've told you I'm sorry. I've told you I was wrong, and that hasn't budged you a bit. So why not listen to the rest of it?"

"Let's see . . . could it be that I'm not interested? Yes, that could be it." She enjoyed hearing the sarcasm in her own voice. It made her feel in charge. "The personal portion of this relationship is over."

"I disagree with that."

He took a step toward her; she took one back.

And the retreat, however slight, made her feel vulnerable all over again. "You want to argue about it?" She shrugged, trying to put a little Cleo into it. "I'm not very good at arguing, but in the interest of putting this aside once and for all, I'll do my best. You treated me like a fool, and worse than that, you made sure I believed you found me attractive, even desirable. And that, Malachi, is contemptible."

"It would be, right enough, if it were true. The fact is I did find you attractive and desirable, and that was a major dilemma for me." He watched irritation cross her face. Irritation he knew was rooted in disbelief. So he ignored it. "And so I made my first of several mistakes. Do you know what started me on that series of mistakes where you're concerned?"

"No. And I don't care. I'm getting a headache."

"You're not. You're hoping you get a headache so you'll have something else to think about. It was your voice."

"I beg your pardon?"

"Your voice. When I was sitting in that auditorium, and your voice was so pretty, just a little nervous around the edges at first, then it got stronger. Such a nice, flowing voice. I admit I was bored witless about what you were saying, but I liked hearing you say it nonetheless."

"I don't see what that—"

"And there were your legs." He wasn't stopping now, not when he could see the nerves tangling up with her temper. "I passed the time listening to your voice and admiring your legs."

"That's ridiculous."

Ah, he considered. Now she was flustered, and flustered was better than irritated, better than nervous. Because a flustered Tia wouldn't be able to stop him from saying things he so much needed to say. "But that wasn't the main thing. I liked how shy and tired and confused you seemed when I came up to you with my book. Oh, so polite you were."

He stepped toward her again, and this time she eased herself around so the couch was between them. "You weren't thinking I was tired, you were thinking how you'd pump me about the Fates."

He nodded. "True enough, I was focused on the Fates, but I had room for both in my head. Then when I lured you away from the hotel and into a walk, I liked seeing how dazzled you were when you started to look around, when you really saw where you were."

"You liked thinking I was dazzled by you."

"I did. I admit it. It was flattering, but still that wasn't the moment things started to shift around so I'd finish off the first of the mistakes."

He moved to the end of the couch, and she backed into the coffee table, flushed, then nearly skipped backward to the far end.

"It was when we got back to your room."

"My trashed room."

"Yes." He caught a whiff of her scent that lingered in the air where she'd been standing. So soft. So quiet. "I was angry over that, and furious with myself, as well, knowing I'd had a part in bringing that on you. There you were, all frazzled and upset, digging for some pill or other, and that thing you suck on like a lolly."

"An inhaler is a medical—"

"Whatever." He was smiling now, pacing her around the sofa. "Do you know what did it for me, Tia? What just slipped right through my defenses and had me starting to moon over you?"

She snorted. "Moon? My butt."

"It was when I looked in the bathroom. That wonderful Finnish bath and I saw all those bottles and packages. Energy this, stress relief that. Special soap and God knows."

"Of course. You were attracted to my allergies and phobias. I've always found them ruthless sexual tools."

He found the prim, damn near prissy tone like music. "I was fascinated that a woman who believed she needed all that to get through the day would have taken herself off, alone, on such a journey. What a brave soul you are, darling, under it all."

"I am not. Will you stop stalking me?"

"My plan had been to see if I could get solid information from you, in hopes you'd lead me to the other statues. Very simple and no harm done. But there was harm. Because I couldn't stop thinking about you."

There was a tickle at the back of her throat, a pressure settling on her chest. "I don't want to discuss this anymore."

"I kept seeing you sitting there, with all your things jumbled around you. And how you talked so calmly to the police even though you were pale and shaken."

Now there was heat, or outrage. "You left me there, left me until you thought I might be of use again."

"You're right. But it wasn't just the Fates I thought of when I came to New York. It wasn't only them I wanted.

Do you remember how I kissed you outside your door? Do you remember how that was?"

"Stop it."

"I made you go inside alone, and closed the door between us myself. If you hadn't mattered, I'd have come inside. I knew you'd let me. But I couldn't, couldn't touch you that way while I was lying to you."

"You'd have come in, and you'd have taken me to bed if you could've stomached making love to someone like me."

He stopped in his tracks, like a man who'd come up sharp against a thick glass wall. "What the hell does that mean? Someone like you. It pisses me off to hear you say that." He moved fast, nearly had her by the arm before she scampered back and away. "And I'm damned if I'll have you believe it. I wanted you that night, too much for my own good, or yours. And I've had the taste of you inside me ever since. The way I see it now, there's only one way to solve all this. I'm having you."

"Having me what?" When he stopped his forward motion, laughed like a loon, it clicked. The blood rushed to her face, then fell away again. "You can't just say something like that. You can't just assume—"

"I'm not assuming, and I'm not just saying. I've been trying to say since I got here, and I'm giving up on words. I want my hands on you. Stop gulping air before you need that sucking thing."

"I'm not gulping air." But she was, even as she raced around to the back of the couch again. "And I'm not going to bed with you."

"It doesn't have to be the bed, though I think you'd enjoy it more if it was." He feinted left, dodged right and grabbed for her arm. He deliberately shortened his reach to let her escape, as he was enjoying himself.

Her color was back now, prettily pink in her cheeks.

"You're not very good at this," he commented when she nearly tripped over her own feet. "I'll wager you haven't had many men chase you around your sofa."

"As I don't date twelve-year-olds, no, I haven't." If she'd hoped to insult him, his chuckle told her she'd missed the mark. "I want you to stop it, right now." She shot a look toward her office, measuring the distance.

"Go ahead and try for it. In the interest of fair play, I'll give you a head start. I want to kiss the back of your neck. Just run my lips over that elegant curve."

He dived for her. With a squeal, she pinwheeled her arms and, overbalancing, flipped onto the couch. More out of luck than design, she kept rolling so he landed flat on the cushions when she hit the floor, butt first.

With a nervous giggle that surprised her more than him, she leaped up and made the dash for her office.

He caught her a step outside the door, spun her around and pressed her back, hard, against the wall. Words rushed into her throat, babbling words that stuck there as she stared into his hot and glittering eyes.

"This is how unattractive, how undesirable I find you."

He crushed her mouth with his, ravaged it, without any of the warm and stirring tenderness he'd shown her before. His body pressed unrelentingly against hers so that the pounding of his heart seemed to ram inside her.

She brought her hands up with some idea of . . . with no idea at all. And they fell limply to her sides again.

He lifted his head, an inch only, so his face blurred in her vision. "Are we clear on that now?" he demanded. When she could do no more than shake her head, he captured her mouth again.

It was like being shot out of a cannon, or torn out of a roller coaster in mid-dive. At least she imagined both those events would whip a rush of color and sound into the brain and bounce the pulse rate screaming high. Turn the limbs to water and cause the system to be trapped somewhere between iced terror and molten exhilaration.

Her ears began to ring, reminding her she was holding her breath. But when she let it out, it sounded like a moan.

That helpless response had him chewing restlessly on her bottom lip before he ended the kiss. "How about now?"

"I . . . I forgot the question."

"Then I'll rephrase it."

He swept her into his arms. Really, she could think of no other way to describe how he plucked her off her feet.

"Oh, God," was the best she could manage when he carried her into the bedroom, kicked the door shut behind them.

"Hold that thought. You know, of course, I'm only doing this so you won't be angry anymore."

"Oh." He laid her on the bed. "Okay."

"I've no personal interest whatsoever in getting you naked and sinking my teeth into you." He straddled her, watching her face as he unbuttoned her blouse. "But sometimes a man has to make sacrifices for the greater good." He skimmed his thumbs, whisper light, over the swell of her breasts. And she began to tremble. "Wouldn't you agree?"

"I, yes . . . No. I don't know what I'm doing here. I've lost my mind."

"I was hoping you would, Tia." He eased her up so he could slip the blouse away. "You're such a pretty little thing."

"I'm not wearing the right underwear."

He'd distracted himself by running a fingertip up and down her torso. Her skin, he thought, was like warm rose petals. "What's that?"

"If I'd known we'd . . . I'm not wearing the right kind of underwear for this."

"Really?" He studied the simple, serviceable white cotton bra. "Well then, we'd best get rid of it right away."

"I didn't mean . . ." She gulped audibly when he slid his hand under her, and undid the bra's catch with two fingers. "You've done that before."

"I confess I have. I'm a cad." He bent down to rub his lips over hers as he tugged the bra aside. "I'm going to take terrible advantage of you now." He used his thumbs again, running them over her nipples until heat balled in her belly. "You should probably call for help."

"I don't think you need any."

With that he scooped her up into a fierce hug. "Christ, you're one in a million. Kiss me back." He brushed his lips over hers. "Kiss me back now. I need you."

In all her life, no one had said those three words to her. The thrill of them spurted through her, flooded her heart and gushed into the kiss. She threw her arms around him, shifting her body so it pressed against his with an abandon neither of them had expected.

Rocked, he dug his fingers into her flesh, struggled for about two seconds to maintain some reasonable control. Then he tumbled her back and did just as he had threatened. He sank his teeth into her.

She rose under him, like a woman riding a wave, and with no thought but the taking, tugged at his shirt. "I want . . . I want . . ."

"So do I." He was breathless now, with muscles quivering. There was the taste of her skin, warm and sweet in his mouth, the feel of it, silky smooth, under his hands. And the surprising, delightful enthusiasm of her as she ran those small, nervous hands over him.

She was so delicately built, and the curves of her so wonderfully subtle. Her scent was a quiet, very female drift that slowly hazed the senses until it seemed as though he could simply breathe her in. Eager to explore, he let his lips rush down her body, back up to those small and lovely breasts.

Back to her warm, willing mouth.

When he did no more than press his hand against the heat and she came with a quick, shocked cry, he felt like a god.

He was murmuring something, or perhaps he was shouting it. There was such a roaring in her head, she couldn't tell. Her system was barraged by a series of long, liquid pulls, of quick, slapping jolts with each sensation rapping so hard into the next it wasn't possible to separate them.

And her body absorbed them greedily, then called for more.

And his, his was so firm and smooth, and hot. Was it any wonder her hands were in such a rush to touch? When she did she could feel the quiver of a muscle, the wild leap of a pulse.

Need. It was need for her.

Then she forgot his need for her own when his fingers slid slickly over her, into her. She could do nothing more than fist her hands in the rumpled bedspread, holding on even as she flew.

His mouth came back to hers, and she opened. Opened everything, so that when he thrust inside her, he entered both heart and body.

He said her name again. It seemed to echo endlessly in his head as he sank into her, into that wet heat. She rose to him, fell away, rose again until the rhythm was like music. He lost himself in it, in her, as the beat became more urgent, and urgency became desperation. And desperation a brilliant pleasure that swallowed them both whole.

WEAK AND WRECKED, she lay under him. In some dim area of consciousness she was aware of his weight, of the galloping race of his heart, even of the shallow breaths he took. But she was much more aware of the lovely limp stretch of her own body, of the hot river of her own blood that swam under her skin.

A part of her mind continued to huddle in a corner and gape with shock and stingy disapproval. She'd made frantic, reckless love with a man she had no business trusting. And at nine o'clock in the morning. A Thursday morning.

Those same basic facts brought on a wave of smugness she knew she should be ashamed of.

"Stop thinking so hard," Malachi said lazily. "You'll hurt yourself. I missed the nape of your neck." He turned his head so he could nibble a bit on her shoulder. "I'll have to make up for that oversight when I can move again."

She closed her eyes and ordered herself to listen to that scolding voice. "It's nine in the morning."

He turned his head, focused on her bedside clock. "Actually, it's not. It's ten-oh-six."

"It can't be. They left at just before nine." It was so nice to be able to run her fingers through his hair, through all that rich, dark chestnut. "I looked at the clock so I'd know when to start worrying if they weren't back." She tried to shift to see the clock for herself, but he stopped the movement with his mouth on hers.

"And when are you scheduled to start worrying?"

"At ten."

"You're running behind, then. Darling, it takes a bit of time to make love if you put any effort into it."

"Ten? It's after ten?" She wiggled, shoved, squirmed. "They could be back any minute."

"So they could." Her movements were perfect, he decided. "So what?"

"They—We can't be in here. Like this."

"Door's closed, and the bedroom's off limits, as I recall."

"They'll certainly know what we've been doing. And we shouldn't have—"

"They will, I imagine. Oh, it's shocking." He snuck a hand up to stroke her breast.

"Don't tease me."

"I can't help it, any more than I can help wanting you again. I like you out of bed, Tia, but I have to tell you." He bit her earlobe and made her shiver. "I surely like you in it as well. I'm just going to take a few more minutes here, and show you."

"We have to get up, right now," she began, but his tongue slid down to her breasts. "Well. Well, I guess a few more minutes won't make any difference."

# Seventeen

GIDEON Sullivan should give lessons on payback, Cleo decided. He should write a goddamn book on it.

### HOW TO MAKE YOUR LOVER FEEL LIKE SLIME IN TEN EASY LESSONS

But there was no way she was going to break. He could be cold; she'd be colder. He could speak in monosyllables. Well then, she'd communicate in grunts.

If he thought the fact that he'd chosen to sleep on the stupid roof rather than share a piece of the bed with her hurt her feelings, he'd miscalculated.

She wished it had rained. Buckets.

They used the subway, which was, Cleo thought, the perfect venue for a stony silence. She sat with her well-developed New York stare into middle distance while he read a tattered paperback edition of *Ulysses*.

Guy should lighten up, she thought to herself. Anybody who chose, of his own free will, to read James Joyce for pleasure wasn't her type anyway.

He probably figured she'd never cracked a book in her life.

Well, he was wrong. She liked to read as much as the

next guy, but she didn't choose to spend her spare time wading through some metaphoric jungle of depression and despair.

She'd just leave that to Slick, who was so goddamn Irish he probably bled green.

She got to her feet at their stop. Gideon simply marked his place in the book and shuffled off the car with her. She was too busy sulking to notice how his gaze swept over the others who got off, or the way he angled his body to shield hers. He followed her through the tunnels to the crosstown train.

He stood patiently on the platform while she tapped her foot, shifted her weight.

"Don't think we were followed," he said quietly.

She nearly jolted at the sound of his voice, which irritated her enough that she forgot to grunt in response. "Nobody knows we're at Tia's, so they can't follow us."

"They may not know we're at Tia's, but someone might be watching her building. I wouldn't want to lead them to her or let them scamper along after us."

He was right, and it reminded her she'd led someone to Mikey. "Maybe I should just throw myself in front of the next oncoming train. Maybe that would be enough penance for you."

"That's a bit over the top, and self-defeating. At least until you get the statue out of the bank."

"It's all you ever wanted anyway."

The platform vibrated with the sound of the crosstown train. "It must comfort you to think that."

She shoved herself, blindly, into the subway car, all but hurled herself into a seat. He took one across from her, opened his book, began to read.

And kept reading when the ride bumped and juggled the words on the page. There was no point in arguing with her, he reminded himself. Every reason not to do so in public. The priority was to get to the bank, retrieve the Fate, get it back to Tia's. Quietly and unobtrusively.

After that a good shouting row might be in order. Though he could hardly see what good it would do. Despite the enforced intimacy they were, at the base, strangers. Two people from different places, with different ideas. And different agendas.

If he'd let himself think of them as more, had let his feelings for her tangle up with the reality of things, that was his problem.

His primary quest, so to speak, had been Lachesis. And so, shortly, that part of the journey would end.

He wished he could go back to Cobh, back to the boatyard and work off some of this excess energy and heat by scraping hulls or some damn thing. But the second Fate was only one of three, and he had a feeling it would be some time before he saw home again.

He felt her move, caught the flash of the blue shirt she'd borrowed from his brother as she rose onto those endless legs of hers. He got up, shoved the book in his jacket pocket.

She strode onto the platform and away as if she were in a great hurry. But then as everyone else did the same, Gideon doubted anyone would take notice. She practically flew through the streets as he scurried after her.

When she reached for the door of the bank he forgot his vow not to touch her, and his hand closed over hers. "You walk in there ready to chew a hole in somebody's neck, people are going to notice."

"This is New York, Slick, nobody notices nothing."

"Chill it down, Cleo. You want a round with me, then we'll have one. But right here and right now, chill it down."

She decided, right there and right then, that the one thing she hated most about him was that he was able to cut through the crap and maintain. "Fine." She offered him a frozen smile. "All chilled."

"I'll wait out here." He stepped back from the door.

He watched the traffic, cars and people. He saw no one who appeared to be interested in him and had just reached the conclusion that anyone who opted to live in a place with so many people and so much noise was either brain-damaged or would be before it was done, when Cleo came out again.

She nodded to him, tapped her fingers lightly on her

shoulder bag. He moved in so the bag and its most recent contents were tucked between their bodies.

"We'll take a cab back," he said.

"Fine. But we're making a stop. Tia lent me two hundred. I need some damn clothes."

"This isn't the time to shop."

"I'm not shopping, I'm buying. I'm desperate enough to settle for the Gap, and that's going a ways for me. We can hike over to Fifth." She was already heading in that direction, giving him no choice but to follow. "Then we'll be sure nobody's tailing us, I grab a couple of shirts, some jeans, we catch a cab and we're home. Then I might just burn the clothes I've been stuck with since Prague."

He might have argued, but was a man who knew how to weigh his options quickly. He could drag her into a cab, then sit on her until they got back to Tia's.

Or he could give her a half hour to do what she felt she needed to do.

"I hate it in here," she muttered the minute they were inside. "It's so . . . pert." She headed for black.

He kept so close to her side, Cleo was tempted to grab something and head to a dressing room just to see if he'd come in with her. She wouldn't put it past him.

Trust was obviously not the word of the day.

She got what she considered the absolute bare essentials. Two T-shirts, a long-sleeved tee, jeans, one sweater, one shirt. All black. Then watched the total ring up to two hundred twelve dollars and fifty-eight cents.

"Arithmetic isn't your long suit, is it?" he asked when she swore under her breath.

"I can add. I wasn't paying attention." She dug out what she had, and was still eight dollars and twenty-two cents short. "Give me a break, will you?"

He gave her a ten, then held out his hand for the change.

"It's less than two bucks." She slapped the money into his hand, swung the bag over her free shoulder. "I'm busted."

"Then you should take more care with how you spend what you have. Mind you take the eight and twenty-two off what I owe you for the earbobs. I'll spring for the taxi."

"You're a real sport, Slick."

"If you want to be kept by a man, you'll have to look elsewhere. I'm sure you'd have no problem finding one."

She said nothing to that. Could say nothing over the ball that lodged in her throat. Instead, with him gripping her arm, she marched to the curb and shot out a hand for a cab.

"I'll apologize for that."

"Shut up," she managed. "Just shut up. We both know what you think of me, so just drop it."

When her head was clear again, she'd thank whatever god of the despairing had a free cab veering to the curb at her feet. She climbed in, snapped out Tia's address.

"You don't know what I think of you. And neither do I."

He let that be the last of it during the ride.

She'd have walked straight into her temporary bedroom when they entered the apartment, but Gideon stopped her. "Let's see the statue first."

"You want to see it." She shoved her purse into his stomach hard enough to knock the breath out of him. "Go ahead."

She made it halfway across the room when she stopped dead.

"Look, Cleo—"

She held up a hand, shook her head frantically. His stomach, already suffering, took a fast dive as he imagined her weeping. But when she turned, her wide, foolish grin had him narrowing his eyes.

"Quiet!" She hissed it out in a whisper, jerked a thumb toward Tia's bedroom. "They're in there."

"Who?" Visions of Anita Gaye or one of her muscle men burst in his brain. Cleo had to leap in front of him.

"Jesus, Slick, open your ears."

He heard it then, the quick, strangled cry that could mean only one thing. When dumbfounded curiosity sent him a few steps closer, he caught the unmistakable sounds of a mattress squeaking.

"Well, Christ." He dragged a hand through his hair and had to swallow a laugh. "What the hell are we supposed to do now?" He whispered it, finding himself grinning back at Cleo. "I can't just stand out here listening to my brother going at it with Tia. It's mortifying."

"Yeah. Mortifying." Snickering, she all but pressed her ear to the bedroom door. "I think they've got a ways to go yet. Unless your brother's one of those get on, get in, get off, get out sort of guys."

"I wouldn't have any way of knowing. And I'd as soon not find out. We'll go up on the roof for a bit."

"Go, Tia!" Cleo murmured as they headed toward the front door. She managed to hold off the laughter until they were safely in the elevator, heading up.

"Do you think they heard us?"

"I don't think they'd have heard a nuclear blast." Cleo caught her breath and walked out with him to take the steps to the roof. She walked into the sunlight, dropped into a chair and kicked out her long legs.

Then felt her mood dip again when Gideon opened her purse. The moment of shared amusement was over, and it was back to business.

He pulled out the Fate, held it up so it glinted and gleamed. "Not much of a thing," he commented. "Pretty enough, and canny, too, when you take a moment to examine the details. You've let it get tarnished."

"It was a lot worse before. It's still only one of them."

His gaze shifted, studied the sun flash on her dark glasses. "It's one Anita doesn't have, and we do. The middle one, the one who measures. How long will this life be? she might think. Fifty years, five, eighty-nine and three-quarters? And what will be the measure of this life in deed? Do you ever think of that?"

"No. Thinking about it doesn't change it."

"Doesn't it?" He turned the statue over in his hand. "I think it does. Thinking about it, pondering over what you'll do, what you won't, those are layers to a life."

"And while you're thinking about it, you get run over by a bus, and so what?"

He leaned back against the wall, studying her as she sat among pots of flowers, pots of greenery. "Is that why you didn't tell me you had it? Because it's nothing more than a means to an end to you? Without any meaning at all?"

"You plan to sell it, don't you?"

"We do. But it's not just money I'm holding in my hand. Now more than ever it's not."

"I'm not going to talk about Mikey." Her voice went thin and quivered before she clamped down and steadied it. "And I'm not going to apologize again for playing it the way I did. You got what you wanted out of me, and some heat in the sheets besides. You've got no complaints."

He stood, Fate curled in his hand. "And what did you get, Cleo?"

"I got the hell out of Prague." She leaped to her feet. "I got home, and I've got the potential for enough money to keep the wolf from my throat for a good long time. Because whatever you think, I'm not looking to whore myself so some guy will pave the way for me. I stripped, okay, but I didn't turn tricks. And I'm not stupid enough to let some guy fuck me over and leave me broke and stranded again like I was after Sidney."

"Who's Sidney?"

"Just another bastard in the perpetual lineup I seem to attract. Can't blame him, though, since I was the one who was stupid. He came on to me, and I fell for it. Told me how he was part owner of this theater in Prague, how they were putting together a show and looking for a dancer— an American dancer who could choreograph and was willing to invest. What he wanted was a patsy, and some free nooky. With me, he got two-for-one."

She tucked her thumbs in her front pockets because what she wanted to do was hug herself, hard, and rock. "He wanted to get back to Europe, and I was his ticket. I sprang for the freight because what the hell. I wanted to try something new. I wasn't making a name for myself here, so I'd make one over there. The more bullshit he pumped out, the more I bought."

"Were you in love with him?"

"Yeah, you're a bone-deep romantic." She tossed her hair back, walked to the wall. Dark hair streaming back, eyes shielded by sunglasses, lips curled in a cynical twist. "He was great to look at, and he had a real smooth line. Lines always sound just a little smoother with an accent. I was gone over him, which is different from being in love. And I was all wrapped up in the idea of someone giving me a shot at choreography."

A shot at something, she thought now, she could be good at. "So I lived the high life in Prague for a few days, then woke up one morning to find he'd cleaned me out. Took my money, my credit cards, left me with a whopping hotel bill I couldn't pay until I pawned the watch and couple rings I was wearing."

"Did you go to the police? The embassy?"

"Jesus, Gideon. What color is the sky in your world? He was gone, long gone. I reported the credit cards stolen, packed up and got a job. And I learned a lesson. When something sounds too good to be true, it's because it's a big, fat lie. Lesson number two? Look out for number one. First, last, always."

"Maybe you should learn one more." He turned the Fate so its face shone like the sunlight. "If you don't believe in something, in someone, what's the fucking point?"

DOWNSTAIRS IN THE apartment, Tia snuggled up against Malachi and thought about taking a nap. Just a short one, a catnap, as she felt very like a cat at the moment. One with a bellyful of cream.

"You have the loveliest shoulders," he told her. "They should always be naked. You never want to cover these up with clothes or hair."

"Anita said men like long hair on a woman."

The name spoiled his dreamy mood and had his mouth tightening. "Don't think about her just now. We'd best get up and see if Gideon and Cleo are back."

"Back?" She sighed, started to stretch. "Back from where? Oh my God!" She sat up straight, too shocked to think about snatching sheets to cover herself. "It's eleven o'clock! Something must have happened to them. What were we thinking!"

She scrambled out of bed, picked up her hopelessly wrinkled blouse and stared at it, mildly horrified.

"If you come back here a minute, I'll show you what we were thinking."

"This is completely irresponsible." She pressed the blouse to her breasts and backed toward her closet for a fresh one. "What if something's happened to them? We should go out and look for them, or—"

She broke off when her bell rang. "That must be them now." Relief was so huge, she grabbed a robe rather than her blouse and bundled hurriedly into it as she dashed for the door.

"Thank God. I was so worried . . . Mother."

"Tia, how many times have I told you, even when you look through the peephole, you should always, always ask who's there." She aimed a kiss an inch above Tia's cheek as she sailed in. "You're ill. I knew it."

"No, I'm not ill."

"Don't tell me." She pressed a hand to Tia's forehead. "Flushed, and in your robe in the middle of the day. Your eyes are heavy, too. Well, I'm on my way to the doctor, so you can come with me. You take my appointment, dear. I'd never forgive myself otherwise."

"I'm not sick. I don't need to see the doctor. I was just . . ." Lord, good Lord, what could she say?

"We'll just get you dressed. I have no doubt, none whatsoever, that you picked up some strange foreign virus while you were traveling. I told your father as much this very morning."

"Mother." Tia hurdled over a footstool and, with the skill of a tight end, did a fast lateral rush in front of the bedroom door. "I feel absolutely, perfectly well. You don't want to miss your appointment, do you? You look a little pale. Have you been sleeping well?"

"When have I ever?" Alma smiled her martyr's smile. "I don't think I've had more than an hour's rest at a time since you were born. Why, it took all my reserves just to get dressed this morning. I'm sure my platelets are low. I'm just sure of it."

"You tell the doctor to test them," Tia urged as she pulled her mother to the door.

"What's the point? They won't tell you when you're really sick, you know. I need to sit down awhile. I'm getting palpitations."

"Oh . . . Then I think you should hurry to the doctor. I think you need to—" She broke off, sagged, when the door opened to Gideon and Cleo. "Ah, well . . . hmmm. You're back. These are associates of mine, Mother."

"Associates?" She scanned the faded jeans, the Gap bag Cleo still carried.

"Yes, yes. We're working on a project together. In fact, we were just about to—"

"You're working in your robe?" Alma demanded.

"Busted," Cleo said under her breath, but one of Alma's many complaints wasn't her hearing.

"Just what does that mean? Just what is going on here? Tia, I demand an explanation."

"That's a bit delicate." Malachi stepped out of the bedroom. He, too, wore jeans and a smile that could have melted an iceberg at twenty yards. He'd tossed on a shirt, then deliberately left it unbuttoned. There were times, he'd calculated, the truth served best.

"I'm afraid I distracted your daughter while our associates were out." He crossed over, took Alma's hand and shook it gently. "Completely unprofessional of me, of course, but, well now, what could I do? She's so lovely. I see now where she gets it."

He lifted the hand he still held to his lips while Alma stared at him. "I've been completely undone by your daughter, Mrs. Marsh, since first we met."

He draped an arm over Tia's stiff shoulders and kissed her lightly on the cheek. "But I'm embarrassing her, and you as well. I'd hoped to meet you and Tia's father under less awkward circumstances."

Alma's eyes rushed from Malachi's face to her daughter's, and back again. "Almost any would be less awkward."

He nodded, adding as much sheepishness as he could manage. "Can't argue with you there. Hardly a good beginning to get caught with your pants down by the lady's mum before you've exchanged how-do-you-dos. I can only tell you I'm enchanted by your daughter."

As gracefully as possible, Tia slipped out from under

his arm. "Maybe you could step into the kitchen for a moment? All of you? So I could have a word with my mother."

"If you like." Malachi cupped her chin, lifted it until their eyes met. "It should be as you like." He touched his lips to hers, lingering over it before he followed the others into the kitchen.

"I demand an explanation," Alma began.

"I think an explanation is superfluous, under the circumstances."

"Who are those people and what are they doing in your apartment?"

"They're associates, Mother. Friends. We're working together on a project."

"And having orgies every morning?"

"No. That was just today."

"What's come over you? Strangers in your home? Strange Irish men in your bed in the middle of the morning? I knew nothing good would come of your running off to Europe. I knew there would be terrible consequences. No one would listen to me, and now look."

"Terrible consequences. Mother, what's so terrible about me having friends? What's so dire about there being a man who wants to go to bed with me in the middle of the morning?"

"I can't get my breath." Alma clutched at her chest and dissolved into a chair. "There's a tingling down my arm. I'm having a heart attack. Call nine-one-one."

"Stop it. You can't call an ambulance every time we disagree, every time I take a step away. Every time," she added, crouching at her mother's feet, "I do something just for me."

"I don't know what you're talking about. My heart—"

"Your heart's fine. You've got the heart of an elephant and every doctor you find tells you the same thing. Look at me. Mother, can't you just look at me? I cut my hair," Tia said quietly. "You haven't even noticed because you weren't looking. All you see when you look at me is a sickly little girl, someone who can keep you company at the doctor's and give you an excuse for a nervous disposition."

"What a horrible thing to say." Shock had Alma forgetting all about the possibility of cardiac arrest. "First you take up with some strange man, and now you say horrible things to me. You've joined a cult, haven't you?"

"No." Unable to help herself, Tia lowered her head to her mother's knee and laughed. "No, I haven't joined a cult. Now I want you to go downstairs. Your driver's waiting for you. Go to your appointment. I'll come see you and Father very soon."

"I'm not sure I'm well enough to get to the doctor's on my own. I need you to come with me."

"I can't." Gently Tia drew Alma to her feet. "I'm sorry. If you want, I'll call Father and ask him to meet you there."

"Never mind." Wrapping martyrdom around her like a stole, Alma walked to the door. "Obviously nearly dying in childbirth, then devoting my life to your health and well-being aren't enough to have you give me an hour of your time when I'm ill."

Tia opened her mouth, then swallowed the placating, agreeable words. "I'm sorry. I hope you feel better soon."

"Boy, she's good." Cleo came out of the kitchen the instant she heard the front door close. "I mean, she's the champion. Hey." She walked over to hook an arm around Tia's waist. "You've gotta shake it off, honey. She was doing a number on you."

"I could've gone with her. It would only have taken a little time."

"Instead you stood up to her. A better choice, if you ask me. What you need is some ice cream."

"No, but thanks." She took a deep breath, felt it catch near her sternum, but resolutely pushed it out. Then turned so she could face all of them at once. "I'm embarrassed, I'm tired, and this time I do have a headache. I'd like to apologize for the entire business, all at once. And I'd like to see the Fate, examine it, hopefully verify it before I take some medication, get dressed and go downtown to see my father."

Malachi held up a hand and showed her the statue his brother had given him in the kitchen.

Without a word, Tia took it into her office, to the desk. There with her glasses perched on her nose, she studied it under a magnifying glass. She felt them hovering behind her as she continued her studies. "We'd be more certain if my father could examine it or, better yet, give it to an expert."

"We can't chance that," Malachi told her.

"No. I certainly won't risk my father by connecting him. These are the maker's marks," she said, tipping the base up. "And, according to my research, they're correct. You and Gideon are the only ones here who've seen Clotho. I've only seen photographs and artists' renderings, but stylistically this is a match. And you see here . . ." She tapped the tip of her pencil on the notches, right and left on the base. "These slots connect her, the middle sister, with Clotho on one side, Atropus on the other."

She glanced up, waited for Malachi to nod. She took a tape measure out of the drawer, noted down the exact height, width. "Another match. Let's check weight."

She took it into the kitchen, used her scale. "It's exact, down to the gram. If it's a forgery, it's a careful one. And the odds of that, given its connection through Cleo, are small. In my not so considered opinion, we have Lachesis. We have the second Fate."

She set it on the counter, slipped her glasses off and set them beside the statue. "I'm going to get dressed."

"Tia. Damn it. Give me a minute," Malachi said to Gideon, then went after her.

"I need to take a shower," she told him and would have closed the door in his face if he hadn't just pushed it open. "I need to change and figure out what I'm going to tell my father and what I'm not going to tell him. I'm not as skilled in this game-playing as you are."

"Are you embarrassed we made love, or embarrassed your mother knows of it?"

"I'm embarrassed period." She turned into the bathroom, took a bottle of pills out of the medicine cabinet. She took one of the bottles of water she kept in the linen closet and downed a Xanax. "I'm upset that I had an argument with my mother and sent her away unhappy with me. And I'm trying not to imagine her collapsing on the street because I was too busy and disinterested to go with her to her doctor's appointment."

"Has she ever collapsed on the street before?"

"No, of course not." She got out another bottle of pills and took two extra-strength Tylenol for the headache. "She just mentions the possibility of it often enough so the image is always fresh in my mind."

With a shake of her head, she met his gaze in the mirror. "I'm a mess, Malachi. I'm twenty-nine years old, and I've been in therapy for twelve years next January. I have regular appointments with an allergist, an internist and a homeopathic healer. I tried acupuncture, but since I'm phobic about sharp implements, that didn't last long."

Even thinking about it made her shudder a little. "My mother's a hypochondriac and my father's disinterested," she continued. "I'm neurotic, phobic and socially inept. I sometimes imagine myself suffering from a rare, lingering disease—or being lactose intolerant. Neither of which is true, at least up till now."

She braced her hands on the sink because saying it out loud, hearing herself say it out loud, made it all sound so pathetic. "The last time I went to bed with a man—other than this morning—was three years ago in April. Neither of us was particularly delighted with the results. So, what are you doing here?"

"First, I'd like to say that if it'd been over three years since I'd had sex, I'd be in therapy as well."

He turned her to face him, then kept his hands lightly on her shoulders. "Second, being shy isn't being socially inept. Third, I'm here because here's where I want to be. And finally, I'd like to ask if when we've got all this business done with, you'd come back to Ireland with me for a bit. I'd like you to meet my own mother, under less touchy circumstances than I met yours. Now look what you've done," he said when the bottle she held slipped out of her hand and hit the floor. "You've got those little pills everywhere."

# Eighteen

ANITA considered the possibility of flying to Athens and personally interrogating every antique dealer and collector in the city. Though there would have been something satisfying in this hands-on approach, she couldn't expect another Fate to simply fall into her lap.

Moreover, she wasn't willing to go to quite that much trouble on the vague memory of a bumbling fool like Tia Marsh. No, as much as she craved action, it wouldn't do.

She needed direction, she needed leads. She needed employees who could follow both so she wasn't required to shoot them in the head.

She sighed over that. She'd been vaguely disappointed that her former employee's murder had warranted no more than a few lines in the *New York Post*. Really, that said quite a bit about the world, didn't it? she mused. When a dead man garnered less press than a pop singer's second marriage.

It only proved that fame and money ran the show. Something she'd known all her life. Those two elements had been her goal even when she'd been moldering in that lousy third-floor walk-up in Queens. When her name had been Anita Gorinsky, when she'd watched her father work himself to a nub for a stingy paycheck her mother had struggled to stretch week by week.

She'd never belonged there, inside those dingy walls her mother had tried to brighten with flea market art and homemade curtains. She'd never been a part of that world, with its rooms that smelled forever of onions and its tacky hand-crocheted doilies. Her mother's wide, fresh-scrubbed face and her father's scarred workingman's hands had been an embarrassment to her.

She'd detested them for their ordinariness. Their pride in her, their only daughter, their joy in sacrificing so that she could have advantages, had disgusted her.

She'd known, even as a child she'd known she was destined for so much more. But destiny, Anita thought, often needed a helping hand.

She'd taken their money for schooling, for clothes, and had demanded more. She'd deserved it. She'd earned it, Anita thought. Every penny of it she'd earned with every day she'd lived in that horrid apartment.

And she'd paid them back, in her way, by seeing that their investment in her produced considerable dividends.

She hadn't seen her parents, or her two brothers, in more than eighteen years. As far as the world she now lived in was concerned—as far as she herself was concerned—she had no family.

She doubted anyone from the old neighborhood would recognize little Nita in the woman she'd become. She rose and walked to the giltwood pier glass that reflected the spacious sitting area of her office. Once her hair had been a long fall of mink brown her mother had spent hours brushing and curling. Her nose had been prominent and her front teeth had overlapped. Her cheeks had been soft and round.

A few nips, a couple of tucks, some dental work and a good hairstylist had changed the outer package. Streamlined it. She'd always known how to enhance her better assets.

Inside, she was exactly as she'd always been. Hungry, and determined to feed her appetites.

Men, she knew, were always willing to set a full plate in front of a beautiful woman. As long as the man believed the woman would pay with sex, there was no end to the variety of meals.

Now, she was a very wealthy widow—who could buy her own.

Still, men were useful. Think of all the contacts her dear, departed husband had put at her disposal. The fact was, Paul was handier dead than he'd been alive. Widowhood made her even more respectable and available.

Considering, she went back to her desk and opened her husband's burgundy leather address book. Paul had been very old-fashioned in some respects and had kept his address book meticulously up to date. In the last years, when his hand hadn't been quite so steady, she'd written in the names herself.

The dutiful wife.

She paged through until she found the name she was looking for. Stefan Nikos. Sixtyish, she recalled. Vital, wealthy. Olive groves or vineyards, perhaps both. She couldn't quite recall. Nor could she recall if he currently had a wife. What mattered was he had money, power and an interest in antiquities.

She unlocked a drawer, drew out a book of her own. In it, she'd noted down everyone who'd come to her husband's funeral, what flowers they'd sent. Mr. and Mrs. Stefan Nikos hadn't made the trip from Corfu, or Athens—they had homes in both places—but had sent an offering of five dozen white roses, a Mass card and, best of all, a personal note of condolence to the young widow.

She picked up the phone, nearly buzzed her assistant to make the call, then reevaluated. Best to make it herself—friend to friend—she decided, and was already practicing the words and tone as she dialed.

She wasn't put through right away, but she held the line and her temper so that when Stefan picked up, her voice was as warm and welcoming as his.

"Anita. What a wonderful surprise. I must apologize for keeping you waiting."

"Oh, no. You didn't. I'm the one who's surprised I'd be able to reach a busy man like you so easily. I hope you and your lovely wife are well."

"We are, we are, of course. And you?"

"Fine. Busy, too. Work's a godsend to me since Paul died."

"We all miss him."

"Yes, we do. But it's wonderful for me to spend my days at Morningside. He's here, you know, in every corner. It's important for me to . . . well . . ." She let her voice thicken, just slightly. "It's very important to keep his memory alive, and to know old friends remember him as I do. I know it's been a very long time since I contacted you. I'm a bit ashamed of that."

"Now, now. Time passes, doesn't it, my dear?"

"Yes, but who knows better than I that one should never let people drift away? And here I am, Stefan, calling you after all this time for a favor. I nearly didn't."

"What can I do for you, Anita?"

She liked the fact that a hint of caution had come into his voice. He'd be a man accustomed to hangers-on, to old acquaintances hitting him up for favors. "Yours was the first name I thought of because of who you are, and your friendship with Paul."

"You are having difficulties with Morningside?"

"Difficulties?" She paused, then let embarrassment, even a touch of horror, color her tone. "Oh no. No, Stefan, nothing like that. Oh, I hope you don't think I'd call this way to ask for any sort of financial . . . I'm so flustered."

She twirled, gleefully, in her desk chair. "It concerns a client, and some pieces I'm trying to track down at his behest. Honestly, your name popped into my mind, a kind of shot in the dark, as the pieces are Greek images."

"I see. Is your client interested in something in my collection?"

"That would depend." She tried a quiet laugh. "You don't happen to own the Three Fates, do you?"

"The Fates?"

"Three small silver statues. Individual, that apparently link together by their bases to make a set."

"Yes, I have heard of them, but only as a kind of story. Statues forged on Olympus that will, if complete, grant the owner anything from eternal life to untold fortunes, even the fabled three wishes, one for each Fate."

"Legends increase the value of a piece."

"Indeed they do, but it was my impression that these pieces were lost, if they ever existed in the first place."

"I believe they existed," she said, running a fingertip over the statue of Clotho, which sat now on her desk. "Paul often spoke of them. More to the point, my client believes it. To be frank, Stefan, he's piqued my interest enough that I've made some inquiries, started considerable legwork. One source, which appears to be valid, insists that one of the statues, the third one, is in Athens."

"If this is so, it's not come to my ear."

"I'm tugging on any line at this point. I hate to disappoint a client. I was hoping you could make some discreet inquiries. If I can possibly get away in the next few weeks, I'd love to take a trip to Greece myself. Combine business and pleasure."

"Of course you must come, and stay with us."

"I couldn't impose."

"The guest house here in Athens or our villa on Corfu are at your disposal. Meanwhile, I'll be happy to make those discreet inquiries."

"I can't tell you how much I appreciate it. My client is somewhat eccentric, and very much obsessed just now with these pieces. If I could locate even one, it would mean a great deal. I know Paul would be so proud to know that Morningside had a part in finding the Fates."

Pleased with herself, Anita made a second, personal call. She glanced at her watch, flipped through her daybook and calculated when she could most conveniently squeeze in the meeting she intended to set up.

"Burdett Securities."

"Anita Gaye for Jack Burdett."

"I'm sorry, Ms. Gaye, Mr. Burdett is unavailable. May I take a message?"

Unavailable? Stupid twit, don't you *know* who I am? Anita set her teeth. "It's very important I speak with Mr. Burdett as soon as possible."

Instantly, she thought. She had a second-tier plan to put into motion.

"I'll see he gets your message, Ms. Gaye. If you'd give me a number where he can reach you, I'll—"

"He has my numbers. All of them."

She slammed down the phone. Unavailable, her ass. He'd best make himself available, and soon.

She wasn't about to let Cleo Toliver and the second Fate slip through her fingers. Jack Burdett was just the man to run them down for her.


HE WAS ON the phone himself. In fact, Jack had spent most of the trans-Atlantic flight on the phone, or on his laptop. For herself, Rebecca watched two movies. Actually, one and a half, as she'd fallen asleep during the second. And had yet to forgive herself for wasting a single minute of the flight in sleep.

She'd never flown first-class before, and had decided it was a method of travel she could easily grow accustomed to.

She wanted to use the phone herself, to call her mother, to call her brothers. But she didn't think the current budget would swing for that sort of expense. And she could hardly ask Jack to pay for it.

At the rate they were going she was a little concerned he'd think she was only interested in his money. That was hardly the case, though she didn't consider his money a strike against him.

She'd liked watching him with his great-grandparents. He'd been so sweet and so gentle with them. Not sappily so, she thought now. So many, to her mind, treated the elderly as if they were children, or inconveniences, or simply oddities.

There'd been none of that with Jack. It said something about a man, in her opinion, when he had an easy and natural way with his family.

Of course he was a bit too bossy for her usual taste, but she had to be honest enough to admit that men who fell in line whenever she snapped her fingers annoyed the very hell out of her.

He was a pleasure to look at as well, and that was no more strike against him than his wallet. And he was smart—more, he was canny. Since she was trusting him with a great deal, it helped knowing she'd put her faith in a canny sort of man.

She shifted, started to speak to him, and saw he was making yet another call. Although a bit annoyed, Rebecca promised she wouldn't point out he'd barely said two words to her in more than five hours.

"Message from Anita Gaye," Jack said suddenly.

"What? She called you? What did she want?"

"She didn't say."

"Are you ringing her back?"

"Eventually."

"Why don't you do it now so we know—"

"Let her stew awhile, that's one. Second, I don't want her to know I'm on a plane, and we're about to start the final approach with all the accompanying announcements. If she's calling, she wants something. We'll just let her want it for a while longer."

NEW YORK WAS a thrill, and though Rebecca didn't want to behave like a slack-jawed tourist, she intended to enjoy every minute of it. There were important things to do, and vital business to attend to, but that didn't mean she couldn't hug the excitement of being there, of finally being *somewhere,* tight against her.

It was everything she imagined. The sleek towers of buildings, the acres of shops, the fast and crowded streets. To see them for the first time while being whisked along in a limousine—a genuine limousine as big as a boat, with seats of buttery leather *and* a uniformed driver complete with cap—was the most delicious of adventures.

She could barely wait to call her mother and tell her about it. And oh, how her fingers itched to flip and fiddle with all the little switches. She sent Jack a sidelong look.

He was sitting, legs stretched out, dark glasses in place with his hands folded restfully over his stomach.

She started to reach up to the panel, snatched her hand back. Perhaps he was sleeping and wouldn't see, but the driver might.

"Go ahead and play with them," Jack murmured.

She flushed, shrugged. "I was just wondering what everything did." She reached up, idly she thought, and toyed with the various light schemes. Then the radio, the television, the sunroof. "It wouldn't be so hard to put all this in an ordinary car," she concluded. "Certainly you could have it in a caravan, and people would feel very plush while they traveled."

She eyed the phone, thought of her family again. "I need to get in touch with my brothers. I don't like not being able to just ring them and tell them I'm here."

"We'll go by and see them in person. Shortly."

The limo glided, quiet as a ghost, to the curb, and Rebecca had her first look at Jack's building. It didn't seem like much, she mused as she stepped onto the sidewalk. She'd expected a man with all his wherewithal to live in some glossy place with fancy touches and one of those soldierly doormen.

Still it seemed a sturdy sort of place to her, and pitted with character. She was neither surprised nor disappointed when he used both keycard and code to gain entrance into the narrow lobby. And yet another card, another code to access the elevator.

"I would have thought you lived alone," she began as the elevator started up.

"I do."

"No, I mean to say not in a flat with neighbors."

"I do," he said again. "I have the only apartment in the building."

"It seems awfully big not to make use of the other space."

"I make use of it."

The elevator stopped. He disengaged locks and alarms, then opened the door into his living space.

"Well." She stepped inside, onto a floor with wide, dark

planks, scanned the biscuit-colored walls, the bold art, the wide windows. "You've made use of this space right enough."

There were gorgeous old rugs. She didn't know enough about such things to recognize Chinese Deco, but she liked the blend of colors and the way they accented the deep hues and deep cushions of the sofas, the chairs, even the heavy polished wood.

She wandered through, noting first it was tidy, then that it was tasteful. And last that it was stylish. She liked the wavy glass blocks that separated the kitchen from the living space, and the framed arches that led to what she supposed were hallways and bedrooms.

"It seems a lot of room for a single man."

"I don't like to be crowded."

She nodded, turned back. Yes, she thought, it suited him. A clever and unusual space for a clever and unusual man. "You can be sure I won't crowd you, Jack. Is there a place I can put my things, maybe have a wash and change before we go see my brothers?"

"Two bedrooms down the hall. Mine's on the right, spare's on the left." He waited a beat, watching her. "Take your pick."

"My choice, is it?" She let out a careful breath as she lifted her duffel. "I'll take the spare for the moment. And I have something to say to you."

"Go ahead."

"I want to sleep with you, and I don't generally have that kind of want for a man on such short acquaintance. But I'm thinking it might be better if we're a bit careful with each other for a while yet. Until we're both perfectly sure that the sex isn't some sort of payment, on either side."

"I don't take sex as payment."

"That's good, and you'll be sure if it's offered it isn't meant as such. I won't be long." She carried her bag through the arch and took the room on the left.

He jammed his hands in his pockets, paced to the window. Then turned and had taken two strides after her when his office line beeped.

He listened to his assistant relay the message that Ms. Gaye had called, again. Maybe he'd let her stew long enough.

He passed through another archway and into the small office he kept in the apartment. Before he placed the call, he checked the phone for tampering, ran a brief systems check, then engaged his own recording device.

Some might have called him paranoid. He preferred thinking of it as standard operating procedure.

"Anita. Jack."

"Oh, thank God! I've been trying to reach you for hours."

He lifted a brow at the frantic tone in her usually unruffled voice and made himself comfortable in his desk chair. "I've been out of reach. What's wrong, Anita? You sound upset."

"I am. I'm probably being foolish, but I am. Very upset. I need to speak to you, Jack. I need help. I'll leave for home right now if you can meet me there."

"Wish I could." Not going to be too easy, honey, he thought. "I'm not in New York."

"Where are you?" He could hear the hardening in her voice.

"Philadelphia," he decided. "Quick job check. I'll be back tomorrow. Tell me what's wrong."

"I don't know who else to call. I just don't know anything about this sort of thing. It's about the Fates. Remember, I mentioned them to you over dinner."

"Sure. What about them?"

"I told you I had an interested client. I've mentioned it to others, made some inquiries, though I'll admit I didn't think anything would come of it. But it has."

"You found one?" He opened his carry-on, took out the protective bag. "That sounds like good news."

"I might have found one. That is, I was contacted about one, but I don't know what to do. Oh, I'm rambling. I'm so sorry."

"Take your time." He unwrapped Atropus, turned her to face him.

"All right." She took an audible breath. "A woman called me, claimed she had one of the statues and was in-

terested in selling it. Naturally, I was skeptical, but I had
to follow through. Even when she insisted on meeting me
outside the office. She insisted I come to the observation
deck at Empire State."

"Get out."

"I know. I was amused, actually. It seemed so film noir.
But she behaved rather oddly, Jack. I think she must have
a drug problem. She demanded an exorbitant amount of
money, and she threatened me. Physically threatened me
if I didn't pay."

A faint frown moved over his face as he turned Atropus
around and around on his desk. "It sounds like you should
talk to the police, Anita."

"I can't afford the publicity. And in any case, what point
is there? They were only threats. She had a picture, I think
it was a scanned print, of what might very well be one of
the Fates."

Interesting, he considered. More and more interesting.
"If it was, you know computer images can be generated
easily. Sounds like a standard con."

"Well, yes, but it looked genuine. The detailing on the
statue. I want to pursue this, but I'm . . . I confess, I'm
more than a little shaken. If I go to the police, I'll lose this
contact for my client."

"How did you leave things?"

"She wants to meet me again, and I've stalled her.
Frankly, she frightens me. Before I arrange any sort of
meeting with her, I need to know who I'm dealing with.
Right now I only have a name, the name she gave me.
Cleo Toliver. If you could find her—"

"I'm not a detective, Anita. I can give you the name of a
good firm."

"Jack, I can't trust this to a stranger. I need a friend. I
know it's going to sound crazy, but I'm sure I'm being followed. Once I know where she is, who she is, I'll know if
I should try to negotiate this deal or take some sort of legal
action against her. I need a friend, Jack. I'm very un-
nerved by all this."

"Let me see what I can do. Cleo Toliver, you say? Give
me a description."

"I knew I could count on you. You'll keep this off the record, won't you? A favor for a friend."

He glanced at the recorder. "Naturally."

IN UNDER AN hour, Cleo let out a whoop of joy. "That's gotta be the Chinese food." The thrill of pot stickers might have had her leaping to the door herself if Malachi hadn't intercepted her.

"Let's just have Tia take a look and be sure."

With some regret, Tia set aside Wyley's journal and walked out of the spare room to the front door. One look through the peephole had her gasping in surprise.

"It's Jack Burdett," she hissed. "He's got someone with him, but I can't really see her."

"Let's have a look." Malachi nudged her aside, looked for himself, then let out his own whoop. To Tia's surprise, he flipped locks, pulled open the door, then yanked the redhead into his arms.

"There's my girl!" He spun her once, kissed her hard, then dropped her back on her feet. "What the hell are you doing here?" he demanded in a lightning change of mood. "What the hell are you doing with him?"

"I'll tell you if you give me two seconds to get a breath." Instead of answering, she turned to launch herself at Gideon. "Isn't this a wonder? The three of us in New York."

"I'd like to know why we are," Malachi continued, "when you should be home."

"So you and Gid can have all the fun? Bollocks to that. Hello, you must be Tia." Smiling broadly, she stuck out a hand, grabbed Tia's and shook hard and fast. "I'm Rebecca, and sorry to confess, I'm sister to these two heathens who can't be bothered to tell you who's walked in your door. It's such a lovely place you have here. It is Cleo?" She turned to the brunette who leaned lazily against the back of the couch. "It's a pleasure to meet you. This is Jack Burdett, as Tia already knows, and we've brought considerable news with us."

The bell rang again.

"That better be the Chinese," Cleo said. "And let's hope he brought extra egg rolls."

"Becca." Gideon drew her aside, lowered his voice as Tia dealt with the delivery. "You've no business running off this way with a strange man."

"Why not?" Cleo demanded. "I did. Tia, I'm going to open some wine. Okay?"

"Yes." Because her head was spinning, Tia leaned back against the door, her arms full of Chinese takeout. Her apartment was full of people, and most of them were talking at once. In very loud voices. She was going to eat food loaded with MSG and would probably die young because of it.

Her mother was barely speaking to her, there was a priceless objet d'art hidden behind the two-percent milk in her refrigerator, and she was sharing her bed with a man who was currently shouting at his sister.

It was exhausting. It was . . . wonderful.

"Been a busy little bee, haven't you?" Jack commented. "Here. Let me give you a hand with those. Anybody order pot stickers?"

"I did." Cleo wandered over to him with an open bottle of wine. "I might share if you can manage to shut those three up."

"I can do that." He angled his head, took a good long look at her. "She didn't do you justice. Didn't figure she would."

"Oh. Who?"

"Anita Gaye." The name, as he'd expected, dropped the room into silence. "She called about an hour ago, asked me to find you."

Cleo's fingers tightened on the neck of the bottle. "Looks like I'm found."

"Why didn't you tell me?" Rebecca demanded.

"Easier to tell it once. She gave me the impression you're a dangerous character," he said to Cleo.

"Bet your ass."

"Good. Let's break out these pot stickers and talk about it."

*  *  *

HER LIVING ROOM was a mess. Correction, Tia thought, her life was the mess. There was a voice inside her head lecturing her to clean it up, this very minute. But it was a little hard to hear it with all the voices going on outside her head.

She now had connections to thieves and murderers. And *two* precious objets d'art in her apartment.

"Cunningham," Malachi said as he studied the two statues. "It just figures. If you think about it all, if you believe the way life spins around, it just figures. There's two of them." He looked at his brother. "There's what we were after."

"We were," Gideon agreed, "at the start of it."

"We're not at the start of it anymore." Cleo surged to her feet, rage trembling through her. "That one's mine, and don't you forget it. I'll see it melted down into a puddle before that bitch gets her hands on it."

"Calm yourself down, Cleo," Malachi advised.

"The hell I will. The three of you want to pay her back, that's your business. But it stopped being about money when she had Mikey killed. He's worth more than money."

"Of course he is." For the first time in days, Gideon touched her, gently, just a brush of his hand against her leg.

"I'm sorry about your friend." Rebecca set down her wineglass. "I wish there was a way to make it right again. It's clear enough we have to think of something else. None of us planned for anything beyond skinning her for money once we found these two. Christ knows why we thought we ever would, and still we have. That must count for something."

"I won't sell it to her. Not for any amount."

"How about selling it to me?" Jack used chopsticks expertly for another bite of pork-fried rice.

"So you can turn around and sell it to her?" Cleo demanded. "I don't think so."

"I'm not going to sell anything to Anita," he said icily. "If you think she'll sell you the one she has, you're nuts." Disgusted, Cleo stretched out on the floor again.

"I'm not buying anything from her either."

"They only achieve their true value as a set," Tia pointed out. "If you're not going to negotiate for the set with Anita, the only way to get the first one back is to steal it."

Jack nodded as he topped off two of the glasses still on the coffee table. "There you go."

"Oh, I like that way of thinking." Pleased, Rebecca sat up straight, shot Jack a warm, approving look. "Still, you have to remember that if it's stolen back, it was stolen from us to begin with. Or, I suppose stolen from Tia in a way, then from us. It's complicated, but it comes down to it being mutually owned, wouldn't you say?"

Tia blinked rapidly, pressed a finger on what felt like a muscle tic just under her left eye. "I don't know what to say."

"I do. It's not enough." Cleo shook her head. "Even if you pull it off, she loses a thing. A thing that wasn't hers to begin with. It's not fucking enough."

"No, it's not," Gideon agreed. "Not any longer."

"You want justice?" Jack lifted his glass, skimmed his gaze around the room.

"That's right." Gideon laid a hand on Cleo's shoulder, then looked at his brother, at his sister, back at Jack when they nodded. "That's what has to be."

"Okay. Justice makes it a little trickier, but we'll work it out."

# Nineteen

NOTHING, Malachi decided, was going to be solved during this first disorganized and impromptu meeting. They needed time to let it all settle in. Time, as Tia had said, to define their direction and their goal.

As usual the brainy and delightful Dr. Marsh had cut through to the heart of the matter. The six people currently scattered around her apartment had a variety of agendas and styles.

The outside force of Anita Gaye had only one.

To win, they would have to meld those six individuals into one single unit. That required more than cooperation. It would demand trust.

Since they had to start somewhere, Malachi decided to explore the new element.

Jack Burdett.

He wasn't entirely sure he cared for the way the man looked at his sister. That was a bit of personal business he intended to wind through the rest as soon as possible.

In any case, Tia was looking more than a little shell-shocked. She did better, to his way of thinking, when she had some time inside her own head. So the first order of the day was to clear out the apartment and give her a bit of room.

"We all need to chew on this for a while." Though he didn't raise his voice, the chatter quieted. It was something Jack noticed, and filed away.

"Fine with me." Jack got to his feet. "Meanwhile, I've got something for you, Tia."

"Something for me."

"Consider it a hostess gift. Thanks for the Chinese." He dug into his bag and came out with a phone. "It's secure," he told her. "And so will the line be, once I hook it up. You can use this line to make and receive calls you don't want our eavesdropping friends to hear. I don't imagine I have to tell you not to give the number out."

"No. But doesn't the phone company have to . . . Never mind."

He flashed a grin at her. "Where do you want it?"

"I don't know." She rubbed her fingers between her eyebrows, tried to think. Her office was out as long as Cleo needed it for a bedroom. Her own bedroom seemed wrong, somehow selfish. "The kitchen," she decided.

"Good choice. I'll take care of it. Here's the number," he added, taking a small card from his pocket.

"Do I memorize it, then eat the paper?"

"You're all right, Doc." With a chuckle he hefted the bag and headed toward the kitchen. Then stopped. "Seems like you're a little crowded in here. I've got plenty of room. Rebecca's staying at my place."

"Do you think so?" Malachi's voice was dangerously soft.

"Stop it," was all Rebecca said, and she said it under her breath.

"I can take one more, if anyone wants to relocate. That evens things up."

"I'll go." Cleo rolled up off the floor, careful not to look at Gideon.

But Jack looked at him, saw the start of surprise, the quick, baffled anger. "Fine. Saddle up. This won't take me long."

"I don't have much." She shot Tia a grin. "You might actually get some work done this way."

She walked off into the office, and Malachi sent his sister a fulminating look that only made her yawn. "You think I'm letting you take up with a man this way?"

"What way would that be, Malachi?" She fluttered her lashes at him, and the eyes behind them were cold steel.

"We'll just see about all this." He lurched to his feet and strode off into the kitchen after Jack. "I'm going to need a word with you."

"Figured that. Just let me take care of this."

Malachi frowned as he watched him work. He had no idea what the man was doing with the little tools and bits of equipment, but it was very clear Jack knew.

"Hand me the small Phillips head bit out of the kit there," Jack asked.

"You screwing this into the wall?" Malachi handed over the bit, watched Jack fit it onto a mini cordless drill. "She won't care for that."

"Little sacrifices, big payoff. She's already swallowed more than a couple of holes in the wall." He fixed the phone jack in place, ran the line, then, taking what looked like a palm-sized computer out of his bag, ran a series of numbers through it.

"You can use this to contact your mother," Jack said conversationally. "But I wouldn't mention to the doc that the phone company's getting stiffed on the long-distance calls. She's a straight arrow. Your mother's phones are clear. Or were when I was there and checked them out. I showed her what to look for, and she'll be doing a check twice a day. She's a sharp lady. I don't think they'll get past her."

"You form impressions quickly."

"Yeah. This is set. Reach out and touch someone," he added and packed up his tools.

"Then why don't we step into my office?" Malachi suggested, and grabbed a couple of beers out of the refrigerator.

From her seat on the sofa, Rebecca had a clear view of small dramas. She watched her two angry brothers split off into opposite directions, Gideon into the little room to the right, where Cleo had gone. The door slammed smartly behind him. And Malachi out the front door of the apartment with Jack. That door closed with ominous control.

"It seems everyone's gone off to argue without us." She stretched, yawned again. The flight had tired her out more than she'd realized. "Why don't I help you tidy up this disaster we've made of your home. You can tell me what's brewing with my brother and Cleo, and what's brewing with my other brother and you."

Tia looked blankly around the room. "I don't know where to begin."

"Pick your spot," Rebecca told her. "I'm good at catching up."


"WHAT DO YOU mean you'll go?" Gideon demanded.

"Makes sense." Cleo stuffed clothes into her bag. "We're crowded here."

"Not that crowded."

"Enough that you're sleeping on the goddamn roof." She heaved the bag onto the daybed and turned. "Look, Slick, you don't want me here, in your face. You've made that crystal. So splitting off makes it easier all around."

"It's that easy for you? The man says I've got room and you jump over to him?"

Her cheeks went ice-white. "Fuck you."

She grabbed her bag again, and so did he. For ten bitter seconds they waged a fierce tug-of-war. "I didn't mean it that way." He wrenched the bag free, heaved it aside. "What do you take me for?"

"I don't know what I take you for." Despite Malachi's earlier advice, she'd had no intention of using tears on him and was furious that they were blurring her vision. "But I know what you take me for. A liar and a cheat, and a cheap one at that."

"I don't. Damn it all to bloody hell, Cleo, I'm angry with you. I've a right to be."

"Fine. Be as pissed off as you want. I can't stop you. But I don't have to have it shoved down my throat every day. I screwed up. I'm sorry. End of story."

She started to shove by him to retrieve her bag, but he caught her arms, tightening his grip when she tried to jerk away. "Don't cry. I didn't mean to make you cry."

"Let go." Tears were spurting out faster than she could blink them back. "I don't blubber to get my way."

"Don't cry," he said again, and his grip gentled to a caress. "Don't go." He drew her in, rocked her in his arms. "I don't want you to go. I don't know what I want altogether, but I know I don't want you to go."

"This isn't ever going to go anywhere."

"Stay." He rubbed his cheek against hers, transferring tears. "And let's see."

She sighed, let her head rest on his shoulder. She'd missed this. God, she'd missed just this simple connection so much it ached in the bones. "You can't go soft on a woman just because she drips on you, Slick. Just makes a sap out of you."

"Let me worry about that. Here now. Here."

He skimmed his lips over her damp cheek, found her mouth and sank in, soft and slow.

The tenderness of it had her muscles trembling and her belly doing one long, lazy roll. Even when he deepened the kiss it was all warmth, without any of those edgy flashes of heat she expected, she understood.

For one of the first times in her life she stood poised on absolute surrender, with a man in total control of her. Heart, body, mind.

It terrified her. And it filled her.

"Don't be nice to me." She pressed her face into his shoulder as she struggled for balance. "I'll just screw it up."

Not as tough as she pretended, Gideon thought. And not nearly as sure of herself. "Let me worry about that as well. You've only one thing to do at the moment," he added, and tipped her face back to his.

"What?"

He smiled at her. "Unpack."

She sniffled, and hoped to get a little of her own back. "Is that how you get what you want? By being nice?"

"Now and then. Cleo." He cupped her face in his hands, watched the wariness come back into those deep, dark eyes. He didn't mind it. If she was wary of him, she was thinking of him. "You're so beautiful. Seriously beautiful. It can be a bit disconcerting. Unpack," he said again. "I'll tell Burdett you'll be staying here. With me," he added. "You're with me, Cleo. That's something we'll both have to deal with."


ON THE ROOF, Jack took stock. One way in and out, he considered. That made this area either a trap or a solid defense. It might be wise to set up a few measures here.

If a man didn't anticipate a war, he always lost the battle.

"Hell of a view," he commented.

"Got a smoke?"

"No, sorry. Never picked up the habit."

"I quit." Malachi rolled his shoulders. "Some time ago. I'm regretting that right about now. Well then, let's have first things first."

"That would be Rebecca."

Malachi acknowledged this with a nod. "So it would. She shouldn't be here in the first place, but since she is, she can't be staying with you."

"Shouldn't. Can't." Jack turned his back on the view and leaned on the safety wall. "If you've used those words with her very often, I bet you've gotten some interesting scars."

"True enough. She's a perverse creature, our Becca."

"And she's smart. I like her brain. I like her face," Jack added, eyes direct on Malachi's. "I like the whole package. That's a problem for you, her being your sister." He took a pull from the bottle of Harp. "I've got one of my own, so I get that. Mine went off and married some guy despite the fact that, in my opinion, she had no business even knowing what sex meant. She's got two kids now, but mostly, I like thinking she found them under a berry bush. Probably in the same patch where my mother found us."

Amused, Malachi dipped a hand in his pocket. "You grow berries in that flat of yours?"

"Let's put it this way. She's taking the spare room. Her choice. It stays her choice, either way. I gave your mother my word I'd take care of her. I don't break my word. Not to someone I respect anyway."

Malachi was more than a little surprised to find himself relaxed. More yet to realize he believed Jack was as good as his word.

Maybe, just maybe, they'd forge that unit.

"I suppose this saves me from a bloody battle with Rebecca. But the fact remains, she's an impulsive, headstrong girl who—"

"I'm in love with her."

Malachi's eyes widened, his thoughts scattered. "Jesus Christ, man, that's fast work, isn't it?"

"It only took one look, and she knows it. That gives her the advantage." He paused. "She'd use an advantage when it comes to hand."

"She would," Malachi agreed, not without sympathy. "If need be."

"What she doesn't know, and what I haven't figured out, is what I'm going to do about it. I'm not a fatalist. I think people drive the train."

"So do I." He thought of Felix Greenfield, of Henry Wyley, and a sunny afternoon in May. "But we don't always choose the tracks."

"Whatever the tracks, we've got our hand on the switch. If that wasn't the way it worked, I'd believe that those statues, the circle they've made, have something to do with what happened to me when I looked at Rebecca. Since I don't, I'll just say I'm in love with your sister. So you can stop worrying that I'll let anything or anyone hurt her. Including myself. That do it for you?"

"I'm just going to sit down here a minute." He did so, drank contemplatively, then set the bottle on the little iron table by his chair. He bounced his palms off his knees while he studied Jack. "Our father's gone, and I'm the oldest, so it falls to me to ask you . . ." He trailed off, dragged his hands through his hair. "You know, I'm just not ready for it. Let's have part two of this particular discussion at some later date."

Jack tipped back his beer again. "Works for me."

"You're a cool one, you are. Better for her that you are. So let's move on to another area. The Fates."

"You've been in charge."

Malachi leaned back, cocked a brow. "This is a family affair for us, Jack."

"Never said different, but you're in charge. When push comes to shove, the others look to you for the answer. That goes for Tia, too. Probably Cleo, though she's the wild card."

"She's had a rough go, but she's steady enough. You have a problem with what you see as the pecking order here?"

"I might have, except I get the impression you know how to delegate, and how to let everyone play to their strengths. I know what mine are. I don't mind taking orders, Sullivan, if I agree with them. And I won't mind telling you to fuck off if I don't. Bottom line, I owe you. Felix Greenfield," he continued. "And I want the Fates. I'll work with you so we all end up with what we want.

"Next on the bill," he added. "It's a little too loose for my liking to keep Cleo's Fate in Tia's refrigerator. My apartment's got the best security money can buy. I want to keep it in my safe there, along with mine."

Picking up his beer, Malachi passed the bottle from hand to hand as he thought it through. Trust, he thought. Without it, they'd never solidify. "I won't argue with the practicality of that, but to say you'd then have two of three in your hands. What's to stop you from going after the other on your own, or even negotiating with Anita? No offense."

"None taken. Going after the other alone would be tricky, logistically. Not impossible, but tricky. Moreover, Rebecca wouldn't like it one damn bit, and that matters. And finally, I don't double-cross people I like. I especially like the doc." His grin was fast and wolfish.

"As do I."

"Yeah, that comes through clear. As for dealing with Anita, I don't negotiate with sociopaths. And that's just what she is. She gets the chance, she'd take any one of us out, cold blood, then go have her weekly manicure."

Malachi settled back again, drank again. "Agreed. So, we won't give her that opportunity. We've all got some pondering to do."

"Why don't we take twenty-four hours? Then we can give Tia a break and meet at my place tomorrow."

"All right." Malachi got to his feet, held out a hand. "Welcome aboard."

"YOU AND MAL were involved in your private and manly discussion for some time." Rebecca angled in the seat of the tanklike SUV Jack had driven uptown. "What was it about?"

"This. That. The other."

"You can start with this, move along to that."

"It comes to mind that if we'd wanted you in on the discussion, we'd have asked you up on the roof."

"I'm as much a part of this as anyone."

"Nobody says different." He turned off Fifth, headed east to Lexington, watching his rearview mirror as a matter of course.

"And as such, I've a perfect right to know what the two of you had your heads together about. This is a team, Jack, not a group made up of roosters and hens."

"It has nothing to do with the way you button your shirt, Irish, so cool the feminist jets."

"That's insulting."

He headed south awhile, then jogged east again. No tail, he decided, and no surveillance on Tia's building that he could spot. That could change, but for now, it was handy.

He let Rebecca stew while he wound his way back home. He circled the building, keyed in the code for the garage he'd had built to his personal specs. The reinforced steel door rose, and he guided the SUV inside.

He had his Boxster stored inside as well, along with his Harley and his surveillance van. A man, he thought, had to have some toys. Storing them in a public garage had never been an option for him, and not simply because the yearly rate would have outstretched the cost of sending a kid through Harvard Law, but because he wanted them close. And under his own system.

He climbed out, reset the locks and alarms on the door, on the SUV, then uncoded the elevator. "You coming up?"

he asked Rebecca. "Or do you want to sulk in the garage?"

"I'm not sulking." She sailed by him, crossed her arms over her chest. "But it would be a natural enough response to being treated like a child."

"Treating you like a child's the one thing I don't have in mind. Okay, take a pick. You want the rundown of this, that, or the other?"

She tipped her head up, wishing she wasn't amused. "I'll take this."

"This would be your brother expressing his concern that you're staying here with me."

"Well, it's none of his flaming business, is it? And a nerve he has, too, when it's plain he's cozied himself up with Tia. And I hope you told him so."

"No." Jack pulled open the elevator door so she could stomp into the apartment. "I told him I was in love with you."

She stopped dead, spun around. "What? What?"

"Which seemed to ease his mind more than it eases yours. I've got some things to do. Be back in a few hours."

"Back?" As if to catch her balance, she threw her arms out. "You can't just leave after you've said such a thing to me."

"I didn't say it to you. I said it to your brother. Stretch out, Irish. You look beat." And with this, he closed the door, locked her in and left her stammering curses at him.

He didn't go far. It was only one flight down to the base he kept in the building. He worked from there when it was convenient, or when he was simply restless in his apartment upstairs and wanted a distraction.

Right now he wanted both the convenience and the distraction.

It was a comfortable space. He'd never seen the purpose in spartan work areas when there was a choice. There were deep chairs, good lighting to make up for the lack of windows, the antique rugs he favored and a fully equipped kitchen.

He went there first, started coffee and, while it brewed,

accessed the messages that had come through on his various lines. He booted up one of the computers ranged over a long L-shaped counter, called up his e-mail and listened to the electronic voice read it out while he fixed the first cup of coffee.

He answered what couldn't wait, put aside what could, then shifted to the personal messages. The e-mail from his father made him grin.

*The aliens, having performed hideous medical experiments—of an embarrassingly sexual nature—on us, have returned your mother and me to Earth. You can hear all about it on Larry King. Now that I have your attention, maybe you could spare five minutes to get in touch. Your mother sends her love. I don't. I like your sister better. Always did. Guess who.*

With a laugh, Jack sat down at the keyboard. "Okay, okay."

*Sorry to hear about the alien experience. Typically, they insert tracking devices in their abductees. You may want to chew on tinfoil while having any personal conversations, as this is known to jam their frequencies. Just FYI. Recently back in NY. Am keeping gorgeous Irish redhead prisoner in my apartment. Possibility of exotic sexual favors from same may keep me busy for the next couple weeks. Love back to Mom. None to you. I'm not even sure you are my father. You guess who.*

Knowing his father would crack himself up reading the post, Jack hit send. Then got down to work.

He ran a modified check on Cleo, enough in his estimation to placate Anita. On a separate computer he started a background check on her for himself.

He'd already come to the same conclusion as Tia, as Malachi. The six of them were going to have to work together as a single entity. He had no problem with teamwork, but he wanted to know all there was to know about the team.

While the data scrolled, he rolled over to the monitors and, telling himself it was best all around if he kept an eye on Rebecca, engaged the cameras he had installed in his own apartment.

She was in his office, at his computer, and she looked steamed. Curious, he turned on audio.

"Bugger you, Jack, if you think I can't get by your bloody passwords and blocks."

"If you can, Irish," he replied, "I'm going to be very impressed."

He watched her awhile, noting the rapid streak of her fingers over the keyboard, the curl of her lip as she met another obstacle.

Most women, in his experience, when left to their own devices in a man's space would poke in drawers, closets, examine the contents of the medicine cabinet or the kitchen cupboards. But she'd gone straight for the information highway.

It did his heart good.

He muted the audio, then busied himself writing a report on Cleo that would convince Anita he was doing her a favor, and offer her nothing helpful.

"That'll set you on the boil," he thought aloud.

He rolled away again to let it simmer before he read it over one last time and picked up the phone.

"Detectives Bureau. Detective Robbins."

"The man with the badge."

"The man with fraudulent ID."

"Not me, pal. You must be thinking of someone else. How's the crime-fighting world?"

"Same old. How's it going in Paranoia-ville?"

"No complaints. Wondered if you wanted to take that twenty I owe you and go double or nothing on the Angels and O's tonight."

"Are you intimating that I, a public servant, gamble?"

"I'll take the O's."

"You're on, sucker. Now that the pleasantries are over, what're you after?"

"Now you've hurt my feelings. But since you ask, I got some descriptions to run by you. Muscle, probably free-lance, certainly local. Thought maybe you could run them through the system for me, see if anything pops."

"Maybe. You got names?"

"No, but I'm working on it. Bachelor Number One.

White male, forty to forty-five, brown hair, thinning, no eye color, pale complexion, prominent nose. About five-ten, a hundred and seventy."

"Lot of guys fit that, including my brother-in-law. Worthless fuck."

"My information is he likes to use his fists and isn't long on brains."

"Yeah, that's my brother-in-law. Want me to haul his ass in and kick him around?"

"Up to you. Your brother-in-law take any recent trips to Eastern Europe?"

"He doesn't move his white, dimpled butt out of his recliner to go to the corner deli. You looking for a world traveler, Burdett?"

"I'm looking for an asshole who's recently back from a little trip to the Czech Republic."

"That's a coincidence. We've got a corpse on ice, fits your general description. Had a passport in the pocket of his fancy suit. Had two stamps on it. One Praha. That's, my erudite friends tell me, Prague, Czech Republic. The other was New York, about ten days old."

Bull's-eye, Jack thought, and swiveled back to a keyboard. "Can you spare the name?"

"Don't see why not. Carl Dubrowsky, Bronx boy. Got a pretty yellow sheet on him—mostly assault—and a skate on a Man One. What do you want with our dead guy, Jack?"

Jack plugged in the name and started a search of his own. "Tell me how he got dead."

"It was probably the four holes a twenty-five-caliber put into him. He turned up stiff in an empty warehouse in Jersey. Let's have a little quid pro quo here."

"I've got nothing right now, but I'll hand it to you when I do." He switched computers, readied to start a second search. "Got an address on that warehouse?"

"Jesus, why don't I just fax you the file?"

"Would ya?"

At Bob's rude response, Jack grinned and noted down the address.

When he'd finished on the phone, he typed up meticulous notes on all the data he'd generated. He was getting to his feet, coffee on his mind, when he glanced at the monitors.

The maniacal gleam in Rebecca's eyes had him moving closer, switching the audio back on.

"Not so smart, are you?" she was muttering. "Not so bloody clever."

"You are," he commented, surprised and, yes, impressed, that she'd gotten past his security. Admittedly he didn't keep anything confidential on that unit, and the blocks were moderate. But they were there, and it had taken a hacker with considerable skill to cut past them so quickly.

"Just as I thought," he said to her image. "We're made for each other."

He got another cup of coffee and went back to work while she raided his hard drive.

Twenty minutes later, he'd done all he felt he needed to do for the moment. And so, he noted as he looked toward the monitors again, had she.

She switched the computer off, stretched, then, looking pleased with herself, wandered out of the room, across the living space and down the hall. Jack shifted his attention to the next monitor, watched her roll the stiffness out of her shoulders, pull the band out of her hair and shake it out.

When she started to unbutton her blouse he reminded himself he wasn't a Peeping Tom. He ordered himself to switch off the cameras.

And he tortured himself by watching her peel the blouse away.

When she reached behind for the bra clasp, he ground his teeth and hit the kill switch.

He got a beer instead of coffee and spent the next half hour filing away his work. And wondering how the hell he could be expected to concentrate.

By the time he walked into his apartment again, he had a number of very interesting fantasies going. None of which involved finding her fully dressed but for her pretty, bare feet in his kitchen with fragrant steam puffing out of a pot.

"What are you doing?"

"Why, I'm climbing the Matterhorn, what do you think I'm doing?"

He stepped in, took another good sniff of the pot. Of her. "It looks suspiciously like cooking."

The shower and change, as well as the session on his computer, had revived her. But while fatigue wasn't a factor any longer, temper was still in play.

"As I had no idea how long you intended to keep me locked in here, I wasn't about to sit around and starve to death. You've no fresh fruit or vegetables, by the way, so I'm making due with canned and jarred."

"I've been out of town. Write down whatever you want, and I'll get it for you."

"I can do my own marketing."

"I don't want you going out alone."

She slid a carving knife out of the wooden block, idly checked its tip with her thumb. Her mother's daughter, Jack thought. Both knew how to make their point.

"You've no say where I go, or when."

"You use that on me, you're going to be really sorry after."

Her smile was every bit as thin and sharp as the blade. "You'd be sorrier, wouldn't you?"

"Can't argue with that." He opened the fridge, took out a bottle of water. "Let me rephrase. I'd prefer you didn't go out alone until you know the lay of the land."

"I'll take your preferences into consideration. And one more thing. If you think that saying you love me is going to have me leaping joyfully into your bed—"

"Don't push that button, Rebecca." His tone had gone hard, very hard and very cold. "You won't like the result."

She angled her head. She found it interesting that drawing the knife had barely made him blink. But she'd ruffled him quite a bit by mentioning love, and sex.

"I don't like you winging something like that out at me, then closing the door in my face."

"I closed it in my face."

She considered that, accepted it. "I'm capable of doing that, if and when I want." With her left hand, she picked up a spoon, stirred the pot. "I don't know what I want just now. When I do, you'll be the first to hear about it. Meanwhile, don't shut me up in here like a parakeet in a cage again. If you try, I'll break all your pretty knickknacks, rip your clothes to rags, stop up your toilet and various other unpleasant things. And I'll find the way out as well."

"Okay, fair enough. When do we eat?"

She huffed out a breath, slid the knife back into its slot. "An hour or so. Enough time for you to go out again and fetch back some French or Italian bread to go with this meal. And something sweet for after it."

She tossed her hair back. "I was pissed off, but not enough to bake."

# Twenty

I T was, Tia told herself, a foolish child who was nervous about walking into her parents' home. But her palms were damp, and her stomach churned as she stepped into the dining room of the Marsh town house.

It was eight forty-five. Her father sat down to his breakfast every morning, seven days a week, at precisely eight-thirty. He would now be on his second cup of coffee and have moved from the front page of *The New York Times* to the financial section. He'd have finished his fruit and would have moved on to the next course. Which, Tia noticed, was an egg-white omelette today.

Her mother would take her herbal tea, her freshly squeezed juice and her first of the daily dose of eight glasses of bottled water—using them to wash down her morning complement of vitamins and medication—in bed. With it, she'd have a single slice of whole wheat toast, dry, and a cup of seasonal fruit.

At nine-twenty, Alma would come downstairs, regale Stewart with whatever physical complaints she might have that morning, ramble off her appointment and task schedule while he checked his briefcase.

They would kiss good-bye, and he would walk out the door at nine-thirty.

It was, Tia believed, as reliable and exacting a schedule as a Swiss train.

There had been a time when she'd been part of that schedule. Or, she thought, had been worked into it. Was it their fault or hers that she'd been so unable to do anything, anything at all, to interfere with its precision?

Their fault or hers that even now the idea of doing so made her queasy?

Stewart glanced up as Tia entered, and his creased brow lifted in mild surprise. "Tia. Did we have an appointment?"

"No. I'm sorry to interrupt your morning."

"Don't be foolish." But even as he said it, he glanced at his watch. "Would you like some breakfast? Coffee?"

"No, thank you. Nothing." She stopped herself from linking her restless fingers together and sat across from him. "I wanted to speak to you before you went in to work."

"All right." He spread a thin layer of butter on lightly toasted whole wheat bread, then blinked. "You've cut your hair."

"Yes." Feeling foolish, she lifted a hand to it. "A few days ago."

"It's very flattering. Very chic."

"Do you think?" She felt her color rise. Foolish again, she decided, to be so flustered by a compliment from her own father. But they came so few and far between. "When Mother saw it, I don't think she was pleased. I imagined she'd have told you."

"She may have." He smiled a little as he continued to eat. "I don't always listen, particularly when she's in a mood. She has been."

"It's my fault, and one of the reasons I wanted to see you this morning. Mother dropped by my apartment on her way to a doctor's appointment. It was . . . an awkward moment. I was with someone." She drew a long breath. "I was with a man."

"I see." Stewart hesitated, frowned, stirred his coffee. "Do I see, Tia?"

"I'm involved with someone. He's staying with me at my apartment while he's in New York. I'm working on a project with him, and some other people just now. And

I'm . . . I'm having an affair with him." She finished on a rush and fell into miserable silence.

Stewart contemplated his coffee another moment. It was a toss-up which of them was more uncomfortable. "Tia, your personal . . . relationships aren't my business, or your mother's. Naturally, I assume anyone you're involved with is suitable and appropriate."

"I'm not sure you'd find him so either, but I do. Surprisingly," she rushed on, "he thinks I'm interesting and attractive, which makes me feel interesting and attractive. And I like it. In any case, Mother was—and I imagine is—very upset. I'm not sure I can smooth things over with her, but I'll certainly try. I'm going to apologize in advance if I'm unsuccessful. I can't and won't order my life to suit her needs. Or yours. So I'm sorry."

"Well." Stewart set down his fork, drew air through his nose. "Well," he repeated. "I never expected to hear that from you. You're saying that though your mother and I may disapprove, may even be angry, you'll do as you please."

She *knew* the pain in her stomach was tension, but couldn't help wondering if she had a tumor. "In a nutshell, I suppose that's it."

"Good. It's about goddamn time."

She forgot all about the possibility of stomach cancer. "Excuse me?"

"I love your mother, Tia. Don't ask me why, as I haven't a clue. She's a pain in the ass, but I love her."

"Yes, I know. I mean, I know you love her—not that she's . . . I always knew you loved each other," she finished.

"You say that as if you weren't part of the equation."

She started to make an excuse, then simply let the truth spill out. "I don't feel I am."

"Then we're all at fault. She's never been able to cut the cord with you. Perhaps I cut it too easily, or too quickly. And you tolerated both actions."

"I guess I did. But you've always been a good father to me."

"No, I haven't." He set his coffee down, studied her astonished face. "And I can't say I gave the matter much thought or attention since you were, oh, twelve or so. But I have since the day you came to ask for Henry Wyley's journal, and I brought it down to you. And you were sitting, waiting for me, and you looked so unhappy."

"I was unhappy."

"And surprised now that I noticed." He lifted a hand, then picked up his cup again. "It surprised me as well, and made me wonder how often I hadn't noticed."

"I made you unhappy," Tia stated, "by not being what you wanted."

"Yes, and my way of dealing with that was to leave you to your mother, as it seemed you had a great deal more in common with her than with me. Strange, I've always considered myself a very fair man. But that was remarkably unfair to all involved. The best thing for you and your mother, in my opinion, is your cutting the cord yourself. You've let her push you around your entire life. Whenever I tried to interfere—and I can't claim I tried particularly hard—one or both of you circumvented that effort."

"You gave up on me."

"You seemed content enough the way things were. Children leave home, Tia. If one's committed to a marriage, then one lives with another person most of one's life. I've structured mine in a way that satisfies and pleases me. You come from two very self-absorbed people. And what are your phobias and nervous disorders but another sort of self-absorption?"

She stared at him, then let out a half laugh. "I suppose you're right. I don't want to stay that way. I'm almost thirty, how much can I change?"

"Whether or not you change, you're still almost thirty. What difference does your age make?"

Nearly speechless, she sat back. "You've never talked to me like this before."

"You never came to me before." He moved one shoulder, elegantly. "It's not my habit to go out of my way, or vary my routine. Speaking of which . . ." He checked his watch.

"I need a favor," Tia said quickly.

"This is quite the red-letter day in the Marsh household."

"It concerns the Three Fates."

The vague impatience that had crossed Stewart's face faded. "You've developed a significant interest in them recently."

"Yes, I have. And I'd like that interest to stay between you and me. Anita Gaye also has a significant interest. She may ask you about them again, try to pick your brain for any detail you might have through Henry Wyley's connection to them. If and when she does, I wonder if you could remember—vaguely, casually—some mention of the third Fate being seen or reputed to having been seen in Athens."

"Athens?" Stewart sat back. "What game are you playing, Tia?"

"An important one."

"Anita isn't a woman who would scruple to break rules if doing so was profitable."

"I'm more aware of that than I can tell you."

"Tia, are you in trouble?"

For the first time since she'd entered the house, she smiled. "That's something you've never asked me. Not once in my life. If I am in trouble, I'm determined to handle it, even enjoy it. Can you find a way to mention Athens to her?"

"Easily."

"And not, under any circumstances, to mention Wyley's journal or my relationship with the man Mother met at my apartment?"

"Why would I? Tia, do you have a line on one of the Fates?"

She wanted to tell him, wanted the thrill of seeing pride and surprise in his eyes. But she shook her head. "It's very complicated, but I'll tell you everything as soon as I can." She got to her feet. "One last question. As a dealer, what would you pay for them?"

"It would depend. Speculatively, up to ten million. If I had an interested client, I'd advise him to go upwards of twenty. Perhaps a bit more. Contingent on testing and verification, of course."

"Of course." She walked over, kissed his cheek. "I'll go upstairs and try to make things up with Mother."

* * *

WHILE TIA WAS stroking Alma's ruffled feathers, Jack dropped in on the Detectives Bureau. He'd have preferred leaving Rebecca in his apartment, but since locking her in was the only way to be sure she stayed there, he'd brought her along. He didn't care to risk coming home to a trashed apartment, and had no doubt she'd make good on that threat.

Bringing her had the added benefit of watching her absorb and file every detail of the cop shop. He could almost hear the wheels turning in her head as they climbed the stairs to the detectives' bull pen. Just as he had the satisfaction of seeing cops give her the same once-over.

He saw Bob at his desk, phone cradled on his shoulder. And watched his friend's gaze shift over, scan Rebecca, then sweep up. There was a question in them when they met Jack's, and the warmth of humor and appreciation.

"Hang here just a minute," Jack told Rebecca, then strolled to Bob's desk. He sat on the corner, exchanged a few nods of greeting with other cops while Bob finished his call.

"Hubba hubba," Bob said. "Where'd you get the sexy little redhead?"

"How's your wife?"

"Smart enough to know when I stop looking at sexy little redheads, it's time to shovel the dirt over my cold, dead body. What do you want?"

"More information about the cold, dead body we discussed yesterday."

"I gave you what I had."

"I need a photo."

"Why don't you just ask for my badge?"

"Thanks, I can get my own. I might be able to shake something loose on it for you, but I need to ID him first."

"Let's try this. You tell me what you know, then maybe I can find a picture of the stiff."

"Want to meet the redhead?"

Bob laid his fingers on his own wrist, nodded. "Yeah, I've still got a pulse. What do you think?"

With a grin Jack motioned Rebecca over. "Detective Bob Robbins, Rebecca Sullivan, the woman I'm going to marry."

Bob's jaw dropped, then he was on his feet. "Well damn, Jack. Damn. Nice job. Hey, good to meet you."

Rebecca smiled as Bob pumped her hand. "Jack has delusions of grandeur. At the moment, we're in the way of being business associates."

"She's a tough sell, but I'm working on it. Irish, why don't you tell our speechless friend here what you found out about the warehouse in New Jersey."

"Of course. Doing a bit of digging last night, it came to light that that particular property, which most recently was the scene of a murder, was sold the day before that unfortunate event by Morningside Antiquities."

"And that should interest me because?"

"Let me show the picture to a couple people," Jack continued. "If my hunch plays, I'll have an interesting answer to that question."

"You got a lead on an open homicide, Jack, you don't dick around with it."

"Follow up on Morningside."

"Anita Gaye," Rebecca said clearly, and had both men scowling at her. "Fortunately I don't have any testosterone muddling my ego. Anita Gaye of Morningside Antiquities. You might want to take a look at her, Detective Robbins. There's no point in going further until we've shown the picture and verified that the man who was killed is indeed the one we think he is."

She shot Bob a brilliant smile. "We're all after the same thing in the end, aren't we, Detective? But if you don't trust this one here"—she jerked a head toward Jack—"I'll figure you have good reasons not to. I'm still working on whether I trust him or not myself."

Bob sucked air between his teeth. "I'll get you a picture."

"Ever heard about keeping an ace in the hole?" Jack grumbled when Bob walked away.

"I have, yes. As I've heard about laying cards on the table when it's time to deal. And my way worked." She scooped her hair back, studied his face. "You throw marriage around pretty freely, Jack."

"No, I don't. You're it. Get used to it."

"Why, that's so flaming romantic, I feel I might swoon."

"I'll give you some romance, Irish. Just pick the time and place."

Not quite as sure of herself as she wanted to be, she folded her arms over her chest. "Just be keeping your mind on the job."

"Consider it multitasking again," he said, then eased off the desk when Bob came back with a file.

TIA DID THE best she could with her mother. A thorough stroking would have taken two or three hours at least, and she just didn't have the time to spare. She had one more stop to make. If she didn't keep on schedule, Malachi and the others would worry and wonder.

There was an odd comfort in that, she realized. Having someone worry about you. She supposed, if she were honest, she'd let herself fall into that comfort zone with her mother. Always. Though the truth was Alma didn't worry about her daughter nearly as much as she worried about herself.

That was her nature, Tia told herself as she stepped out of the cab on Wall Street. All the therapy sessions with Dr. Lowenstein had never pushed her into understanding and accepting that one fact.

It had taken an Irishman, three silver statues and an odd mix of new friends to clear her vision and stiffen her spine.

Or maybe, in some strange way, it had taken Anita Gaye. When all was said and done and her life got back to whatever passed as normal, she'd have to thank Anita for thrusting her into a situation that forced her to test her own abilities.

Of course, if things worked out as she hoped, Tia doubted Anita would appreciate the gratitude.

She hummed as she rode up the elevator in the brokerage firm. Tia Marsh, she thought, scheming, plotting, having regular sex. And all without chemical aids.

Well, hardly any.

She felt rather smug, almost confident. And secretly powerful.

It was even better when she stopped by Carrie's assistant's desk and realized the man didn't recognize her. "Tia Marsh," she said, flustered and delighted when she saw him blink in surprise. "Does Ms. Wilson have a minute to spare?"

"Dr. Marsh. Of course." He stared at her as he reached for his phone. "I'll just let her know you're here. You look wonderful today."

"Thank you."

She was going shopping, Tia decided, at the first opportunity, for an entire new wardrobe to go with the hair. And the attitude.

She was going to buy something really, really red.

"Tia." Carrie hurried out of her office. She looked sharp and smart, and very rushed. "We didn't have an appointment, did we?"

"No. I'm sorry. I just need a few minutes if you can manage it."

"A few is what I've got. Come on back. Tod, I'm going to need the analysis on the Brockaway accounts by noon."

"He didn't recognize me," Tia commented as Carrie led her into her snazzy corner office.

"What? Oh, Tod?" Carrie laughed, shot a look at the computer screen where she'd been working, then headed to her coffeepot. "Well, you do look different, honey. Fabulous, really." She poured a cup, didn't bother to ask Tia if she wanted any, as it was real coffee. Then took a good look at her friend as she sat. "Really fabulous. Not just the hair, either." She set the mug aside, got back to her feet, scrutinized Tia's face.

"You've had sex."

"Carrie! For heaven's sake." Tia closed the office door, quickly.

"You've had sex since I saw you." Carrie wagged a finger. "Spill it."

"I didn't come here to talk about that, and you've only got a few minutes."

To settle the matter, Carrie simply strode to her desk, snatched up her phone. "Tod, hold my calls, and tell Minlow I may be a few minutes late for our ten o'clock. There." She hung up the phone. "Talk. I want details. Names, dates, positions."

"It's complicated." Tia gnawed on her bottom lip. It was like being Clark Kent, she decided, and not being able to tell anyone you were really Superman. She couldn't stand it. "You can't tell anyone."

"What am I, the town crier? It's Carrie, Tia. I already know all your secrets. Or I did. Who is he?"

"Malachi. Malachi Sullivan."

"The Irish guy? He came back?"

"He's staying with me."

"He's *living* with you? I'm going to cancel my ten o'clock."

"No, no." Tia pushed her hands through her hair and laughed. "I don't have time. Really. As soon as I can, I'll tell you everything. But he . . . we're . . . it's amazing. I've never felt so . . . potent," she decided and, unable to keep still, wandered around the office as she spoke. "That's a good word. Potent. He can barely keep his hands off me. Isn't that something? And he actually listens to me, asks my opinion. He makes fun of me, but not in a mean sort of way. He makes me look at myself, Carrie, and when I do, I'm not so stupid, so clumsy, so inept."

"You've never been any of those things, and if he's letting you see that, I'm disposed to like him. When do I meet him?"

"It's complicated, as I said—"

"Oh Christ, he's married."

"No. No, nothing like that. It's a project we're working on."

"Tia, just let me get this out of the way. Is he asking you for money, for an investment of any kind?"

"No, Carrie. But thanks for worrying."

"You're in love with him."

"Probably." She took a deep breath as her stomach fluttered. "I'll think about that later. Right now I'm in the middle of something that's exciting, sensitive and very likely dangerous."

"Now you're scaring me, Tia."

"I mean to." She thought of Cleo's friend. "Because it's vital you don't tell anyone what I've said to you. You don't mention Malachi's name." She reached in her purse and took out a slip of paper. "If you call me about anything that has to do with this discussion, use this number. My phones are tapped."

"For God's sake, Tia, what's this guy dragged you into?"

"I dragged myself. That's the wonder of it. And I need you to do me a favor that might be somewhat unethical. It could be illegal, I'm not sure."

"I can't even think of a response to that."

"Anita Gaye." Tia leaned forward. "Morningside Antiquities. I need to know how much she's worth, personally and with the business. I need to know how much liquid cash she can get her hands on, quickly. And she can't know you're looking. That's essential. Is there a way to get the information without it coming back to you?"

As if to anchor herself, Carrie braced her hands on the arms of her chair. "You want me to look into someone's financials and pass that data on to you?"

"I do, but only if you can do it without anyone knowing you're involved."

"You're not going to tell me why?"

"I'm going to tell you there's a great deal at stake, and I'm going to use the information you give me to try to do something important. And right. I'm also going to tell you that Anita Gaye is dangerous, and likely responsible for at least one death."

"Holy God, Tia. I can't believe I'm having this conversation. Not with you. If you believe this about her, why aren't you talking to the police?"

"It's complicated."

"I want to meet this Sullivan character. Judge for myself."

"As soon as I can manage it. I promise. I know what I'm asking you, and if you can't do it, I'll understand."

"I need to think about it." Carrie let out a long breath. "I need to really think about it."

"Okay. Use the number I gave you when you call." Tia got to her feet. "She's hurt people, Carrie. I'm going to see she pays for it."

"Damn it, Tia, you be careful."

"No," she stated as she walked to the door. "Not anymore."

"GIVE HER A few more minutes," Gideon urged. "What good will it do for you to go running around the city looking for her?"

"She's been gone over two hours." For more than half that time, Malachi had been sick with worry. "I should never have let her go out alone. How did the woman get so hardheaded so fast? When I met her she was pliable as putty."

"You want a doormat, go buy one."

Malachi spun around, burned Cleo with one hot look. "Don't piss me off."

"Well, stop pacing around like an overprotective daddy whose little girl is past curfew. Tia's not stupid. She'll handle herself."

"I never said she was stupid, but as for handling herself, she's no experience doing that, has she? If she'd answer her bloody mobile, I wouldn't have to pace."

"We agreed not to use the mobile except for emergencies," Gideon reminded him. "They're like radios, aren't they?"

"This is a fucking emergency. I'm going to find her." He strode to the door, wrenched it open. Tia all but spilled into his arms.

"Where have you been? Are you all right?" He nearly lifted her and the bags she carried off the ground.

"Worrywart here was about to call out the Marines. Is that food?" Cleo demanded, and strolled over to snag one of the bags. "Hot damn! Lunch."

"I stopped at the deli," Tia began.

"I'm not having it. I'm just not having it." Malachi pulled the other bag out of her hands and shoved it at Gideon. "How much money have you got?" he asked his brother.

"About twenty American."

"Let's have it." Malachi dug into his own pocket. "We're not living off you this way, like a bunch of leeches."

"Malachi, the money doesn't matter. It's just—" Tia stopped when he cut her off.

"So far it's mostly been yours, hasn't it? Well, that stops. We'll have to get in touch with Ma, have her wire some funds over."

"You will not."

When Tia set her jaw, planted her feet, Gideon wagged a thumb toward the kitchen. Both he and Cleo slid silently out of the range of fire.

"I'm not living off a woman under any circumstances, but I'm damned if I'll live off one I'm sleeping with."

"We agreed you'll pay me back. And if you're so sensitive about me fronting the money while we're sleeping together, then we can just stop sleeping together."

"You think so?" Riding on fury, he grabbed her arm and dragged her toward the bedroom.

"You stop it. Stop it right now." She tripped, came right out of her left shoe. "What's wrong with you? You're acting like a maniac."

"I feel like one." He slammed the bedroom door behind them, shoved her back against it. "I'm not giving you up, and that's that." He crushed his mouth down on hers, and she could all but taste frustration and wounded pride. "And I'm not having you pay for every crust of bread I swallow."

She managed to catch a breath. "I bought potato salad, smoked turkey and cannolis. I forgot to pick up a crust of bread."

He opened his mouth, closed it again, then just laid his brow on hers. "This isn't a joke to me."

"It should be. There's a lot more at stake than a grocery bill, Malachi. If you have your mother wire money, it might be traced. It's just foolish."

She ran her hands over his back, kneading the tense muscles through his shirt. "I have money. I've always had money. What I've never had is someone who cares enough about me to be embarrassed to take it."

"I couldn't stand it if you thought I take you for granted."

"I don't." Wanting him to see, to know, she framed his face with her hands, lifted it. "You make me feel special."

"You were gone so long, I was half mad with worry."

"I'm sorry. It's all so strange. All so strange and wonderful." She touched her lips to his, lightly, then again when she felt his heart leap against hers.

Power, she thought, was a lovely thing. She slid her arms around his neck, walked him backward toward the bed.

"I'm going to seduce you." She nipped lightly at his jaw. "It's my first attempt, so you'll have to forgive any missteps." She angled her head, rubbing her lips teasingly over his. "How'm I doing so far?"

"Spot on."

She nudged him down to sit on the bed, then straddled his lap. "About the money," she whispered as she unbuttoned his shirt.

"What money?"

She laughed, spread his shirt open, then ran her hands possessively over his chest. "I can always charge you interest."

"All right. Whatever."

"And penalties," she said, then scraped her teeth over his shoulder. She eased back, peeled off her jacket, but when he reached for the buttons of her blouse, she brushed his hands away.

"No, let me. You just watch."

"I want to touch you."

"I know." She loosened the blouse slowly. "I love knowing it."

She shrugged off the blouse, rose onto her knees to unhook her trousers. "Lie back," she urged, nibbling at his lips once more.

She let her mouth roam, imagining his body as a lovely, private feast. When her tongue slicked over his belly, she felt his muscles tremble.

He was already hard, already desperate. And he knew she wanted to lead the way. He struggled to lie passive as she undressed him, not to simply grab and take as she slowly stripped him.

When she used her mouth, he choked back a groan and fisted his hands in the bedspread.

His mind emptied, then filled with her.

Soft skin, hot mouth, eager hands, and that subtle, quiet scent he would always associate with her; the combination flooded him with need for her.

At the sounds of pleasure that purred out of her throat as she nibbled on him, heat washed into his blood, dewed his skin. She slid over him, around him.

He was drenched in her. Drowning.

She could feel his heart galloping. Almost taste the frenzied beat as she skimmed her lips over his chest. It was a marvel to see how his body quivered even as he clung to control, as he held himself back so she could do the taking.

It was a revelation to know she could take what she wanted, as she wanted. As long as she wanted.

She could hear his breath going ragged, feel the tension in his muscles as she touched and tasted, teased and tortured. All the while she felt so fluid, so agile. So . . . potent.

When he gasped out her name, she rose over him, then leaned down to pleasure them both with a deep and drugging kiss.

"No one ever wanted me like this, or made me want, like this."

A sound, almost a purr, rippled in her throat as she lowered, took him inside her. When his hands came to her hips, fingers digging in, she shuddered.

She rocked, moaning when the pressure built inside her, then rolled through her in a glorious rising swell that

gushed heat and light and need. She took him, took herself, slowly, savoring each ripple of pleasure.

When their eyes met, she smiled and, smiling, watched
his go blind. On a long sigh of triumph, she let her head
fall back, let her body rule, and slid silkily under.

# PART THREE
## Cutting

*We are spinning our own
fates, good or evil, and
never to be undone.
Every smallest stroke of
virtue or of vice leaves its
never so little scar.*

WILLIAM JAMES

# Twenty-one

"THAT's him." Cleo stared at the photocopy image. "He was one of the guys in Prague. The shorter one," she said, glancing up at Gideon for confirmation. "The second guy was taller, broader, and he came after us on foot while this guy went for their car. The bigger guy was the one who I spotted tailing me after I met with Anita."

She took a deep breath to relieve the pressure in her chest as she studied the bland black-and-white photo. "This is the one who must've gone after Mikey. This is the one who killed him."

Gideon laid a hand on her shoulder, left it there in a light, comforting weight. "We got a pretty good look at them in Prague."

"We'll have Bob run his known associates, see if we get a line on the second man." Jack took the photo, pinned it to a board he'd set up.

They were in his building, on what he thought of as the business level. "His name's Carl Dubrowsky. Most of his accomplishments run to assault and larceny. Hired muscle, low on brains. He was found in an empty warehouse in New Jersey, the unhappy recipient of four twenty-five-caliber bullets."

"Do you think his partner killed him?" Tia asked.

"Not with a twenty-five. A guy carries a gun like that, he's going to get laughed out of the KneeCappers Union."

"Anita." Malachi walked over to the board. Jack had a photo of Anita pinned there as well. "She wouldn't have been pleased he stirred up the air by killing Cleo's friend and getting nothing out of it. I didn't realize until now that I believed her capable of murder—by her own hand. But, of course, she is, isn't she?"

"I'd say." The man was cool, Jack decided as he studied Malachi. And steady. Someone he could work with. "The warehouse had just been sold by Morningside. My friend on the force will be having a talk with Anita shortly. What do you think her reaction will be to that?"

"It'll piss her off," Malachi said, then dipped his hands in his pockets and rocked lightly on his heels. "Then it'll please her. Add a bit of spice to the game. She'd never believe herself vulnerable."

"It stops being a game when people die." Rebecca waited until her brother looked at her. "Cleo's lost a friend, and the man responsible for that is dead as well. Are any of us here willing to go that far, willing to kill over a few pounds of silver?"

"That's not what it's about, Becca." Gideon left his hand on Cleo's shoulder. "It's long since gone beyond being about the value of the thing."

"For you," she agreed. "For Mal. For you, Cleo?" she asked.

"I want her to pay. I want her to lose. I want her to hurt."

Rebecca crouched in front of Cleo's chair, stared hard into her eyes. "How far will you go for it?"

"He was a sweet, harmless man. I loved him. How far will I go? All the way."

Rebecca let out a breath and got to her feet, turned to Tia. "And you? You've been scooped up into this thing, had your life tumbled around. If we move forward from here, there's no going back. But you could walk away now and pick up your life as it was before we charged into it."

Could she? Tia wondered. Could she go back to tiptoeing through her life, afraid someone might notice her? Could she bury herself again in the deeds of gods and never have the courage to do? To be?

Oh, she hoped not.

"I've never done anything special in my life. Nothing that really mattered. I've never stood up for myself, not really, not when it became uncomfortable or easier to fade back into a corner again. No one who knows me expects me to. Except the people in this room. She has our property," she said, nodding at Malachi. "Yours and mine, and she doesn't deserve it. The Three Fates belong together, and I . . ." She trailed off, flushing a bit when she realized everyone was looking at her.

"No." Malachi watched her. "Go on. Finish it out."

"All right." She steadied herself as she'd learned to do before a public lecture. "Everyone here has a connection to the Fates and, because of them, to each other. It's like a tapestry. The Fates spun, measured, cut the threads of Henry Wyley, Felix Greenfield, the Cunninghams, even the White-Smythes. The design, the pattern they made is already begun."

"You're saying it's all been ordained," Jack began, but she shook her head.

"It's not as simple as that. Fate isn't black or white, right or left. People aren't just plopped down and made to follow one route in life on the whims of the gods. If that were true, we'd have to say Hitler was only a victim of his own destiny, and therefore blameless. I'm getting off track."

"Uh-uh," Cleo disagreed. "You're going under it. It's cool."

"Well. I suppose what I'm trying to say is we have decisions to make, actions to take, good ones and bad ones that make up the texture of our lives. Everything we do or don't do matters," she said to Jack. "Everything counts at the end of the day. But the tapestry that started with the people who came before us isn't finished."

"Now we're the threads," Malachi said.

"Yes. We've begun to choose the pattern, at least individually, that we hope to make. We've still to agree on, to decide the pattern we want to make together. I believe there's a reason we've come together like this, a reason we have a pattern to make. We have to see it through, try to find a way to complete it. I believe we're meant to try. However foolish that sounds."

"It doesn't sound foolish." Malachi stepped toward her, kissed her brow. "Here we have the heart of the thing," he said. "No one cups the heart of the thing in her hand quite like you do."

"You didn't ask me what I'd do," Jack commented, and Rebecca turned to him.

"I'll speak to this one, Tia. You've set your sights on the goal, and that's it for you. You're a single-minded man, Jack. That's how you've gotten where you are in the world."

"Good call. Now that we've got that settled, we can move on to how we intend to reach that goal."

"That wasn't meant to be an actual compliment."

"I got that, too," he said to Rebecca. "These are photographs of Morningside, and Anita's house. Burdett handled security upgrades on both locations."

"That's handy, isn't it?" Interested, Malachi moved over to study the photos. "That's quite the place she's got there."

"Marry a rich fool old enough to be your grandfather, wait it out till he keels over, and pull in the big pot." Jack shrugged. "Paul Morningside was a good man, but he was deaf, dumb and blind when it came to Anita. And to give her credit, she played the role perfectly. You don't want to underestimate her. She's a smart woman. Her weakness is greed. Whatever she has, it's never going to be enough—"

"That's not her biggest one." Tia nearly jumped when she realized she'd interrupted. "I'm sorry. I was thinking out loud."

Jack angled away from the board. "What's her biggest weakness?"

"Vanity. Well, ego, really, of which her vanity plays a large part. She sees herself as smarter, more clever, more ruthless. More everything than other people. She stole the first Fate from Malachi. She didn't have to. She could have bought it from him. She could have doctored an analysis to convince him the piece was of little value, or some variation of that. She stole it because it was more fun, and it fed her ego. 'Look, I can take this right out of your hand, and there's nothing you can do about it.' She gets what she wants, and she hurts and embarrasses someone. That adds a shine for her."

"That's an excellent psychological profile for a mythologist," Jack commented.

"You spend your life getting walked on, you learn to recognize the tread. Greed is a flaw, but her ego is her true Achilles' heel. Notch the arrow, aim for the ego, and she'll stumble."

"Isn't she a marvel?" Grinning, Malachi grabbed Tia's hand, kissed it lavishly.

"Snatching the Fate from under her nose ought to hit her ego dead center," Jack agreed. "There are a number of steps we have to take before going there. First is to determine whether she's keeping it here"—he tapped the photo of Morningside's entrance—"or here." And the front-on view of her town house.

"Since we can't be sure, at least at the moment, we'll have to work out how to get to it in either place." Gideon moved over to give the board a closer look. "None of us has any experience breaking into a place."

"You're forgetting the time we broke into the basement of Hurlihy's Pub and tapped into that keg of Harp," Malachi reminded him.

"I've worked to forget it for more than ten years, as I came out of it with a head big as the moon."

"And when Ma found out," Rebecca put in, "she knocked your big, stupid heads together, dragged you by the ears to the priest for confession."

"Then we spent the whole of that summer at Hurlihy's beck and call," Malachi finished. "We paid for that lager ten times over." He sent Jack an easy smile. "Not a very good foundation for thievery, I'm afraid."

"That's all right, I'll teach you." At Rebecca's steely stare, he sat, stretched out his long legs. "When you make your living putting up obstacles for thieves, you have to understand the criminal mind, and have a certain amount of respect for it. We'll need to break into both places," he added with a nod to Gideon. "To set her up for the full fall, we'll need to do both."

"Dupe her," Malachi concurred. "Set her up, then put a nice pretty frame around her." With his fingers he traced a box around Anita's photo. "I like the sound of it."

"It sounds awfully complicated," Tia put in.

"Who wants a bland tapestry? We'll have to plan each level," Jack went on. "And connect them. To start, there are four safes in the town house. Double that at Morningside. It'll take some time and effort to circumvent the security, get in, open each safe—if necessary—get the Fate, get out and reestablish the security. I've got some ideas on how to use Morningside to narrow the field. But when we go for the gold, we'll need a little more time and space. If we can get her out of the way for a few days, we minimize the risk."

"I, um, think she might go to Athens." Tia cleared her throat and they all turned to her. "I asked my father if he might casually mention the Athens connection to her. He doesn't know what's going on, but I think he'll do it for me. He seemed sort of intrigued that I asked."

Jack sat back. "Good thinking. And when I give her my report, and tell her one Cleopatra Toliver booked a flight to Athens, that should nail it. We've got a lot to do before we hammer that home. We're going to want to be ready to move on the Fate as soon as she's at cruising level."

"She didn't go to Prague after Cleo," Rebecca reminded him. "Why would she go to Athens? She could send one of her pie-faced goons."

"They failed." Malachi sat on the arm of Tia's chair. "And if she's the one who killed the guy in the warehouse, she's upped the stakes considerably. She won't send an underling this time. At least not if she's convinced she may be able to scoop up both remaining Fates in one go."

"All right, that's logical." Rebecca pursed her lips, studying the board. "We want to have her keep the Fate in her home, I'd think. Far too many places to hide something in a place like Morningside, and I'd have to assume the security would be tighter there?"

"It is." It pleased Jack that their thoughts aligned.

"We'd want her to have a concern, then, that Morningside isn't safe enough." Gideon angled his head. "Do we lift something from there?"

"Think of it as a dress rehearsal," Jack told him.

THERE WAS CONSIDERABLE discussion, some argument. There were diagrams and schematics and more printouts to be pinned to the board. Tia absorbed it all. They were planning to break into one of New York's cultural landmarks, and they were planning to do so for the sole purpose of misdirection.

It was fascinating.

"If we get into the bloody place, why don't we just look for the bloody statue?" Frustration honed Rebecca's voice to an edge.

"We won't get that far. Not without a lot more time and preparation. We can take the time and the prep," he added. "But if we do a simple B and E, snag the statue, we won't be hanging anything on her."

"Rephrase." Cleo spoke coolly. "Hanging her."

"If we work it right," Jack agreed, "the house is doable on short notice. Morningside isn't. Not with amateurs."

"Oh, now we're amateurs."

"Well, Bec." Gideon put his hands on her shoulders, gave her a little shake. "We are that."

"Why don't you speak for yourself—"

"I could use some tea." Tia spoke up, got to her feet. "Is it all right if I use the kitchen?"

"Help yourself," Jack told her. "Wouldn't mind some coffee while you're at it."

"There are better facilities upstairs," Rebecca suggested after catching Tia's annoyed expression. "Why don't we go up and put something together?"

"Cleo?"

Even as Cleo started to protest, she caught Tia jerking her head toward the door. "All right, but we take shifts on the domestic duties."

When they were safely in the elevator heading up, Rebecca turned to Tia. "You wanted to get away from that lot?"

"For a few minutes. It occurs to me that this is new territory for all of us. We hardly know each other."

"I just don't like their superior attitude."

"You mean Jack's superior attitude," Cleo said as Rebecca jabbed in the code and strode out of the elevator into the apartment.

"In particular. He didn't even tell me he had that place down there."

"Before we talk about them, let's talk about us." Cleo dropped into a chair, swung her legs over the arm and settled in. "Any wine around here?" she added.

"There is," Rebecca answered. "But put a hold on that tea and coffee. Let's have a drink and see what the three of us think of each other before we go on with this business."

"WE REALLY SHOULD go back down." Tia bit her lip as Rebecca topped off all three glasses. Again.

"They don't need us at the moment." Rebecca bit into a pretzel, studied it consideringly. "Let them huddle over their blueprints and diagrams for a bit. I can take a look at them later. Those deal with technicalities and are easily refined."

"That's if you know one end of a blueprint from another." Tia sipped. "I don't."

"You won't have to. It'll be put into words for you, and those you understand very well. Malachi thinks you're brilliant."

"Oh well, he's . . ."

"Toast," Cleo said and scooped up dip with a ridged potato chip. "Guy's nuts about you, but he's not a moron. You are brilliant. I never got along with brains before. Your kind of brains," she explained. "The academic sort. I spent most of my school time figuring out what kind of trouble I could get into next, and disliking girls just like the two of you." She grinned as she popped another chip in her mouth. "Funny how things work out."

"Gideon wouldn't be wasting time with you if you

didn't have a brain. He'd have gone for the package," Rebecca added. "But once he'd unwrapped it, he'd have lost interest quickly enough if all you had to offer were nice breasts and long legs."

"Gee thanks, Sis."

"Well, after all, he saw you unwrapped—so to speak—straight off, didn't he? And while we're on that subject, what's it like?"

Cleo only picked up her wineglass, sipped.

"Oh, be a sport," Rebecca complained. "It's a natural curiosity, isn't it? Tia, aren't you wondering what it's like to strip down bare-assed in front of a roomful of men?"

"I never thought about . . ." She trailed off, pinned by a smirking look from Rebecca. "Maybe," she admitted. "But I don't mean to offend you, Cleo."

"You don't. She's a lot nicer than you are," Cleo said to Rebecca.

"She is that. But I wasn't after offending you either. Don't you think that at some point in her life, a woman fantasizes about being built and beautiful and tormenting a lot of men by sliding out of her clothes in public? Knowing they want her but can't have her. It's powerful."

"It can be. It can be powerful, or demeaning and exploitive. It can be fun, or it can be humiliating. Depends on how you look at it."

"How did you look at it?" Tia asked.

"As a paycheck. Bottom line." Cleo shrugged and dug into the chips again. "Modesty's not a big issue for me. Most of the men, they don't see you anyway. They just see tits and ass. For me, it paid the rent and gave me a chance to choreograph and dance. I had some pretty sharp numbers."

"I'd love to see sometime. Not the stripping part," Tia said, going beet red when Cleo laughed. "The dancing."

"See, she's really nice. You know what I think? That stuff you said before, about all of us being meant to come together. That rings for me. The three of us would never be sitting here like this otherwise. That's cool. Now I've got a question for you," she said to Rebecca. "You banging Jack yet, or what?"

"Cleo."

"Oh, like you don't wonder," she tossed back, dismissing Tia's appalled whisper.

"Not yet." Rebecca lifted her glass. "But I'm thinking about it. And now that we've brought up sex, I'd like to continue that area as pertains to Anita Gaye. The boys downstairs, they can play with the toys, study the maps and make manly noises over the technology of the thing. But they don't understand what she is, inside. It takes a woman for that. It takes a woman to really see that sort of female ruthlessness. No matter what they say, a man's always going to imagine a woman's just a bit weaker, softer, easier than he is. We're not. She's not."

"She's cold," Tia said quietly. "All the way through, I think. It makes her more dangerous because she doesn't care—not on any level—about anyone but herself. She wouldn't hesitate to hurt someone to get what she wants. She probably thinks she deserves it. I'm getting analytical again," she apologized. "All those years in therapy, and suddenly I'm a psychologist."

"I think you make sterling sense," Rebecca agreed. "And I haven't met the woman as yet. I'm getting a clearer picture of her from you than I did from Malachi. His description was colored with his own embarrassment, I think, and his anger. Once she knows we've outwitted her—as, by God, we will—what do you think she'll do?"

"She'll try to take it out on at least one of us. Your family," Tia said. "Because it started with Malachi."

"Cleo? You agree with that?"

"Yeah." She blew out a breath. "Yeah, I do."

"As do I. So, we have to make certain she can't reach us. Whatever happens, we have to expose her for what she is. And take away her power."

"I've sort of started working on that." Tia rose, walked into the kitchen to finally start the coffee. "Money gives her power, and if you look at her marriage, you have to conclude money is vital to her. I thought it might be helpful to find out how much she has. Then we'd have an idea how much we need to . . . what's the word?" She stopped with the coffee scoop in one hand. "Hose her for. Is that right?" she asked Cleo.

"Isn't she great? Amateur, my ass. Tia honey, I think you could make a living out of this."

Downstairs Gideon jiggled the loose change in his pocket. "They're taking a lot of time putting together coffee and tea."

Jack glanced at his computer clock, shrugged. "They went up there to huddle. But . . ." He turned to his monitors, danced his fingers over a keyboard and engaged the apartment cameras.

When the women appeared on-screen, Malachi let out a low whistle. "You've spy cameras in your own flat? Does the word *paranoia* have any personal meaning for you?"

"I prefer to think of it as thorough."

"They've crisps up there," Gideon pointed out. "Should've known Cleo would nose out crisps. Almost looks like a party. Christ, they make a pretty picture, don't they?"

"Classy blonde, gorgeous redhead, sexy brunette." Jack scanned the screen. "Covers all the bases. Take a good look because we're going to have to decide how far into this we're going to take them."

"I don't see as we have much choice," Gideon commented.

"There's always a choice."

"You're meaning we can hold things back from them." Malachi had leaned closer to the screen and now straightened. "Keep certain parts of the plan from them, tucking them up, as it were, to protect them from Anita."

"She's responsible for two deaths so far. She's got no reason to quibble about a third."

"It won't do, Jack." Malachi watched Tia pour milk into a small pitcher. "They'd figure it out in any case. Rebecca would, I can guarantee that."

"Too right," Gideon agreed.

"Moreover, I started this thing lying to Tia. I don't want to lie to her again. They deserve the full truth of the matter. We'll just have to find a way to protect them despite it."

"I could keep them in that apartment for a week. Locked in, cut off. A week's about all we need if we move fast and move right. They'd be pissed off when they got out, but they'd be safe."

"Are you serious about my sister?"

Jack shifted his gaze from the screen, from Rebecca, and looked at Malachi. "Down to the ground serious."

"Then take my advice and put thoughts like that out of your head. She'd peel the skin off your face for it, and when she was done . . . Gideon?"

"She'd walk away, erase you from her life the way you do letters on a chalkboard. And as for me, I won't cut Cleo out. She lost a friend and deserves taking part in avenging him."

"If we make a mistake, even one mistake, someone could get hurt." Jack tapped a finger on the screen. "It might be one of them."

"Then we won't make a mistake," Malachi said. "They're coming back down. I'd turn off those monitors if I were you, unless you want your coffee poured down your crotch."

"Good point." He blanked the screen, then swiveled in his chair. "So, it's the Musketeers' thing?"

"All for one," Malachi began.

"And one for all," Gideon finished.

Jack nodded, then disengaged the locks so the women could get in. As he did, the phone rang. He glanced at the light blinking on his multiline unit. "Upstairs, office line."

Behind him, Tia nearly bobbled the coffee when she walked in to the sound of Anita's voice.

"Jack, Anita Gaye. I expected to hear from you by now." The answering machine picked up the irritation in her voice. "It's urgent. This Toliver woman is harassing me, and I want it to stop. I'm counting on you, Jack." There was a pause, then the tone of her voice changed, became soft, shaky. "You're the only one I can count on. I feel very alone, very . . . vulnerable. Please, call me as soon as you can. I'd feel so much better if I knew you were looking out for me."

"And the Oscar goes to . . ." Cleo dropped into a chair. "What a load of bullshit. Oh, Jack." She hitched up her voice, fluttered her lashes. "I feel very alone, very vulnerable." She stretched out, gave Jack a considering look. "Did you ever do her?"

"Cleo! You can't—"

"No." Rebecca waved off Tia's flustered protest. "I'd be interested in the answer to that."

Both Malachi and Gideon became extremely busy with the coffeepot. So much, Jack thought sourly, for all for one.

"Thought about it. For about five seconds. Kept getting this image of one of the vegetable slicers. You know." He made quick, chopping motions with his hand. "And her running my dick through it. Not real appealing," he added as both other men winced.

"Why do you work for her?"

"First, I don't work for her. Her husband hired my company as security consultants. I liked him. Second, a job's a job. Do you only take people on your tour boat who you approve of?"

"Fair enough," Rebecca decided, and offered him the bowl of chips as a peace offering.

"Are you going to call her back?" Tia asked him.

"Eventually. We'll let her stew and steam awhile. I figure my pal Bob will pay her a visit tomorrow. That'll give her more to stew and steam about. She won't like being questioned by the police. Then tomorrow night we'll give her the first real kick in the teeth with the break-in at Morningside."

"Tomorrow?" Tia sat down heavily. "So soon? How can we be ready?"

"We'll be ready," Jack assured her. "Since we're going to fail—or at least, it'll look like we did on first glance. You're going to take the first step tomorrow morning."

"I am?"

Tia listened, stupefied, as her assignment was explained to her.

"Why Tia?" Rebecca demanded. "Of the six of us, I'm the only one Anita or one of her monkeys hasn't seen."

"You can't be sure of that," Jack corrected. "It's very likely she's seen photos of you. Besides, we need you here. Next to me, you're the best tech."

"Tia knows how to think on her feet," Malachi added, and had the woman in question gaping at him.

"I do?"

"And best," he said, taking her hand, "she doesn't even know she's doing it. She's a way of making herself invisible and seeing what's around her. Remembering what's around her. And if she's seen and recognized, no one will think too much of it."

He squeezed her hand. "I'm the one who suggested you for this part," Malachi told her. "I know you can do it. But you have to agree. If you don't want to take it on, we'll find another way."

"You think I can do this?"

"Darling, I know you can. But you have to know it as well."

It was the strangest thing, Tia realized. For the first time in her life she was the object of someone's complete confidence. It wasn't scary at all. It was lovely.

"Yes. Yes, I can do it."

"Okay." Jack rose. "Let's go over the steps."

IT WAS AFTER midnight when Jack and Rebecca stepped into his apartment again. He knew she wasn't completely satisfied by the developing plan. He'd have been disappointed in her if she had been.

"Why do you and Cleo get to be cat burglars?"

He knew that was one of the sticking points for her and was pleased to detect the faintest hint of what he liked to think was jealousy in her voice. Or maybe it was wishful thinking on his part.

"First, to make it look like a genuine attempt at a break-in, I need more than two hands. Want a drink?"

"No, I don't. Why Cleo's hands and not Mal's or Gideon's?"

"They'll be patrolling the area, watching out for cops or bystanders and so on. Sure you don't want a brandy?" he asked as he poured himself a snifter.

"Yes. That doesn't explain—"

"Not finished yet." He swirled, sipped, watched with deep affection as her eyes heated at his interruption. "Despite great strides in equality, a woman wandering the streets of New York in the middle of the night is more likely to get hassled than a guy. So, your brothers take the street watch, you run tech in the van with Tia, and Cleo and I do the job."

It was too sensible to argue with, so she picked another angle. "Tia's nervous about the morning."

"Tia's nervous about her shoe size. It's part of her makeup. She'll be fine. When push comes to shove, she comes through. Besides, she'll make it work because Mal believes she'll make it work, and she's in love with him."

"Do you think she is?" Something softened inside her. "In love with him."

"Yeah. It's going around."

She kept her eyes on his as she stepped forward, took the snifter from him for one short sip. "Well then, we've a busy day ahead of us. I'm going to bed."

"Good idea." He set the brandy down, took her arms and backed her slowly against the wall.

"Alone."

"Okay." He kept his eyes open and on hers as he lowered his mouth to hers, as he took the kiss from a teasing brush of lips into quiet urgency.

When her eyes began to blur, when her hands gripped his hips, he shot them both into turbulent heat. He felt the tremor run through her, through himself, heard the strangled moan that caught in her throat.

And still, he knew, she held back.

"Why?" He jerked her back. "Tell me why."

The ache for him was almost a pain. "Because it matters. Because it matters, Jack." She laid her cheek on his. "And that scares me." She turned her head, just enough to trace her lips over his cheek, then, easing away, walked down the hall and into her room.

# Twenty-two

IT was a perfectly beautiful September morning with the first hint of fall brisk in the air.

At least Al Roker had said so during one of his cheerful reports outside 50 Rock. But when you were caught in the vicious war of pedestrian and vehicular traffic, had already stepped on gum and were on your way behind enemy lines, sparkling air wasn't a major concern.

She felt guilty. Worse, Tia was certain she *looked* guilty. At any moment she expected the people who crowded the sidewalk and street to stop and point their fingers at her.

She stopped at the corner, stared hard at the DON'T WALK signal just to keep herself focused. She had a desperate urge for her inhaler, but was afraid to dig in her purse for it. There was so much else in there.

So much illegal else.

Instead, she counted her own breaths—in out, in out—as she joined the flood that poured across the intersection an instant before the signal changed.

"Half a block more," she said to herself, then flushed when she remembered she was wired. Tia Marsh, she thought incredulously, was wearing a wire. And everything she said, or that was said to her, was being picked up on the equipment in the van that was even now parked in a lot two blocks south of Morningside.

She resisted clearing her throat. Malachi would hear her and know she was nervous. If he knew, then she'd be *more* nervous.

It was like a dream. No, no, it was like sliding into a television show. Her scene was coming up, and for once in her life, she was going to hit her cue and remember her lines.

"Okay." She said it quietly and purposefully this time. "Here we go."

She opened the door of Morningside's main showroom and stepped inside.

It was more formal than Wyley's, and lacked, if she did say so herself, Wyley's quiet charm.

She was aware that security cameras were recording her now. She knew precisely where they were located, since Jack had gone over the diagram with her, again and again.

She walked over to stare blindly at a display of Minton China until she calmed herself.

"May I help you, madam?"

Tia considered it the height of willpower that she didn't simply leap out of her shoes and cling by her fingernails to the ornately plastered ceiling at the inquiring voice.

Reminding herself there wasn't a flashing GUILTY sign on her forehead, she turned to the clerk. "No, thank you. I'd like to look around a bit."

"Of course. I'm Janine. Please let me know if you need any help or have any questions."

"Thank you."

Janine, Tia noted as the clerk slipped discreetly away, was dressed sharply in a black suit that made her look skinny as a snake and nearly as exotic. And quick as that snake, she'd summed up and dismissed Tia as beneath notice.

It stung a bit, even though Tia reminded herself that was the point. She'd worn a dull brown suit and a cream-colored blouse—both of which she intended to throw out as soon as she got home—because they helped her fade into the woodwork.

She wandered to a rosewood secretary and saw out of

the corner of her eye that the other clerk, male this time, was as disinterested in her as Janine.

There were other clerks, of course. She had the layout of Morningside flipping through her mind as she wandered. Each showroom on each floor would be manned by at least two eagle-eyed clerks. And each floor would have a security guard.

They would all be trained, just as they were at Wyley's, to separate the customers from the browsers, and to recognize the signs of a possible shoplifter.

She remembered enough of her own training to have geared her wardrobe and her mannerisms for the job at hand.

The expensive and unflattering suit. The good, practical shoes. The simple brown purse, too small for serious pilfering. They gave her the look of a woman with money but no particular style.

She didn't linger long at any display, but moved from spot to spot with the vague and abstracted air of a browser killing time.

Neither the clerks nor the guards were likely to pay more than minimal attention to her.

Two women came in—a mother and daughter by the look of them, Tia decided. Janine pounced. Tia gave her points for speed and smoothness, as she'd scooped up the two potentials before the male clerk had gotten off the mark.

While attention was focused across the room, Tia slipped the first listening device out of her purse and stuck it under the front lip of a secretary.

She waited for alarms to sound, for men with guns to burst through the door. When the blood stopped pounding in her ears, she heard the women discussing dining room tables with Janine.

She continued around the room, giving a pate-de-verre paperweight in the shape of a frog a long study. And attaching another bug to the underside of the George III refectory table on which it sat.

By the time she'd worked the first floor she felt so competent she began to hum. She plugged another bug under the railing as she walked up to the second level. She brought Jack's diagram back into her mind, located the cameras and did her job.

Each time a clerk approached, she smiled wispily and declined their help. When she reached the third floor, she saw Janine showing her customers a Duncan Phyfe dining room table, seating for twenty.

None of them so much as glanced at her.

She had one bug left, contemplated where it would do the most good. The Louis XIV sideboard, she decided. Angling her body away from the camera, she opened her purse.

"Tia? It's Tia Marsh, isn't it?"

The word *eek* sounded clearly in her head, nearly fell off her tongue as she spun around and stared at Anita.

"I, um, oh. Hello."

"Casing the joint?"

The blood that was pounding between Tia's ears drained into her toes. "Excuse me?"

"Well, you are the daughter of a competitor." Anita chuckled, but her eyes were sharp as sabers as she slid an arm around Tia's waist. "I don't believe I've ever seen you in Morningside before."

In the van, Malachi had to be forcibly restrained from charging out the door. "Hold on," Jack snapped. "She's fine. She'll handle it. She knows this was a possibility."

"I haven't been," Tia managed and felt a smile try to wobble onto her face. Use it, she ordered herself. Use your fumbling ineptitude. "It seems so odd, you know, never having been inside. I had an appointment a few blocks away, so—"

"Oh, where?"

"With my holistic therapist." The lie brought a blush to her cheeks and gave the claim perfect credence. "I know a lot of people think alternative medicine is hoodoo, but honestly, I've had such good results. Would you like her name? I think I have a card."

She started to open her purse again, but Anita cut her off. "That's all right. I'll just call you if I have a need for . . . hoodoo."

"Actually, well, that was just an excuse. I came in because I thought I might run into you. I had such a nice time at our lunch the other day, and I . . . I hoped we might be able to do it again."

"How sweet. I'll check my calendar and give you a call."

"I'd really like that. I'm free most any time. I usually try to schedule my medical appointments in the morning so I can . . ." She trailed off, cleared her throat, took a couple of labored breaths. "Oh dear. Do you have a cat?"

"A cat? No."

"Reaction. Something." She began to wheeze until customers and clerks looked nervously in her direction. "Allergies. Asthma."

The wheezing and gulping air made her light-headed so that her stumble was genuine, and effective. She dragged the inhaler out of her purse, used it noisily.

"Come on. Come with me. For heaven's sake." Anita dragged her into the elevator, jabbed the button for the fourth floor. "You'll upset the customers."

"Sorry. Sorry." She continued to suck on the inhaler while the thrill of success jolted through her system. "If I could sit down. Minute. Glass of water."

"Yes, yes." She dragged Tia through the office suites. "Bring Dr. Marsh a glass of water," she called out, then all but tossed Tia into a chair. "Put your head between your knees or something."

Tia obeyed, and grinned. In Anita's manner was all the impatience and irritation the sturdily healthy feel for the sickly. "Water." She croaked it, then watched Anita's gorgeous shoes march across the gorgeous carpet.

"Bring me a damn glass of water. Now!"

By the time she spun back into the room, Tia had the last bug firmly attached to the bottom of her chair.

"I'm sorry. So sorry." Easing up, Tia let her head fall back weakly. "Such a bother. Such a nuisance. Are you sure you don't have a cat?"

"I ought to know if I have a goddamn cat." She grabbed the water from her assistant's hand and thrust it on Tia.

"Of course you would. It's just usually cats that cause that quick and violent a reaction." She sipped the water slowly. "Then again, it could be pollen. From the flower arrangements, which are lovely by the way. My holistic therapist is putting me on a program that combines herbs, meditation, subliminal reinforcement and weekly purges. I'm very hopeful."

"Great." Anita looked meaningfully at her watch. "Are you feeling better?"

"Yes, very. Oh, you're busy, and I've taken up so much of your time. My father hates his workday interrupted, and I'm sure you're the same. I hope you'll call about lunch soon. I . . . my treat," she added and knew she sounded pathetic. "To thank you for your help today."

"I'll be in touch. Let me walk you to the elevator."

"I hope I didn't disrupt your day," Tia began, then stopped as Anita's assistant got to her feet.

"Ms. Gaye, this is Detective Robbins, NYPD. He'd like to speak with you."

Tia controlled a hysterical urge to laugh. "Oh. My. Well. I should get out of your way. Thank you so much. Thank you for the water," she said to the assistant and hurried to the elevator. She bit the inside of her cheek until it hurt, kept right on biting until she'd gotten to the main show-room and out the door.

New Yorkers were too used to lunatics to pay any attention to a drably dressed blonde giggling hysterically as she ran down the sidewalk.


"YOU WERE BRILLIANT." Malachi all but hoisted her into the back of the van, then caught her in a rib-crushing hug. "Bloody brilliant."

"I was." She couldn't stop the giggles. "I really was. Even though I nearly wet my pants when Anita spoke to me. Then I thought, if I can just get into her office for a minute, I can put the last little mike there. But I kept wanting to laugh. Nervous reaction, I suppose. I just . . . some-body shut me up."

"Happy to." Malachi closed her mouth with his.

"If you kids would settle down, you might want to hear this."

Jack switched the audio on, took off his headphones.

". . . understand what a police detective might want with me. Would you like some coffee?"

"No, thanks, Ms. Gaye, and we appreciate your time. It concerns a property you owned, a warehouse just off Route Nineteen, south of Linden, New Jersey."

"Detective, my husband owned a number of properties, which I inherited . . . Oh, you said 'owned.' I recently sold a New Jersey property. My lawyers and accountants handle most of those details. Is there some problem with the sale? I haven't heard anything to indicate it, and I know the deal was finalized earlier this month."

"No, ma'am. No problem that I'm aware of." There was a slight rustling sound, a pause. "Do you know this man?"

"He doesn't look familiar to me. I do meet a lot of people, but . . . no, I don't recognize him. Should I?"

"Ms. Gaye, this man was found inside the warehouse in question. He was murdered."

"Oh my God." There was a creak as Anita sat. "When?"

"Time of death is often hard to determine. We believe he died very close to the date you sold the warehouse."

"I don't know what to say. That property hasn't been in use for . . . I'm not completely sure. Six months, perhaps eight. This should have been brought to my attention. I'll have to contact the buyers. This is dreadful."

"Ms. Gaye, did you have access to the building?"

"I did, of course. My representative was given all the keys and security codes, which would have been turned over to the purchasers. You'll want to contact my real estate representative, of course. Let me have my assistant get you his information."

"I'd appreciate it. Ms. Gaye, do you own a gun?"

"Yes. Three. My husband . . . Detective." Another pause, longer. "Am I a suspect?"

"These are just routine questions, Ms. Gaye. I assume your three guns are registered."

"Yes, of course they are. I have two at home, one in my office, one in my bedroom. And I keep one here."

"It would help if you'd turn the guns over to us, for elimination. We'll issue a receipt."

"I'll arrange for it." Her voice was stiff now, and frigid.

"Could you tell us where you were on September eighth and September ninth?"

"Detective, it's beginning to sound as if I should contact my lawyer."

"That's your right, Ms. Gaye. If you want to exercise that right, I'll be happy to interview you, with your attorney, down at the station. The fact is, I'd just like to cross my t's here and let you get back to work."

"I'm hardly going to be dragged into the police station to be questioned about the murder of a man I don't even know." There was the slapping sound of paper against paper as she flipped through her desk calendar.

She rattled off times, appointments, business and personal time. "You can verify most of this with my assistant or, if need be, my domestic staff."

"I appreciate that, ma'am, and I'm sorry to bother you. I know it's upsetting."

"I'm not used to being questioned by the police."

"No, ma'am. Case like this, you've got to look at all the angles. It's a puzzler why this guy would go all the way out to New Jersey to get shot. And in that building. Well. Thank you for your cooperation, Ms. Gaye. Some place you got here. First time I've been inside. Some place," he reiterated.

"My assistant will show you out, Detective."

"Right. Thanks."

There were footsteps, the sound of a door closing. Then, for several long seconds, nothing but silence.

"Asshole." It was a vicious whisper and made Jack grin. "Stupid bastard. Idiot. The nerve, the fucking nerve of him coming here to question me like a common criminal. Do I have a gun? Do I have a gun?"

Something fragile broke with a sad tinkling of glass.

"Didn't I leave the goddamn murder weapon behind where a ten-year-old could find it? But he comes here interrupting my day, insulting me."

"Bingo," Jack shouted, then sat back.

"She did it." Tia shuddered as she lowered herself into one of two chairs bolted into the van's floor. On audio, she could hear Anita snap at her assistant to call her lawyer. "I know we believed she did, even knew it on some level. But to hear her say it, just like that, annoyed because she's being inconvenienced. It's horrible."

They listened as Anita swore at her assistant when she reported the lawyer was in a meeting.

"Our Anita's having a bad day." Jack turned in his chair. "And we're going to make it worse. You still in?" he asked Tia.

"Yes." She was pale, but the hand she lifted to Malachi's was steady. "More than ever."

GIDEON WATCHED AS Cleo bundled her hair under a black watch cap, as she stepped back, turned in the mirror to study herself.

"What do you think?" She did a quick pirouette. "It's the latest in nighttime B and E fashion."

"You've plenty of time yet."

"Yeah, but I wanted to check out the look." Dressed in black jeans, black sweater, black sneakers, she gave her reflection one more hard stare. "It works on me. The Gap. Who'd have thought it?"

"You're not nervous."

"Not particularly. How hard can it be *not* to break into a place?" She did a couple of deep pliés to check the give of the jeans. "Too bad there wasn't time to hunt up a cat suit." When he didn't respond, she straightened. "What's up, Slick?"

"Come here a minute."

Willing to oblige, she crossed to him and was surprised when he drew her into his arms, hard.

"Wow. What's this about?"

"There's always a chance something will go wrong."

"There's always a chance a satellite will fall out of the sky and land on my head. Doesn't keep me hiding in the basement."

"When I dragged you into this, I didn't know you."

"Nobody drags me anywhere. Got it?"

"I didn't care about you then. I care about you now."

"That's nice. Don't start making me all squishy."

"Cleo, you don't have to do this. Wait," he said when she started to pull away. "Let me finish. Tonight's not such a big step until you look at the whole. If things work, we'll be taking it up a level. A very big level. The next time you put on that cap, it'll be to break into Anita's house, to take something from her she'll kill to keep."

"Something that doesn't belong to her."

"That's not the point. You heard her on that tape. She killed a man, and she won't hesitate to kill another. She knows who you are."

"She knows who I am anyway."

"Listen to me." His fingers tightened on her arms. "Jack could get you out of this. He'd know the way—people, papers. You could disappear, with the money he'd give you for the statue. She'd never find you."

"Is that what you think of me? The rat who deserts the ship even before it starts to sink?" She pushed away. "Thanks a lot."

"I don't want her to touch you. I won't have her touching you."

The restrained violence in his tone, the bubbling frustration under it, defused her own temper.

"Why?"

"I care about you, damn it. Didn't I say so?"

"Give me another four-letter word."

He opened his mouth. His tongue felt thick. "Hell."

She made a buzzing sound, snapped her fingers. "Wrong answer. Care to try again? You can still win the trip for two to San Juan and the complete set of Samsonite luggage."

"This isn't easy for me. I don't like being in this position." He jammed his hands in his pockets, paced restlessly in the confined space of Tia's little office. "I don't know what I'm supposed to do about it. A man doesn't have time to think under these conditions."

"Yeah, yeah, blah, blah." She pulled off the cap, shook out her hair. "I think I'll grab a snack before we head out."

He stopped her by snagging her hair, wrapping it

around his hand and using it as a rope to yank her back. "Goddamn it, Cleo, I love you, and you're going to have to deal with that."

"Okay." And that slow, liquid warmth inside her became a fast flood as she put her arms around him. "Okay," she repeated, nesting into him. "Okay."

Here, she thought. At last.

"Okay? If that's the best you can do—"

"Shh." She wrapped her arms tighter. "Quiet. This is like a Hallmark moment here."

He let out a sigh. "I don't know what you're talking about half the time."

"I'll make it easy for you. I love you back." She eased away so their eyes could meet. "You get that?"

"Yeah." His grip on her hair gentled until his fingers were stroking through it. "That I got." He brought his lips to hers, slid them both into a long, sumptuous kiss. "We'll need to talk about this, eventually."

"You bet," she said and locked her mouth to his again.

"I want to tell the others we need to find another way."

"No." Now she pulled free. "No, Gideon. I do my part, just like Tia did hers this morning. Just like we're all doing. I owe Mikey that. And it's more," she continued before he could speak. "I'm going to be straight with you. I'm a bust."

"What the devil does that mean?"

"As a dancer. I'm a bust."

"That's not true. I've seen you."

"You saw me strip," she corrected. "A three-minute number where I shake it, peel it and sell it to the crowd. Big fucking deal." She dragged her hair back, huffed out a breath. "I'm a good dancer, but so is every second kid who ever took dance class. I'm not great and never will be. I liked being part of the company when I could get the gig. I liked being part of something. I never had that with my family."

"Cleo."

"This isn't some deep philosophical confession of my unhappy childhood. I'm just saying, I like to dance. I liked being with other dancers because we could make something together. Sort of like that tapestry Tia was talking about before, you know?"

"Yes." He thought of his world in Cobh—family, the business, and the need to hold both together. "I know."

"I spent nearly ten years as a gypsy, and the only real friend I made was Mikey. I gotta figure one of the reasons for that is I was never involved enough. I'd get bored. Same show, same routines, same faces, night after night and twice on Wednesday."

He traced a finger along her eyebrow, over the little mole at its tip. "You needed more."

She shrugged. "I don't know. But I do know that when you're a good dancer with a mediocre singing voice, you better have plenty of drive and ambition if you expect to make a living onstage. I didn't. So when that bastard dangled the idea of the theater in Prague, the chance to choreograph, I jumped. Look where I landed. I had a lot of time to think when I was scraping bottom in Prague. Kept focused on getting back to New York, even though I didn't have a clue what I was going to do once I did. I guess I know now."

She picked up the watch cap, twirled it. "I'm part of something now. I've got friends. Tia, especially Tia. I guess I've got family, and I'm not walking away from it."

She blew out a long breath. "And that concludes the True Confessions portion of our entertainment."

He said nothing for a moment, then took her cap, snugged it down over her head. "It looks good on you."

The back of her eyes stung, but her voice was cocky. "You got that backwards, Slick. I make *it* look good."

THEY TOOK SHIFTS monitoring Morningside. After seven, when the place locked down for the night, it was a boring, thankless job. But they would continue monitoring, listening for any change, any sound, until the job was finished.

At three, Malachi had heard Anita's assistant, whom they'd dubbed Whipping Girl, remind her boss of a salon appointment and her evening's dinner engagement.

Anita had left ten minutes later, after haranguing her attorney over the phone, and hadn't come back.

At midnight, Rebecca was manning the listening post,

from the rear of the van. When Jack climbed in the back, all she could drum up was a scowl.

"My brains are going to start leaking out of my ears if I have to do this much longer."

"We leave in an hour." He leaned down, his head close to hers, to study the readouts. Then sniffed the side of her neck. "What's the perfume for?"

"To drive you mad with frustrated desire."

"Could work." He turned his head so his lips skimmed over hers, came back to linger. "Definitely could work. Do the run for me. Sector by sector."

Could work, she realized, both ways. "I've done it for you, five hundred times already. I know what I'm doing, Jack."

"You've never worked this equipment before. Practice makes perfect, Irish."

She muttered curses, but obeyed. "I like the way you kiss me."

"That's handy because I plan on spending fifty years or so at it."

"When I give a man an inch, that doesn't entitle him to run the mile. Sector one. Alarms—silent and audible—up, motion detectors up, infrared up." She keyed in codes she knew by heart now and scanned the readouts on her monitors. "Exterior and interior doors, secured and on-line."

She continued through the sixteen sectors that comprised Jack's security system for Morningside.

"Shut down alarms in sector five."

"Shut them down?"

"Practice, baby. Take sector five down for ten seconds."

She let out a breath, rolled her shoulders. "Shutting down sector five."

He watched her fingers moving smoothly, briskly, over the keyboard. "There's a beeping inside the sector. Should I—"

"That's normal. Keep going."

"Sector's down." She watched the clock now, counting off the seconds. At ten, she keyed in another sequence and watched the system come back up. "Alarm's up in sector five."

"I told you ten seconds."

"It was ten."

"No, it took four to bring the system back up fully. So that's fourteen seconds."

"Then you should've said—"

"I said ten, so ten's what I needed." He patted her head. "Success is in the details."

She frowned while he opened his bag to give his portable equipment a final check. "If the whole place was shut down, how long to bring security back on-line?"

"Now there's a question. Standard alarms, exterior doors and windows, are instantaneous. Motion, infrared, interiors come on level by level. Four minutes, twelve seconds to bring it up to full scope and capacity. It's a complicated system, with multi-layers."

"That's too long, you know. There's a way to shave it."

"Probably."

"I wager I could shave a full minute off that four-twelve, had I access to the entire system and the time to play with it."

"Looking for a job, Irish?"

"Just saying," she replied as she angled her chair away from him, "timing matters, after all. In all manner of things."

"Is that your way of saying my timing's been off with you?"

"It's my way of saying I like picking my own time."

"Wouldn't hurt my feelings if you shaved some of that off. I'm going to get the others."

# Twenty-three

" A parking place, on the street. Upper East Side."
Jack shook his head. He was driving the van, with
Cleo riding shotgun. "We'll have to take it as an omen."

He maneuvered the van between a late-model sedan and
an aging SUV.

She ducked down to look through the windshield at the
streetlight. "Kinda in the spotlight here, aren't we?"

"Your city taxes at work."

"Yours, maybe. I'm not getting a paycheck these days."
Her eyes widened when he pulled a gun from under his
seat. "Whoa, big guy, you didn't say anything about armed
B and E."

"In for a penny," he said. "Sit tight." He climbed out,
walked casually down the sidewalk, then, turning, shot
out the streetlight with a muffled pop and a musical tinkle
of glass.

"BB gun," he told her when he slid back into the van.
He reached behind him, knocked three times on the partition that separated the cab from the back of the vehicle.

Seconds later the van shifted and the rear door opened.
Closed. In her side-view mirror, Cleo watched Gideon
and Malachi step onto the sidewalk. Gideon headed east,
Malachi west.

"And they're off," she mumbled.

They waited three long minutes, in the dark, in silence, before Jack's walkie-talkie hissed. "For a city that never sleeps," Malachi said, "it's damn quiet out here."

"Clear on the east as well," Gideon reported.

"Stay on this channel." Jack knocked twice on the partition, looked at Cleo when he heard the answering rap from the back. "Ready?"

"As canned ham."

They got out on opposite sides. Jack slung his bag over his shoulder and, when he reached Cleo, slung his arm over her shoulders. "Just a couple of urbanites out for a stroll."

"Cops tend to do a lot of drive-bys in tony neighborhoods like this," she commented. "Just how many years in the pen can you get for what you're carrying in that man-purse?"

"It's a bag. Just a bag. Three to five," he decided, "if the judge is a hardcase. Suspended. I've got connections."

He palmed his walkie-talkie. "Crossing Madison at Eighty-eighth."

"Good to go." From Malachi.

"And here." From Gideon.

"Base copies that," Rebecca reported.

Jack took her hand as they walked by the entrance of Morningside, turned the corner. They worked their way around to the delivery entrance.

As rehearsed, Cleo took out her walkie-talkie while Jack opened his bag. "B and E Central," she said quietly. "James Bond here's breaking out his toys."

"I'm at, what is it, Eighty-ninth between Fifth and Madison," Malachi said. "Looks to be a party in a flat here. A number of people, fairly well pissed, are coming out."

"I'm heading back from Park Avenue," Gideon checked in. "Saw a few street people in doorways, and a goodly amount of traffic for this time of night. No problems."

"Ready to go up?" Jack asked.

She nodded, craned her head to study the four stories. "There's this really good door here. I just want to point that out."

"Odds are she has the Fate in her office safe. It'll make

her more nervous if the break-in targets the upper floors."

He aimed what Cleo thought of as a harpoon, shot out a three-pronged hook and length of rope. "Harness," he said, and shot the second line while she shrugged into her harness. He clicked the safety, attaching her, then repeated the steps with his own.

"On three," he told her. "You were square with me about your weight, weren't you?"

"Just count, pal. One, two."

"Three," Jack said, and pressed the mechanism on his harness.

They went up smoothly, and a bit more quickly than Cleo had anticipated. "Jesus! What a rush."

"Keep your eyes on the roof."

"If that's like telling me don't look down, it's exactly the wrong . . . Oh shit," she whispered as she did, indeed, look down. Teeth gritted, stomach flopping, she fumbled for the ledge, skidding a little as her palms had sprung with sweat, and heaved herself over with no grace whatsoever.

"You okay?"

"Yeah, yeah. It just threw me for a minute. Four stories looks a lot higher when you're up there, without a floor under you. I'm cool." She remembered her next step and pulled out her two-way. "Base. We're on the roof."

"Copy that," Rebecca answered. "Shutting down alarms in sector twelve in sixty seconds. Mark."

"Mark," Cleo echoed as Jack depressed the timer on his watch, nodded.

He tucked the two-way back in his bag, fixed on a headset. "All units copy?" He nodded again when he got affirmative responses. "Got your breath back?" Jack asked Cleo.

"Yeah. I'm solid."

He gave his line, then hers, a last testing tug.

She eased off the ledge, took one huge breath, then let herself slide into the air.

The breath rushed out of her lungs, but she steadied the bag for him as they dangled. Following his directions, she braced her feet on the wall of the building, relaxed her knees.

Jack's watch beeped quietly, and Rebecca's voice came through his headset. "Sector's down. Five minutes. Mark."

A cab drove by on the street below, turned at the corner and headed up Madison.

He attached a portable scrambler to the window glass, punched in a code and waited while the numbers ran. When the display glowed green, he detached it, handed it off to Cleo.

"Window backup system off-line, silent alarm killed." He fixed suction cups to the window, held out his hand like a surgeon. Cleo slapped the glass cutter into his hand. Despite the chill, a line of sweat dribbled down her back.

"Four minutes, thirty," she announced while he meticulously cut through the reinforced glass.

The wail of a siren had her choking back a startled yelp.

"You steady?"

"As Gibraltar."

"Take your end."

She gripped the wire from the suction cup in her gloved hands while Jack mirrored the gesture with the second. At his nod, they lowered the pane inch by inch inside the building until it rested on the floor.

"Going in," he said quietly, and boosted himself inside the window.

"Three minutes, thirty," Rebecca warned him.

He unhooked his harness, stepped carefully around the glass, then moved fast through the office area. Cleo rolled in after him and sprinted in the opposite direction.

Crouched at Anita's office door, Jack took out a lock pick. It took him nearly as long to make what would appear to be a botched attempt at picking the lock as it would have to succeed.

At the top of the steps, Cleo debated briefly between a Baccarat wafer dish and a Lalique vase. With no regret, she tipped over the vase, stepping clear as it shattered on the floor.

"Two minutes, Jack, Cleo. Move out now."

"Copy." They met back at the window, but this time Jack brought his heel down deliberately on the edge of the windowpane to crack it. He attached his line, backed through the opening behind her.

"Down," he said to Cleo. "Use your feet, keep your knees loose. Everybody back to base," he said into his headset.

On the descent, he dropped a spare jammer, attached to a torn belt loop.

"Why, it's a clue!" Cleo said breathlessly as her feet hit the ground. "We got one minute."

"Start back."

"No. I leave with the guy I came with." She unhooked her line, shrugged out of her harness and stuffed it back in the bag as Jack did the same. Then she glanced at the dangling rope.

"Bet that stuff's expensive."

"But not that hard to come by." Once again he draped an arm over her shoulders. They walked. Just a bit faster than a stroll. "It'll look like the thieves ran into security trouble and had to abort, and fast."

"Five-minute mark," Rebecca announced. "System's rebooting. You've got thirty seconds. What did you break?"

"Some vase. Scattered a few whatnots around for good measure."

"Thief's in a hurry, drops loot. Works for me."

"One question," Cleo asked him. "You didn't need a sidekick for tonight. Why'd you bring me?"

"The point was to make it look like no less than two involved. I couldn't have gotten to opposite ends of the fourth floor in the allotted time. Knowing there were two should make Anita a little more nervous."

"One would've made her nervous enough."

"Yeah. But it'll take two to get into the house, into the safe and get out again without any hitch. I needed to see how you held up."

"So, this was like an audition."

"There you go. And you got the part."

"Wait till I tell my agent."

They were a full block away, walking easily now, hand in hand, when the alarms went wild.

* * *

IT WAS JUST past two A.M. when Jack popped the cork on a bottle of champagne.

"I can't believe the whole thing took less than an hour." Tia dropped into a chair. "I'm exhausted, and I didn't do anything."

"We're the tech crew," Rebecca reminded her. "That's essential personnel. And we were superb."

"It's a bit early for back-patting and celebration." Malachi lifted his glass. "But what the hell. Just knowing Anita's going to be wakened by the police is cause enough for a round. We've a lot of work ahead of us yet."

"Don't bring me down." Cleo gulped down the first glass of champagne. "I'm still flying. You think Anita'll drag her ass out of bed and go down there?"

"Count on it. The cops'll notify her, she'll get there quick, fast and in a hurry. First thing she'll do, check her office safe. Or she will if that's where she's stashed the Fate. Once she reassures herself it's where she left it, she'll do a dance with the cops, then she'll start calling me. She's going to be seriously pissed with Burdett Securities."

"But you'll fix that," Malachi said.

"Yep, because the system held. That's number one. They got in, but didn't have time to do the job because the backup system clicked into place, as advertised. Then I'll give her my report on Cleo."

"I bet it's terribly hot in Athens this time of year," Tia mused. "Do you think she'll leave soon?"

"If we have two days to put this all together, I'll be satisfied." He winked at Cleo. "My partner's a natural."

"I think we could've gone all the way tonight." Cleo held out her glass for a second round. "Into her office, into the safe and away with the prize."

"Maybe," Jack agreed. "Be a damn shame if we'd gone to all that trouble and it wasn't there."

"Yeah, yeah, practicalities. But all in all, you know how to show a girl a good time."

"That's what they all say. You should go get some sleep.

All of you. I'll man the recorder. She's going to be calling me in an hour or so anyway."

"I could make you some coffee and sandwiches," Tia offered.

"You're a jewel, you are."

AND SO, TWO hours later almost to the minute, while he polished off a ham and cheese on rye, Jack's home line rang. He smiled, let it ring three times. He'd already heard Anita curse him from her office.

Just as he'd heard her open her office safe, breathe a long sigh of relief.

"Burdett."

"Jack. Goddamn it, Jack. I'm at Morningside. There's been a break-in."

"Anita? When?"

"Tonight. The police are here now. I want you in here, Jack, and I want you in here now."

"Give me twenty minutes," he said. He hung up, and finished his coffee.

BY THE TIME he arrived, the Crime Scene Unit was busily at work. He figured he'd left them enough to keep them that way. He got a minor hassle from one of the uniforms blocking the entrance of the building, and had to flag down a familiar face, then wait to be cleared.

Normally the delay would have been mildly irritating, but in this case he figured it only gave Anita more time to stew. He found her in her office, verbally skinning one of the investigators who'd been unlucky enough to catch the case.

"I want to know what you're doing to find the people who violated my property."

"Ma'am, we're doing everything possible to—"

"*If* you were doing everything possible, someone couldn't have broken a window and climbed into this building. I'd like to know where the police were when thieves damaged my property and waltzed into this building. That's what I'd like to know."

"Ms. Gaye, the first unit responded within two minutes after the alarm—"

"Two minutes is too late." She bared her teeth, and it occurred to Jack that if she worked herself up much higher, she'd use them to bite someone's throat out. "I expect the police to protect my property. Do you have any conception of the taxes I pay in this area? I'm not funneling thousands of dollars into this city so the police force can sit on their asses eating doughnuts while thieves walk off with priceless antiques."

"Ms. Gaye, at this time, we can't be sure if any of your inventory was stolen. If you'd—"

"Through no help of the New York Police Department. Now you and your clumsy, fat-fingered *colleagues* are stomping around my building, making a mess of things, and you refuse to tell me the status of the investigation. Would you prefer I called the mayor—a personal acquaintance of mine—and ask him to speak to your superior?"

"Ma'am, you can call God almighty and I'm still not going to be able to tell you any more than I have. This investigation is just over two hours old. I'd be moving that investigation along a lot faster if you'd give me information instead of slinging abuse and threats."

Jack figured she hadn't painted and polished herself as carefully as usual, and with the furious color staining her cheeks, it was hardly surprising Anita wasn't looking her best.

"I want your name and your badge number, and I want you *off* my property."

"Detective Lewis Gilbert."

Lew was already taking one of his cards out of his wallet. Jack decided to give him a break and distract Anita. He put what he hoped was concern on his face and stepped into the room.

"Lew."

"Jack." Lew laid the card on Anita's desk. "Got the word the security was Burdett."

"Yeah." Jack's mouth went grim. "Where did they breech?"

"Fourth-floor window, rear, far east corner."

"Did they get inside?"

"Yep. Tripped up somewhere, though, sprang the alarm. Left some toys behind."

"They get anything?"

Lew slid a baleful glance in Anita's direction. "Undetermined."

"I'd like to speak with Mr. Burdett. Privately," Anita said coldly.

Knowing it was likely to make her choke on her own bile, Jack held up a finger and continued talking to Lew. "If I could take a look at the breech, I might be able to give you something on it."

"Appreciate that."

"I will not be ignored while you—"

"Just hold on." Jack interrupted Anita's newest tirade and walked out with Lew, leaving her vibrating with fury.

"Piece of work, that one," Lew began.

"Tell me about it. The shit she was dumping on you won't come close to what she'll dump on me."

They walked to the east corner, where the office area opened into an alcove. The chilly early morning air came through the empty window. Crime-scene people were measuring, dusting, picking at the window frame for trace evidence.

"Must've counted on the upper window being most vulnerable," Jack began. "That glass is reinforced and wired. They had to circumvent the primary alarm system to get this far. Serious tech capabilities required for that. How'd they get up here?"

"Rappel lines. Looks like the alarm went, and they took off in a quick hurry. Left the lines behind."

"Huh." Jack frowned, tucked his thumbs in his pockets. "Might be they didn't count on the secondary system." He explained the setup as he and Lew walked downstairs and into the utility area, where the main security panels were installed.

"I should be able to do a run, see how long the system

was down—maybe how it came to be put down—once you guys are finished doing what you do. But I can tell you just from what I've already seen, they didn't do it from down here."

"Who knows the system? This particular one."

"My team. You know how I screen my people, Lew. Nobody who works for me had a part in this. If they did, and were stupid enough not to take out the secondary, hell, I'd have to fire them for it."

Lew gave a snort, scratched his jaw. "Need the names anyhow, you know how it goes."

"Yeah, part of the job description." He blew out a breath. "I'll have to check, see who worked with me on this job. Original system was put in for the old man, Paul Morningside. I've done some upgrading since. The widow insists on the latest, and not just in her designer shoes."

He opened his mouth, then shook his head, shut it again.

"Spill," Lew demanded.

"I don't want to influence the angle of your investigation." As if reluctant, Jack dragged a hand through his hair, glanced toward the stairway. "I just want to point out that the client knows the system—or its basic makeup."

Lew looked decidedly cheered at the notion. "Guess she would, wouldn't she?"

"Now I'm going to have to go up and let her bust my balls."

"Got a next of kin I should notify?"

Jack spared Lew a sour smile, then headed back up.

Anita was just slamming down the phone when Jack walked into her office again. He wondered, fleetingly, who she'd called to berate at five in the morning. Then saw the insurance file open on her desk.

The lady didn't waste any time.

"Have you decided you can spare a moment for me?" Her voice dripped, like sugar laced with strychnine.

"I won't do you any good unless I know what happened. I can't figure out what happened until I see the system and the breach."

"I'll tell you what happened. You were paid to design

and install a security system to protect my business from vandals and thieves. You're paid a monthly retainer to maintain, evaluate and oversee that system, with additional fees for upgrading as the technology becomes available."

"I see you read your contract," he said mildly.

"You think you're dealing with a bimbo here?" Her voice spiked as she stalked around her desk. "You think because I have tits I don't have a fucking brain?"

"I never underestimated your brain, Anita. Or commented on your tits. Why don't you sit down?"

"Don't tell me to sit down." She jabbed a finger into his chest, and her eyes widened in shock when he closed his hand over her wrist.

"Watch it." His voice remained level. "A cop might have to tolerate a civilian's bullshit, but I don't have to tolerate a client's. Pull yourself together."

"Do you think you can speak to me that way?"

And he saw, by her expression and the tone of her voice, that she liked it. Go figure, he thought in disgust. "Slap at me, I slap back. I didn't roll out of bed at four in the morning because you snapped your fingers. I'm here because I stand by my work. Now sit down, and calm down."

He could almost see the instant she decided to change gears, the moment she opted to turn on the tears. "I've been violated. I feel so exposed, so helpless."

My ass, he thought, but played the game with her. "I know you're upset, and scared. Sit down now." He led her to a chair. "Do you want me to get you anything? Some water?"

"No, no." She waved a hand, then dabbed delicately at her cheek with the side of her finger. "It's just so difficult. And the police . . . I can't tell you what it's like. They're so cold, so callous. You understand what Morningside is to me. This break-in, Jack, it's a kind of rape. You let me down. I depended on you to protect what's mine."

"And I have."

"How can you say that? The system failed."

"No, it didn't. It worked. If it hadn't, you'd be filing a

claim for a lot more than a pane of glass. The secondary system kicked in, just as designed."

"I don't know what they've taken," she insisted. "I've been too upset to start checking inventory."

"Then we'll deal with it. I'll be working with the police as closely as possible. Burdett will inspect, evaluate, repair and replace any and all parts of the system as necessary. At our expense. I'll have a team here as soon as the cops clear the crime scene. The secondary would have taken over five minutes after the primary went off-line. Odds of anyone getting much of anything out in that space of time are pretty low. I'd concentrate on checking this floor, and it's mostly office space."

He paused, deliberately scanned her office. "You've got some valuables in here, and in the waiting areas outside. How about your office door. Was it secured?"

She drew a breath, let it out shakily. "Yes. I locked it and set the alarm on it before I left. The police . . . they think someone tried to pick the lock."

He frowned, walked over and stooped to study the lock himself. "Yeah, looks like an attempt. Not a very good one." He straightened. "I can't see why they'd waste time stripping down an office with what's laid out in the showrooms. A few goodies lying around, but nothing worth the time and trouble."

He was watching her as he spoke, and he saw her gaze toward the purse that sat on her desk.

"They'd hardly break into Morningside looking for office equipment," she began. And rose.

In a casual move, he beat her to the purse by two strides. She froze. "I'm going to go over the system, chip by chip," he promised, picking up the elegant and heavy snakeskin bag. "I'm sorry you have to go through this, Anita, but trust me, Morningside is as secure as possible. Now, why don't you fix your face." He handed her the purse, saw her fingers dig possessively into the supple leather. "And I'll drive you home so you can get some sleep before you have to face all this."

"I couldn't possibly sleep," she began, then reconsidered. "No, you're right. I should go home, clear my head."

She tucked the bag and its contents firmly under her arm. "And I'd feel safer with you taking me home."

HE WAS BANKING on catching a couple hours' sleep himself and was surprised to see Rebecca in the living room when he came in.

"I heard the elevator," she said. "I was restless. You've been out?"

"Yeah." He shrugged off his jacket. "She called, on cue. It went so much as expected, I could've written the script. She's locked the Fate in her home safe by now."

"You're sure of that."

"As death and taxes." He filled her in, short and spare, as he walked into the kitchen, pulled out orange juice and drank straight from the carton.

Rebecca was too fascinated to scold him for it. "You were so close to it. I don't know if I could have stopped myself from just planting a fist in her face and walking away with it."

"It's a thought. I've never hit a woman before, but she'd be a satisfying first. It's nearly as satisfying knowing we've messed with her head." He replaced the juice. "Or as satisfying as what's coming next. We'll go back over in a while. Me and my top tech," he added with a wink, "to run a system check personally."

She took the carton back out of the fridge, shook it to show him it was empty, then tossed it in the trash. "And what's my hourly wage?"

"Contingent on performance. How'd you know that was empty?"

"The juice? Because you're a man and I was reared with two of your kind. And after I've completed my brilliance with the security system?"

"I give Anita a report. Then I'll remember about the other little task she asked me to do."

He yawned, rubbed his hands over his face. "But now I'm going to grab a shower, and some sleep."

"You're working awfully hard for this," Rebecca commented as he walked toward the bath. "Risking a great deal as well."

He stopped, turned. "When something matters, you work for it. And the risks don't count."

Alone, Rebecca let out the breath she'd barely been aware she'd been holding. So much mattered, she realized. So much it was almost too much. And the fear of that had held her back.

That was foolish, she thought. You could never have too much that mattered. And a woman who continued to step back from love was wasting valuable time.

In the shower, Jack turned the water to near blistering, braced his hands on the tile and let the pumping spray beat on his head. The adrenaline that had kept him going for a straight twenty-four hours was used up.

His brain felt dull. He couldn't afford to go up against Anita again until he'd had a little time to recharge. Couldn't afford it especially since he was taking Rebecca in with him. He closed his eyes and let his mind empty.

Nearly asleep on his feet, he didn't hear the bathroom door open, or close again with a quiet click. He didn't hear the soft slither of her robe sliding to the floor.

But an instant before she opened the glass panel, an instant before she stepped into the heat and steam with him, he smelled her.

His head snapped up, his body jerked to alert. And her arms slid sinuously around him, her breasts pressed, firm and wet, into his back.

"You looked so tired." Rebecca trailed her tongue up the line of his spine. "I thought I'd offer to wash your back."

"We're naked in the shower because I'm tired? What was that you said earlier about timing?"

"I thought the timing perfect." She slithered around him, slicking her hair back as the spray soaked it, then sliding her gaze down his body. Her lips quirked. "And from where I'm standing, you don't look so very tired after all."

"I think I'm getting my second wind."

"Let's not waste it." She rose on her toes, then sank her teeth delicately into his bottom lip. "I want your hands all over me, Jack. And your mouth. I want mine all over you. I have from the first minute."

He fisted a hand in her streaming hair. "Why did we wait?"

"Because I wanted you from the first minute." She laid her palms on his chest, spread her fingers.

"Your brothers mentioned you were perverse."

"And they should know. Do you want to discuss that now, or do you want to have me?"

"Guess," he said and, lowering his head, savaged her mouth with his.

She was breathless, laughing when he let her breathe again. "Why don't you give me another little hint?"

"Sure." He pressed her back against the tile wall, took her mouth again while steam billowed and water pulsed, almost brutally hot over them.

Then it was just as she'd demanded. Hands and mouths frantic and fast. Flesh sliding wetly against flesh as each of them tried to reach more, take more.

There was a volcano of need in him, bubbling, boiling just under the surface. Recklessly she wrapped herself around him. Clung to him, shuddered and let herself burn.

"This is what I want, Jack." With her bones already melting, she bowed back as his teeth nipped down to close over her breast.

It was everything. Beyond all. Having her reach for him, seeing her surrender. Feeling her body quake with passion was everything and more.

And he could take her now, give to her now. When he ravished her mouth, she met the assault with equal urgency. Desperate for the heat, he plunged his fingers into her, and her hips pumped to match the frantic rhythm.

She came with a fast and frenzied violence that left them both weak.

He felt the long, lean muscles of her legs tremble and tense as he gripped her thighs and hauled her higher. The pure ivory skin flushed with rose and sheened with water against the slick white tiles. And water darkened her hair so it lay like fired gold ropes over her shoulders.

She looked, he thought, like a mermaid rising up out of a white sea.

"You're beautiful." He cupped her hips, lifted them. "So beautiful. Belong to me."

She sighed once long and deep. "I already do."

He slid inside her, filled her. And, with the savage edge dulled, loved her slowly. Long, deep thrusts that thrilled. As she crested, she said his name, lifted her mouth to his. Offered.

Then she wrapped herself around him, cradled his head on her shoulder, and rode the thunder of her own heart as he emptied himself into her.

# Twenty-four

THEY tumbled into bed, still damp, still breathless.

"I have to dry my hair. In a minute. You catch a chill going to bed with wet hair." But she yawned and snuggled against him.

Not only sated, not only satisfied, she realized. But saturated.

"You've a wonderful build, Jack. Next time, I'd like to feel it on top of me. But you get some sleep first."

He tangled his fingers in her wet hair. "Why now?"

She lifted her head. "You're tired. And even such a fierce lover needs a bit of rest."

"Why now?" he repeated so she couldn't pretend to misunderstand.

"All right then." She got up, fetched a towel from the bathroom and, sitting beside him, began to dry her hair.

"In the shower you looked like a mermaid. You still do."

"You don't look like a man who'd think or say such poetic and romantic things." She reached out, traced a fingertip over the scar, over the tough lines of his face. "But you do. I never thought I had a weakness for the poetic and romantic. But I do."

She eased back, continued to dry her hair. "I had a

dream," she said. "I was in a boat. Not a grand ship like the *Lusitania,* nor one of our tour boats. But a white boat, sleek and simple. It slid without a sound over blue water. It was lovely. Peaceful and warm. And inside my head I knew I could pilot that boat anywhere I wanted."

She shook back her damp hair and used the towel to blot water drops from his chest and shoulders.

"I had the freedom for that, and the skill. I could see little storms here and there, blurred on the horizon. There were eddies and currents in the water. But they didn't worry me. If a sail's nothing but smooth, I thought in my dream, it gets tedious. And in my dream, there were three women who appeared in the bow of my boat. This, I decided, is interesting."

She got up again, went to his dresser, opened the top drawer and took out a white T-shirt. "You don't mind, do you?"

"Help yourself."

"I know where you keep your things," she said as she pulled the shirt over her head. "As I've had no respect for your privacy. Now, where was I?"

"You were in your boat, with the Fates."

"Ah yes." She grinned, pleased he'd understood. "The first, who held a spindle, spoke. 'I spin the thread, but you make it what you will.' The second held a silver tape for measuring, and said, 'I mark the length, but you use the time.' And the third, with her silver scissors, told me this. 'I cut the thread, for nothing should last forever. Don't waste what you're given.' "

She sat again, curled up her legs. "And in the way of dream creatures, they faded away and left me alone in that pretty white boat. So I said to myself, well now, Rebecca Sullivan, here's your life spread all around you like blue water with its storms and its peaceful times, its eddies and its currents. And where do you want to go with it, what do you want in the time you'll have? Do you know what the answer was?"

"What?"

She laughed, leaned over, kissed him lightly. "Jack.

That was the answer, and I don't mind saying I wasn't entirely pleased with it. Do you know when I had that dream?"

"When?"

"The night I met you." She took the hand he'd lifted for hers and rubbed his knuckles over her cheek. "Hardly surprising it gave me a bad moment or two. I'm a cautious woman, Jack. I don't grab for something just because it looks appealing. I've been with three men in my life. The first time, it was hot blood and a raging need to find out what it was all about. The second was a boy I had deep affection for, one I hoped I might spend my life with. But as it happened, he was just one of those eddies in the sea. You're the third. I don't give myself lightly."

He sat up, cupped her face in his hands. "Rebecca—"

"Don't tell me you love me." Her voice shook a bit. "Not yet. My heart went for you so fast, I swear it left me breathless. I needed to let my head catch up. Lie down, won't you. Let me snuggle up."

He drew her down with him, settled her head on his shoulder.

"I won't mind traveling," she said, and the hand he'd lifted to stroke her hair froze.

"Good."

She smiled, pleased that he'd tensed. Some things, some right things, might come easy, but they should never come without impact. "I've always wanted to. And I'll expect to know a great deal more about this business of yours. I'm not a sit-at-home-and-iron-your-shirts sort."

"I send mine out anyway."

"That's fine, then. I can't leave Ireland altogether. My mother . . . I miss Ma." Her voice went thick, and she pressed her face against his neck. "Something fierce. Especially now, when I'm in love and can't tell her about it. Ah well, soon enough." She sniffled, brushed a tear away. "Anyway, you can expect me to get my hands into your company."

"I wouldn't have it any other way. I want you in my life, Rebecca. I want in yours."

"I have to ask you a question. Why didn't your marriage work?"

"A lot of reasons."

"That's an evasion, Jack."

"Bottom line? We wanted different things." Different directions, he thought, different goals.

"What did you want that she didn't?"

He was silent for so long, her nerves began to stretch.

"Kids."

With those words she all but melted into a puddle of love and relief. "Oh? How many do you have in mind?"

"I don't know. A couple anyway."

"Only two?" She made a snorting sound. "Piker. We can do better than that. Four should suit me." She tucked the sheet under her chin, shifted, sighed. "You can tell me you love me now."

"I love you, Rebecca."

"I love you, Jack. Go to sleep awhile. I already set your alarm clock for nine-thirty."

She slid into sleep, and into dreams, into the white boat gliding over a blue sea. And this time Jack stood at the wheel beside her.

TWENTY MINUTES BEFORE Jack's alarm rang, Gideon brewed the first pot of coffee of the day. He rooted through Tia's cupboards and found the poppy seed bagels. He was beginning to appreciate the Americans' fondness for bagels. While the others slept, he tucked a bagel into his jacket pocket, poured an oversized mug of black coffee and headed to the door.

He'd have his breakfast, and a morning smoke, up on the roof.

He opened the door and stared at the attractive black woman who had her finger poised to ring the buzzer.

She jumped; he tensed. And when she let out a quick, nervous giggle, he shifted gears smoothly.

"Gave us both a jolt, didn't it?" He offered her a broad smile. "Something I can help you with?"

"I'm Carrie Wilson, a friend of Tia's." She shifted her

gears as skillfully as he, and studied him carefully now. "You must be Malachi."

"Actually, I'm Gideon. Tia's mentioned you. Are you coming in?"

Her measuring gaze narrowed. "Gideon who?"

"Sullivan." He stepped back in invitation just as Malachi came out of the bedroom. "That would be Mal. We're just starting to stir. We had a late night."

Still on the edge of the threshold, Carrie goggled at both men. "Good God, she's got two of you? I don't know whether to be impressed or . . . I'll stick with impressed."

"Actually, one of them's mine." Cleo, wearing nothing but a man's T-shirt, strolled out of the spare room. "Great shoes," she said after giving Carrie the once-over. "Who are you?"

"Rewind." Jaw set, Carrie marched in, shut the door. "Who are *you*? And where's Tia?"

"She's sleeping yet." Malachi aimed a smile that was every bit as potent as Gideon's—and, in Carrie's opinion, just as suspicious. "I'm sorry, I didn't catch the name."

"I'm Carrie Wilson. And I want to see Tia right this minute." She set her briefcase down, pushed up the sleeves of her Donna Karan jacket. "Or I start kicking some ass."

"Start with one of them," Cleo requested. "I haven't had my coffee yet."

"Why don't you pour some for everyone?" Malachi said. "Tia's just sleeping in a bit. We were up late."

"Move aside." Carrie took a meaningful step closer. "Now."

"Suit yourself." He moved out of her path and watched her stride into the bedroom. "I think we're going to need that coffee."

The drapes were drawn. All Carrie saw in the dim light was a lump in the middle of the bed. A tongue of fear licked over her annoyance as she thought of all the things a trio of strangers might have done to her trusting, vulnerable friend.

There'd been a bulge in the dark-haired man's jacket

pocket. A gun, she thought. They were drugging Tia, holding her at gunpoint. Terrified at what she'd find, Carrie tore the sheets away.

There was Tia, buck naked and curled in a cozy ball. She blinked sleepily, started to stretch, then let out a thin scream.

"Carrie!"

"What's going on here? Who are those people? Are you all right?"

"What? What?" With a blush rising from her toes, Tia crossed her arms modestly over her breasts. "What time is it?"

"What the hell difference does that make? Tia, what's wrong with you?"

"Nothing's wrong with me, except . . . Jesus, Carrie, I'm naked. Give me the sheet."

"Let me see your arms."

"My what?"

"I want to check for needle marks."

"Needle—Carrie, I'm not on drugs." Keeping one arm tight over her breasts, she held out the other. "I'm perfectly fine. I told you about Malachi."

"More or less. You didn't mention the other two. And when my best friend, whose toes would fall off if she considered jaywalking, asks me to break the law, she's *not* perfectly fine."

"I'm naked," was all Tia could think of. "I can't talk to you when I'm naked. I have to get dressed."

"Christ." Impatiently, Carrie stomped to the closet, yanked it open. She sniffed, audibly, when she spotted the men's shirts hanging beside Tia's clothes. Then she pulled out a robe, tossed it on the bed. "Put that on, then start talking."

"I can't tell you everything."

"Why?"

"Because I love you." Tia stuck her arms in the robe, dragged it around her. And immediately felt better.

"Tia, if those people are pressuring you into something—"

"They're not. I promise. I'm doing something I need to do, something I want to do. For them, yes, but for me, too. Carrie, I bought a red sweater."

The lecture on the tip of Carrie's tongue fell away. "Red?"

"Cashmere. I don't seem to be allergic to wool after all. I've missed my last two standing appointments with Dr. Lowenstein, and I canceled my monthly appointment with my allergist. I haven't used my inhaler in over a week. Well, once," she corrected. "But that was pretend, so it doesn't count. And I've never felt better in my life."

Carrie sat on the side of the bed. "A red sweater?"

"Really red. I'm thinking about getting a Wonderbra to go under it. And it doesn't matter to him. He likes me when I wear dirt brown and dull underwear. Isn't that wonderful?"

"Yeah. Tia, are you doing what you're doing because you're in love with him?"

"No. I started doing it before I fell in love with him. All the way in love anyway. It's connected, Carrie, but it's not the why. I shouldn't have asked you to get that information on Anita Gaye. I'm sorry I did. Let's forget it."

"I've already got the data." With a sigh, Carrie got to her feet. "You get dressed. I'm going to have some coffee and decide if I'm going to give the data to you." She crossed to the door, turned back. "I love you, too, Tia," she said, then closed the door behind her.

And scanned the trio in the living room.

The woman with the legs was sprawled on the sofa, sipping coffee with her feet propped on the thigh of the hunk who'd opened the front door.

Hunk number two was leaning against the opening into the kitchen.

"You." She pointed at Gideon. "What's the bulge in your pocket?"

"Bulge." Cleo gave a wicked laugh, then poked Gideon's ribs with her toes. "You happy to see me, Slick?"

"It's nothing." Vaguely embarrassed, he dug into his pocket. "Just a bagel."

"Is that the last poppy seed?" Cleo straightened, snatched it out of his hand. "You were sneaking off with the last poppy seed bagel. That's low." She unfolded herself. "Just for that, I'm eating it. No weapons," she added for Carrie's benefit, then strolled into the kitchen.

"Would you like coffee?" Malachi offered.

"Cream, no sugar."

"Cleo, be a pal. Cream, no sugar for Miss Wilson here."

"Work, work, work," came the mutter from the kitchen.

"First question," Carrie began. "Tia claims she can't tell me what she's involved in. Is she protecting you?"

"No. She's protecting you. You don't have to ask the second question, I'll just answer it. She matters very much to me, and I'll do whatever needs to be done to keep her from being hurt. She's the most amazing woman I've ever known."

"Just for that," Cleo said from behind him, "you get half my bagel. You're a friend of Tia's," she continued, nodding at Carrie. "So am I. You've got seniority, but that doesn't mean I'm less of a friend."

Considering, Carrie looked at Gideon. "And you?"

"I love her," he said simply, then grinned a little at the looks he got from Cleo and Malachi. "In a warm and brotherly fashion. Do I get the other half of the bagel?"

"No."

"I'm under constant abuse." He got to his feet. "I'm going up and having a smoke. If Becca or Jack call, let me know."

"Becca? Jack?" Carrie turned to Malachi as Gideon walked out of the apartment.

"Rebecca's our sister. Jack's another friend of Tia's."

"She certainly stockpiled a lot of friends in a short time."

"I guess I was saving up," Tia said as she came out of the bedroom.

Carrie glanced over, sighed again. "I told you red would look great on you."

"Yes." With a little smile, Tia brushed a hand over her new sweater. "You always did."

Carrie went to her, took both Tia's hands, looked hard

NORA ROBERTS

into her eyes. "You wouldn't have asked me to do this if it wasn't important. Really important."

"No, I wouldn't have."

"When you can, you're going to explain everything."

"You'll be the first."

She nodded, then turned to Malachi. "If whatever's going on here hurts her, in any way, shape or form, I'm coming after you. And I'm taking you down."

"I'll hold your coat," Cleo offered and bit into her bagel. "Sorry, Mal, we girls have to stick together."

"I'm probably going to like you," Carrie decided. "All three of you. I sure as hell hope so, since I broke several federal laws acquiring the information I'm about to give you."

"For that, you get a whole bagel. We've got cinnamon, plain and onion."

Carrie offered Cleo her first smile. "I'll live recklessly and go for the cinnamon."


ABOUT THE TIME Carrie was polishing off her bagel and explaining the details of Anita Gaye and Morningside Antiquities' financial picture, Anita was having breakfast in bed.

Now that she'd had time to think, and a bit more rest, she wasn't so upset about the attempted break-in. She'd just consider it a wake-up call.

Nobody and nothing was to be trusted.

It was true that the security had held. But as far as she knew that might have been dumb luck or due to some foolish mistake by the thieves. She'd have Jack Burdett and company go over the system, inch by inch. And when they were done, she'd call in another consultant, have them evaluate the system.

One doctor tells you something's wrong with your body, a smart woman gets a second opinion. Morningside was every bit as vital to her as her own health. Without it, her business and social contacts would start to dry up, and her income would suffer a serious shortfall.

Anita Gaye took care of Anita Gaye.

She sat back against the pillows, sipped her coffee and glanced toward the doors of her walk-in closet. Behind the side panel where her day-wear suits hung in a meticulous, color-coordinated row was a safe even the household staff knew nothing about.

The Fate was tucked away now. She was glad the break-in had jolted her into bringing it here. She'd long since stopped thinking of it as an asset for Morningside, but as a personal belonging.

For the right price, of course, she'd sell it without a moment's sentimental hesitation. But when she had all three, she would wallow in it for a while. Her little secret. And she was considering keeping them for a short time. Perhaps putting them on loan—briefly—and reaping the publicity.

Anita Gaye, the skinny girl from Queens, would have made the biggest find, successfully executed the splashiest coup of the century. You couldn't buy that kind of respect and power, she mused. You couldn't inherit it from your rich, elderly and conveniently deceased husband.

It was going to be hers, she thought. Whatever it took. Whoever had to pay.

After pouring the second cup of coffee from her favorite Derby pot, she picked up the portable phone on her bed tray and called Jack's cell phone.

"Burdett." He was drinking coffee himself, and nibbling on Rebecca's fingers.

"Jack, Anita." She worked tears into her voice. "I want to apologize for my behavior this morning. I had no right to take things out on you the way I did."

Jack winked at Rebecca. "No need to apologize, Anita. You'd had a bad shock, were understandably upset."

"Regardless, you were there for me, just as your system was there for Morningside. I feel dreadful about it."

"It's forgotten," he said while Rebecca mimed strangling herself and gagging. "I'm on my way back to Morningside right now," he began.

"Pants on fire," Rebecca whispered and got a light bop on the head.

"I'm going over the system personally. I've already

called in my best tech to do an analysis. We'll both be there within the hour. Whatever vulnerabilities allowed the system to be breached as far as it was will be corrected. You have my word."

"I know I can count on you. I'll meet you there, if you don't mind. I'd feel better knowing more of what's involved."

"I'll take you through it."

"I'm so grateful. Jack, I wonder if you've had any time to work on that other matter we discussed."

"Cleo Toliver, right?" He gave Rebecca the thumbs-up sign. "As a matter of fact, I got some data just last night. I intended to write up a report for you today. Slipped my mind with the trouble this morning."

"Oh, I don't need anything as formal as a written report. Anything you can tell me—"

"I'll fill you in when I see you. How's that? I'm glad you're sounding more yourself, Anita. I'll see you at Morningside." He clicked off before she could answer.

"Butter wouldn't melt," he commented, and pulled Rebecca into his lap. "What do you want to bet she's figured out a way to scam the insurance claim?"

"I don't take sucker bets." She touched her lips to his, then just sank in.

"We gotta go," he murmured.

"Mmm. I think we've gotten caught in terrible traffic."

His hands slid under her shirt. "It's a jungle out there," he agreed. "What's five more minutes?"

It was fifteen, but he wasn't counting.

By the time Anita arrived, he had Rebecca suited up in coveralls and a gimme cap, running a system check, with a few finesses. He'd measured and ordered the replacement glass for the window and was outside on the sidewalk studying the delivery entrance.

"My assistant said you'd be out here." She looked delicately pale. "I thought the staff would be nervous," she began. "But they seem to be more excited."

"A lot of people react that way, especially when it's not their property that's been violated. How you holding up?"

"I'm fine now. Really. I've got so much paperwork to

do over this, it'll keep my mind busy. Why are you out here?"

"Wanted to take a look. I have to figure they did a study of the building, the neighborhood. Traffic patterns, patrols, angle of vision from residential buildings nearby. And they picked the best spot. Upper window. Calculated risk that would be most vulnerable. Replacement glass will be installed by five. Guaranteed."

"Thank you, Jack." She laid a hand on his arm. "Morningside was Paul's life." She let out a shaky breath. "And he entrusted it to me. I couldn't bear letting him down."

Spare me, Jack thought, but laid a hand over hers. "We'll take care of it for him. That's a promise."

"I feel better knowing that. Let's walk around to the front. I could use the time to clear my head a bit more."

"Fine. I'll go over the system with you. My tech's in there now. If there's a hole, we'll plug it."

"I know. Paul considered you the best. So do I. I trust you, Jack. That's why I asked for your help regarding this Toliver woman. You said you found out something?"

"It was tricky." He gave her hand a quick squeeze. "But I don't like to disappoint a client. Or a friend." He ran through basic information he was sure she already knew, listened to her feign surprise as he mentioned Cleo's parents' names.

"For heaven's sake, I know Andrew Toliver. Slightly, strictly socially, but . . . This woman who threatened me is his daughter? What a world."

"Classic black sheep. Troublemaker," he added, knowing Cleo would grin wickedly at the rundown. "Problems in school, minor brushes with juvie. Hasn't had much luck landing permanent jobs as a dancer. Looks like she's just back in New York from Eastern Europe. I'm still digging into that. It's not a simple matter to get information from that area."

"I appreciate your trying. Did you find an address for her?"

"Address on record's the apartment she had before she took off for Europe. Moved out about eight months ago. She's not living there now. In fact, she's not in New York at all."

Anita stopped dead. "What do you mean she's not in New York? She has to be. She contacted me. I met her here."

"That was then, this is now. Cleopatra Toliver, the one who matches your description and the passport number I was able to finesse, left for Greece this morning. Athens."

"Athens." She turned, and her fingers dug into his arm. "You're sure about that?"

"I've got the airline, flight and ticket number back at my place. Since I figured you'd want to know, I called and confirmed the flight after I talked to you this morning. She's been in the air about an hour." He reached for the door of Morningside. "She's headed several thousand miles away, Anita. You don't have to worry about her now."

"What?" She pulled herself back. "Yes, I suppose you're right. Athens," Anita repeated. "She's gone to Athens."

# Twenty-five

WITH her feet propped on the counter while she paged through one of a stack of computer magazines she'd stockpiled, Rebecca manned the listening post. She paused in the middle of an article, ears pricking as she heard Anita's voice snapping out orders.

Smiling, Rebecca swiveled the chair, picked up the phone. "The rat's taken the cheese," she said. "Tell Tia she's on. Then somebody come relieve me. I'm bored half to death."

"We'll be along." Malachi hung up the secured line. "It's your cue, darling," he said to Tia. "Are you set?"

"I didn't think she'd move so fast." Tia pressed a hand to her nervous stomach and felt the soft nap of her new red sweater. "I'm set. I'll meet you all back at Jack's."

"I could go with you as far as the police station."

"No. I'm fine. Being a little nervous will just make it all the more credible." She slipped on a jacket, then for an extra boost, draped the boldly patterned scarf she'd bought on one of her new shopping sprees over her shoulders. "I think I'm getting good at all this."

"Sweetheart." He wrapped his fingers around the scarf and used it to tug her to him for a kiss. "You're a natural."

She held on to that—the confidence and the kiss—all

the way into the Detectives Bureau at the Sixty-first Precinct.

She asked for Detective Robbins, stood twisting the strap of her handbag, then managed a shy smile when he came to get her.

"Dr. Marsh?"

"Detective Robbins, thanks so much for seeing me. I feel so foolish coming in here, bothering you."

"Don't give it a thought." His face remained polite and blank as he studied her. "I saw you outside Anita Gaye's office. Morningside Antiquities."

"Yes." She tried a slightly embarrassed, slightly fuddled look in response. "I got so flustered when I heard your name and recognized it. I couldn't think how to introduce myself in front of Anita without it all being so awkward and complicated. And I didn't think you'd remember the name, from when I called you about Jack Burdett."

"I remembered. You and Ms. Gaye friends?"

"Oh no." She flushed now. "Not really what you'd call friends. We did have lunch once, and I invited her to lunch again, at her convenience. But she . . . Well, this is all very complicated after all."

"You want some coffee?"

"Well, I . . ."

"I could use some." He gestured, then led her into the tiny break area. "Cream, sugar?"

"Do you have decaf?"

"Sorry, strictly high-test around here."

"Oh, well . . . Actually, if I could just have some water."

"No problem." He poured a cup from the spigot of a tiny sink, and Tia tried not to think of the horrors of city tap water. "Now, what can I do for you?"

"It's probably nothing." She lifted the cup, but couldn't quite make herself risk a sip. "I feel like an idiot." She glanced around the boxy coffee room with its cluttered counters, crowded corkboard and water-stained ceiling.

"Just tell me what's on your mind." He brought his coffee to the table, sat across from her.

"All right. Well . . . I thought of you, Detective, because

I'd written down your information when Mr. Burdett came to see me that day. That was the oddest thing."

He gave her an encouraging nod. "Jack has a talent for odd things."

She bit her lip. "You . . . you did vouch for him, right? I mean you know him and believe he's honest and responsible."

"Absolutely. Jack and I go way back. He's unorthodox at times, Dr. Marsh, but you can trust him right down the line."

"Good. That's good. I feel more confident knowing that. It's just that that day when he told me my phones were tapped—"

"Did he?" He shifted in his seat, straightened.

"Yes. Didn't he mention that to you? You see, he'd tried to call me about something, apparently, and when he did he detected something about the line. I don't really understand how all that works. And I have to admit, Detective, even with you reassuring me about him, I didn't believe him. Why should my phones be tapped, after all? That's just silly. Don't you think?"

"Any reason you can think of why anyone would want to listen to your phone calls?"

"None at all. I live a very quiet sort of life. Most of my calls involve my research or my family. Nothing of particular interest to anyone but another mythologist. But it did unnerve me a little. Even so, I more or less dismissed it until . . . Do you know anything about the Three Fates?"

"Can't say I do."

"They're characters in Greek myth. Three sisters who spin, measure and cut the thread of life. They're also statues. Small, precious silver statues. Another kind of myth in antique and art circles. One of my ancestors owned one, and it was lost with him and his wife on the *Lusitania*. The other two . . ." She spread her hands. "Who can say? They're reasonably valuable separately, but would be priceless as a complete set. Mr. Burdett contacted me because he's a collector, and he'd learned of the connection with my family. My father owns Wyley's. The antique and auction house."

"Okay. So Jack was hoping for a line on these statues through you."

"That's right. In any case, I told him what little I knew about the art pieces. But the conversation sparked an idea for another book. I've started researching. Phone calls," she said. "Collecting data and so on. Then the other day, I was talking with someone, someone I know primarily through my family. I was surprised when she seemed eager to spend some time with me and, I admit, flattered."

Tia lowered her eyes to her glass, turned it around and around with her fingertips. "I didn't think she'd be bothered with me, socially. It wasn't until I was back home again, after we'd talked, that I realized she'd not only brought up the Fates, but . . ."

She breathed deeply, looked at him again. "Detective Robbins, there were a couple of things she said that related directly to my research, to phone calls I've made and conversations I've had. I know it's probably just a coincidence, but it seems very odd. Odder when I put it all together with her inviting me to lunch, with her steering the conversation toward the statues and knowing things she shouldn't have known about my research. And I learned she'd asked both my parents about Clotho."

"Who's Clotho?"

"Oh sorry. The first Fate. The statue my ancestor owned was of Clotho. I don't know what to think. She even let it slip about the third Fate, that would be Atropus, being in Athens."

"Greece."

"Yes, I'd only just tracked down that rumor myself the day before we had lunch, had discussed it with a colleague in a phone conversation. I suppose she could be following the same trail as I am, but it just feels so strange. And when I think of what Mr. Burdett said about my phones . . . I'm very uneasy."

"Why don't we have someone take a look at your phones?"

"Could you?" She sent him a thankful look. "I'd be so grateful. It really would relieve my mind."

"I'll take care of it. The woman you mentioned, Dr. Marsh. Would that be Anita Gaye?"

Tia gasped—hoped it wasn't overdone. "How did you guess?"

"Just one of the tricks they teach us in cop school."

"Detective Robbins, I feel so odd about all this. I don't want to get Anita in any trouble if I'm just imagining things. And I probably am. I probably am because I'm not the type of person this sort of thing happens to. You won't tell her I said anything, will you? I'd be horribly embarrassed if she knew I'd spoken to the police about her. And my parents—"

"We'll keep your name out of it. Like you said, it's probably coincidence."

"You're right." She beamed a relieved smile. "It's probably just coincidence."

IT WAS A lot like planting seeds, Tia imagined. Not that she'd ever, literally, planted seeds, but it just seemed much the same. You stirred up the ground a bit, scattered around what you wanted to grow, then gave it a little boost of fertilizer.

Or in this case, bullshit.

She liked the fact that her team trusted her enough to do so much of the planting.

If, as expected, those seeds sprouted quickly, there was a great deal to do in a short amount of time. She swung into Wyley's with a spring in her step, and the clock ticking in her head.

Before she could ask if her father was available, she heard her mother's voice. Tia winced, and hated herself for it. Guilt had her moving through the showroom to where Alma was haranguing a clerk.

"Mother, I didn't expect to see you here." She laid her lips lightly on Alma's cheek. "What a gorgeous vase," she commented, studying the delicate pansy motif on the vase the clerk was guarding. "Grueby?"

"Yes." The clerk slanted Alma a dubious look. "Circa 1905. It's a particularly fine piece."

"I want it boxed up, gift-wrapped and messengered to my home."

"Mrs. Marsh," the clerk began.

"I don't want to hear any more about it." Alma waved the protest aside. "Ellen Foster's daughter Magda is getting married next month," she said to Tia. "I asked your father repeatedly to bring home an appropriate wedding gift, but has he bothered? No. So I'm forced to come all the way down here to take care of it myself. The man's in here every day. The least he could do is take care of one little thing for me."

"I'm sure he—"

"And now," Alma continued, rolling over Tia, "this young woman refuses to do what she's told."

"Mr. Marsh has given the staff very specific instructions. We aren't permitted to allow you to take any merchandise valued at more than one thousand dollars. This piece is priced at six thousand, Mrs. Marsh."

"I've never heard such nonsense. I'm getting palpitations. I'm sure my blood pressure is spiking."

"Mother." Tia's voice, sharper than either of them expected, had Alma blinking. "This vase isn't an appropriate gift for the daughter of an acquaintance."

"Ellen is a dear friend—"

"Whom you see perhaps six times a year at social functions," Tia finished briskly. "Your taste, as always, is impeccable, but this isn't the right gift. Would you mind telling my father we're here?" she asked the clerk.

"Not at all." Obviously relieved to have reinforcements, the clerk left them alone.

"I don't know what's gotten into you." Alma's pretty face shifted from angry to unhappy lines. "You're so unsympathetic, so harsh."

"I don't mean to be."

"It's that man you're involved with. That foreigner."

"No, it's not. You've let yourself get upset over nothing."

"Nothing? That woman—"

"Was only doing her job. Mother, you can't come into Wyley's and pluck something off a shelf because it's pretty. Now, I'm going to help you find just the right wedding present."

"I have a headache."

"You'll feel better when we take care of your errand." She put an arm over her mother's stiff shoulders and guided her away. "Look at this lovely teapot."

"I want a vase," Alma said stubbornly.

"All right." She led Alma along, and though she was tempted to signal another clerk for help, ordered herself to tough it out. "Oh, this is beautiful." She spotted a footed vase, and prayed her shaky expertise was in gear. If she missed and picked out something even more valuable, the ordeal would snowball. "It's so stunning and classic. I think it's Stourbridge."

Carefully, she angled it, tipped it so she could check the tiny price tag. And breathed a quiet sigh of relief. "What a wonderful gift this would be," she went on quickly as she saw the sulk folding into her mother's face. "You know, if you gave the other as a gift, they wouldn't know what they had, so they wouldn't appreciate the gesture for what it was worth. But something as gorgeous as this, at just the right price, will get full marks."

"Well . . ."

"Why don't I take care of having it boxed and wrapped for you? Then we'll see if Father has time to have some tea. It's been a long time since we've been in Wyley's together."

"I suppose." Alma studied the vase more carefully. "It is very elegant."

"Gorgeous." And at less than four hundred, right in the ballpark.

"You always had good taste, Tia. I never had to worry about that."

"You don't have to worry about me at all."

"Then what would I do with my time?" Alma said, with just a hint of petulance.

"We'll think of something. I love you." Even as Alma teared up, Tia heard her father's footsteps. And saw he looked very harassed, very displeased. Without thinking, she instinctively stepped between him and her flustered mother.

"You've been invaded," Tia said cheerfully. "I dropped by to see you and got the bonus of running into Mother. She needs the footed Stourbridge vase boxed and wrapped as a wedding gift."

"Which?" His gaze narrowed as he followed Tia's gesture. After a brief study of the selection, he nodded. "I'll take care of it. Alma, I've told you to check with me before you pick out anything."

"She didn't want to bother you." Determined, Tia kept her voice bright. "But I couldn't resist. Are you terribly busy?"

"As a matter of fact, it's been a distressing morning. Morningside Antiquities was broken into last night."

Alma pressed a hand on her heart. "Burglarized? I live in fear of that happening here. I won't get a wink of sleep tonight worrying about it."

"Alma, it didn't happen here."

"It's only a matter of time," she predicted. "Crime is running rampant. Why, a person isn't safe walking out of her own home. She isn't safe *in* her home."

"Thank goodness Father's seen you have such excellent security here, and at home," Tia commented. "Mother, you should sit down, catch your breath. I know with your empathic nature, hearing of someone else's misfortune upsets you. What you need is a nice calming cup of chamomile," Tia continued, soothing as she helped her mother to a chair across the showroom.

She got her settled, asked a clerk to see to the tea, then went back to her father.

"When did you learn to do that?" he wanted to know. "Handle your mother?"

"I don't know. I suppose I realized you could use a little help in that area, and I haven't been any. I haven't been a very good daughter, to either of you. I'd like that to change."

"It seems to me a lot of things are changing." He touched her cheek in a rare outward gesture of affection. "I don't know when I've seen you look better, Tia."

"Oh, it's a new sweater and—"

He kept his hand on her cheek. "It's not just the sweater."

"No." And she did something she rarely did. She lifted her hand and covered his. "It's not."

"Maybe it's time we took a break in routine. Why don't I take you and your mother out to lunch?"

"I'd love that, but I can't today. I'm already running behind. Can I take a rain check?"

"Of course."

"Well . . . Ah . . . it's terrible about Morningside. Was anything stolen?"

"I'm not sure. Apparently they did get into the building, but only briefly, as the alarms went off. Anita hasn't completed her inventory check."

"Oh, you've spoken to her."

"I went over this morning, to offer my help and concern. And," he added with a faint smile, "to see if I could pry out more details. It also seemed like the perfect opportunity to mention I'd heard rumors about one of the Fates, and Athens. She seemed very interested. So much so I embellished and told her I remembered something, vaguely, being passed down through the family about Henry Wyley planning on going on to Athens after his trip to London."

"Oh! I didn't think of that."

"I wouldn't imagine. You've never been good at embellishment. Though that, too, might have changed."

"I appreciate what you did," Tia said, evading. "I know it was an odd request. I wonder why you agreed to do it."

"You've never asked me for anything before," he said simply.

"Then I'll ask for something else. Stay away from Anita Gaye. She's not what she seems. I have to go. I'm very late." She brushed her lips over his cheek. "I'll call you soon."

She rushed off in such a hurry, she all but collided with a tall, dark-suited man as he came in. She nearly overbalanced, flushed scarlet, then sidestepped clumsily.

"I'm so sorry. I wasn't watching where I was going."

"No problem." Marvin Jasper watched her dash down

the sidewalk. He took a detour, backtracking until he was away from the entrance of Wyley's. Keeping his eye on Tia's retreating back, he made a call on his cell phone.

"Jasper. Just ran into the Marsh woman coming out of Wyley's."

"Alma? Marsh's wife?" Anita demanded.

"No, the young one. The daughter. In a big hurry. Looked guilty. I can catch up and tail her if you want."

"No. She always looks guilty about something. Do what I told you to do and don't bother me again until you have something."

With a shrug, Jasper pocketed the phone. He'd follow orders and keep the bitch happy. He knew she'd done Dubrowsky but it didn't worry him. Jasper figured he could handle himself, and the Gaye woman, better than his unfortunate former associate.

So much better that when everything shook down, he'd arrange a little accident for the ice bitch. A fatal one. He'd probably have to take care of the Marsh woman, too. And her old man. But once the slate was clean, he'd be the one walking off with those three statues.

Thinking Rio might be a nice retirement spot, he walked back to Wyley's, to follow orders.


JACK MET BOB Robbins at the bar and grill two blocks from the station house. It was too early for the change or end of shifts, so there was only a scatter of cops and civilian customers. The place smelled of onions and coffee. In a few hours, the scent of beer and whiskey would predominate.

Jack slid into the booth across from Bob. "You called," he said, "you buy." He ordered a Reuben, a side of fries and a draft. "What's up?"

"You tell me. Morningside."

"Lew caught that."

"Tell me anyway."

"The B and E got through the first level of security, gained entrance to the target. Secondary kicked in, as designed, and all hell broke loose. Word is the boys in blue responded within two minutes. That's good hustle."

"How'd they get through, Jack?"

"We're doing a system check, a full analysis." He stretched out his legs. "If you're thinking about hassling any of my people over this, you're wasting your time and you'll piss me off. If any of mine had turned on a client, they wouldn't have missed the second level, would have taken out what they went in for and would even now be sunning themselves on a foreign beach where extradition wouldn't be a weighty issue."

"Maybe they did get what they went in for."

Jack picked up his beer when it was served, watched Bob over the foam as he took his first sip. "Which would be?"

"Again, you tell me."

"As far as I know, the client hasn't completed her inventory check. And I can tell you, all my people are accounted for. Burdett hasn't earned its reputation by hiring thieves. You taking this over from Lew?"

"No. I'm working something that might be connected. Couple of things just don't gel for me. Here's the big one. I go years without anyone saying the name Anita Gaye to me. Now, within a short span of time, you drop it on me in connection with some two-bit muscle who ends up dead in Jersey. I hear it from Lew when he catches a burglary attempt at her place of business, which involves your security. And I get it tossed in my lap again today, from a woman who knows you."

Jack leaned back as his lunch slid in front of him. "I know a lot of women."

"Tia Marsh. Says you told her that her phones are tapped."

"They are."

"Yeah, they are." Bob nodded, picked up his burger. "I just checked it out. Question is, why are they?"

"My guess is somebody wants to know who she's talking to, and about what."

"Yeah, ele-fucking-mentary, Watson. She thinks it might be Anita Gaye."

Jack set his beer down, carefully. "Tia Marsh tell you that?"

"What's going on, Jack?"

"I've got nothing solid. But let me tell you this." He leaned forward, lowered his voice. "Whoever got into that building knew enough about the system to get in. And not enough to stay in and finish. I always see to it the client knows as much as he wants to know about the operation. In this case, with this client, she knew the basics."

"She wants something out of her own place, why doesn't she just walk out with it?"

"How the hell do I know? Five minutes, Bob. The primary was down for five maximum before secondary kicked the alarms. Your guys responded in two. Coming in from that section, I can't see how they got squat out of there in under seven minutes. Even if the thing ran smooth as silk while they were inside, they couldn't have gotten much. I'd be real interested to see what she files on her insurance claim."

"Doesn't sound to me you like your client, Jack."

"Can't say I do." He went back to his sandwich. "That's personal. On another level, I've got nothing on her but speculation."

"How do you connect her to Dubrowsky?"

"Round about." He moved his shoulders. "Another client told me how Anita was hassling her about a certain art piece. Enough high pressure that this client was uneasy, and tells me how she's seen this guy following her. Described him to me, I described him to you, and you tell me he's stiff. She ID'd him from the picture you slipped me."

"I want a name."

"Not without her okay. You know I can't, Bob. Besides, all she knows is Anita spooked her, this guy tailed her, and now he's dead."

"What about the art piece?"

"Pieces, actually. They're called the Three—"

"Fates," Bob finished, and Jack registered surprise.

"You *are* a detective."

"Got the decoder ring to prove it. What do these statues have to do with you?"

"I just happen to have one."

Bob's gaze narrowed like pinpoints. "Which one?"

"Atropus. Third Fate. Came through the family, the Brit side of it. Anita doesn't know that, and I want to keep it that way. She wanted me to get some information on them for her, which got me to thinking and led me to Tia Marsh and my other client."

"Why'd she come to you if she didn't know you had one?"

"She knows I'm a collector, and she knows I've got connections."

"Okay." Satisfied, Bob dipped into Jack's fries. "Keep going."

"The Marsh woman's phones are tapped. My client, who's the lead to Lachesis, or Fate number two, is being tailed. And Anita's been pressuring them both. You do the math."

"Plugging a guy full of bullets is a long way from trying to finesse a couple of statues."

"You talked to her. What did you think?"

Bob said nothing for a moment. "What I think is I'm going to dig deeper."

"While you're at it, look into a homicide on West Fifty-third a few weeks ago. Black guy, dancer. Beat to death in his apartment."

"Goddamn it, Jack. If you know something about an open homicide—"

"I'm giving you information," Jack said evenly. "Check the witness descriptions of the guy who went in and out of the building. It's going to match the hired fist you got from New Jersey. Find a way to get a warrant for Gaye's private line. I bet you'll find some interesting calls on it. I've gotta go."

"Stay out of the police work, Jack."

"Happy to. I've got a hot date with a gorgeous Irish redhead."

"The one you brought into the station? Rebecca," Bob remembered. "She your client?"

"Nope. She's the woman I'm going to marry."

"In your dreams."

"There, too." He dug in his pocket, pulled out a box and flipped it open. "What do you think?"

Bob's jaw dropped, nearly bounced off the table as he stared at the ring. "Holy shit, Burdett, you're serious."

"First time around, I went to Tiffany's. But Rebecca, she'll like the heirloom thing. This was my great-great-grandmother's."

"Well, hell." Bob climbed out of the booth and gave Jack a one-armed hug. "Congratulations. How the hell am I supposed to be pissed off at you?"

"You'll find a way. You want to give me a wedding present? Take Anita Gaye down."

# Twenty-six

WHEN he was parked, sitting behind the wheel of Jack's SUV, Gideon was happy enough with his assignment. It was just when he actually had to drive that he cursed his luck. It was bad enough to be swallowed up by the intrinsic anger of New York City traffic and its seemingly mad competition between cars, cabs, the ubiquitous delivery trucks, the kamikaze bike messengers and the always-in-a-damn-hurry pedestrians. But he had to contend with it all from the wrong bloody side of the road.

He'd practiced. Even managed to negotiate the viciously jammed cross streets, the wide avenues where everyone drove as if they were on a raceway, without killing anyone. And so had been elected for this task.

As he sat brooding a half block from Anita's posh house, he wondered whether any of them had considered that driving around with a coach and driving alone—with the express purpose of following a car to the airport—were vastly different matters.

Still, he'd been drafted for it, as he and Rebecca were the only ones whose faces Anita wasn't personally familiar with. And Rebecca was needed at the keyboard.

He'd have felt better if Cleo had been there with him.

Egging him on, or giving him grief or . . . just being there. He'd become entirely too used to having her around.

They'd have to work out what they intended to do about that once they'd dealt with the Fates. With Anita. They'd have to work out the single fact that he couldn't live in New York and stay sane. Visit, certainly, but live in a place so crowded you could barely draw one clean breath? No, not even for her.

Christ, he wanted the sea again, and the quiet rain. He wanted the hills and the sound of cathedral bells. Most of all he wanted to wake up in a place where he knew if he walked down to the quay or the boatyard, or just wandered the steep streets, he would come across people who knew him, knew his family.

Who were family.

She'd probably hate it in Cobh, he thought and tapped his fingers restlessly on the wheel. The very things that sustained him would likely drive her mad.

Why should two people who came from such different places, who wanted such different things, have fallen in love?

One of fate's little jokes, he supposed.

In the end, she'd probably go her way and he his, so the rest of the thread of their lives would spin out with an ocean between them. The thought already depressed him. He was so busy chewing over his own misery that he nearly didn't register the long black limo that glided up in front of Anita's town house.

He tucked away his personal troubles and clicked into gear. "Well now," he said aloud. "Travel in style, don't you?"

He watched the uniformed driver get out, walk to the front door and ring the bell. Gideon was too far away to see who answered, but there was a brief conversation, then the driver returned to the car.

They both waited a full ten minutes by Gideon's watch before another man—the butler, Gideon assumed—came out carrying two large suitcases. A young woman trailed behind him rolling another, smaller case.

While the three of them loaded the trunk, Gideon

pressed the buttons of the car phone. "They're loading the car," he told his brother. "A limo big as a whale, and enough luggage for a modeling troupe."

He got his first in-person look at Anita when she stepped through the door. Her hair was copper bright and sleekly styled around a face that looked to be soft to the touch. Her body—and he could easily see what had appealed to his brother there—was very female with its generous curves.

He wondered, studying her, what had twisted inside her to make her what she was. He wondered, too, why others couldn't see how out of place she was with her polish and gloss in that fine, dignified old house.

Perhaps she saw it, Gideon mused, whenever she looked in the mirror. That might be one more thing that drove her.

And he'd leave the philosophizing to Tia.

"Here's the woman of the hour, just coming out."

"Remember, if you lose them, you've just to go to the airport and pick her up again there."

"I'm not going to lose them. I can drive better on the wrong side of the road than most of the people in this city can on the right side. They're pulling away now. I'll get back to you from the airport."

Malachi hung up, turned to Tia. "They're moving."

"I feel a little queasy." She pressed a hand to her stomach. "But I'm starting to like it. I don't know what I'm going to do when my life gets back to normal."

He took her hand, pressed his lips to her fingers. "We'll have to see it doesn't."

Flustered, Tia pressed the intercom and contacted the garage. "She's on her way to the airport. Gideon's behind her."

"Then let's move out." Jack clicked off.

Tia pushed away from the console, rose.

"Steady?" Malachi asked her.

"Steady enough. Have you ever planted anything?"

"Like a tree?" He stepped into the elevator with her.

"I was thinking more like seeds. Different seeds in different places." She took a deep breath. "It's going to be a very interesting garden when we're done."

"Any regrets?"

"Not so far. And I don't intend to have any." She stepped out into the garage, looked over to where Cleo, Rebecca and Jack were already beside the van. These people, she thought, these fascinating people were her friends.

No, she didn't have any regrets.

"Let's rock and roll," Cleo said.

On this leg, Tia manned the keyboard and Malachi communication. With Jack and Rebecca in the cab, Cleo chilled out with Queen blasting through her headphones.

"I don't know how she can do that," Tia commented. "Relax that way."

Malachi flipped a glance over his shoulder to where Cleo sat back, body swaying to her music. "Storing energy. She'll need plenty of it later." He hit a switch and spoke to Rebecca on her two-way. "Gideon says there's heavy traffic on something called the Van Wyck. He still has them, but they're moving slowly just now."

"That's fine. We're nearly at the parking lot."

"You be careful, darling."

"Oh, I'll be better than careful. I'll be good. Over and out."

Rebecca tucked the two-way back into the holster on her belt. She stored energy her own way as Jack pulled the van into the parking lot. She went over every step of her assignment in her head.

When she got out of the van, walked around to Jack, he held out a hand. "Holding hands as we return to the scene of the crime." She gave an exaggerated sigh. "It's so bloody romantic."

"Nervous?" he said as they walked.

"More revved up, I'd say. That's a good thing."

"Don't rush. We want to move through this stage quickly, but we've got the time to do it right."

"Do your part. I'll do mine."

Together they walked directly to the front entrance of Morningside. Casually, Jack keyed in the new code he'd programmed into his palm converter, then took out the keys he'd had made as the security system shut down.

"We're clear," he said softly, then unlocked the door. After they slipped inside, he relocked the door, reengaged the outer alarms. "And we're in. Go," he ordered, but Rebecca was already dashing for the stairs.

Guided by the beam of her flashlight, she raced up to Anita's office. She took the key out of her pocket and, trusting she and Jack had succeeded in realigning the security, unlocked the door.

After closing the drapes over the window facing Madison, she switched on the desk light, then sat down at Anita's computer. And rubbed her hands together.

"All right, handsome, let's make love."

Downstairs, Jack reconfigured the security system. It would go back on-line, complete and better than ever, after he and Rebecca were clear. While he worked, he listened to Malachi through his headset.

"They're at the airport. She's been dropped off at the curb. Gideon's finding a place to park. He'll pick her up again inside the terminal. What's your status there?"

"Coming along. Put Tia on. I want to run the first checklist."

"You're up." Malachi handed her a headset.

"Jack?"

"I'm giving you the first encryption. Key it in."

Behind her, Cleo yawned. She lifted one earpiece so the muffled sound of bass and drums beat into the air. "Everything cool?"

AT THE KEYBOARD, Rebecca hacked her way through Anita's computer security. It was, she thought with some glee, pathetic. No more than a simple password lock and easily dispatched. She found the insurance file in her first document search. Opening it, she searched out the inventory list and claim form Anita had generated that day.

"Tsk-tsk. Padded the claim already, didn't you? But so conservatively. We're going to improve on that." Out of her pocket she took the short list Jack and Tia had made. And got to work.

As she doctored the claim form, she heard her brother's

voice in her ear. "He's caught up with her. She's just walked into the first-class lounge. There's an hour and fifteen before her flight."

"I'm into the file. I wonder what the devil the Nara period is, and why some plaque from it's worth so flaming much money. Jack, you can check that piece, and the Chiparus figure. Are you going to get to the earbobs?"

"I'll get them. Log them in."

"Don't forget the bugs Tia planted."

"Working on it. Be quiet. Tia, set to run next encryption."

Within fifty minutes, Rebecca finished listing and detailing the items Tia had selected on her wanderings through Morningside, had adjusted the computer's date and time to stamp the work for earlier in the day. At a time, thanks to the little mic under the chair, they knew Anita had been alone in her office.

After printing out the claim, she wiggled her fingers, then signed the bottom of the form with a fine—if she did say so herself—forgery of Anita's signature. She dated it, then typed up a detailed instruction list for the assistant.

She had the clock reset, the computer shut down, the mic Tia had put under the chair in her bag and the drapes open again when she heard Jack coming up the stairs.

"We're set here."

"Check again," he ordered.

"Yes, Mr. Anal-Retentive Sir. Drapes, computer, lamp, flashlight, mic and articles suitable for framing," she added, waving the file in her hand.

She relocked the office door before strolling over to lay the file on Anita's assistant's desk. "Being an efficient soul, the girl will likely have this sent off first thing in the morning. I should tell you she'd already added a couple of things to the claim. Some sort of plate that's apparently worth some twenty-eight thousand American dollars."

"Added to this . . ." Jack tapped the bag on his shoulder. "That takes her claim over two million. She'll sure have a lot of explaining to do. Security's reset. We'll bring it back on-line when we're clear."

"Then our work here is done. Let's go."

"There's one more thing." He dug in his pocket, took out the ring box. When he flipped open the top, Rebecca leaned in to study it in the beam of her flashlight.

"That's a lovely sparkler. Did you steal that from here?"

"No. I brought it in with me. Want it?"

She looked back up at him, cocked her head. "You're asking me to marry you here, in a building we've burglarized?"

"I've already asked you to marry me," he reminded her. "I'm giving you the ring here, in a building we've *technically* burglarized. It belonged to my great-great-grandmother. She was wearing it when your great-great-grandfather saved her life."

"That's lovely. That's all-around lovely, Jack. I'll take it." She tugged off her glove, held out her hand. "And you."

He slid it onto her finger, dipped his head for a kiss to seal the bargain.

"That's a very sweet moment," Malachi said through the headpieces. "Congratulations and best wishes to you both. Now would you mind getting your asses out of there?"

"Oh, stuff it, Mal." Rebecca leaned up for one more kiss. "We're on our way."

When they got back to the van, Cleo slid the partition open so she and Rebecca could change places. "Let's see the bauble," Cleo demanded. Impatient, she tugged off Rebecca's glove. "Whoa. Some rock."

"Save the girl stuff for later." Jack strapped into his seat. "Bring the system on-line."

"Now that we're engaged, he's full of orders." Rebecca stepped through and took over the controls from Tia. "Booting it up."

As she worked, Malachi bent over her, pressed his lips to the top of her head and made her smile. "I'm going to get all gooey and sentimental in just a bit."

"Me, too."

"It's a beautiful ring." Unable to resist, Tia leaned down to get a closer look. The diamond flashed as Rebecca's fingers raced over the keyboard. "I'm so happy for you."

"We'll have a party tonight, won't we? For all sorts of

reasons. Primary's up, backup booting," she announced. "And there we are. All neat and tidy." She leaned back, took the bottle of water Malachi offered. "We've done it."

"Time for Act Two." Cleo propped her feet on the dash. "We got time to grab a pizza?"

GIDEON SAT IN Kennedy Airport, reading a paperback copy of Bradbury's *Something Wicked*. He'd settled into a gate area where he could easily observe the first-class lounge.

The flight to Athens was on time and had already started to board. He was beginning to feel a bit twitchy, yearned for a cigarette.

He shifted in his seat, turned a page without reading as Anita strolled out of the lounge. He let her get another gate down before he rose and wandered after her.

Like dozens of other travelers, he pulled out a cell phone. "She's queuing up to board," he said quietly. "Flight's on schedule."

"Let us know when it, and she, are in the air. Oh, by the way, Becca and Jack got engaged."

"Did they?" Though he kept his attention on the back of Anita's head, Gideon grinned at his brother's news. "Official and all?"

"She's wearing a ring with a diamond fit to blind you. We're heading toward the second target now. If all goes well, we'll meet you back at base on schedule. You can see it for yourself."

"Good thing I've got me sunglasses. She's just going down the jetway. Thirty minutes to takeoff. I'm sitting down here, going back to my book. I'll ring you back."

THEY PARKED THREE blocks away, and waited.

"See, I told you we had time for pizza."

Jack slanted Cleo a look. "Why aren't you fat as a cow?"

"Metabolism." She took a Hershey's Big Block out of her bag, unwrapped one end. "It's the one useful thing my mother passed on to me. So, are you and Rebecca going to live here, or over on the Emerald Isle?"

"Some of both, I imagine, and here and there. We'll work it out."

"Yeah. It's handy you've got a gig where you bounce around a lot."

"What about you? You going back to dancing when this is over? With your cut, you could buy a chunk of the Rockettes."

"Dunno. Probably hang loose awhile." She munched on chocolate. "Maybe I'll open my own club or a dance school. Something that doesn't keep me hauling butt from audition to audition. Right now, I can't think further than making Anita pay for Mikey."

"We've got a good start on that."

"Man. He'd get such a rush out of all this shit. Jack?"

"Yeah."

"What if it's not in there? What if she took it with her or something?"

"Then we go to Plan B."

"What's Plan B?"

"I'll let you know when we get there." He looked at her as Malachi's signal came through his headset. "She's in the air."

"Curtain up," Cleo said, and stepped nimbly out of the van.

"You want to go over anything again? Floor plan, hand signals?"

"No, I got it."

"We've got two people in the building this time," he reminded her. "Two live-in servants. We have to do this quietly."

"I'm a fucking cat. Don't worry. Do you think this is some kind of record?"

"What's that?"

"Breaking into two places, for a total of three B and E's in twenty-four hours, without actually stealing anything."

"We're taking the Fate."

"Yeah, but it already belongs to Mal, and Tia, I guess.

So that doesn't count. I think we could get into the Guinness guy's record book for this."

"A lifelong dream of mine."

They walked by the house once. The lights were off on the second floor. "Looks like they've settled in for the evening. Servants' quarters there, south corner of the house."

"Housekeeper and butler, check. You think they get it on while the boss is away?"

Jack scratched his jaw. "I'd rather not get that image stuck in my head just now. We go up the east side to the bedroom terrace. We'll be exposed about fifteen seconds."

"Takes more than that to shake a former stripper, pal."

"Maybe you could do a number for my bachelor party." He grinned as Rebecca's pithy comment came through his headphones. "Or maybe not. Love of my life? Shut down the alarms."

He ignored the stream of cabs that drove by, and the radio car. At Rebecca's signal, he clamped a hand on Cleo's and pulled her off the sidewalk and into the shadows of the house.

They hooked lines to harnesses and were rising up the side of the building, rolling over the stone rail and crouched on the terrace before another word was spoken.

He gestured for Cleo to stow the gear while he crabwalked to the terrace doors. "Take out the locks, east terrace, second level," he said quietly into his headphones. He waited until he heard them snick, then rose, exposing himself again to deal with the manual locks.

From his jacket pocket, he pulled out a small case, chose his lock pick from it.

"Bet they didn't teach you that in security school," Cleo mentioned in a low voice.

"You'd be surprised."

He dealt with the dead bolt, then, easing the door open, waited for Cleo to slip inside before he relocked it.

A good crime-scene investigator would spot the job, he knew. But he didn't think that was going to come up.

"Obsession." Cleo sniffed the air. "Her perfume. Fits, doesn't it?"

"Lock the doors. Hallway, straight ahead. Master bath on the left."

She moved through the shadowed light to oblige, and continued to whisper. "Should I ask how come you know so much about her bedroom setup?"

"Professional knowledge only." When the doors were locked, he moved directly to the closet.

"Holy shit, this is bigger than my old apartment." She fingered the sleeve of a jacket as she moved inside. "Not bad, either. Think she'd notice if I copped a couple things? I'm rebuilding my wardrobe."

"We're not here to shop."

"Hey, shopping's the only merit badge I ever earned." She snagged one of a pair of snakeskin pumps off a wall of shelves. "My size. It's fate."

"You've got a job to do here, Cleo."

"Okay, okay." But she stuffed the shoes into her bag before she crouched to unroll his tools.

Jack opened the panel to the safe and exposed the security pad. He interfaced his portable computer, engaged the search.

"Sooner or later, she's bound to figure out you're the only one who could pull this off," Cleo commented. "She's going to be really pissed off at you."

"Yeah. I'm shaking." He watched the readout as the first two numbers of the combination of seven locked into place. "What's our time?"

"Four minutes, twenty seconds. We're skating right along." While she waited, Cleo pushed through a rack of suits. "I don't go for the lady-suit look. But hey, this one's cashmere. Bet it'll look sharp on Tia."

She rolled it up, added it to her booty.

"Combination's locked," Jack told her. "Cross your fingers, gorgeous."

She did, on both hands, then stepped behind him. "Son of a bitch." She breathed out audibly when he opened the door. Clotho glinted like a star. "There she is. You copy that, you guys? We've got her." She held out the padded bag for Jack. "Rebecca? I'm giving your man a big, sloppy kiss. So deal with it."

When she was done, she reached for her bag again. "Don't close it yet, Jack. I got a little present for Anita."

"We don't leave anything behind," he began, then stared at what Cleo pulled out of her bag. "What is that? Is that Barbie?"

"Yeah. To replace the statue. I picked out the wardrobe on a quick trip to FAO Schwarz." Gently, Cleo stood the black-leather-clad, buxom blond doll in the safe. "I call her Cat Burglar Barbie. See, she's got a little goody bag. It's got lock picks in it I made out of little safety pins, and this tiny plastic doll, pretty much to scale, I painted silver to represent the Fate."

"Cleo, you're a regular Martha Stewart."

"I got hidden talents, all right. Bye-bye, Barbie," she added, and blew a kiss as Jack closed the safe.

They shut the panel, gathered the tools.

"Okay, once we leave this room, no talking. Hand signals only. Out the door, to the right. Down the steps, to the left. Stay close."

"I'm practically riding piggyback."

"This part's trickier," he reminded her. "We get caught in here, it's all for nothing."

"Just lead the way."

They slipped out of the bedroom. As they couldn't risk flashlights now, they waited for their eyes to adjust to the dark of the second-level hallway. The house was silent, so silent Cleo could hear the ticking of her own heart. And wondered how it had managed to rise up into her throat.

At Jack's signal, they moved forward, footsteps soft over the Karastan runner.

At the base of the stairs Cleo began to think the place was more tomb than house. The air was cool, the rooms soundless, and the street sounds muffled by drape-covered windows.

Then she heard it, the instant before Jack froze and she bumped into his back. The sound of a door opening, a spill of light from the far end of the first-floor hallway and the shuffle of footsteps.

She and Jack moved as one into the cover of the first doorway. There were distant voices, almost a tunnel effect. It took her several sweaty seconds to realize the house wasn't full of people. Television, she decided, then had to swallow a nervous chuckle when she recognized the obnoxious, thrumming music from *Who Wants to Be a Millionaire?*

Perfect, she thought. Dead-on perfect.

When the light went off again, a door closed, she counted to ten until she felt Jack relax beside her. Just as she counted the steps they took down the hall, in case she had to make a dash back to cover.

They melted like shadows into the library and secured the door at their backs.

They moved fast now, and without words.

Penlights guided them to the glass-fronted bookshelves. There was a quiet rattle and creak that sounded like cannon fire in the silence as he opened a case. He cleared a section, passing her volume after volume of a leather-bound collection of Shakespeare. When the safe was exposed, he drew out his portable.

He tapped his watch. Cleo flashed the twenty-minute sign before she crouched, unzipped his bag and carefully took out the items chosen from Morningside.

He placed them in the far reaches of the small vault, behind an impressive stack of fifties, leather files and numerous jewelry cases.

When the safe was closed again, they changed places, with Cleo reshelving the books and Jack stowing all the gear. They both jumped like rabbits when the phone rang.

He gave her the hurry-up sign, then bolted to the door to unlock it, crack it open. Cleo was breathing down his neck when light flooded the hallway. With one bag clutched at her breast like a baby, Cleo dived behind a hunter-green leather winged-back chair. With another bag slung over his shoulder, Jack angled himself behind the door and tried not to breathe as the footsteps came briskly down the hall.

"One thing then another," an irritated female voice uttered. "As if I've got nothing better to do this time of night than take messages."

She shoved open the door. Jack caught the knob with

his hand before it slammed into his crotch and held it there as he pressed himself into the shielding triangle.

Light poured into the room when the woman hit the switch for the overheads.

Rebecca spoke into his ear, warning him they were going overtime.

He heard the housekeeper march to the desk, slap something on the polished wood. "Hope she stays away for a month. Give us some breathing room."

Footsteps, shuffling now, headed back to the door. There was a pause, a soft snort that might have been approval or derision, then the lights went out.

Jack stayed just as he was, willed Cleo to do the same, as the footsteps retreated. He didn't move an inch until he heard the quick slam of a door from down the hallway.

Gently, very gently, he nudged the door open. In the shadowy light he saw Cleo, still huddled behind the chair. Her eyes gleamed in the dark as they met his. She rolled them wildly, then eased to her feet.

They crept out of the library, slipped silently down the hall to the foyer. And walked right out the front door.


"SO I'M PLAYING rabbit behind this chair, and there's Jack doing his Claude Rains impression behind the door, and all I can see are her feet. She's got on fuzzy slippers. Pink ones, and all I can think is I'm gonna get busted by some woman wearing fuzzy pink slippers. It's mortifying."

Because she'd wanted to get horizontal as soon as possible, Cleo had given Rebecca back the shotgun position and was stretched out, as best as possible, on the floor of the van.

"Man. *Man.* I need to take some alcohol internally really soon."

"You were great." Jack glanced in the rearview mirror. "Nerves of steel."

"Yeah, nerves of jelly for a moment there. Oh hey!" She rolled herself over, eased up to a crouched position. "I got you a present, Tia."

"A present?"

"Yeah." She dug into her bag and pulled out the balled-up suit. "Great color for you. Sorta eggplant, I think. Good texture. Cashmere."

"Is this . . . is this hers?"

"So what? Have it cleaned, fumigated, whatever." Cleo shrugged as she dug in the bag again. "It'll look better on you anyway. Just like these shoes are gonna look better on me." She set them aside, dug in again. "Snagged you this little evening purse, Rebecca. Judith Leiber. It's not bad."

"How the hell did you get all that stuff?" Jack demanded.

"Leftover skill from my shoplifting days. I'm not proud of it, but I was sixteen and rebellious. It's a cry for attention, right, Tia?"

"Well . . . don't you think she'll notice this is missing?"

"Hell, she's got half the stock from Bergdorf's in there. What's one outfit? Besides, she's going to be too busy to do a wardrobe check once she gets back and our shit hits her fan."

"You've got such a way with words." Malachi reached down, patted her head.

"Tell me." And she felt the last of the residual tension fade when they drove into the garage and she saw Jack's SUV. Gideon was back, and all was right with her world. "So, we can order pizza now, right?"

# Twenty-seven

"THERE they are." Tia circled the table again. On it, the three silver Fates, linked at their bases, glinted in the late-morning sunlight.

"It almost seemed like a dream," she said quietly. "Like a dream, last night and everything that led up to it. Or a play I somehow stumbled into. But there they are."

"You never stumbled, Tia." Standing behind her, Malachi laid his hands on her shoulders. "You've been rock-steady, through and through."

"That's a dream in itself. They haven't been together for a century. Perhaps two. We united them. That means something. Eternal and secure. That's what's said about them in mythology. We have to see that these symbols of them are just that. Secure."

"They won't be divided again."

"Spin, measure, cut." She touched each, lightly, in turn. "What's in a life and what it touches. These are more than art, Malachi, and more than the dollars anyone would pay to own them. They're a responsibility."

She shifted the base, lifted Clotho, and thought of Henry W. Wyley. He'd held it the same way, had sought the others. And died in the seeking. "My blood and yours are twined in this. I wonder if they understood, even a little, what a long thread she wove for them. It wasn't cut off at their deaths. It's spun out to you and me, and the rest of us. Even Anita."

Still holding the Fate, she turned to him. "Threads spinning out. Two men from opposite arcs of life, starting a circle with this between them. The circle widens with Cleo and Jack, Rebecca and Gideon. And the threads spin on. If we take what these three images represent, if we allow ourselves to believe it, Anita's part in it was meant to be."

"So we give her no responsibility for what she's done?" he demanded. "For the blood she spilled, for nothing more than greed."

"No. The good and bad, the flaws and virtues are woven into the threads. The choices, the responsibilities are hers. And Fate always demands payment." Carefully, Tia set Clotho with her sisters. "And eventually, always collects. I suppose I'm saying she may not be the only one to pay a price."

"You shouldn't be sad today of all days." He drew her into his arms, stroked his fingers through her sunny cap of hair. "We've done most of what we set out to do. And we'll finish it."

"I'm not sad. But I am wondering what happens when we do finish it."

"When we do, the pattern changes again," he said. He rubbed his cheek over the top of her head. "There's something I should have told you before. Something I should've made clear."

She braced, shut her eyes. And the elevator doors opened.

"Okay, break it up. We've got supplies." Cleo, arms loaded with marketing bags, strode into the loft just ahead of Gideon. "Jack and Rebecca are on their way up. He's got word on Anita."


"SHE ARRIVED ON schedule," Jack relayed, "and was driven to the home of Stefan Nikos. Stefan was a friend and client of Paul Morningside, and both he and his wife are known for their art and antique collection, their charitable works. And their hospitality."

"It's olive oil, isn't it?" Rebecca plucked one of the olives from her plate and studied it. "I've read of him in *Money* magazine and *Time* and so on. He's swimming in olive oil. Odd that such a homely little thing could make anyone so rich."

"Olive groves," Jack agreed. "And vineyards, and the various by-products from both. He has homes on Athens, on Corfu, a pied-à-terre in Paris and a château in the Swiss Alps." He plucked one of the olives from Rebecca's plate, popped it into his mouth. "And security by Burdett in each location."

"You've a long reach, Jack," Malachi commented.

"Long enough. I spoke to Stefan last week after Tia planted the Athens seed."

"You might have told the rest of us," Rebecca retorted.

"Didn't know if the seed would sprout. Like I said, he was a friend of Morningside. He's not so fond of the widow. Me," he added with a slow grin, "he likes just fine. Fine enough to do me a favor. He's amused at the idea of stringing Anita along. He'll keep her busy for a couple days with rumors of Lachesis and the tall, sexy brunette who's hunting for the statue."

"Yeah? How am I liking Greece?"

"You're getting around," Jack told Cleo. "Not much time for sight-seeing."

"There's always next time."

"We'll have a week at the outside," Malachi calculated. "For the wheels to turn, to put everything else into play." He paused, scanned the faces around him. "It has to be said, though, and may as well be said now. We could stop where we are. We have the Fates."

Cleo surged up from her slouch. "She hasn't paid."

"Wait now, hear me out. We have what she wants. What she stole, what she's killed for. And we hurt no one. Added to that, we've complicated her life considerably with the insurance claim and in moving those pieces from Morningside into her personal safe."

"She'd already committed insurance fraud," Gideon commented. "We just upped the stakes. There's no guarantee that she won't slither out of it." He laid a hand on Cleo's thigh, felt the muscles vibrating.

"There's no guarantee of anything," Malachi returned. "But we can be sure she won't slither easily, not with those pieces tucked away in her library safe. And Jack's put a bug in the ear of his police friend about her. There's a good chance if we sit back, the system will work."

"Lew will bulldog it." Jack forked up some pasta salad. "Security tapes will show the pieces on her claim form were still in place after the break-in. Her life won't be a picnic while he's on her. The insurance investigator's going to take a really dim view of a claim in excess of two million when the client still has the merchandise."

"Maybe she pays a fine, does some community service. I—"

Jack held up his fork to interrupt Cleo's rant. "Just getting a visual of Anita in a soup kitchen. It's not bad. Doesn't play either, not for seven-figure fraud. Still, if we want her going all the way down, Bob has to tie her to Dubrowsky. If he can't connect her, he can't tie her to the murder, or to Cleo's friend."

"And she'd skate," Cleo said bitterly.

"Yeah, but she could skate anyway. That's where Mal's coming from. With what we did, she gets hit with insurance fraud, does a little time, and her glossy society-widow image ends up smeared."

"Sometimes," Tia said as everyone looked at her, "that sort of notoriety adds a sheen of its own."

"Good point," Jack agreed. "If we follow through with the rest, we skin her financially, and maybe," Jack said again, "we push her into making a mistake that locks it all down. There's a lot of ifs in there. Moving forward puts it all back in the mix."

"Um." Tia lifted a hand, then let it fall. "The Moerae, the Fates, prophesied when Meleager was only a week old that he would die when a brand on his mother's hearth burned out. They sang his fate—Clotho, that he would be noble, Lachesis, that he'd be brave. And Atropus, looking at the infant, that he would live only as long as that brand was not consumed."

"I don't get this," Cleo began.

"Let her finish," Gideon told her.

"Well, you see, Meleager's mother, desperate to protect her baby, hid the brand away in a chest. If it didn't burn out, he'd be safe. So her son grew up, and as a man, Meleager killed his mother's brothers. In anger and grief at the slaughter, she took the brand out of the chest and burned it. So Meleager died. Avenging her brothers, she lost her son."

"Fine. Mikey stands for my brother, but that bitch sure as hell doesn't stand for my kid. So what?"

"The point is," Tia said gently, "revenge is never free. And it never brings back what was lost. If we move forward only for revenge, the price may be too high."

Cleo got up. As Tia had done earlier, she walked over, circled the tables where the Fates stood. "Mikey was my friend. Gideon barely knew him, the rest of you didn't know him at all."

"We know you, Cleo," Rebecca said quietly.

"Yeah, well. I'm not going to stand here and pretend I don't want revenge, and I'm willing to pay the freight for it. But what I said before, the first time we all got together at Tia's, that still holds. I want justice more. So, we've got these, and we're rich. Big fucking deal."

She turned her back on them. "If people just step back from what's right, don't stand up for a friend when it gets tough, what's the damn point? Any one of you doesn't want to get dragged into this, that's cool. No harm, no foul, especially after all this. But I'm not done. I'm not done till she's sitting in a cell cursing my name."

Malachi looked at his brother, nodded. Then he laid a hand over Tia's. "The story you told, darling. There's another meaning to it."

"Yes. Choice determines destiny." She rose, walked to Cleo. "Lives circle around, intersect. Touch and bounce off each other. All we can do is our best, and follow the thread to the end. I don't suppose justice is free either. We'll just have to make it worth the price."

"Okay." Cleo's vision blurred with tears. "I've gotta . . ."

She gave a helpless shrug, then walked quickly out of the room.

"No, let me," Tia said as Gideon started to rise. "I could use a little crying jag myself."

As Tia hurried after Cleo, Malachi reached for his beer. "Now that that's settled, and we're all on the same page more or less, I'm going to bring up other business. Of a more personal sort." He took a deep drink to wet his throat. "The second part of a conversation we had before," he said to Jack. "Well then. As head of the family—"

"Head of the family?" Rebecca gave a shout of laughter. "My arse. Ma's head of the family."

"She's not here, is she?" Malachi said evenly and bristled at having his rhythm broken. "And I'm the oldest, so it falls to me to address the matter of this engagement."

"It's my engagement, and none of your concern."

"Shut your mouth for five flaming minutes."

"I'm getting another beer," Gideon decided. "This should be entertaining."

"Don't you tell me to shut my mouth, you puffed-up, pea-brained monkey."

"I could've done this out of your presence," Malachi reminded her, and the cool tone warned of rising temper. "And saved myself the insults and abuse. And now, I'm talking to Jack."

"Oh, talking to Jack, are you. And I'm to sit here with my hands folded and my head demurely bowed?" She threw a pillow at him.

"You wouldn't know demure if it crawled down your throat and tickled your tonsils." He threw the pillow back, bouncing it off her head. "And after I say my piece, you can say your own. But by God, I'm saying it."

"Rebecca." Jack spoke as she bared her teeth. "Why don't you wait until he's finished before you get pissed off?"

"Thank you, Jack. And first I'll say you have all the pity in my heart for the life you'll lead with this ill-mannered, bad-tempered, violent-natured female." Malachi narrowed his eyes as she made a grab for the jade bowl on the coffee table and Jack clamped a hand on her wrist.

"Han dynasty. Stick with the pillows."

"As I was saying," Malachi continued. "I'm aware money isn't an issue with you, but I want it clear my sister doesn't come to you with empty pockets. She's a quarter interest in our business, which does well enough. Whether or not she decides to continue to work actively in that business, the quarter interest remains hers. And she's also entitled to her share of whatever comes out of this enterprise of ours."

"The money doesn't matter."

"It matters to us," Malachi corrected. "And it matters to Rebecca." He lifted a brow at his sister.

"Maybe you aren't a complete pea brain." And she smiled at him.

"I've seen how things are between you, and I'm glad of it. For all her faults—and they are legion—we love her and want her happy. As far as the Sullivan business is concerned, you're welcome to be as much a part of that as suits you."

"Nicely done, Mal." Gideon sat on the arm of his brother's chair, lifted his glass in toast. "Da would have been pleased with that. And so, Jack, welcome to the family."

"Thanks. I don't know much about boats. Wouldn't mind learning more."

"Well now." Rebecca grinned at her brothers. "I'm just the one to teach you."

"We'll talk about that." He gave her knee a friendly pat before getting to his feet. "I've got one or two errands to run. I could use a hand," he said to the other men.

"If the three of you are going gallivanting, so am I. I'm going to drag Cleo and Tia out to look at wedding dresses. Did I mention I'm wanting a big, white wedding?"

That stopped him. "Define 'big.' "

"Don't waste your breath," Gideon advised him. "She's got that gleam in her eye."

It was still there three hours later when she came back loaded down with brides' magazines, a wedding planner book Tia bought her as an engagement gift and the sexy little nightgown that had been Cleo's gift.

"I still say lilies will make beautiful centerpieces for the reception."

"Right." Cleo winked at Tia. "They're not just for funerals anymore."

"The wildflower nosegays were so charming," Tia put in. "I can't believe I spent all that time in a flower shop and my sinuses stayed clear. I've had an allergy breakthrough."

"What are all those red spots on your face?" Cleo asked her, then roared as Tia made a dash for the Adam mirror in Jack's living area and did a thorough inspection for rashes or hives.

"I don't think that's funny. Not one bit."

"You know how she likes to joke," Rebecca commented, then glanced over toward the archway leading to the bedroom. The bags she held fell to the floor, and she was flying.

"Ma!"

"There's my girl." Eileen caught her, hugged her hard. "There's my pretty girl."

"Ma. What're you doing here? How did you get here? Oh, I missed you."

"What I'm doing is unpacking my things, and I got here on a plane. I missed you, too. Just let me look at you." Eileen pulled her back, studied her face. "Happy, are you?"

"I am, yes. Very happy."

"I knew he was for you when you brought him home for tea." She sighed, pressed her lips to Rebecca's brow while all the years whizzed by in her head. "Now, introduce me to your friends here, who I've already heard so much about from my boys."

"Tia and Cleo, my mother, Eileen Sullivan."

"It's lovely to meet you, Mrs. Sullivan." Malachi's mother, Tia thought, panicked. "I hope you had a pleasant flight."

"I felt like a queen, lolling about in first class."

"Yeah, well, it's a long one though." Uneasy, Cleo tugged on Tia's sleeve. "We'll split and let you rest up. Catch up. All that."

"Indeed you won't." Eileen's smile was friendly, and her mind made up. "We'll have a nice cozy pot of tea and a chat. The boys are down below doing some devious thing or the other, so we'll take advantage of the time. Such a fine, big flat this is," she added, glancing around. "There must be the makings for tea somewhere in it."

"I'll make it," Tia said quickly.

"I'll help." Cleo nipped at her heels all the way into the kitchen. "What are we supposed to talk to her about?" she hissed. "Oh, hi, Mrs. Sullivan. We really enjoy sex with your sons when we're not out breaking into buildings."

"Oh God. Oh God." Tia put her head in her hands. "What did we come in here for?"

"Tea."

"Right. I forgot. Okay." She opened two cupboards before she remembered where she herself had stored the tea. "Well, she has to know. Oh God!" Tia opened the fridge, found an open bottle of wine. She pulled out the stopper and took a pull straight from the bottle. "She has to know something about the other. Either Malachi or Gideon would call her regularly. We know she knows about the Fates and Anita and at least some portion of the plans. As for the other . . ."

Tia tried to calm down as she measured out tea. "They're grown men, and she seems like a reasonable woman."

"Easy for you. She's probably going to be all right with the idea of her firstborn cozied up with a published author with a Ph.D. and an apartment on the Upper East Side. But I don't see her doing cheers when she finds out her baby boy is doing it with a stripper."

"That's insulting."

"Well, Jesus, Tia, who could blame her? I—"

"No, not to Mrs. Sullivan, to you." With the tea canister still in hand, Tia turned. "You're insulting a friend of mine, and I don't like it. You're brave and loyal and smart, and you have nothing to be ashamed of, nothing to apologize for."

"That was well said, Tia." Eileen stepped into the kitchen and watched both women blanch. "I can see why Malachi's so taken with you. And as for you," she said to

Cleo. "It happens I trust my baby boy's judgment and have always admired his taste. And Mal's, as well. I'll start there with the both of you, and we'll see how we get on. See that water boils full before you pour it," she added. "Most Yanks never can get a decent pot of tea made."

When Jack came into the apartment thirty minutes later, he noted three things simultaneously. Tia was flustered, Cleo was stiff. And Rebecca was glowing.

It was Rebecca who rose, slowly, walked to him. She wrapped her arms around his neck, brought her mouth to his for a long, lingering kiss.

"Thanks," she said.

"You're welcome." He kept an arm around her waist as he looked over at her mother. "Settling in all right, Eileen?"

"Couldn't be more comfortable, thank you, Jack. Now, I'm hearing from the three girls here that you've all got more plans for this woman who's after hurting my family. I hope we can sit down and find a way I might help you out with them."

"I'm sure we'll think of something. According to my contact, the woman is even now combing Athens in search of a certain silver lady and a brunette." He came over, sat across from Cleo. "She bought a gun. It was the first thing she did. It's clear she's hoping to track you down, and when she does, she plans to play for keeps."

"She's going to be disappointed, isn't she?"

"And we're going to keep her that way." Gideon came in, Malachi behind him. And there was fury in his eyes. "Whatever plans are from this point, we're keeping you well away from her."

"Hey, listen, Slick—"

"The hell I will. She's not planning on having a chat with you. She's planning on getting what she's after, then killing you. Did you tell her where she got the gun?"

"Black market," Jack provided. "Unregistered Glock. She was careful. She didn't try to get a weapon through customs. Odds are she's not planning on bringing it back through either. She hopes to get her money's worth out of it, then ditch it."

"Like I said, she's going to be disappointed."

"And you're on background duty from here out," Gideon told her. "You help Rebecca with tech, Tia with research. And you stay in this flat or Tia's. You don't go out alone for any reason. And if you argue with me, I'll lock you in a closet until it's done."

"Cleo, before you cosh my son, which I'm sure he deserves for any number of reasons, I'd like to say something." Eileen sat comfortably, as she often did at her own kitchen table. "I've had a different view of things, as I haven't been in the center of it. There's a weak spot—an Achilles' heel, you could say. That'd be apt, wouldn't it," Eileen said to Tia. "This woman knows your face, Cleo. She believes you're holding something she's already killed for. She's focused on you now. That'll change and shift a bit after she comes back here. But you're the one thing she's sure of. If she manages to get to you, she gets to all. Would that be the case, Mal?"

"It would, in a nutshell. We won't risk losing you, Cleo, for your own sake. And I don't think you'll risk the whole of the matter just for the chance to thumb your nose in her face."

"Okay, point taken. I'm a risk, so I stay covered."

"And next time, Gideon," Eileen said, "you might ask reasonably instead of tossing orders about. You make a fine cup of tea for a Yank, Tia."

"Thank you, Mrs. Sullivan."

"Let's just make it Eileen, why don't we? From what I gather here you're a clever girl in other areas."

"Not really. I'm just good at following directions."

"Modesty's very becoming." Eileen poured another half cup of tea from the pot. "But when it's misplaced or untrue, then it's just foolishness. You found a way to get this woman's financial information."

"Actually, it was my friend who . . . Yes," Tia amended at Eileen's lifted eyebrows. "I found a way."

"And so you know how much to demand from her for the Fates."

"We haven't decided, exactly, but I thought . . ."

"Does the girl always worry about speaking her mind?" Eileen asked Malachi.

"Not as much as she did. You're making her nervous."

Though color rose into her cheeks, Tia straightened her shoulders. "She can liquidate up to fifteen million. Twenty, really, but that adds considerable time and complications, so fifteen's better. So I thought we should ask for ten and give her a buffer. The Fates are worth a great deal more. She'll know that with a little work and research she can sell them to the right collector for at least double her investment. My father verified that he, as a dealer, would offer ten. As a businesswoman, she'd think the same way."

"Very sensible," Eileen said with a nod. "Now all you have to do is figure out how to have her turn over that kind of money without giving her the Fates. Have her charged with the insurance fraud and end it all with her being arrested for murder. With that done, we can get down to planning a wedding and get back to running Sullivan Tours. Your cousins are doing a fine job with the day-to-day of it," she told Malachi, "but we need to have our hands back in it again."

"It'll hold a bit longer, Ma," Malachi assured her.

"If I didn't believe that, I wouldn't be here. Just as I believe the lot of you will come up with the solution to the whole of it. You've gotten this far, after all. And speaking of that, isn't it time someone offered to show me the Fates?"


"I LIKE YOUR mother."

Malachi's lips twitched as he watched Tia neatly turn down the bed. "She terrifies you."

"Just a little." Out of habit, she switched on the white-noise maker on the bedside table.

When she moved away to adjust her bedroom air filter, Malachi switched it back off as he did every night. She never noticed.

"Rebecca was so happy to see her. It was a lovely thing for Jack to do, bringing her here." Restless, Tia walked into the bath, carefully removed her hypoallergenic makeup with hypoallergenic cleanser.

"A nice surprise for you, too," she added when Malachi came to the doorway. "I'm sure you've missed her."

"I have, very much." He loved to watch her this way—the tidiness of her, the pretty sweetness of her face without any trace of cosmetics. "You know what they say about Irish men."

"No, what do they say?"

"They may be drunks or rebels, brawlers or poets. But to a man, they love their mothers."

She laughed a little, stood there opening and closing the top of her moisturizer. "You're not any of those things."

"What an insult. I can drink and brawl with the best of them. Sure I've got some rebel in me. And . . . do you want poetry, Tia?"

"I don't know. I've never had any."

"Do you want it quoted or made up?"

She wanted to smile, was sure she could, but it collapsed on her. "Don't do this."

"What?" Baffled, and a little alarmed, he stepped to her. And she stepped away.

"I'm not going to make it difficult for you."

"That's good to know," he said carefully. "Why are you crying?"

"I'm not crying." She sniffed. "I won't cry. I'll be reasonable and understanding, just like I always am," she said and set the moisturizer on the counter with a snap.

"Maybe you should tell me what you're going to be reasonable and understanding about."

"Don't laugh at me. Knowing people laugh at me doesn't make it any less horrible."

"I'm not laughing at you. Sweetheart . . ." He reached out for her and she smacked his hand aside.

"Don't call me that, and don't touch me," she added as she pushed by him and strode back into the bedroom.

"Don't call you sweetheart, don't touch you. You won't cry and you'll be reasonable and understanding." His head began to throb. "Give me a clue here."

"We're almost done. I know it, and I'll finish it out. This is the only important thing I've done in my life, and I won't leave it unfinished."

"It's not the only important thing you've done."

"Don't placate me, Malachi."

"Damned if I'm placating you, and bloody hell if I'm going to stand here arguing without any idea what I'm arguing about. Christ, I'm getting one of your headaches." He scrubbed his hands roughly over his face. "Tia, what is it?"

"You said you should have told me before. Maybe you should. Maybe, even though I knew, it would have been better that way."

"Told you . . . ah." And he remembered what he'd been about to say before Cleo had interrupted them that morning. He frowned, jammed his hands into his pockets. "You know, and it pisses you off?"

"I'm not allowed to have feelings?" she tossed back. "I'm not allowed to be angry. Just grateful? Grateful that we've had these weeks together. Well, I am grateful and I'm angry. I'll be furious if I want." She glanced around. "God! There must be something to throw."

"Don't think about it," he advised. "Just grab the first thing and let it fly."

She snatched up her hairbrush, heaved it. It cracked solidly against the jewel-toned shade of her bedside lamp. "Damn it! Damn it, that was Tiffany. Can't I even have a successful temper tantrum?"

"You should have thrown it at me." He grabbed her arms before she could go clean up the mess she'd made.

"Just let me go."

"I'm not going to do that."

"I'm stupid." The fight went out of her. "All I've done is embarrass myself and break a beautiful lamp shade. I should've taken a Xanax."

"Well, you didn't, and I prefer fighting with a woman who's not hazy on some tranquilizer. These are real feelings, Tia, and you'll have to deal with them. Whether you want mine or not, you'll have to deal with them."

"I've been dealing with them." She shoved at him. "I've

been dealing with them all along. And it's not fair. I don't care that life doesn't have to be fair, because this is *my* life. And I can't make it easy on you, no matter how often I told myself I would. I want you to go stay at Jack's. You can't be here with me, it's too much."

"You're tossing me out? Before I go, I'll know why," he said and grabbed her.

"It's too much, I said. I'll finish what we started, and I won't let the others down. But I won't, I will *not* be the quiet, unassuming lover who makes it convenient for you when it's over and you walk away, when you go back to Ireland and pick up your life where you left it off. Where you leave me off. For once, I'm doing the ending, and I'm telling you to go."

"Have I ever asked you to be quiet or unassuming?"

"No. You changed my life, thank you very much. There." She tried to twist away and was hauled back. "You want more? Fine. It's very considerate of you to be honest enough to tell me it's all temporary—lives bumping together and moving on. You've got a home and a business to run in Ireland. So good luck."

"You're a confusing woman, Tia, and a great deal of work."

"I'm a very simple woman, and extremely low maintenance."

"Bollocks. You're a maze, and constantly fascinating to me. Let's just back all this up, for clarity's sake. In your opinion, I was about to tell you this morning that it's been nice, it's been fun, and very pleasurable as well. I'd probably add that I'm quite fond of you, and knowing you to be a quiet, unassuming woman—ha ha—I'm sure you'll understand that when this business is done, then so are we."

The image of him was hazed through tears. For the first time she wished, viciously, that he was ordinary—to look at, to speak with. To make love with.

"It doesn't matter what you would have said because I'm saying it now."

"Oh it matters," he disagreed. "I'm thinking it matters. So I'll tell you what it is I realized I should have told you before. I love you. That's what I should have told you before. What do you think of that?"

"I don't know." A tear spilled over now, but she didn't notice. "Do you mean it?"

"Of course not." He laughed as her mouth fell open, then scooped her off her feet. "What, I'm a liar now as well? I love you, Tia, and if I changed your life, you changed mine right back. If you think I can pick up where I left off before you, then you are stupid."

"Nobody ever said that to me before."

"That you're stupid?"

"No." She touched his face as he sat on the side of the bed with her in his lap. "'I love you.' No one's ever said that to me."

"Then you'll have to make do with me telling you, until you're tired of hearing it."

She shook her head as her heart swelled. "No one's ever said it to me, so I never had the chance to say it back. Now I do. I love you. I love you, Malachi."

Spinning threads, she thought as she pressed her lips to his. Spinning them into yet another pattern. If her thread was cut short, she could look back at this moment and have no regrets.

# Twenty-eight

S HE was close. She knew it.

She'd spent hours combing trinket shops, more paying calls on antique and art houses with the pretense of doing business. She'd had endless, and so far fruitless, conversations with local collectors she'd tagged thanks to Stefan.

To reward herself Anita enjoyed a long, cold drink at a shady table by the sparkling pool beside the Nikoses' guest house.

Despite his introductions to collectors, Stefan wasn't being as helpful as she'd hoped.

Hospitable enough, she mused as she sipped her frothy mimosa. He and his dull wife had welcomed her with open arms. Another time, she'd have relished the time in the spectacular white house flowing over the hills above Athens, with its acres of gardens, its army of servants and its cool, fragrant courtyards.

It was very satisfying to stretch out here on thick cushions beside a shimmering pool fed by a fountain depicting Aphrodite, to scan the sheltering trees and flowers under a hot blue sky and know that she had only to lift a finger and anything—anything—her appetites craved would be brought to her.

That was the silken shelter of true wealth, true privilege, where there was no need to concern yourself with anything beyond your own immediate desires.

And that was her life's ambition.

In fact, she thought it was time she looked into similar accommodations for herself. Once she had the other statues, and she would have them, she might consider a partial retirement. After all, she'd be hard-pressed to top the coup of acquiring and selling the Three Fates. Morningside would have outlived its purpose for her.

Italy might be more her style, she mused. Some elegant villa in Tuscany where she would live in staggering expatriate style. Of course, she'd keep the house in New York. She'd spend a few months there every year. Shopping, socializing, entertaining and gathering the envy of others like rose petals.

She'd grant interviews. But after the initial flurry of media, she'd slip away. That veil of mystery would be thin, and when she lifted it on her own whim, they'd run scrambling for her.

She would put Morningside up for sale, regretfully. And would reap all the profits due her after the investment of twelve tedious years of marriage.

It was the life she'd been meant for, Anita decided as she eased back on the chaise. One of indulgence, fame and great, great wealth.

God knew she'd earned it.

She'd find that infuriating Cleo Toliver and remove that obstacle from her path. It was only a matter of time. She couldn't hide forever. At least Stefan had been of some help interpreting in a few of the shops, inquiring for her about the brunette and a small silver statue.

The Toliver woman was certainly getting around. And twice now, according to the shopkeepers, Anita had missed her by less than an hour.

It only meant she was closing in, Anita assured herself. Imagine that slut believing she could outwit Anita Gaye.

It was going to be a very costly mistake for Cleo Toliver.

"Anita?"

Still floating on the current of her fantasies, Anita tipped down her shaded glasses and looked at Stefan. "Hello. Beautiful out here, isn't it?"

"Perfect. I thought you might enjoy a fresh drink, some refreshment." He gestured to the trays of fruit and cheese a servant arranged on the table, then handed her another mimosa.

"I'd adore it, thanks. I hope you're going to join me."

"I will."

His silver hair glinted in the sun as he took the chair beside her.

His arms were tanned and muscled, his body fit, and his face interestingly craggy. He was worth, at conservative estimates, a hundred and twenty million.

If she'd been in the market for another husband, he'd have been a top contender.

"I want to thank you again, Stefan, for being my guide and liaison. It's bad enough I'm taking advantage of your hospitality by coming into your home on hardly a moment's notice, but I'm taking up so much of your time. I know how busy a man of your stature and position is."

"Please." He gestured her words away as he picked up his own drink. "It's nothing but a pleasure. And exciting as well, this treasure hunt. Such things make me feel young again."

"Oh. As if you're not." She leaned toward him, offering him a deliberate view of lush breasts barely contained by her thin bikini. She may not have been in the market for a husband, but lovers were always a consideration. "You're an attractive, vital man in his prime. Why, if it wasn't for your wife . . ." She trailed off, tapped a finger on the back of his hand in a flirtatious manner. "I'd make a play for you myself."

"You flatter me." Calculating and pitifully obvious woman, he thought. And felt another twinge for his good friend who hadn't seen this creature for what she was.

"Not in the least. Like wine, I prefer men with a certain

age and body to their credit. I hope, one day, I'll be able to repay you for your kindness."

"What I do," he said, "I do for Paul. And, of course, for you, Anita. You deserve all I can do for you, and more. As it happens, I fear I have not been successful in helping you with your treasure hunt. Naturally, as a collector my interest isn't completely altruistic. What a prize it would be, to add the Moerae to my collection. I trust, when the time comes, we can do business."

"How could it be otherwise?" She tapped her glass against his. "To future dealings, business and personal."

"I look forward to it, more than I can say. I should tell you that on the other front, I have had some small success."

He paused, studied the fruit and sliced off a branch of fat purple grapes. "Will you not sample some? From our own arbors."

"Thank you." She took the branch from him. "You were saying?"

"Eh? Oh yes, yes." He took his time, selected a branch of grapes for himself. "Yes, some small success on the matter of the woman you seek. The name of the hotel where she was booked."

"You found her." Anita swung her legs over the chaise so that her feet smacked against the tiles. "Why didn't you say so? Where is this place?"

"In an area of the city I would never recommend for a lady of your delicacies. Cheese?"

"I need a car and driver," she snapped. "Immediately."

"Of course, all is at your disposal." He cut a thin slice of cheese, added it to the small plate that held the grapes she'd yet to taste. "Ah, but you think to go to this hotel to see her. She is not there."

"What are you talking about?"

Obvious, Stefan thought again. Yes, she was obvious. And now the cat peeked out behind the mask, showing its nasty little fangs and ugly temper. "She *was* booked," he explained, "but has checked out only today."

"Where did she go? Where the hell is she?"

"Alas, I was unable to learn this. The clerk said only

that she checked out, shortly after meeting with a young man. British or Irish, the clerk wasn't certain. They left together."

The color that temper and excitement had thrown into her cheeks slid away until her face was white as bone, hard as stone. "That can't be."

"Naturally, there could be some mistake or confusion, but the clerk seemed cooperative enough, and very certain. I can arrange for you to speak with him yourself tomorrow if you like. He has no English, but I will be happy to interpret. Still I must insist you meet him away from this area. I could not, in good conscience, take you there."

"I need to talk to him now. I need to find her *now*. Before . . ." She paced the hot white tiles around the pool, and thought murderously of Malachi Sullivan.

"Calm yourself, Anita." His tone all comfort, Stefan got to his feet. A servant approached and apologized for the interruption.

Stefan took the envelope the servant held out, then dismissed him.

"Anita, you have a telegram."

She whirled back, the heels of her sandals clicking on the tile.

Ordinarily he would have excused himself to give a guest privacy, but he refused to miss the moment and stood nearby, watching as she ripped open the telegram. And read.

*Anita. Sorry I didn't have time to come around in person and give you my regards. Strangers in a strange land, and so on. But I finished my business in Athens rather quickly, and am by the time you read this escorting some rather attractive ladies to New York. I suggest you get yourself back there as soon as possible, if you're interested in a fateful reunion.*

*I'll be in touch.*
*Malachi Sullivan*

Stefan had the pleasure of hearing her strangled scream as she balled the telegram in her fist. "I hope this is not bad news."

"I have to get back to New York. Right away." The color was back in her face, and raging.

"Of course. I'll make the arrangements for you. If there's anything I can do—"

"I'll do it," she said between her teeth. "You'd better believe I'll do it."

He waited until she'd stormed away, rushing in the direction of the house. Then he sat, picked up his drink, took out his cell phone.

He enjoyed a grape while he made the call.

"Jack. I'll have a very angry woman on my private jet within two hours. No, no," he said, chuckling as he chose another grape. "It's been, my friend, and continues to be, my very great pleasure."


SHE GOT HOME to a pile of messages, many of which were from the police and only served to irritate her. She'd spent the hours in the air devising ways she would dispose of Malachi—all of which ended in his bloody, painful death.

As satisfying as all of them were, Anita was smart enough, and still controlled enough, to know it was essential to find the right time, the right place and the right method.

She wanted him dead, but she wanted the Fates even more.

She ordered her servants out of the house. She wanted the place empty. She showered, changed, then contacted Jasper. She broke one of her own cardinal rules by ordering him to come to her home.

She was dissatisfied with his work and considered disposing of him. It would, she imagined, be simple enough to make it look like a break-in attempt, mock up signs of a struggle. With her clothes torn a bit, a few handy bruises, no one would question her, a woman alone, defending her home and her person with one of her dead husband's guns.

Remembering how it had felt to pull the trigger, to see Dubrowsky stumble, fall, die, she knew the act would be a great stress reliever.

But she'd had enough of the police for a while. And, added to that, Jasper might yet come in handy. She couldn't afford the luxury of cutting him loose quite yet.

He came, as instructed, to the rear entrance. She gestured him in, then walked directly to the library. Appreciating the value of position, she sat behind the desk. "Close the door," she said coolly.

When his back was turned she took the gun she'd placed in the drawer and set it in her lap. Just in case.

"I'm not pleased with your work, Mr. Jasper." She held up a finger before he could speak. "Nor am I interested in your excuses. I've paid you, and paid you well, for your particular skills and talents. In my opinion, they've been sadly lacking."

"You haven't given me a hell of a lot to go on."

She sat back. After the long flight it was energizing to feel the fury, the violence pumping out of him. Better, she thought, than drugs. He believed he was stronger, more dangerous. And had no idea he was only one finger twitch away from death.

"Are you criticizing me, Mr. Jasper?"

"Look, you don't think I'm doing the job, fire me."

"Oh, I've considered that." She stroked a fingertip over the cold steel of the nine-millimeter in her lap. "I'm a businesswoman, and when an employee does unsatisfactory work, that employee is terminated."

"No skin off my nose."

She saw his body shift. She knew he carried a gun under his suit jacket. Was he considering using it on her? she wondered. To intimidate, to rob, perhaps to rape? Thinking she'd be helpless against him, and unable to go to the police.

The idea was absolutely thrilling.

"However, as a businesswoman I also believe in giving

employees certain incentives in the hopes their work will improve. I'm going to offer you an incentive."

"Yeah." He relaxed his gun arm. "Such as?"

"A twenty-five-thousand-dollar bonus if you find and deliver to me a man named Malachi Sullivan. He's in the city, possibly in the company of Cleo Toliver. You remember Cleo, don't you, Mr. Jasper?" She purred it. "She's managed to slip through your fingers a number of times. If you deliver both of them, I'll double that bonus. I don't care what kind of shape they're in, as long as they're alive. I want to be very clear on that point. They must be alive. Your former associate didn't understand that distinction, which is why he was terminated."

"Fifty for the man, a hundred if I get them both."

She angled her head, then used a finger to nudge a large manila envelope over the desk. "There's a picture of him in here, and two thousand for expenses. I will not give you more than two thousand," she said, "until I have some results. There's an apartment building on West Eighteenth, between Ninth and Tenth. The address is also in the envelope, along with keys. The building is being renovated. Renovations will be put on hold as of today. When you have Mr. Sullivan, and hopefully Miss Toliver, you're to take them there. Use the basement facilities. Employ whatever means necessary to restrain them, then contact me at the number I've already given you. Is that all very clear?"

"I got it."

"You get me the man and the woman, and you'll get the money you've asked for. After that, I don't want to ever see or hear from you again."

He took the envelope. "Figure you want to know. Taps are off the Marsh woman's phone."

Anita pursed her lips. "Doesn't matter," she decided. "She doesn't interest me any longer."

"Her old man got real talky when I went in his place and asked about those statues. Sounded like he'd like to get his hands on them."

"Yes, I'm sure he would. I assume he told you nothing particularly helpful."

"Said something about how he'd heard maybe one was in Greece. Athens. But said it was just a rumor, and there were others."

"Athens. Well, that was yesterday."

"Tried getting information out of me, acting like he was just shooting the breeze, but he was digging."

"I'm no longer concerned with that. Get me Malachi Sullivan. You can leave the way you came in."

She figured he didn't have a brain, Jasper decided as he walked out. Figured he didn't have the smarts to find out what was what.

He'd find this Sullivan guy, all right, and the woman. But he'd be fucked if he'd turn them over for a lousy hundred grand. If they were the connection to those statues, they'd tell him about it. And when he had the Fates, Anita Gaye would pay, and pay deeply.

Then maybe he'd do her just the way he figured she'd done that asshole Dubrowsky. Right before he hopped a plane to Rio.

ANITA STAYED AT her desk, going through messages. To entertain herself she tore those pertaining to the police into small pieces. Investigations of homicides and burglaries weren't her job, after all.

She intended to contact the insurance agent very shortly. She expected them to deliver a check for her claim promptly. If they needed to be reminded that she could easily take her hefty annual premiums elsewhere, she would be happy to do so.

The doorbell rang twice. She cursed her miserably inefficient and grossly overpaid staff before remembering she'd dismissed them for the remainder of the day.

Sighing over the annoyance of having to do everything herself, she went to the door. She wasn't pleased to see the two detectives standing on her stoop, but after weighing the pros and cons of ignoring them, she opened the door.

"Detectives, you just caught me."

Lew Gilbert nodded. "Ms. Gaye. May we come in?"

"This really isn't a good time. I've just returned from an overseas trip. I'm very tired."

"But you're on your way out? You said we just caught you."

"Just caught me before I lay down," she said sweetly.

"We'll make it quick, then."

"Very well." She stepped back to let them in. "I didn't realize you were working with . . . I'm sorry, I've forgotten your name."

"Detective Robbins."

"Of course. I didn't realize you were working with Detective Robbins on the burglary, Detective Gilbert."

"Sometimes cases overlap."

"I imagine. Of course, I'm delighted to have two of New York's finest looking into my problem. Please sit down. I'm afraid I sent the servants off, as I wanted the house to myself. But I'm sure I could manage coffee if you'd like."

"Thanks just the same." Lew sat down, started the rhythm. "You said you'd just gotten back from a trip? Something you planned before the break-in."

"Something that came up unexpectedly."

"Overseas?"

"Yes." She crossed her legs smoothly. "Athens."

"Must be something. All those old temples. What's that drink? Ouzo. Had some once at a wedding. Some kick."

"So I'm told. I'm afraid this trip was business, and I didn't have time for temples and ouzo."

"Tough on you, having to take off like that right after the burglary," Bob put in. "You usually do the business travel?"

"Depending." She didn't care for his tone. Not one bit. When this was over, she was going to have a few choice words on the subject with his superiors. "Excuse me, but if we could get to the point?"

"We've been trying to contact you. It hampers the investigation when the victim's incommunicado."

"As I said, it was necessary and unexpected. In any

case, I gave Detective Gilbert all the information I had. I assumed you and the insurance company would handle the rest of it."

"You filed your claim."

"I left the paperwork with my assistant before I left. She assured me it was messengered to my agent. Do you have any leads on my property, or on who broke into my building?"

"The investigation's ongoing. Ms. Gaye, do you know anything about the Three Fates?"

For a moment all she could do was stare. "Of course. They're a legend in my line of work and my field of interest. Why?"

"A tip that maybe that's what the thieves were after. But you didn't list any silver statue or statues on your claim form."

"A tip? From whom?"

"Anonymous, but we intend to follow up any and all leads in this case. I didn't see anything that matches the description of any of these statues on your inventory list."

"You wouldn't, as I don't have one. If I did, Detective, you can be sure I would have had it locked in a vault. The Fates are extremely valuable. Unfortunately, one was certainly lost with its owner on the *Lusitania*. As for the other two . . . No one can substantiate their existence."

"So you don't have one of these statues?"

The anger, the insult of being questioned edged into her voice. "I believe I've already answered that question. If I did own one of the Fates, you can be sure I'd announce it loud and clear. The publicity would be very beneficial to Morningside."

"Well, anonymous tips usually turn out to be dead ends." Lew took the apologetic route. "Just as well. Something like that wouldn't go through the usual channels and fences. Since you weren't available, we got photographs and descriptions of the stolen property from the insurance company. We've been checking all those usual avenues. Jack Burdett's cooperated regarding the security.

But I'm going to be honest, Ms. Gaye, we're coming up empty so far."

"It's very upsetting. I'm trying to be grateful we were fully insured. Though, of course, I hope to have the property restored. But it's very upsetting to know that Morningside was vulnerable. You'll have to excuse me." She got to her feet. "I'm really very tired."

"We'll keep you updated." Bob rose. "Oh, on the other matter? That homicide in the warehouse you used to own."

Not just a few choice words, Anita decided. She would see to it this man was fired. "Really, Detective, I think we've established I know nothing about it."

"Just wanted you to know that we've ID'd a suspect. A man the victim was purported to be working with most recently." Pulled a photo out of his inside pocket. "You recognize this man?"

Anita stared at the photograph of Jasper and wasn't sure if she wanted to laugh or scream. "No, I don't."

"Didn't think you would, but we've got to follow up the angles. Thanks for your time, Ms. Gaye."

As they walked back to their car, the cops exchanged one brief look. "She's dirty," Lew said.

"Oh yeah. Up to her swanlike neck."

The minute the car pulled away from the curb, Cleo pulled out her phone. "She's primed," she said. "Make the call." Then she tucked the phone away and turned to Gideon in the driver's seat. "Let's just hang a few minutes. I bet we'll be able to hear her scream all the way out here."

"We could do that." He passed her back the oversweet soft drink she'd brought for them to share during the stakeout. "And after, I think we could take a little detour to Tia's. No one's there at the moment."

"Oh." Cleo tucked her tongue in her cheek. "What did you have in mind?"

"Tearing your clothes off, tossing you down on the first handy flat surface and having at you."

"Sounds good to me."

Inside the house, Anita stormed up the stairs. She should have killed Jasper. Killed him when she'd had the chance, then hired fresh muscle, one with a brain, to track down Malachi. Now she would have to find a way to do it anyway, and before the police found him.

It had to have been Malachi who'd called the cops about the Fates. Who else could it be? But why? Had he been the one who tried to break into Morningside?

She balled her hands into fists as she paced her bedroom. How could some tour captain circumvent that layer of security? He could have hired someone, she supposed. But the man wasn't rolling in money.

It had to go back to him, all of it. And oh, *oh,* would she make him suffer for it.

She snatched up the phone on the first ring and snarled into the receiver. "What?"

"Rough day, darling?"

She bit back the curses on her tongue and all but cooed. "Well, well. Malachi. Isn't this a surprise."

"The first of many. How did you find Athens?"

"I turned left at Italy."

"Good one. I don't recall you being quick with a joke, but it's nice to see you've your good humor in place. You'll need it. Guess what I'm looking at? Lovely silver ladies. A little birdie told me you were working very hard to find them. Looks as if I beat you to it."

"You want to deal, we'll deal. Where are you? I'd prefer discussing this face-to-face."

"I'll just bet you would. We'll deal, Anita, indeed we will. I'll be in touch with you about the when and where, but I want to give you time to recover from the shock."

"You don't shock me."

"Why don't you go see how your own little silver lady fared while you were turning left at Italy? And stick around the house, won't you? I'll ring you back in thirty minutes. You should be conscious again by then."

When the phone clicked in her ear, she slammed the receiver down. He wasn't going to shake her. So, he had two to her one, but that was all right. All he'd done was save her the trouble of getting them through customs and smuggling them back to New York herself.

She glanced toward the closet and, unable to resist, walked over and inside. Her fingers trembled with fury as she opened the panel, opened the safe.

Cleo was right. At that distance and that angle, they could just hear the scream.

# Twenty-nine

Now that she was naked, facedown on the floor and trying to get her breath back, Cleo figured letting Gideon have at her had been worth the rug burn. In spades.

And since she'd had at him right back, she didn't think she'd hear any complaints from him either.

They had, she thought, a really fine rhythm going between them. The kind she could dance to endlessly.

"Doing okay there?" he asked her.

"I think some of my brains might have leaked out my ears, but I've got more. How about you?"

"Well, I can't see yet, but I'm hopeful the blindness is temporary. Still, ending up blind and brain-damaged doesn't seem like such a high price to pay."

"You sure are a cutie, Slick."

"At such a time, a man prefers being called a tiger or some other sort of wild beast rather than a cutie."

"Okay. You're a regular mastodon."

"That'll have to do. We should get up, put ourselves back together."

"Yeah. We should."

And they lay as they were, a tangled and sweaty heap with clothes scattered around them.

"I heard, through the grapevine, that you're thinking of opening a club or a school or some such."

She managed to move one shoulder in what passed for a shrug. "I'm thinking about it."

"So, you're not set on going back to dancing, spinning around on Broadway and that sort of thing."

"I never did a hell of a lot of spinning on Broadway anyway."

"I think you're a wonderful dancer."

"I'm not bad." She turned her head, rested her cheek on the rug. "But you've got to know when to move on or you end up a blown-out gypsy being bounced from audition to audition."

"So, you're more in mind to stay put."

"You could say."

He trailed his finger up her spine, down again. She had such a lovely, long back. "You know, they have clubs and dance schools in Ireland."

"No kidding? And here I thought all they had were shamrocks and little green fairies."

"You forgot the beer."

She ran her tongue around her teeth. "Could use one right now."

"I'll get us both one, when I can feel my legs again. Cobh's not so big and crowded as New York . . ." Thank the lord. "But it's a good-sized village, and we get lots of tourists. It's not such a ways from Cork City, if there's a need for the urban sort of crowds and traffic. We're very big on dancing in Ireland, whether it's the doing it or the learning it. You know, a dancer's a kind of artist, and we hold our artists as national treasures."

"Is that so?" She could feel her heart begin to thud, but stayed very still. "Maybe I should check it out."

"I think you should." His hand began to rub light, lazy circles on her butt. "So, do you want to get married?"

She closed her eyes a moment, let the honey of it— warm and sweet—slide through her. Then she turned her head, looked him in the eye. "Sure."

Their grins spread, and, laughing, they reached for each other just as the front door opened.

"Oh, Mother of God! My eyes." Malachi slammed his shut, covered Tia's with his hand. "Is it so hard to find the bed in this place?"

"We were in a hurry." Gideon grabbed for jeans and had them nearly to his knees before he realized they were Cleo's. "Just hold on."

Cackling with laughter now, Cleo tossed Gideon his pants, then snagged his shirt for herself. "It's okay. We're getting married."

"Married?" Tia shoved Malachi's hand aside and, caught up in the thrill, rushed over to hug Cleo. "This is wonderful. It's just wonderful. Oh, oh, you can have a double wedding! You and Gideon and Rebecca and Jack. A double wedding. Wouldn't that be fabulous?"

"It's a thought." Cleo peeked around Tia at Malachi, who was staring hard at the ceiling. "Aren't you going to congratulate me, welcome me to the bosom of the Sullivans and all that jazz?"

"This isn't the time to mention bosoms. Put some clothes on. I can't come over there when you're naked."

"I'm only mostly naked." With Gideon's shirt skimming her thighs, Cleo got up, walked to him. "Is this cool with you? Mister Head of the Family?"

He looked down and, relieved the shirt was buttoned, took her face in his hands, kissed both her cheeks. "I couldn't have chosen better for him myself. Now I'm begging you, put some pants on."

"Thanks, and I will. I really need to talk to Tia a minute."

"We've got a lot to tell you about Anita, and what's about to happen."

"Just five minutes," she whispered. "Please. Take Slick up on the roof for a smoke, a man-to-man or something."

"Five minutes," he agreed. "It's all in the timing now." He signaled his brother. "Up on the roof."

"I need my shirt."

"Well, you're not having the one she's wearing and sending me into another heart attack. Your jacket's good enough."

Obliging, Gideon pulled his jacket over his bare chest. "I haven't kissed her yet." So he did, warmly enough to have Malachi looking at the ceiling again. "I'll be back."

"I'm counting on it." When the door shut behind them, Cleo sighed. "Wow, who'd've thought?" She walked back to Tia, dropped down on the floor. "Have a seat."

Curious, Tia sat on the rug facing her. "Is anything wrong?"

"No. Definitely not. Don't cry, okay, because I'll get all choked up. I just want to say . . . Okay, I'm going to get choked up anyway. So . . ." She took a deep, cleansing breath. "I've been thinking about stuff. Takes some longer than you to get down there. You're the brainy one."

"No, I'm not."

"Sure you are. Tia, you're like, deep."

"I am?"

"You get stuff. You see the connections and the layers and, hell, all that neat shit. That's part of what I was thinking about. If it wasn't for the Fates, you and me, we wouldn't be sitting here on the floor together right now. We didn't exactly circle the same wheel. Anyway, I think about what happened to Mikey, and that's hard. Part of me feels lousy because I'm so fucking happy. I know that's stupid," she said even before Tia could speak. "I'm working on it. Anyway, it's like the things I've heard you say. Threads, and what is it, lots?"

"The apportioning of lots. Lachesis."

"Yeah, that one was mine. I never figured this would be my lot, you know? Having a friend like you, having somebody like Gideon love me. And the rest of them. Like a family. I never figured that kind of thing was in the cards for me. I'm not going to screw it up."

"Of course you're not."

"I've screwed up plenty before. I guess I could figure I was meant to. It's weird thinking that I swiped a pair of Levi's when I was sixteen, or tanked a history test so I could get here, mostly naked on your living room rug, sniveling because there's this great man up on the roof who loves me."

She shoved her hair behind her shoulders, swallowed back the tears. "I guess I'd better get my pants on before Malachi comes back in and goes ballistic."

She reached for her jeans, stopped. "There is one more thing. I was wondering if you'd stand up for me. Like the maid-of-honor deal when we get married."

"Oh, Cleo." Tia threw her arms around her, hugged tight. And blubbered. "I'd love to. I'm so happy. I'm so happy for you."

"Jeez." Sniffling, Cleo hugged back. "I feel like such a girl."


AT PRECISELY SEVEN-thirty, Anita walked into Jean Georges. Though she had dressed with meticulous care, and in Valentino, she didn't bother with the ploy of keeping her date waiting.

She turned toward the bar, noted that Jasper was in place. And enjoyed the idea of this being Malachi Sullivan's last meal.

The bastard thought he had her by the throat, ordering her to meet him in this upscale and very public restaurant so that he could lay out the terms of the deal. She'd play him through to coffee and dessert, then he was going to find out who held the cards.

She was greeted by name and shown to the window table where Malachi was already waiting. He was wise, she noted, to sit with his back to the wall. Not that it would help him.

He got to his feet, took her hand and brought it to within an inch of his lips. "Anita. You look very well . . . for a hissing viper."

"And you clean up decently for a second-rate tour guide with delusions of grandeur."

"Well, now that the pleasantries are over." He took his seat, gestured so that the waiter poured the champagne waiting on ice. "It seems appropriate that we have this meeting in pleasant surroundings. No need for business dealings to be uncomfortable, after all."

"You didn't bring your little tart."

He sampled the wine, approved it. "Which little tart would that be?"

"Cleo Toliver. I'm surprised at you. I credited you with more taste than that. She's nothing but a professional slut."

"Don't be jealous, darling. In the slut department, she can't hold a candle to you."

The waiter cleared his throat and continued to pretend he'd been born deaf. "Would you care to hear about this evening's specials?"

"Absolutely." Malachi leaned back. He listened and, before the waiter could slip away to give them time to consider, ordered grandly for both of them.

"You take a great deal for granted," Anita said coldly, when they were alone again.

"True enough."

"You broke into my house."

"Someone broke into your house?" He feigned surprise. "Well then, call the garda. I should say, police. And what, I wonder, would you tell them was taken?"

While she steamed, he reached down and lifted an attaché case. "I thought you might like to see all the pretty silver ladies in a row." He handed her a large color printout of a digital photo his sister had taken only hours before. "Beautiful, aren't they?"

Rage wanted to choke her. Greed trembled straight down to her fingertips. "What do you want?"

"Oh, a great many things. A long, healthy life; a fine, faithful dog. And an embarrassing amount of money. But we don't want to discuss that on an empty stomach. I've individual photos, as well, for you to study. I want you to rest assured you'll get what you pay for."

She studied each photo, and at every new angle she increased the pain level she'd make him suffer before she killed him. She laid the photographs in her lap when their appetizers were served. "How did you get into my house? Into my personal safe?"

"You're giving a lot of credit to a—what was it?— second-rate tour guide. And I must take exception to that estimation, Anita, as you've yet to take a Sullivan tour. We're quite justifiably proud of our little family business."

Anita speared a sautéed mushroom. "Maybe I should have gone after your mother."

Though his blood ran cold, Malachi kept his calm. "She'd fry you up for breakfast, and serve the leftovers to the neighbor's cat. But let's not get personal. You were asking me a question. You want to know how it happened I recovered what it was you stole from me."

"I don't believe you called the police either."

"I made it easy for you, no mistake there. Foolish of me, believing you to be a reputable businesswoman and handing the Fate over to you for, yes, testing and appraisal, it was. Lessons learned." He sampled a bite of crab meat. "You judged that one correctly. How could I go to the authorities accusing the respected owner of the renowned Morningside Antiquities of stealing from a client? And stealing what, by all accounts, was at the bottom of the Atlantic?

"And now," he said, while the waiter moved in silently to top off their wineglasses, "it seems you're in a similar fix. Tough to make a public complaint about losing what should never have been in your possession in the first place."

"You couldn't have gotten in, not to Morningside or my house, without help."

"Puzzle that one out," he said, "and you'll know I'm not without friends. By the way, Cleo sends her regards. Her very low regards. Just think, if you'd paid her price, made a legitimate deal at that point, our positions might be reversed now."

He leaned closer, and all his fake humor was gone. "The man you had killed, Michael Hicks was his name, and his friends called him Mikey. She grieves for him. You're fortunate, Anita, that I can convince her to deal with you now."

Anita nudged her appetizer aside, picked up her wine. "My employee, former employee, was under instructions to extract information. He got carried away. It's hard to get competent help in some areas."

"And did you get carried away when you put the bullets into your former employee?"

"No." She watched him over the sparkling edge of the crystal flute. "I pulled the trigger with a steady, easy hand. You'd be wise to remember that, and to understand how I deal with people who disappoint me."

She picked up the attaché case, slid the photos in as the waiter returned with the salad course. "May I keep this?"

"Of course. I'll tell you what I understand. You don't consider two lives too high a price to pay for what you want. I'm sure you won't find the price I ask out of your reach either."

"And that would be?"

"Ten million, cash."

Anita gave a sour laugh, even as her pulse jumped. So little, she thought. The man was a complete fool. At auction she could command double that. More, considerably more, with the right publicity.

"Do you actually think I'm going to pay you ten million dollars?"

"I do, yes. Three for each lady and one for good measure. So you see the price Cleo asked for Lachesis before you had her friend beaten to death was a rare bargain that won't come 'round again. Oh, and here's the topper." Malachi broke apart a roll. "He knew, Mikey did, where the Fate was being kept and had the means to get it. What does that say to you, Anita?"

She laid a hand on her purse, imagined pulling out the pistol she'd put inside it—just in case—and emptying it into Malachi Sullivan's smug face.

"It says to me that Mr. Dubrowsky deserved what he got. I'll be handling my own negotiations from now on."

"Then I should tell you straight off, our asking price isn't negotiable, so let's not spoil this lovely meal with wrangling. We considered asking for a great deal more, letting you counter and doing the back-and-forth business. But really, we've come too far for such petty behavior, haven't we? You want them, I have them. That's the price."

He bit into the roll he'd buttered. "You'll parlay them for a tidy profit, reap considerable glory on Morningside and yourself. Everyone wins."

"Even if I agreed to the price, that much in cash—"

"Cash is the currency. Or I should say electronic cash. Simpler all around, very little paperwork to contend with. I'll give you two days to make the arrangements."

"Two days? That's—"

"Time enough for a canny woman like you. Thursday, eleven o'clock. You transfer the funds to the account I'll give you at that time. Once it's done, I give you Clotho, Lachesis and Atropos."

"And I'm supposed to trust you to hold up your end. Really, Malachi."

He pursed his lips. "That's a problem, isn't it? Still, I'm trusting you to make the arrangements and not have a couple of rottweilers standing by to tear out my throat and take the prize from my cold, dead hand. That's why we'll make the exchange in a public and civilized arena. The New York Public Library. I'm sure you've heard of it? The one on Fifth Avenue at Fortieth Street. Grand marble lions out front. They have an extensive section on mythology. It seems quite apt to me."

"I need time to think about it. A way to contact you."

"You have till eleven on Thursday to think about it. As for contacting me, well, there's no need. Those are the terms. If they don't suit you, they're sure to suit someone else. Say, Wyley's. The library, the main reading room on the third floor. Excuse me a minute, won't you, darling? I'm just going to make use of the facilities."

He strolled out through the doors that led to the rest rooms and the bar. And kept right on walking, leaving Anita stuck with the check.

"That went well," he said into the mike fixed to the underside of his lapel.

"Well enough," his sister agreed. "We're circling back around. We'll pick you up on the east corner. Cleo wants you to know she's very disappointed you didn't hang through it and bring back a doggie bag."

He chuckled, headed toward the corner. Then felt the honed point of a knife jab at his side, just along his kidney.

"Just keep walking, pal." Jasper's voice was low and even as he gripped Malachi's arm in his free hand. "And keep in mind, I can jam this into you, slice out a good chunk, and nobody but me's going to know the difference."

"If you're after what's in my wallet, you're going to be very disappointed."

"We're going to get in a car half a block up and go to a nice, quiet place I've got all ready for you. Have a nice, quiet talk."

"Talking works for me. Why don't we find a bar and do it over a friendly drink?"

"I said keep walking."

Malachi bit back a hiss as the knife slid through jacket and shirt and into flesh. "That's going to be hard to do if you keep jabbing at me with that pig-sticker."

"Well now," Gideon said pleasantly as he came up behind them. "This is a dilemma. You push that knife into my brother, and I shoot you dead. Hardly anyone's going to be happy with that eventuality."

"Shoot him anyway. He's fucked up my best suit."

"That doesn't seem quite fair. What do you think, Jack?"

"Spill the guy's guts out over the sidewalk, city employees have to clean it up. That means higher taxes for me." He held out a hand. "But if you don't take that knife out of my friend there and give it to me, hilt first, I'm willing to pay."

This time, when the tip of the steel slid out of his side, Malachi couldn't hold back the hiss. "Fuck me, did you have to take so bloody long?"

"Let's have the hardware, too." Jack moved in, smiling cheerfully and, in a move that looked like a friendly embrace, slid the gun from beneath Jasper's jacket and under his own.

"Are you all right, Mal?"

"Oh, I'm fucking dandy." He pressed a hand to his bleeding side. "What the hell were you going to shoot him dead with?"

Gideon held up Tia's inhaler behind Jasper's back.

"Oh perfect. I owe my flaming life to hypochondria." He spotted the van, turned to Jasper and showed his teeth in a sneering smile. "We'll have that nice, quiet talk now." He wrenched open the cargo doors, hauled himself in.

Tia leaped toward him, sobbing his name, but he held up

a hand. "One minute. First things first." As soon as they'd shoved Jasper in behind him, Malachi plowed a fist into his face.

"Oh that's fine, that's good." Wincing, Malachi flexed his fingers. "A broken hand'll take my mind off the fact that I'm bleeding to death."

Shocked steady, Tia eased him into a chair. "Cleo, drive to Jack's. You keep that horrible man down that end," she ordered Gideon. "Jack, do you have a first-aid kit in here?"

"Glove box."

"Rebecca?"

"I'm getting it."

Despite the pain, and the extra jolt of it when she tugged his jacket off, Malachi grinned up at her. "You're a wonder, you are. Give us a kiss."

"Be quiet. Be still." Though her head spun sickly as she saw the blood spreading low on his shirt, she tore it open. She shot one fulminating look toward Jasper, now cuffed and gagged in the rear corner of the van. "You should be ashamed of yourself."


"HE SHOULD GO to the hospital. He should really go see a doctor, don't you think?" Pacing Jack's living room, Tia wrung her hands. "The cut was awfully deep. If Jack and Gideon hadn't gotten there in time . . . If that man had gotten Malachi into the car . . ."

"If a pig had two heads, he'd have two brains. Here now." Eileen held out a tumbler with three generous fingers of Paddy's. "Drink this."

"Oh. Well. I don't really drink. And whiskey . . . well, I used to—sometimes—take just a little sip of some before one of my lectures. But it's not—"

"Tia. Chill."

At Cleo's order, Tia shuddered, nodded, then took the glass and downed every drop.

"That's a girl," Eileen approved. "Now you sit down."

"I'm too frazzled to sit. Mrs. Sullivan . . . Eileen, don't you think he needs to be seen by a doctor?"

"You patched him up just fine. The boy's had worse

wrestling with his brother. Here now, Rebecca's brought you a nice clean blouse."

"Clean . . ." Baffled, Tia glanced down, saw the blood smeared over her shirt. "Uh-oh," she managed as her eyes started to roll back.

"No, you don't. None of that now." Eileen spoke briskly and pushed her into a chair. "No woman who can mop a man up in a moving van is going to faint away at the sight of a bit of secondhand blood. You're not so silly."

Tia blinked to clear her vision. "Really?"

"You did great," Cleo told her. "I mean, you kicked serious ass."

"She was brilliant," Rebecca agreed. "Here, change your shirt now, Tia darling, and we'll soak your nice blouse and see if we can get the blood out of it."

"Do you think they're going to beat him up?" Tia wondered.

"Ugly Mean Guy?" Cleo passed the stained blouse to Rebecca. "Sure hope so."

IT WAS BEING debated downstairs, with some heat, with Jasper in the unfortunate position of being tied to a chair and listening to the arguments pro and con.

"I say we kick his ass, break a few important bones, then talk to him."

Jack shook his head, took the hammer Malachi was thumping rhythmically on the counter, set it aside. "Three to one. Doesn't seem quite fair."

"Oh, we want fair, do we?" Enjoying himself, Malachi stormed over and kicked Jasper's chair. "And was he being fair, I'd like to know, when he fucking stabbed me, right out on the street?"

"Mal's got a point, Jack." Gideon popped cashews out of a bowl and into his mouth. "Bastard stuck a knife in my brother, who was unarmed at the time. That's just not right. Maybe we should let Mal stab him. Not fatally or anything such as that. Just one good jab, to even the score, so to speak."

"Yeah, look at this." Mal lifted an arm, showing off the

bandage riding just above his waistband. "And what about my suit? That's another factor. The shirt, too. Big gaping holes in both, as well as in my person."

"I know you're upset. Can't blame you. But the guy was just doing his job. Isn't that right?" Jack flipped open the wallet they'd taken off him, as if to check the name again. "Marvin."

Marvin let out a choked sound around his gag.

"Well, his flaming job stinks," Malachi ranted. "And I'd think a good thrashing was just one of the employment risks in the field."

"Let's try this. Let's talk to the poor bastard first. See if he cooperates. If you're not satisfied"—Jack gave Malachi a friendly pat on the back—"we'll beat the shit out of him."

"I get first shot. I want to break the fingers on the hand he used to stab me. One knuckle at a time."

The men looked at each other, back at Jasper, whose eyes were bulging, and were satisfied they'd played their parts well.

Jack walked over, tugged down the gag. "Okay, you got the picture. My associates here want to take some pieces out of you. Me, I'm a fan of democracy, and majority rules. You want to avoid that vote, you'll cooperate. Otherwise, I turn them loose, and when we're done, we dump you on Anita's doorstep. She'll finish you off. Gid? Play back that one part of the tape, you know, where she's telling Mal how she deals with unsatisfactory employees."

Gideon walked over to the recorder, turned on the tape he'd already cued up. Anita's voice, cold as death, filled the room as she spoke about steadily, easily putting bullets into a man.

"We'll make sure she gets the opportunity with you," Jack told him. "The three of us, we might cause you some pain, but we're not cold-blooded killers. We'll leave that part to the expert."

"What the hell do you want?"

"You tell us everything you know. Don't spare the details. And when the time comes, you're going to tell the whole thing to a friend of mine who happens to be a cop."

"You think I'm going to talk to the cops?"

"I've seen your sheet, Marvin. It won't be the first time. Nobody's got you on murder yet. You want to give her the chance to twist it around so you take the fall for Dubrowsky, for Michael Hicks?" Jack waited a beat. "That's what she'll do if you don't get there first and have us backing you up. Or we just step back and let her do to you what she did to Dubrowsky."

"Better prison than the morgue," Malachi put in. "You should know we've got our little dance on the sidewalk on tape as well. So we can turn it and you over to the police now and be done with it, and you don't have the edge of going in with—what is it, Jack?"

"Remorse. Remorse and cooperation."

"You won't have that opening with the police. With Anita still free and with money at her fingertips, how long do you think it would take her to hire someone to terminate your employment, on a permanent basis, when you're behind bars?"

"I want a deal." Jasper licked his lips. "I want immunity."

"You'll have to take that up with my friend with the badge," Jack told him. "I'm sure he'll be happy to take your wants and needs into consideration. Now." Jack signaled Gideon to turn on the video recorder. "Let's talk about what it's like to work for Anita Gaye."


ANITA SOAKED IN the tub, bubbles up to her chin. She imagined, even now, Malachi was being softened up. In the morning, when he'd had plenty of time to think, and to suffer, she'd stop by and see him. He'd tell her exactly where he was keeping the Fates, exactly where to find Cleo Toliver, and he'd confirm if her conclusions were correct and it had been Jack or someone working at Burdett who'd helped him get through her security.

Then she'd deal with all of them. Personally.

The candlelight glowed soothingly over her closed lids and she picked up the phone she'd set on the ledge of the tub and answered her private line.

"Yes?"

"I felt I should apologize for leaving so abruptly."

The sound of Malachi's voice had her sitting straight up in the tub. Water and bubbles gushed over the rim and ran a river over the tiles.

"It was very rude of me," he went on. "But I had what you might call a pressing engagement. In any case, I'm looking forward to seeing you Thursday. Eleven o'clock, remember. Oh, and one other thing. Mr. Jasper asked me to tell you, he quits."

When the click sounded in her ear, Anita let out a roar of frustration. She heaved the phone across the room, where it smashed into the mirror.

In the morning when the maid came in to tidy up, she would cluck her tongue and think of seven years' bad luck.

# Thirty

I T would be, at its core, like any sort of play, largely dependent on staging, costumes, props and the actors' zest for their roles. Since Cleo was the team expert on stage work, she took over as director.

With Eileen standing in for Anita, Cleo rehearsed her cast mercilessly.

"Timing, people. It's all about the timing. Jack, cue."

He mimed making the phone call that would set the ball rolling, then walked with Gideon to the elevator.

"I don't see why we have to go down again. We could just pretend to go down."

"Look, Slick, I'm directing this show. Get moving."

He stepped into the elevator with Jack.

"Good luck," Tia called out and shrugged. "Well, that's what I'd say to them if this was real."

"See." Cleo folded her arms. "Tia knows how to rehearse. Okay," Cleo began. "We figure it's eight-fifteen, and time passes. Two of the three prongs are being set. The rest of us wait here, enjoying a nutritious breakfast, until Gideon gets back. Clock's ticking, clock's ticking, and where the hell is he?"

"We'd all be pacing around like cats in a cage and drinking too much coffee," Rebecca put in as she flipped a page in one of her bridal magazines. "Oh, Ma, look at this dress. This may be the one."

"She's not your mother. She's the dreaded and dastardly Anita Gaye. Stay in character," Cleo insisted, then turned as Gideon opened the elevator doors again. "You're late, we were worried, blah blah. And you tell us everything's aces."

"I would, if you'd give me the chance."

"Actors are such children." She grabbed his shirt, jerked him forward for a kiss. "Scene change," she announced. "Library. Interior. Time: ten-thirty. Places, people."

IT WAS RAINING hard when Malachi stepped out of the cab in front of the New York Public Library. The sheets of wet and the traffic it snarled had put them slightly behind schedule.

The weather gave him a little pang of homesickness. It was nearly over now, he thought as he climbed up the stairs between the lions known as Patience and Fortitude. Nearly time to go home again and pick up the threads of his life. The old and the new. He wondered what pattern they would make together.

He stepped inside, into the cathedral-like grandeur and quiet. It was his second visit, as a dress rehearsal sort of business had been demanded of him. He still wondered at the fact that such a huge and stately library should have no books in its entranceway.

He scooped a hand through his hair, scattering wet, then, as planned, took the stairs instead of the elevator to the third floor.

No one seemed to take any particular notice of him. There were those who sat at tables studying or simply browsing through books. Some tapped away at laptops, others scrawled notes on pads, still others roamed the stacks.

As planned, he filled out a call sheet for the book Tia had deemed most appropriate and took it to the proper reference desk.

He liked the smell of the place, of books and wood and

people come in out of the rain. Another time he'd have enjoyed just the being there. And though Gideon was the keenest reader in the family, Malachi would have found pleasure in simply choosing a book and settling down with it in this palace of literature.

He walked by where Gideon was, even now, sitting with his nose in a copy of *To Kill a Mockingbird.* Gideon turned a page in Scout's lyrical narrative, signaling the go-ahead.

They'd considered the fact that Anita would have had enough time to hire a replacement for Jasper. And that her temper might have pushed her to find someone willing to kill an unarmed man in a library.

The odds were small enough, as she'd lose her best chance for the Fates. And though it was a risk Malachi was willing to take, the back of his neck prickled as he walked through the stacks.

He found a quiet table, glanced idly around the area, his gaze passing over Rebecca's head as she bent over her laptop nearby.

Within twenty minutes, a pretty young page delivered his requested book. Then, Malachi settled down to wait.

AT MORNINGSIDE, HAVING spent an hour reviewing security tapes provided by Burdett, Detective Lew Gilbert was already interviewing clerks regarding three particular items of inventory that had gone missing.

Downtown, Jasper was angling for a deal with the DA.

At the wheel of a van chugging through the rain and pissy traffic on Fifth, Cleo tapped her fingers to the Barenaked Ladies and waited to give Tia her cue.

Malachi heard the click of heels, caught the whiff of expensive scent and looked up from his book. "Hello, Anita. I've just been reading about my ladies. Fascinating females. Did you know they sing their prophesies? A kind of mythological girl group."

"Where are they?"

"Oh, safe and sound. I beg your pardon, where are my manners?" He rose, pulled out a chair. "Sit down, won't you? Such a wet day out, it makes a grand place like this almost cozy."

"I want to see them." But she sat, crossed her legs, folded her hands. It would be business, she reminded herself. For now. "You can hardly think I'd pay your exorbitant fee without first examining the merchandise."

"You examined one of them before, and look where that got us. Right? You sent some very impolite men after my brother. I'm very fond of my brother."

"I only regret I didn't send them after you, with less restrained orders."

"Well, live and learn. There was no need to have that friend of Cleo's killed. He wasn't involved."

"She involved him. It was business, Malachi. Just business."

"This isn't *The Godfather*. Business, Anita, would have been meeting Cleo's price for her Fate. If you had dealt squarely, you'd have it in hand right now. And perhaps even the third one. As it is, you've blood on your hands."

"Spare me the lecture."

"If you'd dealt squarely with me," he continued, "instead of letting greed get in the way of good judgment, you'd have all three, for a fraction of what you'll pay now. You started this thread, Anita, when you stole from me and my family."

"You wanted to get laid. I let you fuck me, then I fucked you over. No point in whining about it."

"Right you are. I'm just explaining to you why we're sitting here as we are. Ten million. Have you made the arrangements?"

"You'll get the money, but not until I've seen the Fates. The transfer's ready to go. Once I verify you have what you claim to have, I'll call and put it through to your account."

"One more item of business before we start. Should you, after we complete the transaction, feel compelled to get some of your own back by bringing harm to any member of my family, to Cleo, to me, for that matter, take into consideration that I've documented everything. Everything, Anita, and have that documentation in a safe place."

"In the event of my untimely death?" She gave a short laugh. "How trite."

"Trite but true. You'll get what you've earned for the money. And that will be that. Agreed?"

A woman who had spent a dozen years married to a man who'd revolted her in bed and bored her out of it knew how to be patient. Patient enough, she thought, to wait years, if need be, to implement just the right sort of tragic accident.

"I'm here, aren't I? Let me see them."

He sat back and, keeping his eyes on hers, lifted a hand. Gideon walked over to the table, set a black briefcase between them.

"I don't believe you've actually met my brother. Gideon, Anita Gaye."

Anita laid a hand on the case, looked up. "So you get to be gofer," she said in a silky tone. "Tell me, don't you mind sharing your whore with your brother?"

"We're very big on sharing in my family. Just as well Mal didn't get around to sharing you with me. You're a bit old for my taste."

"Now, now, let's mind our manners." Malachi gestured at the case.

"This is too public for an examination."

"Here, or not at all."

In a bad-tempered move, Anita tried to open the case. "It's locked."

"So it is." Gideon's tone was cheerful. "Combination is seven, five, fifteen." The date the *Lusitania* sank.

Anita set the combination, clicked the lock, opened the lid. Nestled in foam padding, the Fates looked up, placidly.

Lifting the first, Anita examined it. She remembered well the feel, the weight, the shape of Clotho. The satin texture of her silver skirt, the complicated coil of her hair over her shoulder, the delicacy of the spindle in her hand.

She replaced it and lifted Lachesis. There were subtle differences. This dress had a different drape, leaving the curve of one shoulder bare. The gleaming hair was done up in a kind of crown. Her right hand held the end of a tape pulled out of the measuring rule she held in her left. There were notches and Greek numerals etched on the tape.

Anita's heart began to thud as she set the second Fate back in its bed and took out the third.

Atropus was slightly, very slightly shorter than her sisters. And so agreed the legend. Her face was softer, somehow kinder. She held her tiny scissors in clasped hands between her breasts. She wore sandals, the strap of the left crisscrossing twice before disappearing under the flow of her skirts.

Every detail agreed with documented descriptions. The workmanship was magnificent. And more, much more, there was a sense of power that pulsed from them. A kind of quiet underbeat that seemed to echo in Anita's head.

She would, at that moment, have paid anything, done anything, to have them.

"Satisfied?" Malachi asked her.

"A visual exam is hardly satisfactory." She continued to hold Atropus. "Certain tests need to be—"

Malachi plucked the Fate from her fingers, set it inside the case with the sisters. "We've gone that route once. Take it or leave it, here and now."

He closed the case even as she tried to reach out and stop him. And locked it. "You can hardly expect me to pay you ten million after a two-minute look."

He kept his voice hushed, as hers was. Reasonable, as hers was. "It's all you had when first I showed you Clotho. And you knew, just as you know now. Transfer the money and you can walk out with them." He took the case off the table as he spoke, put it on the floor at his feet. "Or don't, and I walk out with them and sell them elsewhere. I've a suspicion Wyley's would pay the price, and happily."

She opened her purse. Malachi closed a hand over her wrist as she reached inside. "Slowly, darling," and his hand stayed on her wrist until she'd pulled out her phone.

"Do you really think I'd take out a gun and shoot you in cold blood in a public place?"

"Everything but the public place fits you as perfectly as that lovely suit you're wearing." He closed her handbag himself, then eased back.

"If you think I'm that ruthless, I'm surprised you didn't go to Wyley's in the first place."

"I figure there's fewer questions and explanations, some of which might be sticky, between you and me."

"Tell your brother to stop hulking over me," she snapped, and punched in a number when Gideon faded back. "This is Anita Gaye. I'm ready to transfer the funds."

Malachi took a folded piece of paper from his pocket, spread it on the table in front of her. She relayed the information on it. "No," she said. "I'll call you back."

She laid the phone on the table. "The transfer's being done. I want the Fates."

"And you'll have them." He nudged the case farther out of her reach. "When I've verified the money's in my account."

From a nearby table, Rebecca answered an e-mail from Jack, sent another to Tia, then continued monitoring the numbered account.

"It's a lot of money, Malachi. What do you plan to do with it?"

"We've all manner of plans. You'll have to come to Cobh sometime, see for yourself just how we've put it to use. And you, what will you do? Start right up on turning a tidy profit, or take a bit of time off to enjoy your acquisition?"

"Business first, always."

Now, Gideon thought as he watched his sister lower the screen of her laptop, it was all in the timing. They'd soon see how well Cleo had choreographed the scene. He tucked his thumbs in his belt loops, tapped his fingers on the front pockets of his jeans.

On cue, Malachi glanced over. "Well, for Christ's sake," he said and frowned at Anita. "We've company. Let me handle her."

"Who?"

"Tia." Malachi let the warmth pour into his voice as he got to his feet. "What a happy coincidence."

"Malachi." She stuttered a little, and it was the excitement of the moment as much as the part she was playing that brought the flush to her cheeks. "I didn't know you were back in New York."

"Only just. I was going to ring you later today; now you've saved me the price of the call." He leaned in, pressed his cheek to hers and lifted his brows at Anita.

"I just came in to do some research on my book." She clutched her briefcase to her breasts. "I never expected to . . ." Tia trailed off, looked startled. "Anita?"

"Of course, you know each other." Malachi's voice lifted, with just enough of a frantic edge to have heads turning irritably in their direction. "I asked Ms. Gaye to meet me here to discuss . . . ah, to discuss a potential purchase for my offices."

"Oh. I see." She looked from one face to the other, her eyes wide and hurt. As if she did see, and very well. "Well, I . . . I don't mean to interrupt. As I said, I was just . . . Oh, are you reading about the Fates?"

She leaned over, a bit clumsily, to turn the book, and effectively blocked Anita's view.

Rebecca strolled up, switched cases smoothly and continued by the table. She spared a quick wink for Gideon, gripped firmly the handle of the briefcase that held the Fates and walked out of the reading room, toward the stairs and down.

"Just passing the time." Malachi tapped Anita's phone when he saw the call light blinking. "I think you've a call coming in, Anita."

"Excuse me." She picked up the phone. "Anita Gaye."

"I, ah, should get to work." Tia stepped back. "It was nice to see you again, Malachi. It was . . . well, good-bye."

"Shattered her maiden's dreams." Laughing lightly, Anita disconnected the call. "The transfer's complete, so . . ."

She reached down for the case, and for the second time Malachi closed a hand over her wrist. "Not quite so fast, darling. I'll just verify that for myself."

He took out his own phone and, as if to confirm what Rebecca had already verified, called Cleo in the van.

"I need to confirm an electronic transfer of funds," he stated curtly. "Yes, I'll wait."

"Rebecca's just getting in the van. Jack should be at Anita's with Detective Gilbert. They got the search warrant."

"Yes, thank you. I'll give you the account number."

"Mal, Rebecca. Jack e-mailed me from his PalmPilot. His friend Detective Robbins is going to bring Anita in for questioning on the murders. He should be at Morningside by now. With the other cop at her house, she's nowhere to go. And here's Tia now, just coming out of the library."

"Excellent. Thank you very much." He tucked his phone back in his pocket. "That seems to be that." He got to his feet, handing her the briefcase. "I can't say it's been a pleasure."

"You're a fool, Malachi." Anita rose. "Worse, you're a fool who thinks small. I'll turn what's in this case into the biggest story in a decade. Hell, in a century. Enjoy your ten million. Before I'm done, that'll be petty cash."

"A nasty piece, that one," Gideon commented as she clipped away.

"Oh well, ever since that house fell on her sister, she's been out of sorts. Let's give her a minute or two to start up her broomstick before we go see all our girls."


THE BROOMSTICK MIGHT have been a New York City cab, but Anita was very near cackling. Everything she wanted—money, power, position, fame, respect—was tucked in the briefcase beside her.

It was Paul's money that had brought her this far. But it would be hers that took her the rest of the way. She was, now, as far away from that row house in Queens as she had ever been.

Inspired, she flipped out her phone to call her butler and arrange for champagne and caviar to be waiting for her in her sitting room.

"Good afternoon, Morningside residence."

"This is Ms. Gaye. Haven't I told you Stipes or Fitzhugh is to answer the telephone?"

"Yes, Ms. Gaye. I'm sorry, Ms. Gaye. But both Mr. Stipes and Mrs. Fitzhugh are with the police."

"What do you mean, with the police?"

"The police are here, ma'am. They brought a search warrant."

"Have you lost your mind?"

"Yes, ma'am. No, ma'am. I heard them say something about an insurance claim, and some items from Morningside." The excitement in the girl's voice was palpable. Anita couldn't know the internal war being waged between admitting to listening at the door and risking being fired, or passing on the information.

"What are they doing? Where are they?"

"In the library, ma'am. They went into your safe and they found things. Things that were supposed to be stolen from the store."

"That's ridiculous. That's impossible. That's . . ." And the pieces began to fall, to shuffle into place. "The son of a bitch. The son of a bitch!" She tossed the phone aside and, with trembling fingers, unlocked the briefcase.

Inside were three puppets. Even through the haze of fury, she recognized Moe, Larry and Curly.


"SHE WON'T APPRECIATE the full irony of the Three Stooges."

Gideon reached over and stole the slice of pizza out of Cleo's hand. "It's a pie in the face. That point's clear enough, even to her."

"I never understood the humor. I'm sorry," Tia said when all three men stared at her. "All that eye-poking and head bashing."

"It's a guy thing," Jack told her. "They should have her downtown by now," he added, checking his watch. "Her lawyers can dance till they drop, but they're not going to tap their way around the insurance fraud."

"And Mikey?"

Jack looked back at Cleo. "Jasper gave them chapter and verse. The courts may look dubiously on a guy with his sheet, but the phone records will back up the connection. Start welding those links together, you've got a hell of a chain to wrap around her neck. She's accessory before and after the fact. She'll pay for Mikey. She'll pay for it all."

"Thinking of her in that really ugly orange jumpsuit— nasty color with her hair—brightens my day." Cleo lifted her beer. "Here's to us."

"It was a hell of a party." Gideon rose, rolled his shoulders. "I've got to go out."

"Where are we going?"

"You're not invited." He leaned down to tap Cleo's nose. "I'm taking Mal and Ma so I can have both male and female advice on a proper ring."

"You're getting me a ring? Aw, you traditional sap." She leaped to her feet to kiss him. "Then I'm going, too. I should pick it out since I'm the one who's going to wear it."

"You're not going, and I'm picking it out, as I'm the one giving it to you."

"That's pretty strict, but I think I can live with it."

"We'll walk down with you." Jack took Rebecca's hand. "We'll head downtown, see what we can wheedle out of Bob on the status. He might be able to resist me, but he won't be able to resist Irish face-to-face."

"A fine idea." Rebecca snagged her jacket. "When we're done, we'll make reservations at some hideously expensive restaurant. We'll have the mother of all celebration dinners. We'll just help Tia clean this mess up."

"No, that's all right. I'd rather know what's going on quicker. And I want to see Cleo's ring."

"Me, too." Cleo stretched on the sofa. "Enough that I'll help clean up. Don't be afraid to go for gaudy," she told Gideon. "I can live with it."

When she was alone with Tia, Cleo rolled over on her stomach, crossed her legs in the air. "Sit down a minute. Those pizza boxes aren't in a hurry."

"If I keep busy it won't seem like so long before everyone's back. You know, I've eaten more pizza in the past month than I have in my whole life."

"Stick with me and you'll discover all the joys of fast food."

"I never thought I'd enjoy having crowds of people in my apartment. But I do. It never seems quite right when they're not around."

"I was just wondering if you and Mal were going to go for it, too."

"Go for what?" She looked at the Three Fates, even now standing among empty bottles and pizza boxes. "We've already gone for it, haven't we?"

"No, I mean, you know, 'till death do us part.' "

"Oh. We haven't talked about it. I imagine he's anxious to get home, to get back to the family business, to figure out what to do with his share of things. Maybe after . . . maybe in time he'll feel more settled and we'll talk about it."

"Time's part of it, isn't it?" Cleo lifted Clotho. "Seems to me for all the fate and destiny stuff, sometimes you have to do the job yourself. Why don't you ask him?"

"Him to what? To . . . to marry me? I couldn't. He's supposed to ask me."

"Why?"

"Because he's the man."

"Yeah, yeah. So what? You love him, you want him, so you ask him. Then we can plan a triple wedding. Strikes me like that's how all this was meant to shake down."

"Ask him?" The idea rolled around in Tia's brain before she shook her head. "I'd never have the nerve."

When the phone rang, she carried empty boxes into the kitchen and picked up the nested portable on the counter. "Hello?"

"Doing research, you bitch?"

A whipsnap of ice slapped up Tia's spine. "Excuse me?"

"What did he promise you? True love? Devotion? You won't get it."

"I don't understand." She walked quickly back into the living room, signaled Cleo. "Is this Anita?"

"Don't play dumb with me. Game's over. I want the Fates."

"I don't know what you're talking about." She tipped the phone so Cleo could bump heads with her and listen.

"If you don't, it's going to be very sad about your mother."

"My mother?" Tia jolted up straight, instinctively gripping Cleo's hand. "What about my mother?"

"She's not feeling well, not well at all. Are you, Alma?"

"Tia." The voice was weak, and thick with tears. "Tia, what's happening?"

"Tell her what I'm doing right now, Alma dear."

"She's . . . Tia, she's holding a gun to my head. I think, I think she shot Tilly. Oh God, my God, I can't breathe."

"Anita! Don't hurt her. She doesn't know anything. She's not involved in this."

"Everyone's involved. Is he there with you?"

"No, Malachi's not here. I swear to you, he's not here. I'm alone."

"Then come, alone, to your mommy's house. We'll have a nice cozy chat. You've got five minutes, so you'd better run. Five minutes, Tia, or I shoot her."

"Don't, please. I'll do anything you want."

"You're wasting time, and she doesn't have much."

Even as the phone clicked in her ear, Tia was tossing it aside. "I have to go now. I have to hurry."

"Jesus Christ, Tia, you can't go over there. You can't go by yourself."

"I have to. There's no time."

"We'll call Gideon, Malachi. We'll call Jack." Cleo muscled Tia away from the door. "Think, damn it. Think. You can't go rushing over there. We need the cops."

"I have to. She's my mother. She's terrified, maybe already hurt. Five minutes. I only have five minutes. She's my mother," Tia repeated, pushing Cleo aside.

"Stall her." Cleo rushed out the door behind Tia. "Stall her, I'll get help."

Tia called out her mother's address and ran. She hadn't known she could run that fast, that she could streak through the rain like a snake through water. Drenched, terrified and chilled to the bone, she hurled herself up the steps to her parents' door and, desperate, lifted a hand to beat on the wood. Her fist pounding, she pushed the door, already slightly ajar, open.

"Mother!"

"We're up here, Tia." Anita's voice floated downstairs. "Close and lock the door behind you. You just made it, you know. Thirty seconds to spare."

"Mother." She hesitated at the base of the stairs. "Are you all right?"

"She struck me." Alma began to weep. "My face. Tia, don't come up. Don't come upstairs! Run!"

"Don't hurt her again. I'm coming." Tia gripped the banister hard and started up the steps.

At the top, she turned and saw Tilly lying in the hallway, blood seeping into the rug beneath her. "Oh God, no!" She rushed forward, threw herself down to check for a pulse.

Alive, she thought, nearly weeping. Still alive, but for how long? If she stalled Anita long enough for help to come, Tilly might bleed to death.

You're on your own. She ordered herself to get to her feet. And you will do whatever needs to be done.

"Tilly is badly hurt."

"Then your father will just have to call the agency and find another housekeeper. Get in here, Tia, before I start splattering your mother's blood in this overly rococo bedroom."

Without taking time for one last prayer, Tia stepped into the doorway. She saw her mother, tied in a chair. And behind her, Anita holding a gun to her already bruised temple.

"Hold your hands up," Anita ordered. "Turn a slow circle. Look at this," she continued when Tia obeyed. "She didn't even take time for a raincoat. Such daughterly devotion."

"I don't have a gun. I wouldn't know how to use one if I did."

"I can see that. Soaked to the skin. Come all the way inside."

"Tilly needs an ambulance."

Anita lifted her brows, pushed the barrel of the gun more firmly against Alma's temple. "Want to make it two?"

"No. Please."

"She came to the door," Alma sobbed. "Tilly let her in. She was coming up to tell me, and I heard that terrible sound. She shot poor Tilly, Tia. Then she came in here, she struck me. She tied me up."

"I used Hermés scarves, didn't I? Stop complaining, Alma. I don't know how you stand this woman," Anita said to Tia. "Seriously, I should put this bullet in her brain and do you a favor."

"If you hurt her, I won't have any reason to help you."

"Apparently I judged you right on some level." She rubbed the barrel of the gun against Alma's bloodless cheek. "I never would have figured you to lie, cheat, steal."

"Like you?"

"Exactly. I want the Fates."

"They won't help you. The police are at your house, at your business. They have warrants."

"Do you think I don't *know* that?" Anita's voice pitched up, like a child's about to throw herself into a tantrum. "You think you're so clever, planting stolen merchandise in my safe. You think I'm worried about a little insurance fraud?"

"They know you killed that man. First-degree murder. They know you were paying him when he killed Mikey. Accessory to murder." Tia moved forward as she spoke. "The Fates won't help you with that."

"You get them, and I'll worry about the rest. I want the statues and the money. Call that Irish prick and get them back, or I kill her, then you."

She'll kill us all for them, Tia thought. Even if she were to hand them over to Anita now, she would still kill them all. And maybe, somehow, find some hole to hide in.

"He doesn't have them. I do," she said quickly when Anita jerked her mother's head back with the barrel of the gun. "My father wanted them. You know what a coup it would be. I wanted Malachi. So we tricked you out of the money. My father would buy them. I get Malachi, and Wyley's gets the Fates."

"Not anymore."

"No. I don't want you to hurt my mother. I'll get you the Fates, and my share of the money. I'll try to get the rest. I'll get you the Fates right now if you stop pointing the gun at my mother."

"You don't like it? How's this?" Anita shifted her aim so the gun was pointed at Tia's heart.

And seeing the gun aimed at her daughter, Alma began to scream. In an absent gesture, Anita rapped the side of her fist against Alma's temple. "Shut the fuck up or I'll shoot both of you for the hell of it."

"Don't. Don't hurt my Tia."

"You don't have to hurt anyone. I'll get them for you." Moving slowly, Tia eased toward her mother's dressing table.

"Do you think I'm stupid enough to believe they're in there?"

"I need the key. Mother keeps the key to the lockbox in here."

"Tia—"

"Mother." Tia shook her head. "There's no use pretending anymore. She knows. They're not worth dying for." Tia opened the drawer.

"Hold it, step back." Gesturing with the gun, Anita moved forward as Tia stood by the open drawer. "If there's a gun in there, I'm putting a bullet in Alma's kneecap."

"Please." As if staggering, Tia laid a hand on the vanity for balance and palmed a small bottle. "Please don't. There's no gun."

Anita used her free hand to riffle through the drawer. "There's no key either."

"It's in there. Right—"

She slammed the drawer on Anita's hand, then tossed the contents of the bottle in her face. The gun went off, plowing a hole in the wall an inch from Tia's head. Through the screams—her mother's, Anita's, her own— Tia leaped.

The collision with Anita knocked the breath out of her, but flying on adrenaline, she didn't notice. But she felt, with a kind of primeval thrill, her own nails rake the flesh of Anita's wrist.

And she scented blood.

The gun spurted out of Anita's hand, skidded over the floor. They grappled for it, Anita clawing blindly as the smelling salts Tia had flung at her stung her eyes. A fist glanced off her cheek and made her ears ring. Her knee plowed into Anita's stomach more by accident than design.

When their hands closed over the gun at the same time, when they rolled over the floor in a fierce, sweaty tangle, Tia did the only thing that came to mind. She got a handful of Anita's hair and yanked viciously.

She didn't hear the glass shattering as they rammed into a table. She didn't hear the shouts from downstairs or the pounding of feet. All she heard was the blood roaring in her own head, the fury and elemental violence of it.

For the first time in her life, she caused someone physical pain, and wanted to cause more.

"You hit my mother." She gasped it out and, using Anita's hair as a rope, slammed her head over and over against the floor.

Then someone was pulling her away. Teeth bared, hands fisted, Tia struggled as she stared down, watching Anita's bloodshot eyes roll back in her head.

Gideon stepped over, picked up the gun, and Malachi turned the still struggling Tia into his arms. "Are you hurt? Jesus, Tia, there's blood on you."

"She kicked her ass." Cleo sniffled her way through a grin. "Can't you see, she kicked her fat, sorry ass."

"Tilly." The adrenaline dumped out of her system and left her limbs feeling like water. Her voice was weak now, her head starting to spin.

"Ma's with her. She's ringing an ambulance. Here now, here now, darling, you're going to sit down. Gideon, help Mrs. Marsh there."

"I'll do it. She's frightened." Holding on, Tia stayed on her feet. Her knees wanted to buckle, her legs to give, but she took the first step. The second was easier. "Get her out of here, please. Get Anita out of here. I'll take care of my mother."

Stepping around the unconscious Anita, Tia hurried over to untie her mother. "You're not going to be hysterical," Tia ordered, pressing a kiss to her mother's bruised face as she dealt with the knots. "You're going to lie down. I'm going to make you some tea."

"I thought she would kill you. I thought—"

"She didn't. I'm perfectly fine, and so are you."

"Tilly. She's dead."

"She's not. I promise." Gently, Tia helped Alma to her feet. "An ambulance is coming. Lie down now. Everything's going to be fine."

"That horrible woman. I never liked her. My head hurts."

"I know." Tia brushed Alma's hair back from her bruised temple, kissed it. "I'll get you something for it."

"Tilly." Alma gripped Tia's hand.

"She's going to be all right." Tia leaned down, put her arms around her mother. "Everything's going to be all right."

"You were very brave. I didn't know you could be so brave."

"Neither did I."

To Tia's surprise, her mother insisted on going to the hospital with Tilly. And was just as forceful in sending Tia home again.

"She'll drive the doctors crazy. At least until my father gets there and calms her down."

"It shows a good heart"—Eileen set a cup of tea in front of Tia—"that she was more concerned with her friend than anything else. A good heart," she added, touching Tia's sore cheek, "goes a long way. Drink your tea now, so you're steady when you talk to those policemen."

"I will. Thank you."

She closed her eyes as Eileen left the room, then opened them and looked at Malachi.

"I never thought she could hurt you. I never thought she'd—I should have."

"It's no one's fault but hers."

"Look at you." He cupped her face gently. "Bruises on your cheek and scratches as well. I wouldn't have had it, not for all the money in the world, not for the Fates, not for justice. I wouldn't have had one mark on you."

"There are more on her, and I put them there."

"That you did." He lifted her to her feet to hold her. "Smelling salts dead in the eyes. Who but you would think of it?"

"It's done now, isn't it? All the way done?"

"It is. All the way done."

"Then, are you going to marry me?"

"What?" He eased away, slow and careful. "What did you say?"

"I asked if you're going to marry me or not."

He let out a short laugh, raked a hand through his hair. "I thought I would, it being agreeable with you. As it happens, I was on the point of deciding on a ring when Cleo rang on Gideon's mobile."

"Go back and get it."

"Now?"

"Tomorrow." She wrapped her arms around him and sighed. "Tomorrow's just fine."

# Epilogue

*Cobh, Ireland*
*May 7, 2003*

THE Deepwater Quay at water's edge was unchanged from the time of the *Lusitania,* the *Titanic* and the great, grand ships that once plied the waters between America and Europe.

Here, tenders from those ships had come to get mail and passengers from the Dublin train, which often arrived late.

Though the Quay still functioned as a train station, the Cobh Heritage Centre, with its displays and shops, ran through its main terminal.

Recently an addition had been added to serve as a small museum. With security by Burdett. The focal point of that museum were three silver statues known as the Three Fates.

They gleamed behind their protective glass and looked out at the faces—perhaps the lives—of those who came to see, and to study.

They stood, united by their bases, on a marble pedestal, and in the pedestal was a brass plaque.

### THE THREE FATES

On loan from
the Sullivan-Burdett Collection
In memory of

HENRY W. AND EDITH WYLEY
LORRAINE AND STEVEN EDWARD CUNNINGHAM III
FELIX AND MARGARET GREENFIELD
MICHAEL K. HICKS

"It's good. It's good that his name's on there." Cleo blinked back tears. "It's good."

Gideon draped his arm over her shoulders. "It's right. We did what we could to make it right."

"I'm proud of you." Rebecca hooked her arm through Jack's. "I'm proud to stand here beside you, as your wife. You could have kept them."

"Nope. I got you. One goddess is enough for any man."

"A wise and true answer. It's time we went to the cemetery. Cleo?"

"Yeah." She laid her fingers on the glass, just under Mikey's name. "Let's go."

"We'll be right behind you," Malachi told them. "Button up." He began doing up the buttons of Tia's jacket himself. "It's windy out."

"You don't have to fuss. We're fine."

"Expectant fathers are allowed to fuss and fret." He laid a hand on her belly. "Are you sure you want to walk?"

"Yes, it's good for us. I can't sit in a bubble for the next six months, Malachi."

"Listen to her. Not a year ago you were barricaded against every germ known to man."

"That was then." She leaned her head on his shoulder. "It's a tapestry. Threads woven in a life. I like the way my pattern's changing. I like standing here with you and seeing something we helped do shining in the light."

"You shine, Tia."

Content, she laid her hand over his. "We made justice. Anita's in prison, probably for the rest of her life. The Fates are together, as they were meant to be."

"And so are we."

"So are we."

She held out a hand and felt unreasonably strong when his linked with it. They caught up with the others and walked up the long hill in the May wind.

Can't get enough of Nora Roberts?
Try the #1 *New York Times* bestselling
In Death series, by Nora Roberts
writing as J. D. Robb.

Turn the page to see where it began . . .

# NAKED IN DEATH

S HE woke in the dark. Through the slats on the window shades, the first murky hint of dawn slipped, slanting shadowy bars over the bed. It was like waking in a cell.

For a moment she simply lay there, shuddering, imprisoned, while the dream faded. After ten years on the force, Eve still had dreams.

Six hours before, she'd killed a man, had watched death creep into his eyes. It wasn't the first time she'd exercised maximum force, or dreamed. She'd learned to accept the action and the consequences.

But it was the child that haunted her. The child she hadn't been in time to save. The child whose screams had echoed in the dreams with her own.

All the blood, Eve thought, scrubbing sweat from her face with her hands. Such a small little girl to have had so much blood in her. And she knew it was vital that she push it aside.

Standard departmental procedure meant that she would spend the morning in Testing. Any officer whose discharge of weapon resulted in termination of life was required to undergo emotional and psychiatric clearance before resuming duty. Eve considered the tests a mild pain in the ass.

She would beat them, as she'd beaten them before.

When she rose, the overheads went automatically to low setting, lighting her way into the bath. She winced once at her reflection. Her eyes were swollen from lack of sleep, her skin nearly as pale as the corpses she'd delegated to the ME.

Rather than dwell on it, she stepped into the shower, yawning.

"Give me one oh one degrees, full force," she said and shifted so that the shower spray hit her straight in the face.

She let it steam, lathered listlessly while she played through the events of the night before. She wasn't due in Testing until nine, and would use the next three hours to settle and let the dream fade away completely.

Small doubts and little regrets were often detected and could mean a second and more intense round with the machines and the owl-eyed technicians who ran them.

Eve didn't intend to be off the streets longer than twenty-four hours.

After pulling on a robe, she walked into the kitchen and programmed her AutoChef for coffee, black; toast, light. Through her window she could hear the heavy hum of air traffic carrying early commuters to offices, late ones home. She'd chosen the apartment years before because it was in a heavy ground and air pattern, and she liked the noise and crowds. On another yawn, she glanced out the window, followed the rattling journey of an aging airbus hauling laborers not fortunate enough to work in the city or by home 'links.

She brought the *New York Times* up on her monitor and scanned the headlines while the faux caffeine bolstered her system. The AutoChef had burned her toast again, but she ate it anyway, with a vague thought of springing for a replacement unit.

She was frowning over an article on a mass recall of droid cocker spaniels when her telelink blipped. Eve shifted to communications and watched her commanding officer flash onto the screen.

"Commander."

"Lieutenant." He gave her a brisk nod, noted the still-wet

hair and sleepy eyes. "Incident at Twenty-seven West Broadway, eighteenth floor. You're primary."

Eve lifted a brow. "I'm on Testing. Subject terminated at twenty-two thirty-five."

"We have override," he said, without inflection. "Pick up your shield and weapon on the way to the incident. Code Five, Lieutenant."

"Yes, sir." His face flashed off even as she pushed back from the screen. Code Five meant she would report directly to her commander, and there would be no unsealed interdepartmental reports and no cooperation with the press.

In essence, it meant she was on her own.

BROADWAY WAS NOISY and crowded, a party that rowdy guests never left. Street, pedestrian, and sky traffic were miserable, choking the air with bodies and vehicles. In her old days in uniform she remembered it as a hot spot for wrecks and crushed tourists who were too busy gaping at the show to get out of the way.

Even at this hour steam was rising from the stationary and portable food stands that offered everything from rice noodles to soy dogs for the teeming crowds. She had to swerve to avoid an eager merchant on his smoking Glida-Grill, and took his flipped middle finger as a matter of course.

Eve double-parked and, skirting a man who smelled worse than his bottle of brew, stepped onto the sidewalk. She scanned the building first, fifty floors of gleaming metal that knifed into the sky from a hilt of concrete. She was propositioned twice before she reached the door.

Since this five-block area of West Broadway was affectionately termed Prostitute's Walk, she wasn't surprised. She flashed her badge for the uniform guarding the entrance.

"Lieutenant Dallas."

"Yes, sir." He skimmed his official CompuSeal over the door to keep out the curious, then led the way to the bank of elevators. "Eighteenth floor," he said when the doors swished shut behind them.

"Fill me in, Officer." Eve switched on her recorder and waited.

"I wasn't first on the scene, Lieutenant. Whatever happened upstairs is being kept upstairs. There's a badge inside waiting for you. We have a homicide, and a Code Five in number eighteen-oh-three."

"Who called it in?"

"I don't have that information."

He stayed where he was when the elevator opened. Eve stepped out and was alone in a narrow hallway. Security cameras tilted down at her, and her feet were almost soundless on the worn nap of the carpet as she approached 1803. Ignoring the hand plate, she announced herself, holding her badge up to eye level for the peep cam until the door opened.

"Dallas."

"Feeney." She smiled, pleased to see a familiar face. Ryan Feeney was an old friend and former partner who'd traded the street for a desk and a top-level position in the Electronics Detection Division. "So, they're sending computer pluckers these days."

"They wanted brass, and the best." His lips curved in his wide, rumpled face, but his eyes remained sober. He was a small, stubby man with small, stubby hands and rust-colored hair. "You look beat."

"Rough night."

"So I heard." He offered her one of the sugared nuts from the bag he habitually carried, studying her, and measuring if she was up to what was waiting in the bedroom beyond.

She was young for her rank, barely thirty, with wide brown eyes that had never had a chance to be naive. Her doe-brown hair was cropped short, for convenience rather than style, but suited her triangular face with its razor-edge cheekbones and slight dent in the chin.

She was tall, rangy, with a tendency to look thin, but Feeney knew there were solid muscles beneath the leather jacket. But Eve had more—there was also a brain, and a heart.

"This one's going to be touchy, Dallas."

"I picked that up already. Who's the victim?"

"Sharon DeBlass, granddaughter of Senator DeBlass."

Neither meant anything to her. "Politics isn't my forte, Feeney."

"The gentleman from Virginia, extreme right, old money.

The granddaughter took a sharp left a few years back, moved to New York and became a licensed companion."

"She was a hooker." Dallas glanced around the apartment. It was furnished in obsessive modern—glass and thin chrome, signed holograms on the walls, recessed bar in bold red. The wide mood screen behind the bar bled with mixing and merging shapes and colors in cool pastels.

Neat as a virgin, Eve mused, and cold as a whore. "No surprise, given her choice of real estate."

"Politics makes it delicate. Victim was twenty-four, Caucasian female. She bought it in bed."

Eve only lifted a brow. "Seems poetic, since she'd been bought there. How'd she die?"

"That's the next problem. I want you to see for yourself."

As they crossed the room, each took out a slim container, sprayed their hands front and back to seal in oils and fingerprints. At the doorway, Eve sprayed the bottom of her boots to slicken them so that she would pick up no fibers, stray hairs, or skin.

Eve was already wary. Under normal circumstances there would have been two other investigators on a homicide scene, with recorders for sound and pictures. Forensics would have been waiting with their usual snarly impatience to sweep the scene.

The fact that only Feeney had been assigned with her meant that there were a lot of eggshells to be walked over.

"Security cameras in the lobby, elevator, and hallways," Eve commented.

"I've already tagged the discs." Feeney opened the bedroom door and let her enter first.

It wasn't pretty. Death rarely was a peaceful, religious experience to Eve's mind. It was the nasty end, indifferent to saint and sinner. But this was shocking, like a stage deliberately set to offend.

The bed was huge, slicked with what appeared to be genuine satin sheets the color of ripe peaches. Small, soft-focused spotlights were trained on its center where the naked woman was cupped in the gentle dip of the floating mattress.

The mattress moved with obscenely graceful undulations to

the rhythm of programmed music slipping through the head-board.

She was beautiful still, a cameo face with a tumbling water-fall of flaming red hair, emerald eyes that stared glassily at the mirrored ceiling, long, milk-white limbs that called to mind visions of *Swan Lake* as the motion of the bed gently rocked them.

They weren't artistically arranged now, but spread lewdly so that the dead woman formed a final X dead-center of the bed.

There was a hole in her forehead, one in her chest, another horribly gaping between the open thighs. Blood had splattered on the glossy sheets, pooled, dripped, and stained.

There were splashes of it on the lacquered walls, like lethal paintings scrawled by an evil child.

So much blood was a rare thing, and she had seen much too much of it the night before to take the scene as calmly as she would have preferred.

She had to swallow once, hard, and force herself to block out the image of a small child.

"You got the scene on record?"

"Yep."

"Then turn that damn thing off." She let out a breath after Feeney located the controls that silenced the music. The bed flowed to stillness. "The wounds," Eve murmured, stepping closer to examine them. "Too neat for a knife. Too messy for a laser." A flash came to her—old training films, old videos, old viciousness.

"Christ, Feeney, these look like bullet wounds."

Feeney reached into his pocket and drew out a sealed bag. "Whoever did it left a souvenir." He passed the bag to Eve. "An antique like this has to go for eight, ten thousand for a legal collection, twice that on the black market."

Fascinated, Eve turned the sealed revolver over in her hand. "It's heavy," she said half to herself. "Bulky."

"Thirty-eight caliber," he told her. "First one I've seen outside of a museum. This one's a Smith and Wesson, Model Ten, blue steel." He looked at it with some affection. "Real classic piece, used to be standard police issue up until the latter part of the twentieth. They stopped making them in about twenty-two, twenty-three, when the gun ban was passed."

"You're the history buff." Which explained why he was with her. "Looks new." She sniffed through the bag, caught the scent of oil and burning. "Somebody took good care of this. Steel fired into flesh," she mused as she passed the bag back to Feeney. "Ugly way to die, and the first I've seen it in my ten years with the department."

"Second for me. About fifteen years ago, Lower East Side, party got out of hand. Guy shot five people with a twenty-two before he realized it wasn't a toy. Hell of a mess."

"Fun and games," Eve murmured. "We'll scan the collectors, see how many we can locate who own one like this. Somebody might have reported a robbery."

"Might have."

"It's more likely it came through the black market." Eve glanced back at the body. "If she's been in the business for a few years, she'd have discs, records of her clients, her trick books." She frowned. "With Code Five, I'll have to do the door-to-door myself. Not a simple sex crime," she said with a sigh. "Whoever did it set it up. The antique weapon, the wounds themselves, almost ruler-straight down the body, the lights, the pose. Who called it in, Feeney?"

"The killer." He waited until her eyes came back to him. "From right here. Called the station. See how the bedside unit's aimed at her face? That's what came in. Video, no audio."

"He's into showmanship." Eve let out a breath. "Clever bastard, arrogant, cocky. He had sex with her first. I'd bet my badge on it. Then he gets up and does it." She lifted her arm, aiming, lowering it as she counted off, "One, two, three."

"That's cold," murmured Feeney.

"He's cold. He smooths down the sheets after. See how neat they are? He arranges her, spreads her open so nobody can have any doubts as to how she made her living. He does it carefully, practically measuring, so that she's perfectly aligned. Center of the bed, arms and legs equally apart. Doesn't turn off the bed 'cause it's part of the show. He leaves the gun because he wants us to know right away he's no ordinary man. He's got an ego. He doesn't want to waste time letting the body be discovered eventually. He wants it now. That instant gratification."

"She was licensed for men and women," Feeney pointed out, but Eve shook her head.

"It's not a woman. A woman wouldn't have left her looking both beautiful and obscene. No, I don't think it's a woman. Let's see what we can find. Have you gone into her computer yet?"

"No. It's your case, Dallas. I'm only authorized to assist."

"See if you can access her client files." Eve went to the dresser and began to carefully search drawers.

Expensive taste, Eve reflected. There were several items of real silk, the kind no simulation could match. The bottle of scent on the dresser was exclusive, and smelled, after a quick sniff, like expensive sex.

The contents of the drawers were meticulously ordered, lingerie folded precisely, sweaters arranged according to color and material. The closet was the same.

Obviously the victim had a love affair with clothes and a taste for the best and took scrupulous care of what she owned.

And she'd died naked.

"Kept good records," Feeney called out. "It's all here. Her client list, appointments—including her required monthly health exam and her weekly trip to the beauty salon. She used the Trident Clinic for the first and Paradise for the second."

"Both top-of-the-line. I've got a friend who saved for a year so she could have one day for the works at Paradise. Takes all kinds."

"My wife's sister went for it for her twenty-fifth anniversary. Cost damn near as much as my kid's wedding. Hello, we've got her personal address book."

"Good. Copy all of it, will you, Feeney?" At his low whistle, she looked over her shoulder, glimpsed the small gold-edged palm computer in his hand. "What?"

"We've got a lot of high-powered names in here. Politics, entertainment, money, money, money. Interesting, our girl has Roarke's private number."

"Roarke who?"

"Just Roarke, as far as I know. Big money there. Kind of guy that touches shit and turns it into gold bricks. You've got to start reading more than the sports page, Dallas."

"Hey, I read the headlines. Did you hear about the cocker spaniel recall?"

"Roarke's always big news," Feeney said patiently. "He's got one of the finest art collections in the world. Arts and antiques," he continued, noting when Eve clicked in and turned to him. "He's a licensed gun collector. Rumor is he knows how to use them."

"I'll pay him a visit."

"You'll be lucky to get within a mile of him."

"I'm feeling lucky." Eve crossed over to the body to slip her hands under the sheets.

"The man's got powerful friends, Dallas. You can't afford to so much as whisper he's linked to this until you've got something solid."

"Feeney, you know it's a mistake to tell me that." But even as she started to smile, her fingers brushed something between cold flesh and bloody sheets. "There's something under her." Carefully, Eve lifted the shoulder, eased her fingers over.

"Paper," she murmured. "Sealed." With her protected thumb, she wiped at a smear of blood until she could read the protected sheet.

ONE OF SIX

"It looks hand printed," she said to Feeney and held it out. "Our boy's more than clever, more than arrogant. And he isn't finished."

EVE SPENT THE rest of the day doing what would normally have been assigned to drones: She interviewed the victim's neighbors personally, recording statements, impressions.

She managed to grab a quick sandwich from the same Glida-Grill she'd nearly smashed before, driving across town. After the night and the morning she'd put in, she could hardly blame the receptionist at Paradise for looking at her as though she'd recently scraped herself off the sidewalk.

Waterfalls played musically among the flora in the reception area of the city's most exclusive salon. Tiny cups of real coffee and slim glasses of fizzling water or champagne were served to those lounging on the cushy chairs and settees. Headphones and discs of fashion magazines were complimentary.

The receptionist was magnificently breasted, a testament to the salon's figure sculpting techniques. She wore a snug, short outfit in the salon's trademark red, and an incredible coif of ebony hair coiled like snakes.

Eve couldn't have been more delighted.

"I'm sorry," the woman said in a carefully modulated voice as empty of expression as a computer. "We serve by appointment only."

"That's okay." Eve smiled and was almost sorry to puncture the disdain. Almost. "This ought to get me one." She offered her badge. "Who works on Sharon DeBlass?"

The receptionist's horrified eyes darted toward the waiting area. "Our clients' needs are strictly confidential."

"I bet." Enjoying herself, Eve leaned companionably on the U-shaped counter. "I can talk nice and quiet, like this, so we understand each other—Denise?" She flicked her gaze down to the discreet studded badge on the woman's breast. "Or I can talk louder, so everyone understands. If you like the first idea better, you can take me to a nice quiet room where we won't disturb any of your clients, and you can send in Sharon DeBlass's operator. Or whatever term you use."

"Consultant," Denise said faintly. "If you'll follow me."

"My pleasure."

And it was.

Outside of movies or videos, Eve had never seen anything so lush. The carpet was a red cushion your feet could sink blissfully into. Crystal drops hung from the ceiling and spun light. The air smelled of flowers and pampered flesh.

She might not have been able to imagine herself there, spending hours having herself creamed, oiled, pummeled, and sculpted, but if she were going to waste such time on vanity, it would certainly have been interesting to do so under such civilized conditions.

The receptionist showed her into a small room with a hologram of a summer meadow dominating one wall. The quiet sound of birdsong and breezes sweetened the air.

"If you'd just wait here."

"No problem." Eve waited for the door to close then, with an indulgent sigh, she lowered herself into a deeply cushioned chair. The moment she was seated, the monitor beside her blipped on, and a friendly, indulgent face that could only be a droid's beamed smiles.

"Good afternoon. Welcome to Paradise. Your beauty needs and your comfort are our only priorities. Would you like some refreshment while you wait for your personal consultant?"

"Sure. Coffee, black, coffee."

"Of course. What sort would you prefer? Press *C* on your keyboard for the list of choices."

Smothering a chuckle, Eve followed instructions. She spent the next two minutes pondering over her options, then narrowed it down to French Riviera or Caribbean Cream.

The door opened again before she could decide. Resigned, she rose and faced an elaborately dressed scarecrow.

Over his fuchsia shirt and plum-colored slacks, he wore an open, trailing smock of Paradise red. His hair, flowing back from a painfully thin face, echoed the hue of his slacks. He offered Eve a hand, squeezed gently, and stared at her out of soft doe eyes.

"I'm terribly sorry, Officer. I'm baffled."

"I want information on Sharon DeBlass." Again, Eve took out her badge and offered it for inspection.

"Yes, ah, Lieutenant Dallas. That was my understanding. You must know, of course, our client data is strictly confidential. Paradise has a reputation for discretion as well as excellence."

"And you must know, of course, that I can get a warrant, Mr.—?"

"Oh, Sebastian. Simply Sebastian." He waved a thin hand, sparkling with rings. "I'm not questioning your authority, Lieutenant. But if you could assist me, your motives for the inquiry?"

"I'm inquiring into the motives for the murder of DeBlass." She waited a beat, judged the shock that shot into his eyes and drained his face of color. "Other than that, my data is strictly confidential."

"Murder. My dear God, our lovely Sharon is dead? There must be a mistake." He all but slid into a chair, letting his head fall back and his eyes close. When the monitor offered him refreshment, he waved a hand again. Light shot from his jeweled fingers. "God, yes. I need a brandy, darling. A snifter of Trevalli."

Eve sat beside him, took out her recorder. "Tell me about Sharon."

"A marvelous creature. Physically stunning, of course, but it went deeper." His brandy came into the room on a silent automated cart. Sebastian plucked the snifter and took one deep swallow. "She had flawless taste, a generous heart, rapier wit."

He turned the doe eyes on Eve again. "I saw her only two days ago."

"Professionally?"

"She had a standing weekly appointment, half day. Every other week was a full day." He whipped out a butter yellow scarf and dabbed at his eyes. "Sharon took care of herself, believed strongly in the presentation of self."

"It would be an asset in her line of work."

"Naturally. She only worked to amuse herself. Money wasn't a particular need, with her family background. She enjoyed sex."

"With you?"

His artistic face winced, the rosy lips pursing in what could have been a pout or pain. "I was her consultant, her confidant, and her friend," Sebastian said stiffly and draped the scarf with casual flare over his left shoulder. "It would have been indiscreet and unprofessional for us to become sexual partners."

"So you weren't attracted to her, sexually?"

"It was impossible for anyone not to be attracted to her sexually. She . . ." He gestured grandly. "Exuded sex as others might exude an expensive perfume. My God." He took another shaky sip of brandy. "It's all past tense. I can't believe it. Dead. Murdered." His gaze shot back to Eve. "You said murdered."

"That's right."

"That neighborhood she lived in," he said grimly. "No one could talk to her about moving to a more acceptable location. She enjoyed living on the edge and flaunting it all under her family's aristocratic noses."

"She and her family were at odds?"

"Oh definitely. She enjoyed shocking them. She was such a free spirit, and they so . . . ordinary." He said it in a tone that indicated ordinary was more mortal a sin than murder itself. "Her grandfather continues to introduce bills that would make prostitution illegal. As if the past century hasn't proven that such matters need to be regulated for health and crime security. He also stands against procreation regulation, gender adjustment, chemical balancing, and the gun ban."

Eve's ears pricked. "The senator opposes the gun ban?"

"It's one of his pets. Sharon told me he owns a number of nasty antiques and spouts off regularly about that outdated right to bear arms business. If he had his way, we'd all be back in the twentieth century, murdering each other right and left."

"Murder still happens," Eve murmured. "Did she ever mention friends or clients who might have been dissatisfied or overly aggressive?"

"Sharon had dozens of friends. She drew people to her, like . . ." He searched for a suitable metaphor, used the corner of the scarf again. "Like an exotic and fragrant flower. And her clients, as far as I know, were all delighted with her. She screened them carefully. All of her sexual partners had to meet certain standards. Appearance, intellect, breeding, and proficiency. As I said, she enjoyed sex, in all of its many forms. She was . . . adventurous."

That fit with the toys Eve had unearthed in the apartment. The velvet handcuffs and whips, the scented oils and hallucinogens. The offerings on the two sets of colinked virtual reality headphones had been a shock even to Eve's jaded system.

"Was she involved with anyone on a personal level?"

"There were men occasionally, but she lost interest quickly. Recently she'd spoken about Roarke. She'd met him at a party and was attracted. In fact, she was seeing him for dinner the very night she came in for her consultation. She'd wanted something exotic because they were dining in Mexico."

"In Mexico. That would have been the night before last."

Yes. She was just bubbling over about him. We did her hair in a gypsy look, gave her a bit more gold to the skin—full body work. Rascal Red on the nails, and a charming little temp tattoo of a red-winged butterfly on the left buttock. Twenty-four-hour facial cosmetics so that she wouldn't smudge. She looked spectacular," he said, tearing up. "And she kissed me and told me she just might be in love this time. 'Wish me luck, Sebastian.' She said that as she left. It was the last thing she ever said to me."